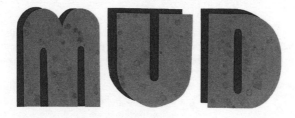

EMILY THOMAS

ANDERSEN PRESS

First published in Great Britain in 2018 by
Andersen Press Limited
20 Vauxhall Bridge Road
London SW1V 2SA
www.andersenpress.co.uk

2 4 6 8 10 9 7 5 3 1

British Library Cataloguing in Publication Data available.

ISBN 978 1 78344 689 6

Typeset by Palimpsest Book Production Ltd, Falkirk, Stirlingshire

Printed and bound in Great Britain by Clays Limited, Bungay, Suffolk, NR35 1ED

For my brother, James.

1979

Saturday 9th June

This diary is the last birthday present Mum ever gave me, three years ago when I was ten. I didn't have to write in it every day, she said, just when a noteworthy event or feeling happened. At the time I thought my life mostly extremely boring, and I didn't know how to write about my feelings, which seemed to change every ten minutes.

Now I'm nearly thirteen and finally something noteworthy HAS happened. In fact, it's more of a bombshell, which the dictionary says is either 'a very attractive woman' or 'an unexpected and surprising event. *Especially an unpleasant one*'.

Yesterday at 6.00 p.m. my father appeared in our TV room, which my parents have described as a fleapit, or a slum or a scrap-metal yard. Only instead of old car doors and broken fridges, there are plates with half-eaten food on, peeling paint, pen drawings on the walls, bits of furniture that's falling apart, broken Airfix kits, old Lego under the sofa, and limbs that once belonged to dolls.

Mum said we could do what we liked in the TV room – but she wasn't cleaning up after us and it was up to us if we sat in squalor. My sister Elsa, who is eighteen and more responsible, used to make me help her remove old apple cores and bits of toast and biscuit from down the back of the sofa, but we began to notice that my older brothers Sam and Harry never lifted a finger. Elsa said that in the spirit of fairness we should not allow ourselves to become slaves to lazy boys, so we've given up bothering. Luckily we have a cleaning lady called Alice, who sometimes sneaks into the TV room in the day and takes dirty plates away after she's had a sit-down in front of the one o'clock news.

I was already in my pyjamas on the sofa eating toast and watching telly when Dad's beard and nose appeared around the door.

'Hello, Lydia,' he said. 'May I interrupt for just two minutes?' He moved further into the room and examined himself in the mirror above the fireplace. Mum would often refer to Dad as 'Your Dandy Father', because he liked to wear flamboyant ties and interesting shirts and jackets. He hasn't bothered so much with all that sort of business over the past couple of years, but he does check his beard every so often.

'What is it?' I said, startled to see an adult had roamed into our domain and wondering if something terrible had happened to the cat. 'Has Bob been run over?'

'Bob?' said my father. 'No, no . . . that creature is immortal.' He hesitated, and then he said, 'But could you turn the TV off, I have some news.'

Loudly sighing I got up and turned the telly off. And then I turned it off again. You have to turn off our television twice before it properly turns off, as it was made in the 1960s and is like an old person who's hard of hearing and needs things repeating. When I returned to my spot on the sofa, Dad came and sat next to me, wincing as he perched on a loose spring.

He looked around the room. 'Big old house, isn't it?' he said, and I followed his gaze up to a decayed piece of omelette that Sam had recently flung at the ceiling – just left of the hanging lampshade, where no one could reach it.

'I suppose so,' I said. 'Is that your news, Dad?'

'Well, no . . .' he said, now staring at the fireplace. 'What I mean is that, thinking about it, we don't *really* need all this space, all these rooms . . . And also . . . I'm in a bit of trouble.'

You know when an adult has slipped up in front of you and forgotten you are not one? Well, this is typical of my father. Also, he starts off annoyingly unclear and then comes right out with it, without the tactful element in the middle.

'What do you mean, "trouble"?'

'Money trouble,' he said. 'Bit of an economic downturn. Life can be very expensive, you know, Lydia.'

'Is this to do with income tax?' I said, as I've often heard this talked about in our house as though it is the bane of all our lives.

'In a way . . . Well, it's really more to do with mortgages . . . and other things,' he went on. 'And what with Kate and her children . . .'

Kate is what Alice calls 'your dad's lady friend', and who he's known about a year and a half. Worse than this, Kate has three children – Sally who is nine and Erica who is seven, and a boy called Jake who is only a year older than me and a year younger than Sam. Sam is quite hostile to Jake for reasons I don't completely understand and Elsa will hardly acknowledge that any of them are alive, but especially Kate. Harry is more pleasant about it all, but he's the eldest

3

so he's more mature. And I am someone, Elsa says, who tends to be a people-pleaser and am super nice to everyone, only because I want them to like me back. I must admit I am a bit.

Anyway, it now appears that Kate and Dad's friendship has already got to the stage where her feelings are judged as important as mine, and Elsa's and Harry and Sam's.

'What do you mean . . . about Kate?' I asked, though not really wanting to know the answer.

'Well, she and— Well, they'll be living with us soon enough, and what with all the bills and inflation and things like that—'

'Hang on.' I held up my hand. 'You can't just say things like that suddenly.'

'What do you mean?' He looked genuinely puzzled.

'That you're in trouble and now Kate and her kids are coming to live with us . . . You can't just say things like that *suddenly*.'

'Oh. Yes,' he said. 'Well, we – Kate and I . . .' He paused to push his glasses further up his nose. 'The thing is, it's not just the bills. We've actually *completely* run out of money . . .'

At this point I began to get that tight anxious feeling I get when I'm about to go to the dentist.

'Anyway,' he went on, more cheerily. 'The point is . . . I've sold this house, and I've bought a big boat. A lovely old Thames Barge. They had an important part to play in Dunkirk . . . you know, on D-Day and all that.' Dad patted my knee.

'I don't care about Dunkirk and D-Day,' I said rudely.

'Well . . .' He looked disappointed. 'What I mean is she's a piece of history. Her name is *Lady Beatrice*, and we're all going to go and live on her, hopefully in a few weeks. Just in time for the summer!'

For a long time there was silence, except for a bird chirruping outside the window. I'll always remember that bird.

'Gosh . . .' I said finally, as calmly as I could. 'I hope this is one of your jokes, as this will absolutely, completely, ruin my life. Sorry. No.'

'Lydia, I'm afraid there is no other choice,' he said. 'I've thought of all the alternatives. It hasn't been an easy decision.' He rubbed my shoulder. 'Sam and Harry are actually quite pleased, and Elsa . . . well, I'm sure she'll come round to the idea . . . eventually.'

Of course Sam and Harry are quite pleased, I thought. They're boys, who find discomfort somehow enjoyable.

'This *is* actually as bad as Bob being run over,' I told my father. 'It might even be worse.'

He sighed. 'Perhaps one day you'll understand . . . Being a parent is not very easy, and one doesn't always get it right.'

No, I thought. One does not. And actually being a child isn't that easy either.

'What about school?' I said.

'I'm afraid you'll have to go to a new school,' he said. 'As the barge is moored in Maling-on-Sea, near the coast. But Oaks in Maling is a jolly good school, and you'll make new friends. Better friends, even . . .'

Dad was referring to Donna Taylor, who is my friend

and my enemy at the same time, as she is spoilt and bossy and often mean.

'Hmmm.' I glowered at him, only very slightly cheered by the thought of getting away from Donna.

'It's a new start,' said Dad, getting up off the sofa. 'I know change is worrying, Lydia, but sometimes it really is for the best. Silver linings and all that.'

'I'm switching the telly back on now,' I said, not wanting to hear any more of his wisdom and annoyed that he was trying to turn this around as though he was actually doing me a favour.

Of course, as soon as Dad had gone, I went straight upstairs to find Elsa.

'Leave me alone!' I heard her yell as I pushed open her bedroom door and had to duck underneath a volume of the *Encyclopaedia Britannica* being flung at the wall.

'Oh, it's you,' she said, flustered. Then she caught sight of my expression. 'Has he told you?'

'I just can't believe it, Elsa.'

'It's unspeakably selfish.' Elsa released her hair from its band so that it fell like a wild, dark, curly halo around her head. She stood there in her pyjamas, with her baggy Inca socks and her pretty face furious.

'A boat though?' I went to sit on her bed. 'What will become of us?'

'Lord knows,' she said tetchily. 'Thankfully, I'm off to university soon, though you may end up getting put into Care.'

'Thanks very much,' I said glumly. Sometimes Elsa says

spiteful things like that just to scare me. I know deep down she doesn't actually mean them.

Elsa sighed, looking a bit guilty.

'The thing is, how can Dad have spent all his money?' I went on. 'Aren't adults supposed to know about things like that?'

'I think Mum was in charge of the finances,' said Elsa, coming to sit down next to me. 'You know how useless Dad is at practical things.' She shook her head. 'But also that *woman* has clearly bewitched him. It's like living with someone who has joined a cult, or has mild brain damage.'

'Well,' I said doubtfully, not sure that Kate was really at the bottom of this. 'Maybe she'll change her mind and chuck him, once she realises about the poverty and deprivation that is coming.'

'Or with any luck she'll accidentally fall overboard,' Elsa said. 'And get swallowed up whole by the stinking mud.'

'Yes,' I said, eager to join in. 'She is slowly sucked down to the sea bed whilst at the same time being devoured by flesh-eating piranhas.'

'The piranhas are rather unlikely,' said Elsa, wrinkling her nose. 'Which is unfortunate.'

We looked at each other then, and I suddenly felt hysterical and started to laugh, and then Elsa started, and we couldn't stop. We were making so much noise that Dad stuck his head round the door and smiled warily at us.

'Oh good,' he said brightly. 'You're OK.' And then he disappeared in case he'd got that wrong.

Elsa and I must have worn ourselves out with all our hysterics, because I woke up much later on her bed with her asleep beside me, one arm wrapped around my stomach. It was very dark and the house was silent, and I thought I might possibly have dreamed everything. But then I saw the *Encyclopaedia Britannica* lying splayed on the floor and I knew I hadn't.

I got up then, and went back to my bedroom, which is where I am writing everything down, because doing that does make it slightly less overwhelming. Also, though I do love Dad, and would never want to hurt him, one day I may be very reluctantly forced to take him to court and sue him for wilful damages to a minor. Or something like that.

This morning on the school bus, Donna was sitting at the very back chatting with a girl called Kim Tym about Kim's new haircut, which is like Purdey's from the *New Avengers*. It didn't feel the appropriate moment to say about us moving away for ever and me never seeing Donna again.

Instead I sat down on my own in the seat in front of Kim and Donna, and took Dad's *Times* newspaper out of my bag and finished reading an article I'd started at breakfast, about a poor old lady who was so agoraphobic that she couldn't even leave her house to buy cat food so her Persian Blue ate her toes and in the end she died. Then I thought about Bob, who does seem overly interested in my earlobes at times.

Behind me, every so often Donna lightly kicked the back of my seat and poked at my shoulder with the ruler from her pencil case.

I don't really know how Donna and I came to be friends. It was an accident. 'A fatal encounter,' Elsa says. Donna and I were sat together on day one of our first year at Brainhill Comprehensive School (the name of Brainhill couldn't be more of a joke by the way. There are probably about three people in the whole school who are actually brainy. Elsa is definitely one of them. I am definitely not).

Anyway, I was nervous, and so was Donna. This was before she started wearing bras and got flicks in her fringe. She wasn't so mean then, and we sort of clung together for the first weeks of term, since there is safety in numbers in certain zones at school, such as the girls' toilets. Apart from being a First Year, I was often under attack because of my voice, which had been marked out as Posh. This meant that I was known as Snob Lydia. Donna had two special names, which were Metal Mouth and Jaws, because of her brace.

Donna's mum and dad liked the sound of me, Donna said, as they didn't want her getting in with tarty girls who hadn't been brought up properly. Donna's dad is a senior accountant who works in London, and they live in a big house with a locked gate that you have to wait outside of while they look at you in a camera before letting you in. Donna's mum used to be a hand-model but is now a house-wife who devotes her days to organising Donna's after-school activities and coffee mornings for all her neighbours.

I've never been quite sure what Donna meant by 'brought up properly' as our house is so untidy and these days no one ever tells us off, as Mum always did that and Dad doesn't know how to. Donna's mum is obsessed with cleaning, and everything being shiny and with no creases, like the trousers Donna wears to school, which are polyester. My mum told me once that polyester is a horrible man-made fabric that I would be wearing over her dead body. She went on to say that polyester is very dangerous and highly flam-mable and that people have been burned alive wearing it, just from leaning against a heater, or a hot oven.

Of course, now I can wear as much polyester as I like. I think that's what's known as a 'hollow victory'.

As soon as we got off the bus, Donna rushed off with Kim, and I walked to our form room, having a satisfying fantasy about when I do tell Donna about us moving, and her tearful remorse at the thought of losing me – someone she has completely taken for granted and overlooked as anyone important.

Monday 18th June

Elsa is fighting what my father is calling the Cold War against him and has not spoken to him for days. Even on Saturday night, when Dad took us out for an Indian meal at the Tandoori Tavern on the high street as a treat, Elsa just sat at the table, angrily snapping a poppadum into little pieces and glaring at Sam.

Being the family dustbin, Sam took full advantage of Dad's guilty conscience, and ate his own food as well as everyone's leftovers, and made annoying comments about real hardship being starving people in Africa living in shacks with no clean water and that Elsa and I were once again making a mountain out of a molehill.

As I have not complained directly to Sam about Dad's terrible plan, I was quite indignant that he had automatically lumped me in with Elsa. But obviously I do completely agree with her.

Sam is one of those devious types, who is crafty about never looking badly behaved in front of adults, but does horrible things in secret. I have still not forgiven him for when he borrowed Harry's air rifle and put three of my old dolls on a tree branch in the garden to practise on. I used to really like Sam when I was a small child, but now nearly everything he says and does infuriates me.

Not even Harry, who is calm and kind and a year older than Elsa, knew what to say to her, and in the end she stormed out, just before the hot flannels arrived.

When Dad was paying the bill, he told the rest of us,

'Elsa's at a pivotal age. She's not really a child any more, but she still needs her mother.' He looked very troubled by this, adding, 'There's nothing I can do about that. I wish I could.'

I felt quite affected by Dad's words, and pondered that behind her spikiness a part of Elsa is still a kid, like me. Somehow her feelings are all coming out as angry and not sad, though. Perhaps it is easier to be angry than sad?

At breakfast today, Dad tried again for a ceasefire and asked Elsa if there was anything of Mum's she'd particularly like to keep as before we move the rest is going to Mum's sister, Lorna, in Berkshire.

Sam and Harry had not yet appeared. Sam normally leaves it till the very last minute before he gets up, and then he buys sweets from the newsagents for breakfast, on his way to the school bus stop. Sam is worried that I will talk to him in public, so he makes sure he catches the last bus to avoid unnecessary embarrassment. This suits me down to the ground. Harry is never at breakfast because he's left school now and uses the time to do his hair and choose which T-shirt he's going to wear under his leather jacket. Mum always said that Harry is 'a dandy, just like his father'.

'Yes. I want to keep everything,' said Elsa stubbornly. She was dressed entirely in moody black, and drinking black coffee, just in case we didn't realise that she was really hacked off.

'Really?' said my father. He folded his paper. 'There's an

awful lot. I thought we could give some things to Lorna to keep.'

'You just want to get rid of it all.' Elsa stared intently at the table so that she didn't see the awful look on his face. 'Get rid of my mother.'

'Elsa!' said Dad, taking off his glasses. 'How can you say that?'

Elsa shrugged. 'Because it didn't take you very long to forget about her, did it?'

There was an awkward silence. Dad has never properly explained how he met Kate. 'In a brothel,' Elsa said once, though when she'd caught my expression she'd given me a funny smile, as though that was just one of her dark jokes. Kate is a bit younger than Dad and wears tight jeans and T-shirts and cheesecloth shirts that seem to be bursting open all the time at the boobs area. Sexy clothes. The kind of thing that one of Harry's girlfriends might wear. To be fair, Kate is pretty and slim, so she doesn't look bad or anything. Personally I can't see what she sees in Dad, who is almost a geriatric and is always getting bits of food stuck in his beard.

'OK. That's enough, Elsa,' Dad said, breaking the silence. 'You're upsetting everyone.'

Elsa's face turned a grey colour, and her mouth pinched so that it looked like a slit below her nose. 'You're the one who's upsetting everyone,' she said. 'You're a very selfish man.'

He went quiet.

'What do you think Mum would say if she knew about all this?' I asked, heaping strawberry jam on my toast.

Dad laughed quite sadly. 'She would probably have something to say about it, I expect,' he said. 'But I think she would understand.'

'Well, she's dead,' said Elsa coldly. 'So we'll never know, will we?'

Mum died two years ago. It seems like a hundred years ago and yesterday at the same time. She'd been feeling ill for months, and honestly, she had looked ill too, but nobody had ever talked about it. It was as though talking about it made it serious and real. But it didn't stop me being scared. Dad was probably more scared though, because Mum refused to admit she was properly sick. And being him, he never actually insisted that she saw a doctor.

He should have insisted, because then maybe she would be here now and she would have stopped him from spending so much money and we wouldn't have to move. But in fairness Mum was quite stubborn and formidable, and in the end I suppose no one can force anybody to do anything they don't want to do. Maybe Dad hoped it would all just go away. When I'm really frightened, I kind of can't move, my brain seems to freeze and waits for the fear to go away before it resumes activity. It probably explains why my maths homework is always late, as well as wrong.

One October morning, Dad took Mum to hospital before the rest of us had woken up. And I only saw her one more time after that, when she was lying in a bed, small and thin, with tubes coming out of her. I don't like remembering that day if I can help it. I stood by the bed and saw someone so tiny and shrunken and confused. Mum was the one who told us off and did things for our own good and who I always lived a bit in fear of. Staring at her in her hospital nightdress, she looked like a little bird. The room had smelled awful too, like someone had been boiling fish up for weeks.

Actually, I don't want to think about Mum too much because it's like thinking about how Outer Space goes on and on into infinity. The more you think about that, the more your brain flips out.

Except, how could she just go? She must have known that, left to his own devices Dad would probably go and do something stupid.

I have decided to empty my post office account for buying Personal Items and for Survival Money – in case I need to run away at some point. Unfortunately, I need an adult present to do this. It is Dad who has been putting bits of money in the account over the years and I am not yet considered old enough to make decisions about it. I do find this ironic since it is obviously my father who makes bad decisions about money in our house, but there's no way round it.

'How much have you actually got in your account?' he asked when I'd told him my plan, leaving out the bit about running away and Survival Money.

'About fifty pounds,' I began, before the look in his eye made me suspicious. 'Why?'

'No reason,' he said.

'Will fifty pounds make any difference, Dad?' I asked. 'Will it solve our money problems and help us keep the house?'

'No, my love. Very kind of you to offer, but you must keep it,' he said. 'Get yourself a nice treat.'

Strictly speaking, I hadn't offered it, but I let it pass because Dad was being quite sweet.

'We can pop along to the post office first thing tomorrow morning,' he went on. 'How about that?'

'Thanks, Dad,' I said, as my stomach let out a rumble.

We were sitting at the kitchen table, waiting for Elsa to

put in the lasagne she had made earlier, but there was no sign of her.

'Shall I do it?' I asked.

Dad appraised it. 'Best wait for Elsa,' he said. 'She's good at that sort of thing.'

Elsa is really good at recipes. She's obviously got that from Mum. I am useless at cooking, but very good at eating. When I am older I want a household full of servants, who will prepare my meals and bring them to me on silver trays while I lie under a satin bedspread. If I never make a casserole or a Yorkshire pudding in my life it won't bother me at all.

'Elsa will be gone soon,' I said. 'Having the time of her life at Cambridge University.'

'So she will,' said Dad, frowning. 'Never mind. Kate's an excellent cook too.'

'Hmm,' I said, having no evidence of this thus far.

I was having a wave of homesickness for Elsa, even though she hadn't gone yet. We argue a lot and sometimes I want to kill her and she wants to kill me, but I can always rely on her to stomp around the kitchen making nice food, and on special occasions she lets me try on her clothes and sit in her bedroom. I let the homesick wave build and fall heavily over me.

'I'll miss Elsa,' I said.

Dad squeezed my shoulder. 'Me too.'

'It's not fair.'

'I know,' he said.

He tried to tell me more about the boat, but I was sick

to death of hearing about the stupid boat and I didn't want to listen.

I mainly remember 'old' and 'characterful' and most awful of all, '*Swallows and Amazons*'.

Saturday 23rd June

This afternoon we all went to see *Lady Beatrice*. Elsa and I sat in the very back seats of Dad's car, amongst all the crabbing nets and Wellington boots. Sam, Harry, Jake, Sally and Erica were squeezed up in the other two rows of seats with Erica sitting on Sally's knee. They both kept looking in fright at my brothers, who were pretending to be invisible.

I was counting out notes and change from my little leather purse. I had already spent some of my post office money in the chemist's on Holly Hobbie moisturiser and I had forty-two pounds left. I liked counting my money; it made me feel safe to have it close to me – just in case.

'Bit flush, aren't you,' said Elsa. 'What's all that for?'

'Things,' I said.

'Like what?'

'I don't know yet – make-up, maybe.'

Elsa raised an eyebrow.

'Seventeen foundation and some eyebrow tweezers,' I added.

'You haven't got any eyebrows, you fool.' Elsa smiled cattily.

'Not now maybe,' I said. 'But in a couple of years I'll have great big bushy ones like yours.'

Elsa rolled her eyes.

'Elsa,' I whispered, closing my purse and hugging it to me. 'How about I come to Cambridge and live with you? I could sleep on the floor.'

'Don't be daft,' she said, as kindly as Elsa can. 'You need to go to school and stuff. You'll be OK.'

I won't, I thought, imagining the years ahead of me. Outcast and alone. I thought of leaving my bedroom, my double bed, the proper windows opening onto a proper roof.

I was really trying not to be pathetic and cry, but it happened before I could stop it.

Erica was leaning over from the back seat, staring at me. 'Are you crying?' she said in a tiny voice.

'Mind your own business,' Elsa said crisply, and Erica slunk back down out of sight. 'Come on, Lydia.' Elsa was stern now. 'It's bad enough that Dad has gone mad. Pull yourself together.'

I stared out of the car window, thinking it was easy for her to say when she wasn't really going to have to live on *Lady Beatrice*, just visit sometimes. Lucky Elsa.

'I'll try and come back now and then,' she said, reading my mind. 'In the meantime, read a lot of books. They're very useful when you're miserable.'

This is true. Elsa and I are avid readers, though she likes books about murders and ghosts, and I'm more keen on stories about orphaned youngsters who endure great deprivation, but then discover at the end that they're the secret love child of rich aristocrats and live happily ever after in luxury.

We'd arrived at Maling and were driving down a big hill, where I could see the estuary. The tide was low and it was all marshes and thick mud of a sort of dreary brown colour with an awful smell like farts. I looked at it and wondered what its purpose was.

'We're here!' my father announced jauntily, stopping the car.

Kate seemed to make a point of smiling at me, and I felt a bit bad about Elsa and I imagining her being sucked down into the mud so unpleasantly. I smiled back nervously, aware of Elsa prickly beside me.

'Bear in mind that it's going to be done up very nicely inside,' Kate said. 'It will be really quite stylish.'

Elsa made a quiet gagging sound.

One by one, we got out of the car and stood on the grey concrete quay. Boats of all sizes were moored alongside the edge. A flock of seagulls shrieked above our heads. It was overcast and a bit nippy. The tinkling sound of little flags knocking against metal masts felt quite deafening.

Harry had already wandered off and now lit a cigarette by a steel fence. Ignoring the rest of us, he looked over at a couple of teenage girls, wearing matching bum-skimming denim ra-ras, who walked past with their dogs, sneaking glances at him and giggling as he drew slowly on his fag. Like he was James Dean or something.

'Look at him,' said Elsa witheringly. 'Twit.'

Safe to say, Elsa was in a very unpleasant mood.

Kate and my father stood at the top of the wobbly-looking wooden gangway, which led to the boat's deck. At the front of the barge there was a pretty wooden sign that said, *Lady Beatrice*. Behind *Lady Beatrice* was another Thames Barge called *Philomena*.

From the outside, our boat looked quite nice. It was

enormous, and had a huge mast with a brownish-red sail wrapped around it. Beneath this, Dad said, was a large cabin area called the saloon, which is like a living room. At one end of the boat was a painted wooden shed that looked a bit like my old Wendy house.

'That's where the wheel is,' said Sam, pointing at it. 'The wheelhouse.'

'See,' said my father, looking gratefully at Sam. 'Not so bad, eh?'

'Are you really expecting me to get excited about a hut with a wheel in it?' said Elsa.

Dad and Sam laughed, which I don't think was the reaction Elsa wanted, because she pushed past them and stomped on board.

Erica and Sally were staring mutely at the gangway. Erica was clutching an old blanket, edging it closer to her nose for a good sniff. I could have done with a blankie myself. I often regret being persuaded to throw mine away. I knew I might need it again one day.

'I want to go home,' bleated Erica.

'Yes, well, join the queue,' called my sister.

'And your cabin is through there,' said Dad, pointing at a doorway that led through to a corridor-type thing. I wandered through the narrow aisle, noticing a large built-in cupboard to my right. At the end of the small corridor was a door. My cabin, I presumed. I tried the handle, but the door wouldn't open.

'It's locked,' I said.

Dad appeared behind me. 'No, darling, *that's* not your cabin, behind that door is Elsa's cabin.' He gestured around us with his hands. '*This* is your cabin.'

I blinked. It seemed as if we were standing in a corridor. This couldn't be right. It was definitely a corridor. But then my eyes travelled into and up inside the large cupboard I had passed, and finally I saw it: a thin mattress lying atop the length of the cupboard, with about a foot of space between it and the roof. A bunk.

It is the tiniest room I have ever been in, apart from our downstairs loo at home. And it smells. Musty and mouldy, like a garden shed.

'It's going to get a lick of paint, of course,' said my father brightly. 'And we'll put in a door, and a little lamp. And look . . . here's a table that folds down from the wall!'

I was speechless.

'What do you think then?' Dad asked, sounding less bright, more nervous now.

What did I think? This was one of the worst surprises of my entire life so far. Much worse than the flippers and mask I had got for my birthday when I was eight when I'd been hoping for a Ballet Sindy. In fairness, I had grown to love those flippers – in fact, I used to like wearing them around the house – but I really couldn't ever see a day when I would grow to love this damp dark cave I was standing in.

'Lydia . . .' Dad was anxious. 'Say something.'

'It's fine,' I said finally in a small voice, while trying not to breathe in the smell. I noticed a streak of water running down the wooden wall.

He patted my shoulder. 'Everything's going to be OK. You'll see.'

There was a strange creaking noise coming from somewhere. I looked at Dad.

'Ah,' he said. 'That must be the special chair in the saloon. You'll like the chair.'

Dad really is demented, I thought as I followed him out of my grisly corridor-cabin. I didn't dare look back at it, in case it was even more horrible on second viewing.

Inside the big room that is called the saloon, there was one of those chairs that looks like half a giant egg made out of wicker, hanging from a hook in the ceiling. Sam was sitting in it, whirling himself round and round.

For a few minutes I forgot about my miserable cabin, as the egg-chair did look like fun. 'Can I have a go on that?' I said, trying to stop Sam's whirling with both arms.

'In a minute,' he said, annoying as ever. 'Wait your turn.'

Dad looked delighted that I was distracted by the chair. 'The kitchen – no, the *galley* – is through there,' he said, pointing to another long narrow corridor with no windows and shabby old lino on the floor. 'And beyond that is the bathroom.'

I dragged myself away from keeping guard over the egg-chair at this point as bathrooms are extremely important and a proper inspection was required.

I wasn't quite prepared for what I saw. The bath was sitting on top of a kind of wooden cabinet, about three feet from the floor.

'The hot water is slightly erratic just at the moment,' said

Dad a bit awkwardly. 'But nothing wrong with a lukewarm bath from time to time. I know you girls like boiling yourselves alive, but it's not good for you, you know.'

Elsa appeared behind him in the doorway. 'When you say "lukewarm",' she said, 'do you really mean cold?'

'I'm getting a man in to have a look at the boiler,' Dad said. 'Try not to catastrophise absolutely everything, Elsa.'

Elsa gave him a look of fury, which he didn't see, as he purposely wasn't meeting her eye. She marched over to inspect the toilet area.

Dad got out his handkerchief and gave his forehead a wipe. He does this when he's feeling a bit jumpy, I've noticed.

'Good grief.' Elsa was now peering at a pump thing with a handle next to the toilet bowl.

At this point, Sam came into the bathroom. 'It's a bilge pump,' he said a bit too gleefully, and as though he was an expert.

'What's a bilge pump?' I asked suspiciously.

'It's the pump that gets rid of toilet waste,' said Sam.

'You mean you can't flush the toilet?' I said. 'You have to pump your . . . poo . . . away.'

'Fraid so,' said Sam, and his shoulders quivered slightly.

'Oh!' was all I could say in that moment. 'How disgusting.'

Sam stopped trying to hold in his laughter and had to bend over, as his stomach was obviously straining with it.

'It's really not as bad as it sounds,' said Dad, despite the fact that it obviously was.

Sam was now out of control and in fits of laughter.

Sometimes it's like he's not a human being but a kind of disgusting swamp monster.

'Sam,' said Elsa dismissively as he irritates her a lot too these days, 'I suggest you go and sit in that stupid egg-chair thing again.'

'Probably best, Sam,' said Dad, giving him a look that I've noticed men and boys often give each other when women and girls are in their eyes close to making a scene about something.

I kind of agreed with Elsa, but I still have hopes that Dad will sort it all out somehow.

'It's a death trap,' she went on, after Sam had slunk off. 'Imagine if you died falling out of the bath? Better off having a sink wash, to be honest.'

'No one is going to die,' said Dad. 'And I'm afraid I can't really do anything about the bath. It's the water pressure . . . or something like that.'

'Oh well. At least you know how it all works, that's so reassuring,' said Elsa sarcastically. 'Not to mention the fact that I have to climb up a ten-foot rickety old ladder to get out of my cabin.' She stared stonily at my father. 'Seriously, murderers in high-security prisons have better living conditions than your own children. Good job, Dad. Well done.'

Dad and I looked at each other and I could see he was trying not to laugh, as Elsa can be quite funny when she goes too far and is being horrible.

'Oh, Elsa,' he said, and he looked a bit tired. 'What am I going to do with you?'

Friday 29th June

Dad has announced that as it's my birthday tomorrow we are all going to Windsor Safari Park, which is like a giant wildlife theme park. Dad obviously thinks it's a great treat for me and has forgotten that I am no longer eight years old. Lately I seem to do a lot of pretending to my father that I am not as disappointed about things as I really am, so as not to hurt his feelings, but I would much rather just go to the cinema or watch telly and have presents instead. Even worse, we have to get up at six o'clock in the morning to drive to the other side of London. And Dad has invited Kate, Sally, Erica and Jake, without even asking me. I am losing control of my birthday now, on top of everything else.

'But you used to love all that,' said Dad on sight of my expression, which I'd forgotten to change to an excited one. 'All the animals and the rides. Oh, the tears when it came to time to leave!'

'Yes, Dad, but that was when I was younger,' I said.

'Never too old for that kind of thing,' he said. 'You'll enjoy it once you get there. I know you like to make a bit of a fuss about things.'

I opened my mouth, on the point of outrage, but Dad was obviously not having any of it because he put his glasses on, picked up *The Times* and started reading.

'Also,' his voice came from behind the paper, 'you'll get a nice surprise to top up your post office account again.'

This was much more like it. 'Oh, thanks, Dad,' I said,

coming to terms with Windsor Safari Park. 'But where did you get the money from if the bank's getting it all?'

There was a short silence before he lowered *The Times* and then said, 'Well, I have had to sell off a few things, things we don't really need but are worth a bit of money.'

'Nothing of Mum's?' I asked suspiciously.

'No . . . not your mother's. Just some bits and bobs.' He quickly started reading the paper again.

'What bits and bobs?' I persisted. 'Tables and chairs and things?'

'No . . . those are going into storage,' he said.

'What then?'

Dad sighed. He folded up his paper and put his glasses back in his case. 'Well, I managed to pawn your silver Christening mug and got rather a lot for it, in fact.'

'I . . .' My heart was beating a bit faster. Maybe I had heard it wrong? Had my father actually taken something that belonged to me and sold it for money to give back to me? 'Dad,' I said, still hoping that I'd misunderstood. 'Did you say my silver Christening mug?'

'Well, yes,' he said. 'But it's not for ever. You know what pawning is? When you pawn something you get money in return for it, but then you can buy it back when you are able to.' He smiled nervously. 'So, it's actually a situation in which you can't lose.'

'Yes, I know what pawning is . . .' My throat was dry because my human rights had been completely violated. This couldn't be right. That mug was mine, not Dad's. It was stealing. Surely he had broken the law?

'Don't panic. You'll get it back,' said Dad, who obviously does think I am still eight years old.

'But that . . . that's not it.' My father had done something quite wrong and it felt like the floor was slipping under my feet. 'It wasn't yours, you shouldn't have done it.'

'Done what?' said Elsa, who had appeared in the study with her hair in a towel.

I didn't answer her. I just looked at Dad. If I told Elsa, then she would be furious and might use it against him for years to come and, in a strange way, even though I felt completely betrayed by him, I didn't want to make him feel worse.

'Nothing,' I said. 'Nothing really.'

Elsa looked a bit suspiciously at both of us, but she didn't say anything, just took off the towel and started rubbing her hair.

Dad gave me a look of gratitude, which annoyed me intensely so I scowled back at him. I felt ashamed of him. And that is probably the worst thing you can ever feel about your dad.

I am in bed early because of bloody Windsor Safari Park and wondering if I can ever be resigned to what I found out about Dad today.

No sooner had we got onto the motorway this morning than it poured with torrential rain, and it didn't stop all the way to Windsor. And when we got there, half the animal enclosures were closed because of refurbishment or staff shortages or something, and Erica was sick on the Big Dipper ride at the funfair, so Kate was furious with Sam who had persuaded her to go on it, even though it says it's not suitable for children under ten. Of course, Dad was weird and stiff with me all day, for obvious reasons, and every time I thought about where the money for my post office account was coming from I felt like being sick too.

I think Elsa noticed I was out of sorts but she must have put it down to the crappy birthday treat, while Sam, who is attracted to danger and life-threatening activities, only cared about his own enjoyment. Harry somehow got out of coming altogether, which I didn't really blame him for, and at least it was one less person to ask, 'What's the matter with you? It's your birthday, misery guts!'

The rain stopped about lunch time and the sun came out, which is when Elsa disappeared. I eventually found her sitting in the Safari Café reading a book, with her bare legs up on a chair to get a tan.

'Thanks a lot,' I said. 'You could have told me you'd come to sunbathe.' I sank down onto a bench opposite her which was designed to look like a tree trunk.

'This is bloody hell,' said Elsa, inspecting her legs, which because of her olive skin were already brown. 'Another terrible idea of Dad's.'

'I suppose he thought I'd enjoy it,' I said. 'I always used to. But it's not the same as when you're a child.'

'You *are* a child,' said Elsa.

'Actually, I am now a *teenager*,' I said. 'It's very different.'

Elsa laughed, then pulled her little hessian bag towards her and got something out of it: a brown paper bag. 'Here,' she said. 'Happy Birthday.'

Inside the bag was a little box, and inside that was a delicate silver chain with a little green stone heart hanging off it.

'Elsa! Thanks!' I said, stroking the green heart. 'This is the best present I've ever had.'

'It's jade,' said Elsa. 'A jade heart.' She smiled. 'Put it on.'

She clasped it for me around my neck and I looked down at it, feeling this was a properly suitable present for a person of my age.

'I love it so much,' I said and tried to hug her.

'Yes, all right,' she said, resisting. 'Someone had to get you something nice. Glad you're pleased.'

'I'm never going to take it off.'

It's funny how someone can do something nice and everything feels completely different.

'You've looked so sad all day,' said Elsa. 'Is it this dreadful place or have you got your period or something?'

I was very tempted to tell Elsa about what Dad had done then, but I didn't. I'll just have to keep it inside.

'I'm fine,' I said. 'You know what I'm like.'

'Yes,' said Elsa, picking her book up. 'I certainly do.'

Dad and Kate had a minor argument over something I couldn't quite hear on the way back, which Elsa looked quite smug about, then he dropped her, Jake, Sally and Erica off at Hammersmith tube station in London and drove the rest of us home. But he didn't come inside with us – he just wandered around outside looking at bushes and trees.

I watched him from Mum's old studio window upstairs, wondering if now Kate really would chuck him because of Sam being so irresponsible with Erica and because she's realised Dad's old and poor. I'm still angry with him over the Christening mug, but suppose I will have to find it in my heart to forgive him. It's easier to tell myself it's because he was trying to give me a treat and there was no other choice, even though deep down I still know he was wrong.

Dad went across the cobbled drive to the apple tree as though he was going to pick an apple. But he just stood there, staring at it, and then he got his handkerchief out and covered his face with it. His shoulders were moving and I realised he was crying. And then I remembered that the apple tree was Mum's pride and joy and I thought I was going to cry too.

I touched my little jade heart and moved away from the window in case he saw me watching him.

Thursday 12th July

Because I have been procrastinating for too long, Sam said that it would be his pleasure to tell Donna on my behalf that we're moving away, as he can't stand her. This was very tempting but I knew I should do it tonight. Donna said on the bus this morning that I had to come over to hers as her mum Gina and her dad Tony were off to someone's birthday dinner and drinks party and it was boring being alone in the house.

'Mum's doing sausage and mash for us,' said Donna as an incentive, because she knows it is one of my favourites. 'And you know what my mum's mash is like?'

'Lump-free,' I said, which is true. Gina's mashed potato is very creamy and smooth. The thought of sitting around their dining table, and Donna's mum looking me up and down while I try to have good manners is very tiring though, even if it is the last time I will ever have to do it.

'And afterwards we can go up to my room and listen to *Horizon*, if you like?' she said, referring to her favourite Carpenters album.

'Brilliant,' I said, trying not to sound flat. 'Only I can't stay that long as it's school tomorrow.'

'Nice one,' said Donna. 'And I'll sit next to you on the bus and at lunch the whole of next term, as a special treat.'

After sausage and mash, Gina brought out some Angel Delight from the fridge and my heart sank. I think I might be the only person in the world who hates Angel Delight, which is a disgusting blancmange-type pudding out of a packet. Even the butterscotch flavour makes me gag. Luckily, Donna loves it, so she started eating mine as soon as she'd finished hers.

'Mustn't be greedy,' Gina said, patting Donna's stomach. 'You're getting a bit tubby round the middle as it is.'

'I'm becoming a woman, Mum,' said Donna. 'It's not because of Angel Delight.'

'Hmmm,' said Gina, putting her hands on her own tiny waist. 'Am I going to have to put you on a diet, sweetheart? My mum had me on thirds when I was your age.'

'What's that?' I said.

'Only eat a third of your meal,' said Gina matter-of-factly. 'It's the best way to keep trim. And we need to watch our weight in this family. Nana Beverley was sixteen stone by the time she was thirty-five.'

'Oh my God,' said Donna mid-mouthful. She put down her spoon and pushed away my helping of Angel Delight.

'Evening, my princesses,' Tony said, coming into the kitchen and making a bit of a show of nuzzling Gina's neck.

'Ugh,' said Donna. 'Please don't do that.'

Gina giggled. 'Tony, we're embarrassing our baby.'

And me, I thought, going red.

'Don't worry, we're off in ten minutes' – Gina shrieked as Tony pinched her bottom – 'so you girls can settle in for a nice evening. I've put out some digestive biscuits for later.'

'Funny enough I've lost my appetite,' said Donna. 'You two make me feel sick.'

Eventually Donna's mum and dad left, and I was wondering how I was going to get through another hour in Donna's company, let alone two, or maybe even three. But as soon as the front door shut behind them, Donna grabbed me.

'Upstairs,' she ordered. 'Mum and Dad's bedroom.'

'Now?' I said. 'My sausage and mash hasn't properly gone down yet.'

'I've got to show you something,' she said, and her eyes were fizzing. 'It's really disgusting.'

'Oh,' I said. 'Really?'

I followed her upstairs to the landing and we stopped outside Gina and Tony's bedroom.

Donna opened the door, tiptoed over to the bed and sat down. She reached out and slid open the top drawer of their bedside table and beckoned to me as I hovered by the door.

Before I knew it, she'd pulled a magazine out and shoved it in my face.

I was blinded by the sight of a woman's bare bottom.

'Ugh,' I said, pushing it back at her. 'Donna, I really don't want to see it.'

Donna ignored me and started flicking through the magazine, which I could see, even upside down, was called *Hot and Heavy*.

'Calm down. It's just women with really big knockers with their knickers down by their ankles,' she said. She paused at something she'd seen, then made a face and dropped *Hot and Heavy* on the floor. 'There's other stuff in there too, all to do with "doing it".' She made a disgusted face, but at the same time she sort of looked like she was enjoying herself. 'My mum and dad are perverts,' she said. 'I can't believe that my mum makes me breakfast after she's looked at all this with Dad. Like nothing is out of the ordinary and she's just normal. She needs help.'

'Maybe it's a mistake?' I said. 'And they ordered the wrong one from the newsagent's?'

'Lydia,' said Donna. 'Mum and Dad are sex maniacs, it's obvious.'

I was silent then, really trying not to think about Gina and Tony 'doing it'.

'Your dad probably does it with his girlfriend,' said Donna, dragging my family into it.

'Definitely not,' I said, shaking my head. 'My dad doesn't do it now. He's old.'

'Don't make me laugh, muggins!' Donna said. 'Course he does!'

After Donna had put the magazine back and we'd made sure we'd left no grubby marks in the bedroom, Donna said we could go downstairs and have some of her dad's Harvey's Bristol Cream if I wanted, which I didn't because it looks like cold custard. I was desperate to get away from her and try and get the thought of her mum and dad and my dad and Kate doing all that stuff out of my head, but I agreed to watch a repeat on telly of a Roald Dahl's *Tales of the Unexpected* episode as Donna gets scared watching things like that on her own, and *Tales of the Unexpected* are always about people getting their come-uppance in a very creepy way and often ending up being murdered. Donna kept hiding her eyes behind her hands, so she missed most of it. Meanwhile, I couldn't really concentrate as I couldn't get the picture of the woman's bottom from that magazine out of my head.

By the time it had finished it was nearly dark outside, and we had eaten all the digestives her mum had left out, even though I had no appetite because of earlier.

But something was suddenly very clear to me.

'Donna?' I said. 'We're moving.'

Donna had been examining the bottles in her mum and dad's drinks cabinet and was sniffing a bottle of rum. She stopped. 'What?' she said. 'Where?'

'To Maling-on-Sea.'

'That's thirty miles away,' she said. 'How are you going to get to school on time?'

'I'm going to Oaks,' I said. 'In September.'

Donna shoved the bottle of rum back in the cabinet. 'Blimey,' she said. 'That means you can't do Ballroom any more.'

Donna does ballroom dancing every week, as it's part of her mum's organised after-school activities for her. Whenever her cousin Sue can't make it, I'm drafted in to be her partner. I hate ballroom dancing and I'm rubbish at it, which secretly pleases Donna, of course.

'Sorry,' I said.

'Probably for the best anyway,' she said. 'Not being funny, but I'm Advanced, and you're definitely a Beginner.'

Typical that after all my anxious procrastinating, Donna was only put out for selfish reasons.

'Anyway,' I said. 'Just thought you should know.'

'Bet you're off to some big swanky house,' she went on. 'I mean, your dad must have a bit of money, what with all you lot and that mansion you live in.'

'Not exactly,' I said. 'Actually, we're going to live on a boat.'

Donna gaped at me. 'No way.'

'Yes,' I said. 'Dad's on an economy drive.'

'He's not a gambler, is he?' said Donna suspiciously. 'My Uncle Derek is a gambler. He lost his house in the end and my Auntie Carol chucked him out last Christmas. He's living above a chippy in Brentwood now.'

'Dad's definitely not a gambler,' I said, though thinking about it that would explain a lot. 'It's just money problems.'

'Well,' said Donna. 'Thirty miles is a long way away. I doubt we'll keep in touch.'

'Suppose not,' I said, wondering why I'd put off telling her so long since she obviously wasn't bothered. 'I'd better go. I've got Sam's bike outside and the lights are a bit hit and miss.'

'Please yourself,' said Donna. 'And don't tell anyone about all that stuff I showed you. I don't want other people thinking I'm the child of sex freaks?'

'Course not,' I told her.

'You're disgusted, aren't you?' she said.

'No, Donna,' I lied. 'It's nothing I didn't know already, to be honest.'

'Nice evening round lovely Donna's?' asked Elsa. She was lying in her favourite place, the inglenook, flipping through a magazine. I'd just got home and was hoping to rush upstairs and forget the evening had ever happened.

'Not really,' I said, subdued. 'But I did finally tell her we're moving.'

'Excellent,' said Elsa, still looking at her magazine. 'How did she take the news?'

'I don't think she cared at all.' I took off my anorak. 'It was a weird evening, Elsa. She showed me a horrible magazine in her parents' bedroom.'

'Oh?' Elsa perked up. 'A dirty magazine?'

I shuddered. 'I don't really want to talk about it.'

Of course, this didn't put off Elsa. 'Her mum and dad are a dark pair, I've often thought,' she said. 'You can tell. *She* looks like butter wouldn't melt.'

'Hmmm,' I said, pretending to yawn.

'It's always the ones you don't suspect,' she went on. 'Those two look much too clean for my liking. Always a sign.'

'Anyway . . .'

'But it reminds me of when I found that book in Dad's cupboard,' Elsa kept talking. 'I'd only gone in to borrow some shoe polish for my Doctor Martens, and there it was . . .'

'Where was what?'

'*The Joy of Sex*,' she said. 'Horrific.'

It was one of those moments when you want to put your fingers in your ears and stick your tongue out while loudly humming. I didn't, because this would only encourage Elsa.

'Dad can't possibly still do all that any more,' I said in disgust.

'Have you not seen him leering at Kate?' she said. 'It's obscene.'

I *had* actually seen this. Once, when Kate and Dad were in the study and he had his hand on her thigh and rubbed it. I had just stood there in front of them, furious, as though my poisonous psychic energy could stop them.

'The world has changed,' I said dramatically. 'Everyone has changed.'

'You're going to change too,' Elsa said. 'You're changing right now, but you don't know it.'

'You're wrong, Elsa,' I said. 'I will never change.'

Elsa picked up her magazine and hugged it to her chest, keeping her eyes on me. For once she wasn't mocking me, or annoyed. In fact, she looked a bit upset.

'Actually, I hope you're right,' she said seriously. 'It would be sad if you changed too much.'

I was waiting for her to start cackling like a witch, but she didn't. Instead she gave me one of her rare sweet smiles.

I went to bed quite troubled about the evening, and wondering if there was any way you could have a baby without having to do what those people were doing in the magazine at Donna's house.

Friday 20th July

I had an interview with the deputy headmaster at Oaks today and have missed the last day at Brainhill.

They are assessing me on my overall intelligence. I could have saved them the bother as I have a good idea of what that is. I had English first, which was quite easy, but when I saw the maths test – upside down, admittedly – on Mr Frank's desk, I knew the game was up. I am subnormal at maths. My brain freezes up at anything more complicated than simple addition and subtraction. Long division should be renamed Long and Hard as far as I'm concerned.

'You've got half an hour,' said Mr Frank, smiling like a penguin. He's got a smile that doesn't show his teeth – his mouth bends like a banana at each end. 'Though most pupils don't need as long.' He pushed a pencil at me across his desk. 'It's all fairly straightforward.'

I nodded, doubting that was true in my case. Already little beads of sweat were forming on the back of my neck and even my Brainhill school shirt, which is certainly not brand new, felt as stiff and constraining as cardboard.

'Thank you,' I said, taking the pencil and the test.

'You can sit over there, Lydia.' Mr Frank pointed at a smaller desk by the door to his office. 'I'll be back in half an hour.'

He got up and waddled, also like a penguin, to the door, shutting it behind him as he left.

'Oh dear,' I whispered to myself.

I had to go and sit in the canteen and read a book until I got my results back a couple of hours later. I fiddled quite a bit with my jade necklace and looked out of the window at all the Oaks pupils, wondering which one might become my best friend, and then eventually Mr Frank and another teacher – a man called Mr Turing who is head of maths – called me back in to another office.

Apparently my English is exceptional but my maths is so poor they are not sure what to do with me. Not news to me, of course. Mr Frank and Mr Turing examined my results in front of me, glancing at each other with a fair bit of frowning.

'I can't understand it. You're clearly not an unintelligent girl,' said Mr Turing. 'But you don't even have a grasp of Roman numerals.' He held out my paper which contained a variety of made-up numerals. 'What on earth is this?'

I held my breath. I am used to being a matter of concern to teachers. Sam sometimes helps me with my maths homework, because his brain seems to be the opposite of mine – he's not keen on books or writing, but absolutely fascinated by logarithms and cosines. Sam knows about my frustrated tantrums because I can't seem to understand what's going on, and he is actually quite patient, if annoyingly determined that I work things out for myself rather than use a calculator. But even Sam has almost given up on me.

It's not just maths either. It's facts in general. They go in one ear and out of the other. I know there's something not right with me. I tried to explain it to my mother a long time ago back when I was at St Helen's Primary School, after we moved out of London, but Mum wouldn't entertain the thought that a child she had given birth to might not be a genius. Though I think she might have wondered a bit when I started at St Helen's and I came home the first lunch time because I got mixed up about what school dinner money was for. I decided in the end that it must be for paying to *leave* school and go home for lunch, and not for an actual school lunch, but when I turned up at the back door and tried to explain that, Mum put her hands on my shoulders and stared at me as though I was an alien. She just gave me a Kit Kat and sent me back to school though, so she can't have been that worried.

After a lot of muttering with Mr Turing, Mr Frank delivered his verdict. 'We're going to put you in the top band for now,' he said uncertainly. 'And we'll see how you get on, shall we?' He exchanged a look with Mr Turing. 'But you might want to see about getting extra help with some subjects. I foresee some issues with mathematics and the sciences . . .'

I am going to fail at all those and more, I thought. If only there was some kind of special test that could really find out who I am. And prove that I'm not really stupid, only different. Even better if the test also reveals that I am, in fact, adopted too. But I have my mother's eyes so that is unlikely.

I wonder if there is any chance I can be home schooled like Laura Pitt, whose mum took her away from Brainhill in the second week of First Year. I might look into it.

Dad has refused point blank to home school me. He said that apart from the fact that nobody would be able or willing to do it, children who spend that much time only with adults become 'socially stunted'. I did try and argue that this wouldn't really affect me, and that Laura Pitt does it, but Dad says Laura Pitt is no doubt precocious and odd and it will do me no good in the long run to be hothoused that way. Sam, who was listening in, practically wet himself laughing when Dad said 'hothoused'.

There is obviously no way out of going to Oaks, and to add to my worries this evening Elsa and her friend Anna took it upon themselves to cut my hair. I now look like Mrs Fitch from next door but one, who is eighty-five. You can see Mrs Fitch's scalp through her hair, which I believe is common amongst old people, but not amongst young people.

Saturday 28th July

Yesterday Kate and Dad got married.

Dad told us all last weekend that they had booked the wedding in a registry office and it was happening quite soon.

Me, Elsa, Harry and Sam had been finishing off breakfast on Sunday and I was halfway through a chocolate-spread sandwich when he just said suddenly, 'Kate and I have decided to get married – it's nothing extravagant, just the registry office in Chelmsford at three thirty next Friday.'

He said it so quickly that we all just blinked and stared, and then the chocolate-spread sandwich got stuck in my throat.

'This is the last straw,' said Elsa, shocked. 'I can't believe it.'

I saw Harry and Sam look at each other and then at Elsa, whose face was a thundercloud. 'Bit quick, isn't it?' muttered Harry. 'What's the hurry?'

'Listen,' said Dad. 'I'm asking this lovely woman to turn her life and her family upside down for me, so the very least I can do is offer her the security of marriage.' It was like Dad had been rehearsing this or something because he sounded very forthright.

'How gentlemanly of you,' said Elsa. 'What about us? Suppose we don't get any say in the matter.'

Dad looked at her. 'Well . . . I was hoping you would be happy for us,' he said, as though he hasn't lived with Elsa's obvious hatred of Kate for the past year or so. 'It won't make any difference to anything.'

'Why are you doing it then?' Elsa couldn't even look at him; she just stared down at her porridge.

'Because,' said Dad, 'she makes me happy.'

This was a really unfair thing for him to say, and Elsa might be right about him being selfish.

'You just seem to be making a lot of decisions really quickly,' said Elsa. 'Without thinking them through.'

Harry and Sam were silent. Somehow they never speak out loud what they're really thinking – they usually leave that to Elsa, which might be for the best, but on the other hand might be a bit cowardly. There was something else that I had to ask though. I couldn't help myself.

'Dad,' I said. 'You won't love her more than us, will you?'

He looked at me and his face fell a bit, and he put out a hand and gripped my arm. 'Absolutely not,' he said. 'That will never happen.'

I caught Elsa raising her eyes to heaven.

I shrugged off Dad's hand and chewed on the rest of my sandwich without enjoying it at all.

'Well,' said Elsa. 'Good job you're broke, isn't it, as it's not like she can take all your money when you get a divorce.'

'Elsa . . .' said Dad.

But Elsa got up and walked out, dumping her porridge in the sink on the way.

Kate and Dad's wedding was not at all what I imagined. It was in a room like a box with lots of chairs, in a big modern building off a main road in Chelmsford. There wasn't a priest or a vicar, just a woman with glasses wearing a cardigan, who conducted the ceremony. Only a few of Mum and Dad's old friends came, and my Aunt Lorna was supposed to come but she said at the last minute that she wasn't well, at least that's what Dad said, but Elsa says it was obviously out of loyalty to our mother.

'The whole thing is an insult to Mum,' said Elsa the night before. 'I don't blame Lorna. I'm only coming because of you.'

I'd looked at her, a bit surprised, but Elsa didn't meet my eye. She just sniffed and picked up her latest horror novel and started reading it.

Kate said she was wearing a nice red dress for the ceremony, and she went out and bought me, Sally and Erica some quite garish long red tartan dresses to match, which I only agreed to because I was intrigued by the pampering session she said the four of us were having at a local beauty salon just before the wedding.

Sam told me that no way was he wearing anything smart, but in the end he turned up in his army surplus shirt and his school trousers and Dad said he really appreciated it, even though in the end Sam kept yawning the whole way through the ceremony.

This brings me to the only thing about the wedding that wasn't gloom and doom, as, for the first time in my life I got my hair done at the hairdresser, which Kate organised as part of the pampering.

Antoine the hairdresser took one look at my funny short hair and did a little low whistle, and I thought perhaps I was beyond hope. 'Let's just tidy this up, shall we?' he said in a sing-song voice, and snipped at it with his spindly scissors. And then he turned the hairdryer on and the next time I looked in the mirror I had this really shiny, blow-dried hair. It was still quite like a boy's, but now it was glossy and smooth and straight. I couldn't stop looking at myself and thinking in a shallow way about how very unfair hair is. How the wrong hair can make your life so much worse and that I might be able to cope with everything better if I just had nice hair.

Maybe I just needed something to think about other than that Dad had a new wife who wasn't my mother, because I allowed my new hair to make me happy, even though it would definitely go back to its normal scarecrow appearance as soon as I washed it.

For after the ceremony, Dad had booked a section of the restaurant in the Boar's Head Hotel next door, and we all trooped round, including Alice our cleaning lady, who Dad had invited after some deliberation. Alice was very quiet, and didn't want any of the champagne that Dad popped and then poured for everyone. I thought that this must be quite strange for Alice as she and Mum used to get on well. The week after Mum died, Alice came round every day with a casserole, or a pie, and checked that we had milk and bread, and one day I found her in our study, polishing the mantelpiece and all of Mum's knick-knacks with a tissue in her free hand. Today Alice looked like a mouse in a room full of rats, but every so often I caught her looking at me in my dress, trying to smile but not quite managing it.

It was a sea of grown-ups whispering to each other, and

looking over at Dad and Kate, who didn't really seem to notice anyone else except each other. Sally was scratching at her arms in her tartan dress, while a quite large lady who must work for the hotel – she had a uniform on, with a gold badge pinned to her waistcoat – was trying to persuade Erica to hand over her tattered old comfort blanket. The blanket wasn't fitting for the occasion, I suppose, but Erica wouldn't let go of it, even though the large woman was tugging at it. Having won, Erica then stomped off to hide behind Kate, pushing her face into the back of Kate's red dress, and I thought that I would quite like to hide behind someone too.

I saw the sign for the Ladies just above Sally's head, and I decided it would be a good time to go and check that my hair hadn't reverted to normal already.

'I'm going to go to the Ladies toilets,' I told Sally, as I walked past her. 'Do you want to come too?'

The toilets smelled very strongly of perfume and had scented tissues in pink boxes and a basket of tiny soaps by the sinks. Sally and I immediately took three soaps each and then I noticed a rash, like a huge strawberry mark, all over Sally's neck.

'What's that?' I said, a bit tactlessly in hindsight.

Sally touched her neck. 'It's called hives,' she said. 'It's probably the itchy dress.'

We looked at each other then, and I remembered Elsa telling me that hives happen when you're anxious or upset. Sally's only young, she's not even ten yet, I thought.

'It'll be OK,' I said. 'I know it's strange and unfamiliar

right now.' I didn't know that it would be OK at all, but it seemed important to make Sally believe that.

She looked quite grateful for the kindness, but began itching at the front of her dress again.

I examined my hair in the mirror above the sinks. It was still glossy and blow-dried. I thanked God for small mercies.

'I like your normal hair,' Sally said in a tiny little voice. 'I wish I had curly hair. My hair is so boring and straight.'

I am used to people saying this, and usually they don't mean it at all and are smug in the knowledge that they will never have my hair. I said thanks though, because Sally was only trying to be nice.

'I might go and get a sausage roll now,' she said, clutching her little soaps. 'I'm supposed to be looking after Erica anyway. She doesn't really know what's going on.'

Poor Sally, I thought after she'd gone. Who's going to look after her? It isn't going to be me, that's for sure. I mean, I don't not like her or Erica, but I'm not a child any more, and I don't really want to be anyone's older sister and give out advice and things like that. It's not actually fair that I should be expected to do that when I have a lot on just thinking about myself.

I could happily have stayed in the Ladies toilets and just looked at my hair for the entire reception, but I forced myself to go back out into the room. At least there was a buffet, which Sam was stuffing his face with, not talking to anyone. I've noticed Sam's appetite is never affected by anything. I stood next to him and ate a crumbly mushroom pastry thing, and when one of the hotel staff went past us with a tray of more champagne I took one without her noticing and drank a big mouthful of it and my head swooned and everyone's bodies and faces shimmered. It was awful and quite nice at the same time. Sam was too busy eating his fourth fried chicken wing to notice, but then I felt boiling hot in the itchy tartan dress and thought some fresh air would make me feel better.

Just as I was walking to the door I saw Elsa sitting stiffly on a chair reading her book, wearing a faded old T-shirt with a massive rip in the shoulder and a denim skirt that came up to her thighs. She had made no effort at all to dress up and looked out of place, as everyone else was wearing smart clothes and suits and ties. I tried to will Elsa to look up and see me, but she didn't. She was as still as a statue, and I'm sure she wasn't really reading her book. Harry, who was wearing a jacket and a quite-creased white shirt, was by the fireplace, being forced to talk to an elderly man with a moustache and hearing aid. Harry looked like a trapped bird. But as he is quite good at being polite to people and is good-natured, it's often hard to know what he's really thinking.

No one noticed that I just walked out of the hotel into the broad daylight.

I stood outside the doorway and watched all the people going past on the pavement. Mothers with babies in push-chairs, and two girls about Elsa's age in pencil skirts and blouses, eating sandwiches while walking along. People just doing normal things, completely unaware that my father had lost his mind. I wanted a time machine so that I could be one of them and not have to be here, feeling woozy and helpless.

A few doors down from the Boar's Head Hotel is a toy shop that I'd been in before, as Dad used to take me to get trolls from there, back when I was young and I was fixated with them. I had a really big one with bushy pink hair, and then loads of smaller ones with assorted hair colours. We'd not been back for years, because obviously I have now long since grown out of the trolls, but also because last time I knocked over a toddlers' books display carousel and Dad had to pay for some mangled Miffy books that got squashed underneath it and we left in disgrace. But still, I smiled in remembrance of the trolls and Dad, who had been my friend then.

'Running away, are you?' said someone behind me, interrupting my thoughts. When I looked it was Jake, who was trying to get his tie off. Unlike Sam and Harry, Jake looked really smart, with creases ironed in his trousers, which matched his jacket, and polished shoes.

I looked down at my dress. 'Probably not in this outfit.' I tried not to burp out all the bubbles that were coming up my throat.

Jake laughed. 'It's not really *you*, is it?' he said, looking at my dress.

'I'm not a dress person, no,' I said. 'They just get in the way of everything.'

Jake nodded and finally got his tie off. 'They look a lot more comfortable than trousers though. Boys don't get a choice.'

I smiled awkwardly. I couldn't imagine Sam ever admitting he hankered after wearing a dress.

'I'm sorry about your mother,' Jake said then. 'But my mum's all right really.'

I didn't know what to say to that. Even though Elsa couldn't hear, I felt it would be traitorous even to entertain the idea that Kate was anything else but an interloper.

'And you've still got Charlie,' said Jake, as though having one deranged parent left was compensation.

'What happened to your dad?' I asked then. 'He's not dead too, is he?' I wondered if that was what my father had meant by absent.

'I don't know,' said Jake. 'I haven't seen him for four years.'

'Not once?' I said. 'Not even on your birthdays?'

'Nope.' Jake shrugged. 'He just left one day and never came back.'

Of course, I can't stand thinking of my mother not coming back, but she died and she couldn't help it. Imagine knowing your father is alive, but not where he is? How selfish, just to leave people worrying about you. And worse, not even remembering their birthdays.

'He and my mum were never married,' Jake went on. 'I think he left her for another woman. He might have a new family by now. More kids maybe . . .'

'Oh, gosh,' I said, quite shocked.

At this point a cheer went up inside the hotel, and I heard Dad's voice and then clapping. I ignored it. It felt wrong that Dad was having a nice time while me and Jake were talking about never seeing our other parents again.

'It doesn't seem right that people can just start loving someone else, does it?' I said. 'It means love is pointless and people are very fickle.'

Jake looked a bit stumped, but I'm sure he knew what I meant. Even though I was really talking about Dad, the same thing has happened to Jake, and Sally and Erica, and they never even got to say goodbye.

We stood there for a minute a bit awkwardly. I can't bear silences so I had to start talking again.

'At least today's nearly over,' I chattered, as we watched a few guests departing the hotel. Kate and Dad were the last to come out of the hotel, with Sally and Erica behind them. Neither of them noticed that me and Jake were standing up the road gawping at them, or that Sam and Harry were now loitering over by the bus stop, looking like two people who'd escaped from prison. And Elsa was leaning against the hotel railings with her book in her hand, yawning, as though the whole thing was too boring for words.

'The depressing thing is,' I said to Jake, 'that tomorrow I'll have my old hair back again. Life is extremely unfair.'

Jake stared at me for a second and then burst out laughing. I felt quite happy that I'd made him do that, even though my hair is not a laughing matter in the slightest.

Afterwards, Kate and her three went back to her house in London as Dad obviously can't afford a honeymoon or anything. He said they'll stay until we all move as they have to do their own packing. And then, after that, our lives will never be the same again.

When I got into bed after it was all over, and tried to write about it, it was really hard, and at first the words didn't come. Most of all, I looked at my diary and remembered what Mum had said about 'noteworthy events', and I wondered if ever in a million years she would have thought Dad might marry someone else and that I'd one day be writing about it as a noteworthy event.

Saturday 4th August

I woke up today for the last time in my bedroom in our house and already there was the sound of bustle all around me.

'Sam,' Dad called from somewhere. 'Can you please either box up all those old half-made Airfix kits under your bed and label them for charity, or label them for taking with us? You can't possibly be interested in them any more.'

Sam growled something unclear from somewhere else in the house. I looked at the clock beside my bed. It was 9.00 a.m. and Sam would be in a vile mood at this hour.

'Elsa, Harry. You won't have room for all those records,' Dad called again. 'Perhaps you could find out how much you can get for them at the second-hand record exchange in Colchester?'

There was silence as Elsa and Harry don't usually wake up before midday at weekends.

I had carefully labelled all my belongings one way or the other. It had been really hard and sad, and took all my good nature and I was wondering why I'd bothered to be so cooperative. Obviously there was some bargaining power to be had, and as usual I had completely overlooked it.

I lay there, hoping that if I staged a protest by not getting out of my bed at all today, Dad would decide we could put off leaving until I was ready to get up.

But he was at my bedroom door at 9.15 a.m. 'Come on, Lydia,' he said jovially. 'Rise and shine.'

Bob slipped in behind him, padding over to my bed and

leaping up to take his position on my stomach. I reached out and stroked his soft ears, and he purred contentedly, settling down for another nap.

'Bob's tired,' I said.

But my father was unusually on the ball today. He wasn't having any of it. 'That cat is permanently comatose,' he said briskly. 'Come on, up you get.' He smiled at me and then disappeared to shout at Harry and Elsa again.

I pushed back the sheets and blankets, already missing them. Apparently we will be sleeping under things called continental quilts, or 'duvets', from now on. I'd seen the duvets in Habitat with Elsa when we went with Dad to choose boat-proof kitchenware recently. They're like big cotton sleeping bags, but without the zip.

'But look, Lydia, you can choose your own duvet cover!' my father had said brightly. 'Look at all the lovely colours. Wouldn't you like a nice rainbow-striped one?'

I had to admit the duvet cover patterns were actually quite nice, but Elsa and I had agreed that we couldn't let Dad think that anything about the move was in any way appealing.

'Don't give in,' Elsa had hissed a reminder in my ear. 'Be strong.'

'I'm not sure I like any of them,' I'd told him stiffly. 'They're not really my style.'

Dad looked quite exhausted. He shook his head and began heading to the till with his trolley full of enamel and melamine mugs, bowls and plates.

'Well, Erica and Sally have already chosen theirs,' he said craftily, as the kitchenware was placed in paper bags.

'We'd rather sleep under towels,' declared Elsa, who hadn't actually asked me. 'But thanks all the same.'

'I'm not sure I do want to sleep under a towel, actually,' I whispered to her as we walked out to the car park.

'Trust me,' replied Elsa, lifting her chin. 'The point here is to let Dad know that we cannot be bought off with mere rainbow-striped duvet covers.'

I wasn't sure where making this point would get us, but hadn't the wherewithal to argue just then.

Dad had gone back and bought us duvets and covers anyway, whilst Elsa and I weren't at home. They were downstairs, with seven others. He'd chosen a bright blue cover for me, decorated with orange stars: the kind of pattern a seven-year-old might like. Elsa's plan has backfired on me and I am now stuck with a duvet cover designed for a small child. I am beginning to realise that as much as I want to trust her in these matters, Elsa isn't always right.

After I'd got up and got dressed, and taken all the sheets and blankets off my bed, I looked around at my old bedroom and how bare it all was, and I now know what it means to have a lump in your throat from emotion. I've got used to not seeing my mum coming through my bedroom door, but I would never again sit in the dark and watch the bats on the roof with Sam. Or lie in front of the fireplace reading. The family who were moving in on Monday would probably change my swallow wallpaper too. I put my hand out and touched one of the swallows, I don't know why.

Then I did my daily examination of my dreadful hair in

the mirror above the fireplace, picked up my little rucksack and made myself go, shutting the door behind me.

Forty minutes before we were supposed to leave for ever, Sam said we should go and see the garden one last time, and we walked down past the pond and the landscaped lawn to the bottom, 'the wilderness' as it was known. Mum had deliberately left this bit to grow untamed, so that it is like coming across a little wood, the ground covered in broken-off branches and twigs, and big bits of bushy foliage growing wherever it chooses. The best bit about this part of the garden is the brook at the end, where our land stops. In summer, shaded by the trees, we sit with our feet in the water after school. It is far enough away from the house that we feel detached from the adults – a place where we have some privacy – but close enough to run in for some refreshments and bring them back out again.

It has always been our place – me, Sam, Harry and Elsa. None of us have come down here much since Mum died. It always reminds me too much of her, because she loved our garden.

We stopped at the edge of the wilderness, and Sam looked up. Following his gaze I saw a familiar-looking bike, though missing a wheel, dangling from the tree above us.

'That's my old bike!' I glared at Sam. 'You told me it got stolen from the shed when we forgot to lock it that year when Mum was ill. All the time you knew exactly where it was!' I crossed my arms. 'What's *wrong* with you!'

He made one of his innocent faces, where his eyes go

very wide, as if he hasn't got a clue what you're talking about, but I know his lying face off by heart.

'You never rode that bike anyway,' he said after a bit, as though this excused him. 'And you know I like taking things apart. I was planning to get it down and put the wheel back on, but then I kind of forgot about it . . .' He trailed off, and his smirk disappeared. Suddenly the stupid bike didn't seem to matter as much any more. Sam hadn't come back to make amends because of what had happened to Mum, and I couldn't really blame him for that.

I sighed. 'I don't mind *that* much.'

'Sorry, Lyds,' Sam said, as though he really meant it. 'Sorry about all the stuff I've stolen from you and wrecked.'

'It's OK,' I told him.

'No more wilderness,' he said.

'Maybe one day we can come back?' I suggested hopelessly.

'Not very likely.' Sam kicked at a fallen branch and quite a few beetles scuttled out from underneath it in fright. He looked at me. 'You're not being half as brattish as I thought you'd be about all this. Harry and I had bets on you running away, or trying to set the house on fire. But you've been pretty good about it.'

'There's not much point in being a brat, is there?' I said. 'It's so obvious that Dad is in a bind. It would only make it worse.'

Sam looked at me, and then he did something he hasn't done for a long time. He grabbed me with both his arms and hugged me very tightly.

'Sam,' I said. 'What will become of us all?'

'It's character-building, Lydia,' he said. 'One day you'll be able to tell your grandchildren all about your amazing adventures as a child with your crazy family.'

'That's about a hundred years away,' I said, boggling at the idea of being anyone's granny. 'And to be honest I don't actually think my character needs any more building. If anything, I wish some of it would disappear.'

'Lydia! Sam!' called Dad from the top of the garden. 'The van's here and loading up. We'll need to leave in half an hour!'

Sam let go of me and shivered. And I blew a kiss to the wilderness.

'Goodbye, wilderness,' I said.

It was time to go.

Tuesday 7th August

The Lady Beatrice, Maling-on-Sea, Essex

I haven't been able to write for a few days as I have had no electricity in my cabin and so Bob and I have read by candlelight at night, which only illuminates the garish orange star pattern on my continental quilt. I really wish I had ignored Elsa and been there while Dad was buying them and chosen my own. But no point in crying over spilt milk now, I suppose.

We've been living here four days, and so far it's a bit like a bad dream that is actually happening while you're awake. Thank goodness I have mostly kept Bob to myself and forced him to sleep in my bunk with me. But Bob has struggled, as he likes to sleep with his back to a wall always for some reason (this started because of the swallow wallpaper in my bedroom) and my wall has streaks of rusty water running down it where it leaks, and in the mornings Bob's tail is damp and he looks even more miserable than me. Bob despises discomfort.

Harry explained again that *Lady Beatrice* is a wooden boat, and all wooden boats leak, and as soon as one leak is dealt with another one springs up.

'But won't the whole thing just rot away one day?' I said.

Harry could only agree with a nod.

'*Lady Beatrice* must have been really cheap,' I said. 'I suppose whoever owned it before was glad to get rid of it.'

Harry sighed. He looked a bit pained by the wall next to my bunk. 'I'm sorry,' he said. 'If Dad hasn't got the time,

I'll see if I can make it better.' He looked in the cupboard below. 'It's dry in here though,' he said. 'You can unpack, you know.'

Bob, who was parked on top of the quilt, gave me a bit of a doubtful look as Harry left my cabin. I stuffed the last of my clothes in the drawers under the bunk and hoped Harry was right about the cupboard staying dry. There's a little pinboard above the fold-down table, and in the middle of it someone had stuck a small mirror. I took my photos out of one of the cardboard boxes on the floor and started pinning them up. I put the one of Mum with me as a baby right next to the mirror so I would always see it. I haven't looked at it for a long time, and felt a bit overwhelmed suddenly by the strangeness of my mother just not existing any more. There was nothing to be done though. Mum wasn't coming back. She didn't know where I was and what had happened, and in a way I was glad as she might find it upsetting.

Erica and Sally have been looking quite shell-shocked and tearful since we arrived. I am trying to adapt to the fact that they are younger than me and that I am no longer 'the baby who gets away with murder', as my brothers and sister have complained about often, and despite being tested to the limit I myself haven't cried or screamed since we got here. Not once.

Kate gathered us all in the saloon at about 7.00 p.m. yesterday to talk about 'housekeeping', which sounded like nothing I want anything to do with, but apparently very much is. We all have duties, Kate said, and will take it in turns to clean and wash up and take stuff to the launderette until we get a washing machine. Kate made it clear that gone are the days of a cleaner and that we are all responsible for our own cabins. This wasn't sounding so bad, to be honest, but then she told us about the 'dinner rota'.

'I'll put it up in the kitchen,' said Kate, pointing at the galley. 'But I've made up a weekly rota of evening meals and I'd be very grateful if you didn't make a fuss about it as we have to save some money and there'll be none of the cordon bleu meals you might be used to.'

Elsa, who had been deliberately filing her nails, looked up at Kate with a very flinty expression on her face. 'What do you mean, *cordon bleu*,' she said coldly. 'Are you suggesting that there was something wrong with the food our mother made us?'

Kate fixed her with a look. 'Did I say that?' she said.

'You implied it,' went on Elsa. 'I don't mind cooking, if that is what you're worried about. My mother did teach me a thing or two about cooking, you know.'

A bit unnecessary from Elsa, though I have to admit the first thing I spotted on the bit of paper Kate was holding out was 'Cauliflower Cheese', which makes me gag. Elsa makes a brilliant fish pie. I peered forward to see if 'Fish Pie' was on there. It wasn't.

'That's very sweet of you, Elsa,' said Kate, with one of those unnatural smiles on her face. 'But I am very capable of cooking. I've been doing it for twenty-odd years now, all by myself.'

Elsa's nostrils flared and she went back to filing her nails.

Kate opened her mouth to say something else, but then shut it again and walked into the galley and pinned her rota to the corkboard above the work surface.

We all rushed to examine the rota, and my heart sank. Along with cauliflower cheese, there was macaroni cheese, and pork pie and salad, and beans on toast, and soup – which is not even a meal. No lasagne. No fish pie. No beef Wellington – my next favourite after lasagne.

'Ugh,' muttered Elsa. 'All meals that a simpleton could make.'

To be fair, Kate made a good show of pretending she hadn't heard that as she turned to finish folding the pile of washing back from the launderette.

'Thank God I'm only going to be stuck here another few weeks,' Elsa went on, quite selfishly. 'I'll think of you all, while I eat whatever the hell I like.'

Elsa is going travelling with Anna at the end of August, and has been quite smug about it. I have slightly shut it out of my mind because I am jealous. It will be years before *I* can escape.

Erica and Sally gave Elsa a scared look. They are frightened of her whiplash tongue in much the same way as I used to be and sometimes still am.

Dad seems to be pretending to be completely unaware of any tension on the *Lady Beatrice*, and keeps walking around smiling and reminding us that this and that is going to happen to make living here better, but I am not sure how, as he hasn't got any money, which is why we've ended up here. I had thought that when he sold our house he would have money left over, until Sam reminded me that most of it has gone to the bank.

'I don't really mind, Dad,' I lied. 'Just as long as the telly works and I can use the hairdryer.'

But the telly has already been compromised by the electricity supply being overloaded, or cutting out whenever it rains, and Sam and Harry have been out there at least three times with torches, and wellies and waterproofs on, trying to fix it. Luckily Sally and Erica are miserable about the telly business too, so for once I don't look like the arch-complainer in the family now and Kate is a bit more interested because of E and S. Kate is a lot better at making people do things than Dad, who always takes Sam's or Harry's first answer of I'll Do it Later. Even so, I foresee many frustrations ahead.

What am I going to do if the TV stops working altogether and Dad can't afford to buy another one? We will become like one of those experiments where families try living like they did in the eighteenth century, without any of life's modern conveniences and luxuries, but with plenty of hardship. Though I would definitely call the TV a necessity, not a luxury. More now than ever. And books. At least you don't have to turn a book on, you just have to open it and read it. That's so brilliant when you think about it.

Friday 10th August

There is no real privacy on *Lady Beatrice*, and trying to concentrate on reading a book is hard. This is annoying as I am halfway through *Octavia*, a romantic novel by a writer called Jilly Cooper.

Octavia is the kind of book my mother would probably have thought frivolous rubbish, but Aunt Lorna has sent me all of my cousin Lizzie's Jilly Cooper novels and I have become a bit obsessed with them. *Octavia* is one of about six books all about girls leaving home and living in rented flats, going to big grand houses at weekends, where they shoot clay pigeons and have tempestuous flirtations with brooding men who don't seem very nice but are somehow very attractive. The thought of leaving home and living like Octavia, or Bella, or Prudence is the light at the end of my tunnel. One day I will share a flat in London with the best friend I have yet to make. To be honest though, now that I have read a few of the Jilly Cooper books, the story does seem to be more or less the same in each one and the girl always ends up with the brooding man, who turns out to have been in love with her all along but has been hiding this because he is shy or has been privately heartbroken in a previous relationship.

Even though I don't plan on having anything to do with it myself, I was curious to see if some actual sex would appear but it is mostly some intense kissing and then waking up the next morning and getting breakfast in bed, which was a bit of a let-down.

'Oh, I read those,' said Elsa, picking up *Octavia*, which is now quite dog-eared and damp because I've been reading it in my cabin. 'Quite entertaining, but very unrealistic.'

Elsa then went on about the false expectations of life and of men in particular that are described in Jilly Cooper books and that I would be better off reading something by Fay Weldon or Erica Jong if I wanted to know what life is *really* like for women. I'm not too sure I do want to know, as I am already experiencing what life is really like for girls and if that's anything to go by, the future looks a bit gloomy for me. But because Elsa probably knows what she's talking about when it comes to this kind of thing, I did look at one of her Fay Weldon books – one called *Praxis*.

I understood from the summary on the back of *Praxis* that it was about two sisters and the different turns their lives took after a troubled childhood, which seemed very relevant to our situation, but a few chapters into *Praxis* something rather disturbing and weird happened and made me feel strange, so I'm not sure what Elsa's on about. Maybe I'll go back to *Praxis* later.

Sunday 12th August

Last night, after dinner of pea soup and brown bread and cheese, I was just propping my book up against the salt and pepper pots on the saloon table to continue reading when Jake came and sat down next to me with a magazine.

As I have mentioned, I'm not sure what I think about Jake. He's nothing like Harry or Sam. Even though at fourteen he is only a year younger than Sam, he is much more advanced in certain ways and seems to care quite a lot about what he looks like, and he has a lot of friends. I know this because before we left our house in Cottlesham, I eavesdropped on Kate saying to my father that Jake had invited fifteen people from his school to their flat in London for a leaving-party, including a girl called Simone who was his girlfriend. Kate said Jake had spent an hour in the bathroom getting ready before everyone arrived.

Sam, however, hardly ever had friends round to our house, except for a boy called Felix who he's known since primary school. Sam and Felix would spend hours in Sam's bedroom looking up Sam's telescope and discussing stars or astrophysics, things like that, or make submarines out of Airfix kits. Sam has never shown any interest at all in girls or in having loads of friends, whereas Jake has already put up posters in his cabin of girls in skimpy tennis outfits, or in bikinis and drinking cocktails on a beach. The girls mostly have prominent boobs. He's also lined up all his shoes in his cabin in a neat row and I saw him iron his T-shirt once.

Dad has said that Jake is the 'gregarious' type. 'Not unlike how I was at that age,' Dad said. 'I was quite keen on girls as a teenager.'

'Who can Sam take after then?' I said. 'He's so belligerent!'

Dad laughed. 'Belligerent, is he? Well.'

I was quite pleased with myself using this word in conversation, though wondered if I had used it wrongly. But Dad just added, 'Sam's a late developer. Too much time with his head in a school book probably. He's a good boy though. Underneath.'

I am not so sure about Sam being a good boy, but secretly I am glad he is a bit strange, as Jake makes me feel slightly self-conscious. Not on purpose, but whereas I've never particularly cared about being frilly and feminine and wearing perfume before, I wonder if I might seem a bit plain to Jake. I will never ever look like those girls in bikinis drinking cocktails. I only bought eyebrow tweezers because I thought they might be useful for other things too. I'm not sure I'll ever be ladylike.

Anyway, Jake had put some sticky gel stuff like you can get in Boots the chemists and Woolworths in his hair, to make it stand up slightly stiffly on his head.

Jake took my book and peered at the cover, which was a picture of a glamorous girl, with glossy lipstick, wearing sunglasses and a fur coat.

'It's a romance,' I said, hoping that this would make me appear more mature.

'Looks awful,' he said, grinning. 'You read a lot, don't you?'

'Quite a lot,' I said. 'Life seems better in books.'

Jake gave me a funny look. 'Does it?' he said. 'But it's all made up.'

'So what?' I looked over at the cover of his magazine, which showed a bicycle and there was a big flash at the bottom that featured a competition to win pannier baskets. 'Wow,' I said. 'I can't wait to enter *that* competition.'

Jake laughed out loud. 'You're quite amusing,' he said.

'Thanks,' I said. Since I'm pretty sure I'm not a looker, being quite amusing is compensation. If I looked like Elsa, then I could probably be really dull and it wouldn't matter. Of course, Elsa is not dull and she is also pretty. Life is unfair like that.

'Sally likes reading,' said Jake. 'You two are quite similar, actually.'

As Sally has long, straight, neat hair and is much quieter than me, and she is still a child, I didn't agree about this.

'How do you mean?' I asked.

'Just . . .' Jake shrugged. 'I don't know. It's just something about you.'

I turned round to look at Sally who was sitting with her arm round Erica on the sofa, reading a *Famous Five* book. Erica was huddled into her, holding her blanket thing. Sally looked patient, I thought, which I'm not. But she also looked kind, which I appreciate in a person. I prefer to pretend Erica doesn't exist as she has taken my place as youngest in the family.

'It's a bloody drag having to go to a new school,' said Jake, looking at a page in his magazine.

'Are you going to miss your friends?' I said.

'Yep,' said Jake. 'What about you?'

'I didn't really have any friends,' I said. 'I am a friend-repeller. I'm sure it's something to do with my hair.'

Jake laughed again. 'I'll be your friend.'

'Thanks. But I don't think you can be my friend as well as my brother.'

'Who says?' he said, just as Bob jumped up onto the bench next to us and started rubbing his face against Jake's arm. 'It's not like we're blood-related, and loads of my friends in London were girls.'

'Hmm,' I said, a bit intimidated.

'And I like your hair,' Jake said. 'You remind me of Addie Loggins from that film *Paper Moon*.'

Jake could not know that *Paper Moon* is pretty much my favourite-ever film. It's all about a young girl being driven across America to her relatives by a con man, and they squabble and pretend not to like each other, but then they become partners in crime. Addie Loggins had short hair and wore dungarees. I watched *Paper Moon* on TV with Dad, who observed that Addie had 'guile, hidden beneath tomboyish innocence'. I wasn't exactly sure what that meant, but I really wanted to be the same as Addie Loggins. I couldn't imagine a boy liking *Paper Moon*. Sam had found it boring because there were emotions in it.

'I love that film so much,' I said.

'Yeah, me too,' said Jake.

'Well . . .' I said, suddenly a bit shy. Jake had said more civilised words to me in those last ten minutes than Sam had ever in the whole of our lives.

Still, I reminded myself, as Bob was now curled up on Jake's lap completely ignoring me, I must watch out that Jake doesn't become too close to Bob, as Bob is unofficially mine and no one is going to take him away from me.

I have noticed that cats are easily swayed by other sources of affection, so I'll have to stay alert to this.

Tuesday 14th August

Kate took me to buy my new school uniform today. She said we should get it early, as if you leave it too late they might have run out of sizes. I wasn't keen – I don't want to think about school yet – but Kate said we might as well get it over and done with.

'I took the girls to get theirs last week,' she said. 'It occurred to me that your father might forget.'

This is true. Dad wouldn't have a clue. Mum took control of all that – she'd even made me my uniform for Brainhill before she went into hospital and I'd made it last for two years after that.

Me and Kate walked up the high street to the special shop that does uniforms for Oaks in the school colours of navy blue and grey. Why are all school uniforms in such drab colours? Wouldn't a uniform in orange or bright green be a bit more cheerful? But then, not everyone looks good in orange. Elsa might because she is darker-skinned and looks nice in everything, but I would look awful – it would only make my cheeks look more red, though Dad insists my cheeks are 'rosy' and not red and that I should be grateful for being such a pretty, healthy-looking girl. I think all parents lie to their children and tell them they are more attractive than they are, but I wish they wouldn't, as it doesn't help in the long term.

It was a mixed experience. On the one hand I was getting a uniform that would be exactly the same as everyone else's and I'm not going to stand out by wearing one made out of wool or cotton, natural fibres such as Mum dictated. On the other hand, this has made me much sadder than I thought it would, as it is dawning on me that Mum only wanted me to have nice clothes, even if she didn't really want to know when I told her about the teasing. I still miss watching her at her sewing machine, making my school dresses and skirts. I didn't dwell on this for too long though because at last I don't have to have a duffel coat for winter! Kate allowed me to choose a belted winter coat that actually makes me look like a grown-up rather than Paddington Bear.

'You'll need to protect these,' said Kate as the assistant packed the shirts and skirts up. 'The girls already have rust stains on their school shirts.'

We stopped off at the dry cleaners on the way back and got some of the thin plastic they wrap clothes in and some metal hangers too. I was quite grateful to Kate for anticipating potential disaster, and felt a bit of guilty pleasure when she then said we should buy some cakes from the bakers to take home and cheer us all up. I hoped that Elsa wouldn't be around when we got back as she would doubtless think I have been disloyal and have passed over enemy lines. That will never be true, but it is a relief not to be constantly resisting people when they're probably only trying to help.

But just before we started down the hill to *Lady Beatrice*, Kate decided to have a 'woman's conversation' with me, which was unexpected and a bit embarrassing.

'Have you got everything you need, Lydia?' she asked. 'I mean, what about your periods – have they started yet?'

'Oh. That's all in hand,' I said awkwardly. Bodily functions are not much discussed in my family. Elsa does sometimes refer to my periods, but she has never once asked me if I need help with anything like that. I've had to steal her old bras for instance, because I am mortified at the thought of asking my father to buy me some of my own. Elsa's bras are far too big for me, so I do without most of the time, something that it seems Kate is on to.

'Well, if you need sanitary towels, you must ask,' she said. 'And . . .' she glanced down at my chest, 'you probably need a bra.'

This was good news. I hadn't even had to ask. I smiled at Kate and thanked her, though I felt that I was betraying Elsa at the same time.

'Don't worry,' said Kate, as if reading my thoughts. 'This is just between us.'

I couldn't wait to get home and examine how my new coat looked from every angle in the bathroom mirror, which is the only one big enough to see most of your body, though it cuts off your head unless you squat down, which actually I don't mind. I wonder if head transplants will be a regular thing in the future. If so, I will ask for one similar to Elsa's friend Anna's head, including her hair. In the meantime, I hope to grow into my face, and that my hair will somehow straighten through hormonal changes, which I have heard is a possibility.

Friday 17th August

It's suddenly a heatwave and *Lady Beatrice* has kind of come into its own. We've all been lying around on deck, trying to ignore the tourists who seem to be constantly trailing past and gawping at us because of the whole Dunkirk and Second World War thing when barges like *Lady Beatrice* sailed to France to rescue soldiers. Looking at *Lady Beatrice* now, I can't imagine it would get as far as France as it creaks so much, and has holes in it everywhere. But we are living on a 'working antique', and tourists love antiques and the stories behind them, according to Sam, who is very proud of *Lady Beatrice*'s heritage and makes sure he is coiling ropes or climbing the mast for no reason when people are watching, much to Elsa's amusement.

For the past couple of days Elsa has sunbathed a lot in a bikini, refusing all Kate's food and only drinking Coke out of the bottle through a straw and eating handfuls of peanuts while reading books. She is now very brown and glamorous, and secretly views the tourists from behind her sunglasses, so that she can adjust her position if ever a young good-looking male goes past. I can see her doing this – I know Elsa's little ways. She doesn't talk to me, as I am still not fit to converse with properly, it seems. So I have had no choice but to hang around with Erica and Sally, who cling together like Siamese twins, plaiting each other's hair. I'm relieved to see that they are both still deathly pale like me despite hours of exposure to the sun.

I know this is a mean thing to say but I find it hard to be interested in Erica. She's all right, but she doesn't really do much without Sally – she just presses that blanket against her face and doesn't really speak.

But I have to admit, Sally is actually a nice person. She asked me if I am still sad about my mother and think about her. Nobody in my family talks about what happened to Mum, particularly Dad, so this made me warm to her, and I feel I may have overlooked Sally's virtues.

'I bet you miss your bedroom too?' said Sally. 'All the books and things you had to leave behind.'

'A bit,' I said. 'Quite a lot at the moment. But they're just things.'

'Important things though,' said Sally.

I looked at her and noticed properly that she has freckles on her nose and is actually very pretty. Normally this would not endear me to a person, but in Sally's case somehow it has the opposite effect.

'Our flat was really small,' went on Sally. 'So I didn't have much. And Mum was always on night shifts so we had a babysitter. Charlie's changed everything.'

I mainly only ever think about myself to be honest and how *my* life has changed. Now I wondered what it would be like to live in a tiny flat with your family and never see your only parent. It probably explains why Sally and Erica are stuck together like glue all the time.

'I didn't know any of that,' I said. 'Dad probably didn't tell me because I was annoyed about you. It can't have been very nice.'

Sally smiled at me. 'I was really hoping you wouldn't hate us. I'm glad you're my sister.'

I was taken aback by this and didn't know what to say, which is unusual for me as I am not often lost for words and have been told many times that I would be better off shutting up.

Then I glimpsed Elsa looking over at us suspiciously, and I felt a pang. Elsa is my real sister, the one I've had all my life, but then Sally is more like me in some ways. I felt an awful sad feeling, which was ridiculous – I can only describe it as thinking you are both losing something and getting something at the same time, and not feeling very comfortable about it.

At about four, Kate came up on deck with a huge tray of tea and biscuits – she'd even bought shortbread and not digestives, which seem to be the standard boring biscuit in all families – so she was trying. Even Elsa snuck a bit of shortbread when she thought no one was looking, and Sam was making a valiant effort not to be unfriendly to Jake, who wanted to help with the rope coiling and mast climbing.

And then Dad appeared, and stood looking at Sam and Jake with a relieved expression on his face. He noticed me sitting with Sally and put out his hand to pat my head.

'Good girl, Lydia,' he said vaguely, and then went to join Kate who was pouring tea out into mugs by the hatch.

With the afternoon sun and the clinking of metal masts and the tide coming up over the stinking mud, it didn't seem so bad to be here, not at that moment. Bob came along and curled up happily between me and Sally and I allowed myself to consider the possibility that it might all turn out OK.

Monday 20th August

Elsa's gone. She's flying from Heathrow airport to Lisbon in Portugal, and she and Anna are travelling around Europe before Elsa goes to Cambridge at the end of September. She didn't even move all of her things into her cabin on the *Lady Beatrice* when we left the house – most of them have been stored in Anna's spare room.

'No point in moving stuff,' she'd said. 'I'm only going to move it all out again soon.'

No one had argued with her about this at the time, but today I felt deserted. Somehow I still had a hope that Elsa would rescue me too and take me with her. That at the last minute somebody would say, 'This girl can't live in a place like that!'

Dad and I drove Elsa to the airport. Elsa looked really happy. It was sickening.

'I'm afraid the boat's telephone is still a bit erratic,' said Dad to Elsa. 'But I'll get the number of the pub in case of emergencies.'

The one telephone on the boat looks like one of those things sailors send out SOS messages in code on. It is huge. Like a public phone. It is kept in the wheelhouse, where no one goes. This means that even if Elsa did get through, no one would hear the phone, so it seems pointless to me.

'OK,' said Elsa next to him in the front passenger seat. She was staring out of the window with a calm smile on her face, the breeze lifting up her curls. She wore large dark sunglasses and suddenly she looked like an adult.

'Or postcards,' I said. 'Send us postcards.'

'I'll do my best,' said Elsa, 'but I'm back in England in a few weeks, hardly seems worth it.'

'Still,' said Dad. 'I'd like to know you're OK. Two girls travelling on their own. You need to be careful. I worry about you.'

'Oh do you?' said Elsa, still staring out of the car window.

'Of course I do.' Dad frowned. 'I'm your father.'

'Right,' said Elsa, finally turning to him. 'I forgot.'

Dad looked hurt. And though I silently agreed with Elsa that it was a bit rich him suddenly being the concerned parent, Elsa was going to get on her plane after this and leave me to have to be nice to Dad to make up for her need to tell the brutal truth at all times. Somehow Elsa gets away with her moods and her directness in a way that I'm sure I couldn't. Elsa doesn't care enough about being thought well of. I've noticed that people like that usually have everyone desperate to be their friend.

'I do understand, Elsa,' said Dad after a pause. 'You children have had to put up with a lot. I wish things had turned out differently . . .'

Elsa groaned and pushed her head back on the seat.

Dad shut up then and turned on Radio 4. Nobody spoke until we arrived at Departures.

Saying goodbye to people is the worst thing ever. Worse even than after they've gone. And though Elsa and I are not exactly best friends, she has been there since I was born, so it felt like something else was being pulled out from underneath me.

To my surprise, as soon as she had checked in, Elsa hugged me. Really tightly, for a long time.

'Look after yourself, Lyds,' she said. 'Try and have an adventure of your own, won't you?'

'How?' I said.

'I mean, something outside of all this,' she said mysteriously, and she blinked her brown eyes at me. 'Something that's yours.'

I nodded. 'Bye, Elsa,' I said. 'Please don't drown or talk to weirdos.'

Elsa laughed, still holding onto me. 'I'll try not to,' she said. 'And please don't drown or talk to weirdos either.' She released me and we all realised that her plane was boarding; it was up on the board and being announced over the Tannoy.

Dad looked really upset, and reached out to touch Elsa's hair. Normally Elsa would flinch at this kind of thing, as she's not one for public shows of affection. But her eyes looked a bit watery and she was making a face as though she had a peach stone stuck in her throat.

'I'll try and call, and write, Dad,' she said. 'Don't worry.'

I just wanted her to go now. This was unbearable.

'Come on.' I hooked my arm through Dad's. 'I'm sad.'

Elsa and Dad looked at each other, and then he put his hand in his back pocket and took out his wallet and pulled out a fifty-pound note. He pressed it in to Elsa's hand.

Elsa looked shocked but she still held onto it.

'Can you afford that?' she said half-heartedly.

Dad just smiled. 'I want you to have it for emergencies,'

he told her. 'But if you don't absolutely have to spend it, then you can give it back . . .'

Elsa rolled her eyes, but then she stood on tiptoe and kissed Dad's cheek.

'Keep an eye on each other,' she told us. 'I'm counting on you.'

In the car, Dad waited a few minutes before starting the engine and we sat there, outside Departures, watching people hurry inside with their suitcases.

'Are you OK, Dad?' I asked, feeling a bit worried.

He smiled. 'I'm absolutely fine,' he said sadly, and then he looked at me. 'Whatever happens, remember I love you all dearly, won't you?'

'OK,' I said, watching as he wiped at his face with his handkerchief. 'I will.'

I'm not like Elsa, I don't think I'm strong like her. I got into bed with Bob tonight and tried very hard not to miss my difficult, spiky sister. But everyone has to grow up, don't they? Everyone has to go away one day.

Tuesday 4th September

Sam walked part of the way to Oaks with me this morning. He's catching the bus from the high street to Brainhill, where he's still going. He's halfway through important exams and Dad thought he might as well stay there rather than have the disruption of settling into Oaks.

'You'll be OK,' he told me, quite kindly for Sam. He was carrying my bag for me. I had packed spare socks and pants, along with all the books and other paraphernalia, just in case I needed to suddenly run away. When I'd mentioned my contingency plans to Elsa before she left for her travels, she said she thought that was really sad.

'I suppose it depends what you mean by OK,' I told Sam.

'Well . . . Jake's in the year above you,' he said, scrunching up his eyes as though it hurt to acknowledge Jake in any way. 'You can walk to school with him tomorrow. He'll look out for you.'

I know Sam is only trying to help for once, but he doesn't get it either. I mean, it has already become clear that I smell. As I trudged up the hill with Sam, I caught the musty whiff of mould and something else, a kind of inky metal odour.

'Diesel oil,' Sam said, looking at me with my nose against my blazer. Depressed, I ignored him and looked to my left. We had climbed as far as the church with its huge graveyard and were just passing the gates. I gazed inside, thinking about all those bodies under the earth. The grass around the stones and tombs looked uneven, as though zombies burst out every night, patrolling the town, looking for humans to drag down into the underworld. It occurred to me that being dragged into the underworld would not be the very worst thing to happen right now.

'Lydia,' Sam was saying. 'Can you hear me?'

'What?' I snapped.

'The smell. It's diesel oil, from the engine,' Sam said cheerfully. He himself was dressed in school trousers and a scruffy white shirt, beneath which you could just glimpse a T-shirt with a 'Punk Skunk' transfer ironed across his chest. Elsa and I had been obsessed with this transfer, which was on special offer at Woolworths last summer. We had bought loads of them and enthusiastically ironed them onto every T-shirt in the house. Harry had been furious on finding his carefully faded plain black T-shirt emblazoned with the motif of a cartoon skunk with a Mohican.

'Great,' I said. 'Smelling like a petrol station on my FIRST DAY AT SCHOOL.'

'It's not that bad,' Sam said, patting my shoulder. 'Only if someone's standing right next to you.'

My form teacher is called Miss Grant, and she's very tall and willowy. Today she wore a floaty skirt down to her ankles and a matching top with no bra that made her chest wobble when she moved. It was quite difficult not to look at her chest. I can't imagine what it must be like to have a chest with enough there to wobble so I probably stared a bit too much. Miss Grant has also gone a bit overboard with henna. She has henna tattoos all up her arms and her hair is that special orangey-red and smells of clay. Miss

Grant smiles far too much to be normal; she's one of those really positive people that get on your nerves.

'Welcome, Lydia,' said Miss Grant, looking over at me from her desk. She was leaning against it. 'Everyone, be nice to Lydia. She has just moved to Maling and she has an amazing story to tell about where she lives. Isn't that right, Lydia?'

I was trying so hard not to go red, I couldn't speak. I just tried not to make one of my faces.

Miss Grant was looking at me expectantly, along with the rest of the form. All eyes were swivelled in my direction.

'Not really,' I managed, after what seemed like a year.

'Are you a gypsy?' whispered the girl sitting next to me. She's called Nadine and she's petite with black hair that gleams. She'd spent the last ten minutes tidying her pencil case. I saw that everything in the case was purple.

'No,' I whispered back.

'Come on, Lydia, tell us all about it,' urged Miss Grant, who was smiling in a forced kind of way.

'I live on the *Lady Beatrice*,' I said at last, staring into the middle distance, avoiding eye contact. 'Down on the quay.'

'Wonderful.' Miss Grant looked round the class. 'Isn't that wonderful, everyone?'

You stupid woman, I thought, wanting to pull out her silly hair and scratch off her tattoos.

No one said anything.

'Well, *I* think it's wonderful,' said Miss Grant. 'I do quite a bit of sailing myself.' She looked a bit wistful.

Luckily though, it seems the general opinion in my form

is that living on the *Lady Beatrice* is very *uninteresting* indeed. Thank goodness.

First days at a new school are mixed because on the one hand no one expects you to do much work as you are new, but on the other hand, everyone has already made friends and there didn't seem to be anyone who looked like they wanted to be mine. Maybe there will be someone, who's nothing like Donna, I don't know.

Tonight in bed I am cuddling Bob and being grateful for small mercies, such as no one commenting on the smell of diesel oil or laughing at my hair.

Wednesday 12th September

A postcard arrived for me this morning from Elsa; the picture was of a place called Myrtos, on a Greek island called Crete, with a bright blue sea and a white-sand beach, and a lot of craggy rocks. Elsa said she'd been bitten all over by mosquitos and had to go to a hospital because of a bite that got infected and that she'll be quite relieved to come back to England as the insects are getting a bit much in the Mediterranean and if she never sees Feta cheese again it will be too soon. Right at the very end she remembered to say, 'I hope everything on *Lady Beatrice* isn't too awful', and that she'd definitely be back with us for Christmas, after her first term at Cambridge, and love to Dad and Harry and Sam but no one else.

Christmas is ages away. I have never not seen Elsa for that long.

I sniffed the postcard for an exotic holiday smell, and then I put it inside *Harriet*, which is the last of the Jilly Cooper books from Lorna and which I've nearly finished. Then I was just packing my school bag up ready to go and looking for an apple, when Sally came into the galley in her pyjamas.

'Aren't you going to school, Sally?' I asked.

'I don't feel very well,' she said, in the familiar frail voice of one who is pretending to be ill. I have used this voice myself many times. But though Sally looked a bit pale, she looked more upset, as though she'd been crying.

'Is it school?' I said. 'Are you being teased about *Lady Beatrice*?'

Sally's lip wobbled slightly and her eyes got even more glassy, but she didn't say anything. She just half shrugged, half nodded.

'Don't take any notice,' I told her. 'You don't have to be like everyone else anyway. It's much better to be different.' I put my school bag over my shoulder, feeling a bit of a fraud as this is not something I believe myself. In fact, it is the kind of pointless advice that older people give you when they don't have a clue or have forgotten how awful it is to stand out in a crowd.

But Sally did look a bit cheerier. 'Thanks, Lydia,' she said.

I don't think it matters that what I'd told Sally was rubbish. The point was being kind enough to give her rubbish advice.

At lunch I went and tried to hide behind one of the prefab classrooms on the edge of the playing field and read my book on my own, but then this girl from my form called Juliet appeared and said that Miss Grant had asked her to keep an eye on me.

'She's a bit worried that you haven't made any friends,' said Juliet, who has long reddish hair like Rapunzel's. She sat down next to me and unwrapped a soggy-looking egg tart thing from some tinfoil. I noticed she had a name tag at the top of her socks which said her whole name: Juliet Huntley-Smith. Her socks were very white and her legs were very pale, with freckles blobbed all over them.

I turned my attention back to *Harriet*, which despite

being predictable is approaching a gripping climax, but still Juliet started talking about how she and her mum went past the quayside in their car the other day and saw an older boy in a leather jacket who was quite good-looking winding up ropes on the deck of *Lady Beatrice*.

'Is that boy your brother then?' said Juliet. 'He looks like James Dean.'

I am so bored by all the girls being interested in Harry, and almost wish he didn't exist so that I could test out whether people really like me for *me*. Harry doesn't do anything ever to get girls to like him, except stand there smoking a fag or winding a rope, and everyone seems to find that utterly fascinating.

'Yes, that is my brother Harry,' I said, holding *Harriet* right up to my face, even though the words were blurry and much too close-up to read.

'Gosh,' said Juliet. 'There's loads of you, isn't there? Like The Waltons or something. My mum gets all the gossip from her cousin who's a member of the Yacht Club.'

'They're not *all* related to me,' I said, wanting to put matters straight. 'My dad got remarried because my mum died.' I had decided that I would tell this in a matter-of-fact manner as soon as possible because otherwise it's too awkward. Best to just get it out of the way and hope that people change the subject.

'Oh,' said Juliet. 'Sorry.'

'It's OK,' I said quickly, as I can't be bothered with all the condolences.

'I don't know what I'd do if my mum died,' went on

Juliet. 'Since my dad moved to Thailand, it's just Mother and myself. I'd probably go and live with my aunt on her estate in Yorkshire.'

'Your aunt lives on an estate?' I said, confused, as Juliet is quite plummy.

'She inherited it from my uncle, who died,' said Juliet. 'He was stinking rich.'

'Oh, that kind of estate,' I said. 'I thought you meant a council estate?'

Juliet looked a bit blank when I said that.

I thought then how I'd like to go and live with my Aunt Lorna, who is definitely not stinking rich, but who lives in a nice stone cottage in Berkshire and spoils us when we visit. We could sit and drink tea and eat Jamaican ginger cake, which Lorna always buys from her local Spar shop for me and Sam as a treat because Mum never allowed us to have it at home. And I could take Lorna's Yorkshire terrier out for walks and have chats with Lorna in the evenings, with no one else to interrupt us. Dad might even be relieved to be rid of me as it would be one less person to have to take care of.

Juliet ate more of her soggy tart, which I now noticed had bits of asparagus and red pepper in it.

A group of boys walked past us then, and behind them was a very tall girl with dark, curly hair and strong features and quite large boobs for her age. She was eating a bag of proper chips from a chip shop.

'Oh dear,' said Juliet, looking at her too. 'Kay Palmer. She's in our year, and she's really odd. She eats chips every lunch time practically. Extremely unhealthy.'

Juliet sounded like someone's meddling old granny, I thought, as I watched her fold the rest of her soggy tart into the foil wrapping. Then with a mean little smile on her face she said, 'Kay's family are quite insane, and they've got an absolutely ridiculous dog, which is about the same size as a human being.'

'Like Scooby Doo?' I said.

'Yes, ridiculous,' repeated Juliet.

Just then Kay Palmer looked over at us, and she saw Juliet, and then she looked away again very quickly, and I thought I knew exactly how she felt, as it's how I felt at Brainhill all the time, as though there was something wrong with me and no one would say it to my face.

I shut my book and followed Kay's progress. She went round the tennis courts and onto the playing field, and then she sat down on the grass and opened up her chips. I could see them glistening a bit, probably with plenty of salt and vinegar on them.

If I had to choose between a chips person and a soggy asparagus tart person, I know which I'd prefer. I made a private note to investigate Kay Palmer.

Back at *Lady Beatrice*, Kate is already organising Christmas and a bit of a row broke out tonight between Sam and Jake. Kate says that in *her* family they don't open Christmas presents till after lunch, which in *her* family is not until 3.00 p.m.

When Mum was here, I opened my Christmas presents

before my parents had even properly woken up and then we'd watch TV and eat Terry's Chocolate Oranges till one o'clock, when we had our lunch. The thought of being awake all night and then most of the next day waiting for your lunch and presents is totally unfair. Sam obviously thought so too because he said that she could do it her way, and we would do it our way, and then Jake said something like 'That's the spirit' in a sarcastic way and Sam kicked Jake's bike (which Jake had parked at the bottom of the hatch stairs) and Jake looked like he was going to explode.

'That's enough!' said Kate. 'As I'll be cooking the Christmas dinner and buying the presents, then I decide what happens. Is that clear?'

Sam muttered something about her not being his mother and having no rights to boss him around, and Jake rolled his eyes and then glared at me even though I hadn't said anything (though for the record, I am on Sam's side. It's unfair that our feelings are not taken into consideration).

It's hard not to notice the obvious warring factions on board the *Lady Beatrice*. Sam and Jake don't like each other at all, and Erica and Sally are stuck in the middle, like me. But you have to side with your own family, don't you? Even though we are all supposed to be one big one.

But one thing I have noticed is that Dad is never around to see all these cracks appearing. He's at work all day and looks really tired when he gets home and then starts reading the paper. Meanwhile, Kate's face is beginning to look slightly like frosted glass.

Wednesday 3rd October

Things are already going wrong with my subjects at school. I'm getting more of a foggy brain than ever and keep asking for things to be repeated. I am always the last one to finish work during lesson times and other people have started to notice. Now when Mr Turing comes round to collect the papers in maths, everyone turns round to see if I'm still writing, which I always am. Mr Turing is not good at hiding his impatience, which only makes me panic more.

I'm really worried they are going to put me in the remedial band as all the issues that were foreseen by the deputy headteacher have come to pass. No one in the remedial band ever leaves school and does something with their lives: they all end up shelf-stacking in a supermarket. The thought of going through all this just to end up in Safeway is terrible.

'I'll help you,' said Sam, who seemed quite affected when I told him about my worries. 'But you really need to concentrate, Lydia. You can't just start yelling when you don't understand something. You really have to try and work it out.'

'Mr Turing said I was lazy,' I said. 'But it's not that.'

'What is it then?' said Sam.

'I just . . . everything fogs up in my head,' I said, feeling ashamed. 'And I can't remember anything I've been told in lessons. Sometimes, for about ten minutes I understand it, but then it's gone.'

'Hmmm,' said Sam, looking at me intently. 'Did you ever tell anyone that?'

'I tried once, at St Helen's, but you know what the nuns were like . . .'

Sam shuddered. 'OK, so this means you have to try even harder, and do something over and over again until it is imprinted on your brain. Like learning to talk, or learning to read . . . You learned to read, Lydia. And you could read much earlier than me. Think about that.'

'That's true.' I felt immediately better. I could learn, I'd already done it. I'd just have to try harder.

'Every night we're going to do one maths exercise until you get it. Even if it takes hours.'

'Thanks, Sam,' I said.

'But I'm not doing it if you start yelling or throwing stuff around. It's like teaching a chimpanzee.'

Now that just leaves history, geography, drama, physics, biology and chemistry. I'm quite good at art, well doodling, anyway. And really, drama is just standing around being dramatic and putting on voices, and that might be my best subject after English.

Thursday 18th October

I had detention after school today. I was caught in the crossfire of Juliet Huntley-Smith passing a note to a girl called Annie in history. It's the second time that I have been implicated in note-passing, and Mr Prescott did say that if he caught me again there would be consequences – even though it is not me that starts the notes. I just always seem to be caught with one in my hand. Juliet, who is more cunning than me, is invisible to Mr Prescott. Mr P is small and weedy and looks like he wouldn't say boo to a goose. Even when he marked me down for detention he was sorry about it. It was a bit sad really. Especially as the notes are mostly about how pathetic he is.

I was secretly pleased about the detention as it puts off going home for a while. Kate and Dad are already bickering about Dad being too soft and bringing us – me, Sam and Harry – up to be 'feral', and Kate says she spends all her time clearing up after us and that she didn't marry Dad and agree to move here so that she could be his live-in house-keeper. Going on the silence at meal times, it really doesn't seem like they have anything in common. Thank goodness they've stopped touching each other though. That was repulsive.

Miss Dark, who teaches drama, was supervising detention and arrived late outside the classroom at four, a bit flustered.

She looked at me, a boy called Justin in my year who is always in trouble and a girl in Band C who apparently refused to take off her nail polish when requested yesterday, then she looked at her watch.

'We've got one more pupil to come,' she said, looking down the corridor, just as Kay Palmer came round the corner.

Since I first saw Kay, I have found out that she is in my band, which is good news, but not in any of my lessons, except for P.E. Kay is always on her own, but she doesn't look lonely or very bothered about it. Yesterday she was sitting by the school bandstand on the steps reading a book, which I saw was called *The Incredible Journey* and had a picture of a dog on the cover.

'Hurry up please, Kay,' Miss Dark said. She unlocked the door to the detention classroom and pushed us all in, though I dawdled as I wanted to start a conversation with Kay.

'Hello,' I said.

'Hello,' said Kay.

'Why are you in trouble?' I asked her.

'I accidentally knocked Mr Prescott's hairpiece off with my bag in the corridor,' she said, straight-faced but quietly, so that Miss Dark couldn't hear. 'I was only trying to get it over my shoulder and told him I can't help it if I'm tall and I didn't do it on purpose, but he didn't believe me. He's obviously got me down as a troublemaker.'

I smiled at her and would have laughed but Miss Dark was eyeing us.

'Go on then. Inside,' she ordered, and as I went past her I got a waft of perfume and saw she was wearing really bright red lipstick. Miss Dark sighed as she looked at some notes she had in her hand.

'Right, two sides on the Nuremberg Trials,' she said, looking around. 'That's you, Kay, and you, Lydia. You two' – she spoke to Justin and Nail Varnish Girl – 'can write an essay on your strengths and weaknesses.'

I'd taken in hardly any information about the Nuremberg Trials during history, so I knew I'd just have to make something up. I'd much rather have had an essay on my strengths and weaknesses as at least half that essay would be extremely easy.

She handed us out paper and told us to start working and we all sat and, in my case, stared at the blank bit of paper, panicking. Kay was sitting at the desk next to me.

Miss Dark was sorting through her bag, muttering and sighing, looking for something.

'Bugger,' she hissed, and then looked up at us. 'I need to go and collect something from the staffroom,' she said. 'So I'll need to leave you alone for five minutes . . .' She slung her little handbag over her shoulder and picked up some keys. 'I expect you to behave yourselves. And no one is to leave the classroom. Understand?'

As soon as she'd gone, I resumed sweating at the essay I had to write, yet again hoping for a miracle.

Justin and the girl with the nail varnish, seemed to already be flirting. Which left me and Kay silently sitting next to each other. I sighed and looked sideways at her – I saw she'd already written a few sentences, but she must have felt my eyes boring into her because she looked up and then looked down at my blank piece of paper.

'Are you stuck?' she said.

'I'm not really confident on the Nuremberg Trials,' I whispered back.

'Prosecution of Nazis after the Second World War . . .' said Kay. 'Except for Hitler and Himmler and Goebbels, who'd topped themselves by then . . .' She rolled her eyes. 'Don't know why we have to write two sides on it though, as that's pretty much it.'

The door to the classroom opened and Miss Dark appeared back in the room. I smiled gratefully at Kay and quickly scribbled down what she'd just told me along with some other things I had suddenly remembered somehow from one of Prescott's lessons. I wrote in the biggest hand-writing I could without it looking suspicious, so that it took up just over a page, but at least I'd written something. The way Kay had explained it made much more sense than what Mr Prescott says. Why do teachers have to make everything so dull and difficult, when it's actually quite straightforward?

Once detention was over, Miss Dark rushed off as though the place was on fire, and Justin had already started snogging the girl with nail varnish by the time we were all out in the corridor.

I looked at Kay. 'Thanks,' I said. 'I'm not brilliant at remembering facts. You saved me another detention.'

'No bother,' said Kay. 'To be honest, I don't mind deten-tion. It's better than going home sometimes.'

'Why's that?' I asked, eager to hear about someone else's dreadful life.

'My mum,' said Kay. 'She's always having a go at me

about something. She cares more about the dog than she does about me.'

'What about your dad?' I asked. 'Doesn't he care about you?'

Kay laughed. 'S'pose he does. But he does what my mum tells him. Everyone's a bit scared of my mum.'

'My name's Lydia,' I said then.

Kay looked at me. 'I know who you are. You live down on that boat. The one opposite the pub? I saw you on it when I walked the dog once. You had your nose stuck in a book.' Kay laughed, a really nice slightly uncool laugh as though a friendly dragon had just heard a joke. 'I thought about talking to you, but you lot are a bit intimidating.'

'Why?' I said, going even redder.

Kay shook her head. 'Is that your brother, the one with the leather jacket?'

'Yes,' I said, without enthusiasm.

'Wish I had a brother,' Kay went on. 'There's just me.'

'Well, my family's a bit weird really,' I blurted. 'And we're not intimidating. If you knew us.'

'Listen,' said Kay, 'my parents are straight-up lunatics. My mum's nearly forty-five and she collects *soft toys*. She's got the spare room full of them, like it's a shrine, and she lines them up on the bookshelves instead of books. They've all got names. I think she has conversations with them when no one else is there.'

Kay was so matter-of-fact as she said this that it was really hard not to laugh. But then she laughed and so we stood in the corridor really laughing about her mum's soft

102

toys until one of the caretakers appeared in the corridor and said, 'Don't you have homes to go to?'

Kay and I walked outside, and she went to go through the back gate while I carried on to the front and we both turned round at the same time and smiled at each other.

Thursday 1st November

It's been snowing for days. Having watched a documentary about Scott of the Antarctic recently, and the effects of frostbite and hypothermia on the human body, I worry I may not have any toes or fingers by the time Christmas comes. My cabin is like an igloo; I have actual icicles in my skylight, and frost where the damp on the wall by my bed has frozen. Dad has bought more hot water-bottles and has suggested that I add a sleeping bag to my duvet in order not to freeze to death. He didn't actually mention 'freezing to death' but it's obvious I am in a life-threatening situation. I am reminded of Victorian times and people dying of consumption. It always seemed romantic watching it on telly, but in real life it is not at all romantic, it is the most uncomfortable I have ever been. I can only hope that the saying 'What does not kill you makes you stronger' is not a complete lie.

At least the saloon has a wood-burning stove, which makes it very toasty after it has been alight for a few hours. I have taken to getting home from school and sitting with my back as close to the stove as possible, and have singed my clothing a few times. Sam says I must have skin like asbestos.

Sally has got quieter and quieter and spends all her time with Erica after school, and some mornings she doesn't eat her breakfast and I've heard her tell Kate that she's got stomach ache and doesn't feel well.

I used to have that stomach ache all the time when I was

at St Helen's because it was mostly run by very strict nuns and none of the girls in my class wanted me as their friend. I'm sure it was my foggy brain and my long dark-blue wool socks, which Mum made me wear because she looked down on white nylon ones. But every time I ask Sally about school she closes up and won't talk about it. That's another thing I remember doing. Not telling anyone how awful I felt.

I suppose I should confide all my observations in Kate, but lately she has developed a bad cough and wears a blanket round her shoulders most days and it never seems like the right time to bother her. I wonder if Kate is regretting having met Dad now? I mean, her life before must have been quite lonely and desperate for her to see all this as a better alternative.

But I did want to ask Kate about Kay coming over. Even though me and Kay are not in the same form, we bump into each other in the corridors quite a bit and Kay smiles at me now.

'I really don't think that's a good idea,' Kate said when I did finally ask her. 'The last thing I want to do in this weather is entertain someone.'

'But you wouldn't have to,' I said. 'We can amuse ourselves.'

Kate did manage to smile. 'I know, Lydia, but it's just so bleak at the moment . . . Perhaps in the spring.'

It felt quite unfair that I couldn't even have a friend round, but then Kate asked me if I wanted a cup of tea, and while she was making it she said something that has stuck in my head and feels like a worry.

'I hadn't expected your father to be so caught up in his

work,' she said, handing me my tea. 'But he's gone all day and then working late. I know he can't help it, and Lord knows he needs his job, but it means I am having to sort a lot of things out on my own . . .' She rummaged around in a jar and got out some Ginger Nuts and put them on a little plate for us. 'I'm doing my best, Lydia. I'm sorry.'

There wasn't much I could say after that, but the bit about Dad working late sort of bothered me, because he's never done that before. He's quite important in his job and once when I asked him what exactly he did all day he just said, 'Make unpopular decisions and have meetings, really,' in a weary voice. And when Mum was here he'd always be back for dinner by 7.00 p.m., and Mum would have a pink drink with ice cubes in it waiting for him.

But if I were my father I might not be in a hurry to come home either. *Lady Beatrice* isn't homely, and there are no more pink drinks, or little bowls of nuts. There's just seven other people in varying degrees of bad moods all trying not to notice the cold and the deprivation.

We had girls-only badminton last thing at school today and yet again Juliet appeared by my side. I don't know why she's attached herself to me, though not many other people seem to like her, possibly because of all the home-made egg tart things she brings to school that are quite pungent.

I had spotted Kay over at the other side of the gym, standing next to a girl who is known as Rat, but whose real name is Louise. Rat has jet-black hair and the whitest skin I've ever seen and she's got an appliqued badge on her school bag with SIOUXSIE AND THE BANSHEES on it. Rat hardly ever speaks and I saw that her and Kay were standing by the far wall in the gym, just staring into space, while Miss Mendez the P.E. teacher shouted and blew her whistle at any unruly pupils. I wanted to swap places with Rat, as Juliet honestly does not stop talking about herself and her pony called Silverstreak, and her mum's conversion to vegetarianism.

Then Miss Mendez announced that we would be playing doubles and me and Juliet were opposite Kay and Rat!

'Oh no,' said Juliet. 'But on the other hand, those two will only make us look better. What with all the fried food Kay Palmer eats, she's not exactly athletic. My mother only buys fresh vegetables and we never have anything out of the freezer. I doubt Kay knows what fresh spinach actually looks like, she's probably only ever seen it in frozen form.'

Luckily Miss Mendez blew her whistle again then, so Juliet shut up for a bit and the four of us played a useless game of badminton in which we were all as bad as each other, though I deliberately only batted my shuttlecock to Kay and it kept bouncing off her head and a couple of times we were reprimanded for not even trying and for laughing too much, and I could feel Juliet being resentful about it, even though I purposely didn't look at her.

As soon as Miss Mendez turned away to bother other people, Kay lifted her P.E. skirt and showed me her knickers, which were not the regulation navy-blue stretchy ones, but purple with Minnie Mouse's face printed across the front.

'What do you think of my pants then?' she called over the net.

I grinned, but Rat rolled her eyes and Juliet let out a gasp.

'That underwear is revolting,' she said beside me. 'I think the Palmer family are actually travellers . . . gypsies, you know?'

I'd had enough of Juliet.

'So what if they are?' I said, irritated. 'I live on a rotting old boat, with no home comforts whatsoever. In fact, *Lady Beatrice* seems to leak every day, even when it hasn't been raining, and at the moment my cabin skylight has frozen because it is so cold and one side of my bed is so damp that if I accidentally roll over in the night I wake up with wet pyjamas. On top of all that it smells. But my dad hasn't got enough money to fix it properly, so we've just got to put up with it.'

Juliet looked quite shocked as I have never said this much to her all in one go.

'And,' I added, 'we've got a weekly dinner rota of food that is really cheap to make because there's so many of us now. Some of it is frozen food too, Juliet. Nearly all my clothes have orange stains on them from the water dripping off the metal supports inside the boat. Not to mention the smell that you can't get out of your clothes, however much you wash them.'

I left out the part about Dad and Kate becoming a bit miserable and weird, even though that part is almost the worst part.

'Oh. But . . . but *Lady Beatrice* is so characterful,' said Juliet, a bit flustered. 'Kay lives in a council house, doesn't she? It's not the same.'

What she meant was that I was posher than Kay so it wasn't as bad. Even I know this is ridiculous, and that being posh doesn't help you at all when you're poor; in fact, in a way it makes it worse.

I was about to reply but Juliet had already set her sights on Kay again. 'What happened to your proper gym knickers?' she asked her loudly. 'Did that giant dog of yours eat them?'

Kay just shrugged. 'They're very uncomfortable,' she said. 'I prefer these ones. Mum bought them in packs of five from Debenhams a couple of years back. I've got pretty much all the Disney characters now – Goofy, two of the Seven Dwarfs . . . loads. They're getting a bit small, but they cheer me up. It's hard to feel miserable when you've Minnie Mouse knickers on.'

'Oh my God,' said Juliet, while I tried not to laugh too much. 'You are such a weirdo, Kay Palmer.'

'And you're such a cow,' Kay said calmly, putting on a snooty voice to match Juliet's. 'To be honest, I'd rather be a weirdo.'

'Whatever you say, Kay,' said Juliet, trying not to seem affected at all.

Rat slunk off to the girls' toilets at this point, though she did give Kay an admiring look before she went.

'Oh, and we don't live in a council house,' Kay added, and Juliet blushed beetroot-red. 'My dad owns it. But even if we did I wouldn't care. At least my parents have jobs. Your mum just spends all day on your couch at home reading magazines about vegetables, or getting her hair done and telling other people how they're doing everything wrong.'

Juliet opened her mouth but no words came out; then she looked at me, picked up her badminton racquet and turned and stalked off back to the changing rooms by herself.

'Did I go too far?' said Kay, but looking only slightly remorseful.

'Quite far,' I said, smiling.

Kay sighed. 'Shall we go to the Wimpy and get a Coke after we've changed?' she said. 'I need to restore my equilibrium.'

In the Wimpy on the high street, Kay and I sat at the counter by the window and watched all the kids from Oaks hurrying home, and I found myself telling her all about everything on *Lady Beatrice*, and it being like the North Pole.

'Blimey. I would say come and live at ours,' Kay said

sympathetically when I'd finished. 'But my mum is walking frostbite these days. Just a look from her can freeze you to death. She reminds me of the Wicked Queen in *Snow White*.'

'Is she that bad?' I asked.

'She's all right sometimes,' said Kay. 'But you never know when she's going to turn.'

'Do you feel cold inside?' I said.

'That's exactly how I feel,' said Kay. 'Don't know what's worse, inside or out?'

'Or both,' I said, with a sinking feeling.

1980

It's been ages since I've written. I've already used up loads of this diary and I've been trying to ration my entries but I've got to write down about our first Christmas on the *Lady Beatrice*.

Elsa came home two days before Christmas Eve with her nose pierced – she's had a tiny diamond stud put in and I wondered whether maybe she'd done it to annoy Dad, but if she did then it only backfired as he kept saying how wonderful it was. I asked her how she got it out to clean it and then Sam took that one further, telling her she might die of nose poisoning, which was so ridiculous that it really made Elsa laugh. It was the high point of Christmas, seeing Elsa laugh like that, and Sam looked quite pleased with himself. Dad, who was cleaning some proper wine glasses, stood watching us, with this huge smile on his face. It was almost like the old days.

Until Christmas Eve.

Kate and Elsa argued the whole evening about the food. Elsa said we should have a goose, rather than a 'huge, dried-up old turkey' and Kate said that Elsa was welcome to cook one if she liked, but she, Kate, would be putting a 'huge, dried-up old turkey' in the oven. Dad hovered around looking scared every time Elsa picked up a cooking utensil, and in the end the turkey won.

At least Dad got a Christmas tree, which looks quite pretty, though it was a bit big and we had to cut the top off because of the low ceiling and couldn't put the angel on top. It's OK if you just look at the middle of the tree and not upwards. I'd been quite excited to see a large box-shaped present underneath it with my name on, despite Sam saying not to expect much this year. I was really hoping it was one of those big ghettoblaster things like Miss Dark the drama teacher uses sometimes; you can play tapes on them but with stereo sound. I've been dropping hints about this for a while now, but when Elsa asked about presents Dad went a bit quiet and said he had done his best and he hoped we wouldn't be too disappointed.

I waited until three in the afternoon on Christmas Day before I opened my present, and when I did I realised that Dad had just used the large box to make it look like his gift WASN'T the new edition of *Grimm's Fairy Tales*, but something a hundred times better than that.

'Great, thanks,' I said, sniffing the pages, which smelled slightly of sick.

'You'll have that for a lifetime,' said Dad cheerily. 'You can pass it on to your own children in years to come.'

'Yes, thanks,' I said again, not meeting his eye.

'Very appropriate,' said Elsa dryly. 'Particularly the GRIMM bit.' She was sitting behind me in her socked feet and prodded me in the bottom with her toes to try and make me laugh.

'I can't laugh about this yet,' I said quietly, turning round.

'Righty-ho,' said Elsa, sighing. 'Here.' She handed me something wrapped in gold paper with a red satin ribbon. It was obviously a book, but I have to admit the wrapping did cheer me up.

It was a novel called *I Capture the Castle* by Dodie Smith.

'I discovered it in a charity shop in Cambridge,' said Elsa, as I noticed it was a second-hand copy. 'I read it in two hours it was so good. I know you'll love it. It's just your sort of thing, Lyds.'

'Thanks.' I was very touched and stroked the cover, thinking this present was really precious. But then I looked up and caught my father's hurt face and felt like a brat.

To be fair, nobody else got brilliant presents either. Sally and Erica got a joint one of a tent, for instance, but I couldn't help thinking of how amazing Mum had always made Christmas for us with the roaring open fire in the living room and carpets and proper windows and curtains. Bob was always in heaven, fat and contented, having eaten up all the spare food he could get his paws on. Everything was so cosy and dry. I'll never take being dry for granted ever again.

Instead of watching the feature-length Agatha Christie on Christmas night, I started reading *I Capture the Castle* in my cabin, with a Terry's Chocolate Orange that Jake had got me. The family in the book are in a very similar predicament to us, except for a very noble love interest – Stephen, the housekeeper's son – which has got me thinking in a slightly different way about boys. Perhaps.

Bob fell overboard on Boxing Day, which was very embarrassing for him. Luckily the tide was low, but Jake and Sam had to temporarily stop bickering to fish him out of the mud with a net and then hose him down as his fur was plastered in muddy spikes. Bob's face of fury at such indignity was so awful but so funny that Jake and I were in fits of laughter in front of him and even Sam was grinning, though Bob might never forgive us for being so callous.

Elsa seemed quite distracted by something that she wouldn't divulge and I wonder if has something to do with a boy at university because she went to the Admiral pub to use the phone there every night, and then came back and slipped through the skylight in her cabin and went to bed. As her cabin is right next to mine I spent a bit of time pressing my ear against the locked door between us, trying to hear if she was crying. Dad said I shouldn't interfere when I confided in him, and that Elsa was just 'coming of age', but then on the night before she went back to Cambridge I did hear her sobbing.

To think this could all get worse, that your family are not the only people who can cause you pain . . . What is it all for?

It's the last day of the holidays, and I borrowed Jake's bike and cycled down the prom. It was bitter and the fresh water pool was frozen over, but I honestly felt like cycling away and never coming back. I went right down to the end, where you can just about see the North Sea at the end of the estuary, and the big power station in the distance and all the little boats bobbing and shivering in the wind. I got off the bike and sat on the bench, thinking about the big wide world and whether it was really worth it.

I think the teachers are despairing of me now. Yesterday in assembly when the nominations for Third Year Prefects were announced, practically everyone but me was picked. I am obviously considered too irresponsible even to stand at the front of the dinner queue for the canteen and let ten First Years through at a time.

'I have no wish to be a prefect,' said Juliet Huntley-Smith, who is one. 'I've got better things to do than look after First-Year idiots. So oppressive.'

We were standing by the lockers after the last lesson, and I had spent the whole day trying not to feel rejected.

I could tell that Juliet wanted to carry on pretending she was somehow dismayed at being made prefect for the third year running, but I didn't want to talk about it any more, and instead dashed off to leave school by the back entrance, which leads out onto the other side of town. This is where all the rough kids live, apparently, and it's not nice according to Juliet.

I needed time to think and come to terms with the day's giant snub.

I followed a group of kids down the road at a distance, risking them noticing me and stealing my school bag or trying to strangle me with my school tie, but luckily they were engrossed in themselves and I meandered quite peacefully down Burnham Road, passing houses that didn't seem that bad. Some of them had nice well-tended gardens and neat paths. But then the kids suddenly turned off right, leaving me to go further and further down the road, and now the houses were getting more and more scruffy, with old mattresses and ovens in the front gardens and wood in the windows where the glass had been broken.

I stopped and a group of girls leaned out of a window and started calling out and spitting at me. I decided I'd gone far enough and was turning back round – when I walked straight into Kay, who was running from school.

'Crikey!' she yelled, clutching at her chest. 'Watch out!'

'It's me, Kay,' I said. 'Lydia.'

Kay huffed and puffed a bit before calming down. 'What are you doing round here?'

'I just needed a think on my own.'

'Go on, kiss your lesbian girlfriend!' shouted one of the girls hanging out of the window. 'Kissy kissy!'

Kay rolled her eyes. 'Shut it, Keeley, or I'll set the dog on you!' she shouted up, at which point the girl and her friends stuck their heads back inside and shut the window.

'That's Ruth Porter's cousin, Keeley,' said Kay. 'Ruth's the worst bully at Oaks. All the Porters are psychopaths. One day that family will be in the papers for doing something really bad and I will say I told you so.'

'Is Ruth really that bad?' I said.

'She's worse,' said Kay. 'Something went very wrong with that girl at some point.'

I vowed to keep out of Ruth's way, suspecting I might be a magnetic attraction for girls like her.

'What do you need to think about then?' Kay said. 'What big thoughts do you have?'

'Just that I was the only one who wasn't made a prefect,' I said. 'The only one in the whole school!'

'Well, that's not true,' said Kay. 'I wasn't made one either.'

'Are you telling the truth?' I said. 'You really weren't made a prefect.'

'Swear on my mum's life,' said Kay. 'And I couldn't care less either.'

'What's wrong with us though?' I said. 'Why are we considered so incapable of looking after people?'

'It's the system,' said Kay, hauling her school bag up on her shoulder. 'It's meant for boffins and creeps. Don't take it personally. No one will give a stuff whether you were a prefect in years to come.'

'That's not what they said in Assembly,' I pointed out. 'They made out that Further Education people count being a prefect as an actual qualification. It speaks volumes about your capacity for commitment, they said.'

'Load of rubbish,' said Kay. 'They just tell you all that so they can sit in the staffroom and have an extra cup of tea while you do their job for them.'

'That really does make sense,' I said, relieved. 'Thanks, Kay.'

'Any time,' said Kay, looking at her watch. 'I'd better get a move on though as I'm dogsitting tonight. Mum's at bingo and Dad's got this big job on the high street, doing all the plumbing for the re-opening of the Regal.'

The Regal is this really old cinema that has been shut for years with the front all boarded up. Developers had been going to turn it into flats but loads of people in Maling had signed a petition and now it's going to show films again.

'I love the cinema,' I said, remembering how me and Donna had gone to see *Grease* four times at Brainhill Odeon, as we both had huge crushes on Danny Zuko, played by John Travolta, who's very handsome.

'Me too,' she said. 'Mum used to take me on Saturday mornings when all the cartoons were on years ago. I'm not sure what they're showing now, but to be honest two hours of peace and quiet is the main thing.'

'You sound like you're fifty years old,' I said.

'You've not met my mum,' said Kay, laughing. 'Anyway, one day we can go to the Regal, you and me. If you want.'

'We can go to the new *Star Wars*!' I said. 'Or any film starring John Travolta.'

'Yuck,' said Kay, grinning. 'John Travolta?'

By the time I got home I was feeling much better. It helped to know that Kay was also considered a school pariah and Kate, who was ironing in front of the TV, was in an unusually good mood. When I sat down and got out my incomprehensible science homework, I gave my usual sigh of doom.

'Chemistry,' said Kate, craning to see my text book. 'I never could get to grips with that. She folded a shirt and put it on a pile, and then quite unexpectedly she smiled at me.

There has been a disturbing incident with Dad and his car.

When we were a lot younger, me and Sam used to love going out in the car with Dad. He had a really old one called a Bentley, with a roof that collapses like an accordion. Sam and I would constantly argue over who was going to sit in the front or the back. Sitting in the back meant that in the summer you got to sit right on top of the long leather seat and feel giddy at the idea of possibly tumbling backwards out of the car. Sitting in the front meant you got to play with the cigarette lighter and could take everything out of the glove compartment, examine it and then put it back, as it was always quite disappointing. And of course in the front, you got to sit next to Dad, who always smelled of cologne, and wore very dark glasses and sang along to the radio, sometimes quite loudly, especially if we slowed down through a village and people stared at us, wondering who the madman-driver in charge of children was. It was slightly embarrassing, but at the same time Sam and I were sure that he wasn't mad or unsafe – he just enjoyed singing loudly in the car. To us, he was completely normal.

'A sense of the ridiculous is essential to existence,' he'd always say seriously. 'Don't let anyone tell you otherwise.'

I remembered about all this yesterday, because at five-thirty Kate was summoned to the police station at the top of the high street from a phone call via the Admiral pub.

Dad, who had taken the afternoon off work to take his car for an MOT, had been stopped by the police for dangerous driving, Kate said, and she had to go and sort it out.

'Probably just him being Ridiculous,' I said, as she was putting her coat on and looking very sour-faced. 'You know, silly?'

But Kate didn't understand what I meant.

'Ridiculous is one way of putting it, I suppose,' she said, putting her bag over her shoulder. 'I don't know how long I'll be, but there's cold chicken and salad things in the fridge if I'm not back by seven.'

Sam had just emerged from his cabin after a period of doing some homework when Kate brushed past him, heaving another sigh as she went.

Sam glared at her back. 'Pity she isn't taking a couple of suitcases with her,' he said a bit too loudly.

'Sam.' I sighed at his ongoing campaign to force Kate out. 'She's gone to fetch Dad from the police station.'

'What?' said Sam, now looking quite alarmed. 'Why? Has he been robbed or something?'

'No,' I said. 'But possibly being Ridiculous in the car.'

Sam laughed. 'I didn't think he was Ridiculous any more . . . not since he met Her.'

'Me neither,' I said sadly. 'And I do think it's a bit much to arrest Dad for that.'

'Oh.' Sam's eyebrows shot up. 'Has he been arrested?'

'We'll have to wait and see,' I said, as if I was an expert.

'I'm sure Kate will get him out as the police must have better things to do, such as catching real criminals.'

Sam didn't say anything else about it. Instead he surprised me by offering to make me hot chocolate. 'Don't panic,' he said, noticing my suspicious face. 'I'm not going to put something horrible in it . . . not that you'll notice anyway.'

Sam is not naturally a comforting or nurturing person. Elsa says that she's found most boys aren't good with emotions, and Sam is even worse than most boys in that regard. So I did appreciate the hot chocolate and the two bourbon biscuits he got for me, even though he was restless soon afterwards and muttered something about going for a bike ride.

I suspected that he really wanted to go and privately think about Dad.

After Sam had gone off, and just as I resigned myself to an evening of stewing, Jake came home. Jake spends at least an hour hanging around in the car park after school with his friends; I think they all sit on a wall with graffiti on it and talk about records and girls.

'It's very quiet around here,' he said, dumping his school bag on the floor and collapsing into the egg-chair. 'What's up with you?'

'Me?' I felt quite affronted that everyone seems to know exactly what I'm feeling just because of my face. 'Nothing. Except your mum's gone to fetch my dad from the police station for something to do with the car.'

Jake swung round a bit in the chair and frowned. 'Are you all right?'

I was taken aback. This is not a question I am often asked by my family, in case the answer is No.

'What?' Jake said, seeing my perplexed face.

'Dad won't go to prison, will he?' I blurted.

Jake shook his head. 'Very unlikely,' he said. 'Unless he's killed someone, he won't go to prison.'

'That's a relief,' I said. 'Thank you.'

Jake looked at me again. 'You worry about your dad, don't you?'

I was about to retort 'not really' but that would be a lie, so instead I did a nonchalant shrug.

'I worry about Mum sometimes too,' Jake said. 'So I know how you feel.'

Jake's confiding in me was quite unexpected. 'Maybe we're just the type of people who worry,' I said. 'It's annoying, isn't it?'

'Very,' said Jake, and then he took off the denim jacket he wears over his blazer. 'Shall we watch telly?'

I switched on the TV and settled myself on the sofa and Bob trotted over and sprang up to sit on my lap, rolling over onto his back. Then Jake came and sat down next to me and tickled Bob's stomach, which Bob adores. We stared down at him, with his furry stomach and his paws up in the air, flexing his vicious claws, and then we smiled at each other.

At 6.15 p.m. Jake and I were still watching TV when Sally and Erica were dropped off home from their piano tuition and we all sat around eating the cold chicken with iceberg lettuce and tomatoes from the fridge, which tasted like nothing at all.

Sally asked worriedly, 'Where's Mum?'

'Police station,' I said robotically, which was a bit brutal of me as Sally and Erica then looked upset.

'Nothing to worry about,' Jake told Sally. 'Just a misunderstanding, I'm sure.'

'Oh,' said Sally. 'She probably won't be long, will she?'

I looked at hers and Erica's forlorn little faces. 'Probably not,' I said, trying to be kind too.

When Harry came home from the boatyard a bit later, Sally and Erica went off to play a game in their cabin, and neither Jake nor I had time to tell Harry about Dad, as he disappeared quite sharpish to do his nightly preparation for going out to meet one his girlfriends.

In one way, I was sure that nothing really bad had happened, because Kate or a policeman would have come and told us. But the part of my brain that imagines the worst feared that Dad might have died for some reason. Ever since Mum left our house and then died and never came back, I can no longer tell myself that this possibility is outlandish, as I know now it's not.

I didn't confide this to Jake though, as it seemed childish, and I still felt a bit strange about our earlier conversation. But after a couple of hours of telly, including a boring documentary about sheep, Jake went off to his cabin and I must have fallen asleep, because the next thing I knew, Kate and Dad were back.

Kate immediately went into the bathroom and tried to run a bath, but before he went out Harry had used all the hot water as he likes to soak and top up for hours. It's one of Harry's few selfish habits, baths. Kate stormed back into the saloon.

'The water is freezing and all over the floor!' she hissed at Dad, who was leaning back on the sofa with his eyes shut and may have been asleep. 'Have any of your children grasped civilised consideration for others? Anyone would think they'd been brought up in the bloody Brazilian rain forest.'

Sam had arrived home and was scraping mud off the bottom of his shoes so that it formed a little sticky pile by the bench. Kate glared at that too.

'The thing is,' said Sam calmly, 'every time you say something like that you are insulting my mother, which is quite insensitive, and inconsiderate in itself, when you think about it.'

I was silent, though pleased that for once Sam had managed to make a good point without being too rude and ruining his argument.

Kate shook her head, obviously not having the heart to answer Sam back.

Meanwhile, Dad confirmed he was asleep by letting out a loud snore and twitching slightly.

'What did the police say?' I asked her. 'Did they arrest him?'

She opened her mouth to say something angry, but then she bit her lip and her shoulders slumped slightly. 'No,' she said eventually. 'They didn't arrest him . . . they just asked him a lot of questions, and certain . . . tests were carried out.'

'Tests?' asked Sam, who looked a bit hollow-eyed. 'What tests?'

Kate glanced around to double-check that Sally and Erica weren't up and loitering in their pyjamas, and then she sat down on the bench at the table and sighed.

'Your father was well over the limit, it seems,' she told us. 'He was driving on the wrong side of the road down Maling high street. At four o'clock in the afternoon.'

'Over the limit of alcohol consumption?' I clarified, feeling my heart beating loudly.

'Yes,' said Kate, and frowned again. 'Luckily for him no one was hurt. But he will very likely lose his licence, which is particularly annoying.' She had an expression of grave disappointment on her face.

Sam looked over at Dad, who was still snoring, oblivious. Neither of us could think of what to say, but thoughts were racing around my head.

'Why was Dad drunk at four in the afternoon?' I said to Sam, when Kate had gone in to the galley. 'That's not very normal, is it?'

Sam didn't speak, but he looked pale and worried. 'Maybe he just stopped off at the pub and had one too many?' he said then. 'I think it's quite easy to go over the limit, as they're pretty strict about how much you can drink and drive.'

Never before in the whole of my life has Dad been

stopped by the police for dangerous driving, not in the middle of the afternoon and when most other adults are still at work. I knew Sam didn't really believe what he'd just said, and nor did I.

Sam's really trying with me and the maths homework and I'm really trying to concentrate, but tonight Kay came back with me after school, because her mum and dad were going over to see her grandma, who's in a care home out of town.

'It gets me down going to see my nan,' said Kay. 'It's so creepy in the care home and Nan always thinks I'm my Aunt Elaine. Last time she started yelling at me about my skirt being too short. Especially for "a woman of your age".'

'Has she got senile dementia?' I asked.

'Something like that, it's a word I can't remember.' I could see Kay was trying to be casual about it. 'I'm sure Nan is why Mum is so bad-tempered most of the time, as it is all a bit tiring.'

'That's sad, isn't it?' I said.

'Yes,' said Kay. 'But it's too sad to get my head around.'

I never knew any of my grandparents, because of my parents being quite old when they had kids. I wondered what it must be like to see somebody so old going a bit mad like that. Then I thought of Dad and wondered if I'd have to visit him in a care home one day not that far away.

I warned Kay that I had my special maths tuition with Sam, and that it was unbelievably boring.

'You're always saying Sam's a pain,' said Kay. 'But that's nice of him to help you. I mean, he must have the patience of a saint.'

I laughed. 'I suppose he has,' I said. 'But that doesn't mean he isn't also an idiot.'

Sam looked a bit uncomfortable when I came home with Kay, but she promised she wouldn't listen or interrupt and had brought a book with her so 'don't mind me'.

It wasn't a great session as Sam kept looking over at Kay and his mind wasn't on it, even though I actually got a few things right without having a meltdown.

Despite her implying she was going to mind her own business, Kay laughed quite a few times at Sam's unfunny jokes which encouraged him to make more, and once or twice she actually had a short conversation about the correct formula for one of my maths puzzles, which was beyond the pale as far as I was concerned. Sam however was puffed up like a peacock.

'Why aren't you at our school?' Kay asked him, when we'd finished at about 7.00 p.m. 'Are you at some kind of posh school then?'

'No way,' said Sam. 'I'm at Brainhill. It's literally the worst school in the country. Lydia went there before we moved.'

Kay laughed. 'Maybe that explains Lydia's maths then.'

'That's not the school so much as Lydia's brain,' said Sam.

I bristled. Sam was showing off to Kay at my expense, and she seemed to be joining in.

'OK, you can stop now, Sam,' I said coldly. 'You're not funny.'

Then Kay and Sam smiled at each other infuriatingly.

'We would ask you to stay for dinner, Kay,' he said. 'But you'd never come again if we did.'

I was really annoyed. What was Sam talking about? Why was he suddenly behaving like a respectable human being?

'That's OK,' said Kay. 'Mum will make tea when they get home from seeing Nan. Thanks though.'

'That's OK,' said Sam, just looking at her.

I realise that there is something worse than your brother making your friends feel unwelcome, and that is when he acts like a creep and makes them feel too welcome.

'Better be off then,' said Kay.

'I'll walk up the hill with you,' I said to Kay. Out of the corner of my eye I saw Sam still staring at her as though he'd never seen a girl before.

'See you, Kay,' he said as we got up to leave.

'See you, Sam,' said Kay cheerily.

Up on deck, Kay was trying to get to grips with crossing the gangplank just as Dad arrived home, with his tie a bit loose and his top shirt button undone underneath his mackintosh, which I noticed already had a bit of mildew along the hem.

'Ah!' said Dad, doing the embarrassing little bow that he often does in front of girls or women who are not members of our family. 'You must be Lydia's new friend. Lovely to meet you.'

'Likewise,' said Kay, looking like she was going to do a curtsey.

Dad smiled at her, and patted me on the head.

'Blimey, I feel like I've just met the Duke of Edinburgh,' said Kay as Dad went on his way down below. 'I'll have to tell Mum I've met a distinguished person at last.'

I laughed, relieved that Kay didn't judge Dad for the things I have reported to her about him.

Kay and I fell a bit quiet as we walked up the hill and I resumed stewing over Sam's behaviour. He is awful in lots of ways, but he belongs to me, not to Kay. And Kay is *my* friend, not Sam's. I knew I was being petty, but I felt worried that something else might be taken away from me.

'Kay,' I said when we got to the top of the hill, and I felt unable to keep it in any longer. 'You don't fancy Sam or anything, do you?'

Kay gawped at me. 'No way!' she said. 'No offence, but Sam's a boffin. I'd prefer a boyfriend who's a dimwit so I can order him around and feel cleverer than he is.' She paused. 'Sam is not my type at all. Definitely not.'

'Oh, phew,' I said. 'It's just that Sam never normally acts like that with girls. He's usually really rude. I thought he might be flirting with you.'

'I didn't notice,' said Kay. 'But then my mum's always saying I should be more feminine, and boys like girls to giggle and flirt with them, and I don't do that. Mother reckons I'll always be the bridesmaid and never the bride, but I'm not bothered to be honest.'

Though I was now reassured that Kay didn't like Sam in that way, I was less sure about Sam. The way he'd looked at Kay wasn't exactly like he was looking at a friend.

I don't know, maybe I'm letting my imagination run away with me, as I am wont to do.

When I got home, everything about Sam and Kay got forgotten because Dad has been in the Magistrate's Court today because of 'the incident' and now he has been banned from driving. On the way home, he'd bought himself some cigarettes, which Kate was extremely disapproving of. Dad gave up smoking years ago, and it was a bit of a surprise to see him now sitting at the table reading the newspaper with one in his hand.

'I'm not having my girls breathing in your smoke,' said Kate, waving her hand back and forth in front of her face a bit melodramatically.

'Please,' Dad said calmly. 'I've been told I'm not allowed to drive for six months; the one thing that gives me any pleasure in life has now been withheld. One cigarette won't hurt anyone.'

'I disagree,' said Kate. 'And you've only got yourself to blame about the driving. I'm as furious as you are about that, but clearly for different reasons.'

'Oh, well . . .' Dad glanced up then, and saw that Sam, Jake and me were all pretending not to hear them, and then he frowned at Kate. 'If you could perhaps not openly criticise me in front of my children, I'd really appreciate it.'

Kate huffed, and started noisily laying the table for dinner.

Sally was trying to read a book at the other end of the table, but she looked up at Kate and Dad and heaved a sigh that I don't think she knew she was heaving.

When Kate went back into the galley, I came and sat opposite Sally, and started saying something about how reading is brilliant for going into another world and forgetting about real life for a while and that I have always found it a great comfort in times of sadness and upset. I actually believe this wholeheartedly, but I was also saying it to be nice to Sally and so she knew that I was someone she could talk to about things.

Sally gave me a tiny weak smile and opened her mouth to say something, but just at that point Kate came bustling back out of the galley with a bowl of broccoli and dumped it on the table.

'Put your book away now, Sally,' she said wearily. 'And you should probably wash your hands.'

So Sally got up without saying whatever it was she was going to say, and I thought how funny it was that even in a family as big as ours is now, finding someone to talk to about anything important is really hard.

When Jake sat down he chewed on his lip for a moment and then said to Dad, 'Sorry about the car, Charlie. I know how much you like driving.'

Dad stubbed out his cigarette and looked in surprise at Jake. 'Your mother's right, of course. All my fault . . . As is everything, apparently.'

The thing is, I should really have felt sorry for poor put-upon Dad, being nagged by Kate and made to feel like a naughty child. But he'd ruined it by being sarcastic. Didn't either of them care that we were all listening?

I thought jealously for a minute of Elsa cycling round the streets of Cambridge and going to glittering parties with her friends, and experiencing romance. I pictured her in her rooms with a roaring fire, having interesting conversations and choosing exactly what she wanted for dinner every night. I was torturing myself.

Kate had made toad-in-the-hole, which is my eighth favourite meal in the world, though it was slightly annoying as Dad had lit another fag and kept blowing smoke across the table while the rest of us were eating. The only bright spot was when Sam and Jake did the dishes together and I overheard Sam say gruffly to Jake, 'Thanks for earlier,' as Jake had been sympathetic to Dad.

Then they went back to the washing-up in silence, and I thought, Oh well, *some* things might be getting better, even if other things are getting worse.

When I went to bed, for old times' sake I re-read Enid Blyton's *The Magic Faraway Tree*, which always used to really cheer me up as a child. But it just seemed a bit stupid and young, and the things I once thought were brilliant about it were boring. This made me quite melancholy.

'I'm old before my time,' I told Bob, who as usual wasn't bothered about anything but himself.

Saturday 15th March

Sam told me and Dad after breakfast today that he doesn't think he's going to university after all; he wants to join the Merchant Navy and travel the world instead.

'Really, Sam?' said my father. 'I thought you wanted to be a scientist, something like that?' Dad broke off two chunks of his Bourneville chocolate bar to have with his coffee. He's trying not to smoke and has stockpiled bars of Bourneville in the galley larder for whenever he craves a cigarette.

'I might do that later on,' said Sam. 'But I've been reading up about the Merchant Navy and you get to see all these places like Australia and the Philippines. Also,' he added, 'it's what I like most, boats and being at sea, and all the food and accommodation is free, so you can save loads of money. I've worked it all out, and I could buy a house before I'm thirty.'

Personally, I couldn't think of anything worse than being trapped on a cargo boat for months with lots of people I don't know, even if you did get off every so often and explore the pyramids in Egypt, but I suppose someone has to do that job.

Dad was chomping slowly on a chunk of Bourneville, thinking.

'I see,' he said then. 'Very sensible, Sam. When I was your age I can't say I gave much thought to things like money and buying houses, but I suppose it's not a bad idea to think ahead.'

'Yes. If I save all my wages for a couple of years,' Sam went on. 'I won't have to worry about being poor.'

A look passed between him and Dad and I realised that what Sam was actually saying was that he had no intention of ending up like Dad, who has never planned ahead and has ended up with no money. I can see what Sam means, but if Dad was a sensible planning-ahead type of person then he wouldn't also have been Ridiculous, and we would never have got all those unexpected presents that Dad used to buy us spontaneously before, like the brand-new Chipper bike I once got that Mum was furious about as it wasn't even my birthday; and in general we would not have laughed as much as we have and Dad would be boring.

If he was hurt by Sam's big plan, Dad tried not to show it. He just got up and went to put the other half of his Bourneville bar in the larder for later. And when he came back out of the galley, he patted Sam on the back.

'Whatever you do, and however much money you've got,' he told Sam, 'I would never be more or less proud of you. Life isn't all about money, you know. It's also about taking risks . . . and seizing happiness, even when it's inconvenient.' Dad then picked up his crossword and his coffee and went to sit up on deck.

'Don't listen to Dad about taking risks,' Sam said to me. 'That's a terrible idea. I don't know what he's talking about.'

I was beginning to get confused about all this risks business, and wondered if that was just the difference between my father and my brother. Dad doesn't see things in a straight line, while Sam only ever sees things that way.

Suddenly, from up above us, there was a bit of a commotion going on, and then the sound of someone pounding down the stairs. The door to the saloon opened and Elsa was standing there with her hair in a bun, holding a rucksack and wearing a little short tiered skirt and woolly tights.

'Elsa!' I shrieked.

'Surprise!' said Elsa.

'What are you doing here?' said Sam, in a not very friendly way.

'I've only come for the day,' said Elsa. 'I've got a party back in Cambridge tomorrow.'

'All right for some,' Sam said sourly.

'Don't mind him,' I said to Elsa. 'Sam's got a bee in his bonnet about being responsible in life.'

'That's rich,' said Elsa, laughing. 'Coming from someone who has spent years causing trouble.'

Sam was affronted. 'I don't cause trouble,' he said. 'You're the one who does that.'

'Oh, whatever,' said Elsa, fiddling with her bun and then yawning.

'You'll see, both of you, when I'm a millionaire and you two are living in poverty,' Sam said peevishly. 'Don't expect me to lend you any money.'

'What has come over him?' Elsa said, as Sam sloped off, no doubt to do more homework. 'He's so touchy all of a sudden.'

Come to think of it, I have noticed Sam being a bit irritable lately. Quite nitpicky.

'Maybe he's fallen in love?' Elsa pondered on. 'That can make a person very out of sorts.'

'That's preposterous!' I said, and Elsa laughed.

'Yes, you're right,' she said. 'It *is* preposterous.'

I was anxious to change the subject as it made me uneasy. 'Now that you're here and it's a Saturday,' I told Elsa, 'we can go to the shops in the high street, and the market in the car park behind Tesco – there's jewellery stalls and stuff like that.'

'Wow,' said Elsa sarcastically. 'It sounds incredible.'

'Actually,' I said, ignoring her tone as I'd just had a brilliant brainwave, 'the real reason I want to go to the market is the pet stall.'

'But we've already got a pet,' said Elsa. 'The cantankerous old monster known as Bob.'

'I know,' I said. 'But every week there seems to be a new batch of kittens at the stall and I was wondering if a new kitten would really do us all good.'

'Good luck with that,' said Elsa. 'Apart from anything else, Bob will want to kill it immediately.'

'I'm sure not,' I said. 'It will be a companion for him.'

Elsa sighed. 'I suppose it's better than hanging around here with *her*. Where is Kate, by the way?'

'She went to the launderette earlier,' I said. 'The machine's conked out because of all the thousands of things it has to wash every day. Then her and Dad are going to a child's party with Sally and Erica.'

Elsa looked relieved, then she said, 'Does Dad seems a bit sad to you? When I arrived just now he was super pleased to see me, I thought he was going to burst into tears or something.'

I wondered whether to bring up Dad's coming home late from work and the dangerous driving.

'Lydia?' said Elsa. 'What's going on?'

'Nothing really,' I said. 'I mean, well, Dad and Kate are arguing a bit, and he does come home from work quite late now, and . . . he was caught by the police for drunk driving a few weeks ago.'

'What?' said Elsa.

'I know,' I said.

I'm used to Elsa having an answer for everything, but she just stood there chewing her cheeks.

'Well,' she said eventually. 'The penny has dropped at last.'

'What do you mean?'

'It's finally occurred to Dad that he's married a shrew,' said Elsa matter-of-factly. 'The scales have fallen from his eyes and he is now taking refuge in the pub.'

I thought because of Elsa's lasting vendetta against Kate she would seem delighted about the penny-dropping, but she didn't look happy at all; she looked a bit angry even.

'Shall we go to the market now then?' I said, thinking of cheerier things, such as bringing home a kitten. 'It closes at lunch time.'

'Oh, all right then,' said Elsa. She dragged a crumpled suede blazer out of her rucksack and put it on. 'Maybe I can get some nice food at the market for lunch.'

I was going to say, 'I don't think Kate will like that, Elsa,' but I didn't want to cause an argument as she wasn't going to be here very long. And maybe Kate won't mind, I thought. It's not as though she really likes cooking anyway. She's always moaning about it.

The boy manning the pets stall was sitting with his feet up on a hutch of rabbits, reading the *Daily Mirror*.

'Excuse me,' I said. 'Can I look at the kittens?'

The boy lowered his paper indifferently. 'All of them?' he said. 'Or just the one?'

I looked again at the cage. Four of the kittens were playing a game of clawing each other to death, as cats do, letting out the occasional screech. They were all adorable, but it was the smallest, quietest kitten in the corner that caught my eye. It wasn't like the others, as apart from being smaller and quieter, it had a sad look in its eyes as it watched its siblings play, cocking its little head this way and that.

'This one.' I pointed at it. 'Can I see this one?'

The boy moved extremely slowly up out of his chair as though he might have some kind of physical disability, though he was obviously just lazy. It took him a very long time to open that cage and pluck the little kitten out. When he did, it fitted perfectly into the palm of one hand.

'It's a boy,' he said. 'Runt of the litter. Probably needs injections and that.'

He handed the furry bundle over to me, where the kitten's shivering little body nestled in my hands and his big green eyes gazed mournfully up at me. He dug his claws into my palms.

I winced, but stroked his fur with my thumbs. 'Poor little runt,' I said. 'How much is he?'

The boy shrugged. 'Fiver?'

I glanced behind me at Elsa, who was trying on some rings at the ethnic jewellery stall. I had some money on me, a bit of mine and a bit left over from a couple of pounds Dad had given me to go to the launderette in the week after the machine broke. I'd saved by not using the dryer and also by shoving everything, all squashed up, into one washer.

'Three pounds and I'll take him,' I said firmly. I handed back the kitten and got out my leather purse and emptied all my change into the boy's outstretched hand, and he sighed quite heavily.

'You can count it if you like,' I told him. 'It's all there and probably a bit more.'

He rolled his eyes. 'Go on then,' he said.

Elsa looked slightly aghast when she saw the kitten. 'Do you think he might be diseased?' she said, poking at him. But then his tiny little paws snapped around her finger, and she smiled. 'He is quite sweet though. What shall we call him?'

'Eugene,' I said after a bit of thought, as it's something exotic, and embarrassing for Harry and Sam to say.

'Excellent name,' said Elsa. 'But Bob will loathe him even more.'

After Elsa had got some vegetables and other stuff for lunch, and tried on a ratty old fake-fur coat at the second-hand clothes stall, we wandered back down the high street to *Lady Beatrice*, and I was beginning to get a bit nervous that I had so rashly bought another creature that needs feeding and looking after, and that not everyone thinks cats and kittens are irresistible, seeing as I am the only one apart from Jake who has any affection for Bob at all.

When we got back at 1.00 p.m., *Lady Beatrice* was deserted except for Harry, who was quite pleased to see Elsa, and the two of them went off to listen to a moany-voiced old singer called Neil Young on Harry's record player.

I took Eugene out from where I'd been hiding him inside my coat and tried to play with him on the sofa, but the excitement of being adopted must have really tired him out as he fell asleep almost straight away. I carried him into my cabin and tucked my quilt over him and hoped nobody would make me take him back.

Back in the saloon I tried on Elsa's suede jacket, which was tiny and I could hardly get my arms into the sleeves. I thought Elsa must really have shrunk a lot and I hadn't properly noticed earlier.

Dad and Kate returned at 2.00 p.m. with Sally and Erica. Sally looked really glum and was clutching a party bag with glitter on it and said she wanted to lie down and not have any lunch, which Elsa had made and was lentil salad and goats cheese with some kind of sweet brown vinegar on it. Elsa said the vinegar was from Italy and called Balsamic and she'd brought some bottles home from when she was travelling in Europe last summer.

'What kind of person goes on holiday and brings back

vinegar?' asked Sam, who then heaped a forkful of vinegary food into his mouth.

'A civilised person, Sam,' said Elsa.

Dad looked at them bickering with a peaceful expression on his face.

Though it didn't look it, after a couple of mouthfuls Elsa's lunch was actually nice. Even Kate said, 'Thank you, that was very thoughtful,' to Elsa, who could only shrug as she is mainly just prepared for battle with Kate, and isn't used to being nice to her.

I waited until we'd finished eating to tell everyone about Eugene. I was expecting Kate to be furious and give me a lecture on irresponsible behaviour, but although she didn't seem overjoyed about it, she did say, 'Well, the girls will love it I suppose. I'll take him to a vet on Monday, but you have to promise that you'll look after him properly, Lydia. I've got enough to do without housetraining an animal.'

I nodded eagerly, very relieved.

'That kitten is obviously *doomed*, then.' Next to me, Sam couldn't help himself from butting in as usual.

'You're a fine one to talk,' Elsa told him. 'You can barely dress yourself.'

I smirked at Sam and then caught Dad's eye, and he gave me a wink, though I realised he hadn't actually said a thing the whole time we were at the table.

Afterwards, I went and got Eugene and took him into Sally and Erica's cabin, where they were huddled together on Sally's bunk.

'Here,' I said, handing him over. 'He's all of ours now.'

And Sally looked at me and smiled properly, for the first time in weeks. I felt like a very virtuous person.

I am in bed at last, and as Eugene is with Sally and Erica I am trying to be extra nice to Bob so that he doesn't feel rejected. I feel like today was quite a good day in some ways, and mostly because of Eugene, except for Dad being so quiet. Sometimes it feels like Dad is just watching all our lives in a kind of a daze and he's completely forgotten how to join in any more.

Thursday 3rd April

I have stumbled across a brilliant solution to the bane of my life, and that is a miraculous hair dye called Sun-Dazzle, which you just spray on your hair and then you are a radiant blonde. You don't even have to squeeze out that purple stuff that brings you out in a rash and makes your scalp and nose itch. I can't believe it's so easy, and nor can Kay, or Sam, who told me when I got home tonight not to get my hopes up.

I only came across Sun-Dazzle by accident as I'd gone into Woolworths after school today to get some Pick 'n' Mix and straightaway spotted Kay, who was speedily filling a small plastic bag with mini Refreshers and Mars bars. I've never seen someone move so fast.

I prodded her in the back. 'Kay!'

Kay turned and nearly dropped the contents of her plastic bag all over the floor. 'Lydia,' she shrieked. 'You've got to stop doing that. They make you buy stuff you drop on the floor, you know.'

'Sorry,' I said, taking an empty bag from the dispenser. 'Great minds think alike though.' I looked down at her bag. 'I'm not keen on Mars bars. I'm more of a Crunchie person myself.'

'Oh, fascinating,' said Kay, but she smiled.

'I wish you were in my form.' I was shoving some Rolos in my plastic bag. 'Do you think if I asked they'd move me?'

'Don't go down that road,' said Kay. 'They ask creepy questions about why, and are you comfortable with your form teacher and are you being bullied and stuff. And then everyone thinks you're a moaner and they write it down somewhere to use against you later on. Believe me, I tried it in the First Year, and it's not worth it.'

I sighed. 'Oh well. At least we've got Woollies and the Pick 'n' Mix after school.'

'True,' said Kay. 'I've got to get some shampoo for my mum from the Hair and Beauty aisle. Come on.'

And this is when we came across the Sun-Dazzle. Past all the expensive hair dyes and in with the shampoos: an orange bottle claiming to make you 'a beautiful golden blonde without the need for bleach and plastic gloves'.

Kay, whose hair is rich, dark brown, wasn't interested, but my hair is turning from blonde to mousey over the years, and I was now convinced that Sun-Dazzle would change my entire life for the better.

'It's only one ninety-nine,' said Kay suspiciously. 'Bit cheap, considering.' I was already lost in a hair fantasy though, so I disregarded this.

'I've still got my post office money,' I said.

'Fair enough. And if it doesn't work out, you can always get a wig.' Kay pointed at some joke wigs on sale in the Toy aisle across the way.

We laughed, though of course I was quite sure I wouldn't need a contingency plan.

Friday 4th April

I did the Sun-Dazzle application after dinner tonight and following the instructions on the bottle, made sure to put the hair dryer on extra hot as it said this activates the chemicals. It smelled a bit funny, even Bob and Eugene bolted from my cabin quite quickly, rather than settle themselves somewhere on my bunk for the night – a long way apart from each other, of course. But I am too excited to mind about that. The bottle said to lightly spray a coating of Sun-Dazzle on your hair, but I put two coatings on – just to make sure.

I looked up at the skylight this morning and all I could see was dirty clouds and streaks of rain and then a drop of water splashed off the side of my bunk from a tiny crack in the Perspex and bounced onto my face. Also, a petrol-like smell was coming from somewhere, not quite the same petrol smell as usual. I lay in my bunk like a bad-tempered gnome.

Neither Bob nor Eugene had come near me since last night, and I had one of my feelings of dread. Though I have been mocked for it, I am often right when I get these feelings of impending disaster and can sense bad things are going to happen before they do. I think I might make quite a good fortune-teller, much better than Delphina Crystal the Clairvoyant who sits in the crystal-ball booth on Clacton Pier. Our family still laughs about Delphina Crystal, who told Elsa once that she could see her future clearly and that it most definitely lay in a caring profession, such as St John's Ambulance or voluntary work overseas, and everyone agreed that Delphina Crystal was rubbish and it was a complete waste of the seventy-five pence session fee.

For a moment I was cheered up by having the gift of Second Sight, even though it has not been a very uplifting gift so far, but then Sam practically burst through the door into my cabin, with Bob dangling from one hand. I sat up on my elbows. He dropped Bob brutally on the floor and then looked up at me, and a smirk appeared on his face.

'What?' I said.

'Your hair . . .' said Sam. 'It's—'

'Yes, Sam,' I said. 'I am aware of my awful hair. I've lived with it all my life.'

'It's not . . .' Sam started to say, and then he paused. 'Maybe you should go and look in a proper mirror.'

A sudden coldness, an ice cube shooting through my veins, went through me. I put my hands up to my head.

'Don't touch it,' said Sam, trying not to laugh now. 'It might be radioactive.'

Bob, who had been recovering from the indignity of being manhandled by Sam by frantically licking his fur, was now also looking up at me suspiciously, as though I was very unfamiliar to him.

Something terrible had happened with the Sun-Dazzle.

I raced down the ladder, pushed past Sam and locked myself in the bathroom to look in the big mirror.

'Good lord,' said Dad, when I appeared in the saloon, still not changed out of my pyjamas, having spent half an hour in the bathroom examining my hair. He waved a hand at my hair. 'Is this all the rage then . . . this . . . sort of thing?' He was drinking a cup of coffee on the sofa, with the *Tides Timetable* in one hand.

As suspected, the worst possible outcome had occurred with Sun-Dazzle. My hair was certainly not radiant blonde; it was a lurid ginger colour. There is some ginger hair that is nice, like naturally ginger hair. Sun-Dazzle had made the colour of my hair look like the surface of Mars or Jupiter does when they show ultraviolet pictures of the planets on the news and the colours are like acid and hurt your eyes and you almost have to look away because it's blinding.

Sam started to whistle quietly. To be fair, this was a prime opportunity for him to stick the knife in or turn the screw, or whatever the expression is, but he seemed to be trying to control himself.

'Obviously it has gone wrong,' I told my father. 'No one would ever want to look like this.'

'Oh dear,' said Dad, glancing at Sam. 'Never mind, I'm sure it can be corrected. It's not the end of the world.'

It feels like it, I thought, as Dad resumed examining his tide timetables, dismissing me as though this was just another one of my over-reactions.

'It's all your fault,' I told him, as a burst of rage came over me. 'If we didn't live here, I would be happier and more accepting of the diabolical hair I have obviously inherited from your side of the family, because there would be other things to make me feel better, like a dry bed and a window with curtains and clothes that don't smell and no arguing. I would be really happy to just have those things and I wouldn't be so desperate for things that promise to change my life for the better but have actually completely ruined it . . .' I was crying and angry both at once.

Sam stopped whistling and stared at me. And Dad took his glasses off and was sort of rubbing at his beard with his hand. Any moment now he's going to get his handkerchief out and wipe his forehead, I thought, and then I think I might start hitting him.

'Lydia—' Dad started to say something, but Sam, who

knows from experience when I've reached my limits and am about to explode, interrupted him.

'It's only hair, Lyds,' he said, and came and put a hand on my shoulder, and I was too distraught to shove him off as I would normally do.

'It's not *only* hair.' I couldn't help giving Dad another resentful look, even though I could see that he was still recovering from my outburst.

And then Kate walked in, carrying a couple of bags from the supermarket.

'What's going on here?' she asked, seeing Dad looking bewildered on the sofa and Sam hovering next to me as though I might suddenly start attacking everyone and need restraining. Then she caught sight of me, and took in my hair. But in a split second, before her face had time to make an expression of horror, she put on a huge smile.

'Oh . . . Oh, look at that colour,' she said, putting her bags down. She came over and looked properly at my hair, and tucked some of my fringe behind my ears. She was pretending not to see my face, which I'm sure was puffy from anger and crying. 'I'm sure they won't allow it at school, but it does suit you, Lydia,' she said. 'I used to love experimenting with my hair like this.'

I just gaped at her, quite thrown.

'Funnily enough, I'm going to get my hair cut this afternoon . . .' Kate went on. 'Sally and Erica too. Why don't you come along and see if they can make the colour a bit more . . . natural . . . for school?'

'Really?' I said, taken aback by this unexpected kindness,

as Kate is not always kind and I know even haircuts are a luxury these days, let alone getting hair coloured.

'Won't that cost quite a lot?' Dad said quietly behind her. 'All four of you?'

'I've got some post office money,' I said.

'No. You should keep that . . . for other emergencies.' Kate didn't even turn round to look at Dad. 'I've been given a bit of money by my parents actually . . .' she said. 'More than enough to cover all of us. I was going to suggest it to Lydia anyway.'

'Well . . . that seems like a good solution,' Dad said, but he didn't look exactly happy; in fact, he looked a bit depressed, like a child that's been told off.

'Thank you, Kate,' I said. 'I'd really like that.'

'Lovely,' she said. 'We're booked in for this afternoon, about two.' She glanced back at her supermarket bags. 'In return you can help me unpack some of this shopping.'

Kay was walking her dog Gerta, who is definitely the size of Scooby Doo, down at the quayside later, at about 5.00 p.m. She had yards of hosepipe coiled round her shoulder. I'd been back from the hairdressers about ten minutes and was examining my hair in Sally's Barbie mirror up on deck on *Lady Beatrice*. I was quite pleased with it now that it was more a kind of strawberry blonde, and they'd even put in little gold streaks and trimmed it, and though I was convinced it was ever so slightly green in parts too, at least it was no longer acid-ginger.

Kay wolf whistled when she saw me, whilst trying to

stop Gerta from digging her teeth into the dangling hose-pipe.

'The Sun-Dazzle worked out all right then?' she said, dropping to sit with her legs dangling over the quay, and Gerta sunk down next to her. 'I must admit I was a bit worried it would turn out ginger or something.'

I made a face. 'It did, Kay. I applied it last night, and this morning it was hideous. I've had to go to the hairdresser and get it fixed.'

'I suspected it might be a bit cheap and cheerful.' She nodded in a knowing way. 'But you were so carried away I didn't have the heart to say anything.'

I sighed. 'But you'll never guess who saved the day?'

Kay looked blank.

'Kate,' I said. 'She was actually kind. She even pretended the ginger was nice. She didn't make a big deal out of it either, just said she was getting her hair done anyway and why not me too.'

'Blimey,' said Kay.

'Yes,' I said.

We sat in silence for a while, mesmerised by Gerta who had spotted something in the mud and was growling at it, a string of drool coming out of her jaw.

'What's the hosepipe for?' I asked then.

'Dad's been told by Mum to keep our grass nice and watered,' said Kay. 'She's ordered a swanky new barbecue set out of the catalogue and says this summer she's going to have proper garden parties on the lawn, like the Queen.' Kay rolled her eyes. 'We have this every year. And every year she loses interest. But her wish is Dad's command, and he gave me some money at lunch time on Thursday, and told me I could keep the change if I went out and bought the hose today; it's the wrestling on telly on Saturday afternoons and he never misses the wrestling. He's got a bet on Giant Haystacks.'

I felt a small stab of jealousy at something so normal as a garden and a garden party, and I really would have given anything to see our garden again – even Mum's religious statues that she used to get in auctions and dot around the walls, which I'd always thought a bit creepy.

'I miss my mum,' I said out loud.

Kay was stroking Gerta's ears, but she stopped and looked stricken. 'Oh,' she said. 'I don't think sometimes.'

'No . . .' I opened my eyes very wide to stop myself from crying, which is a good trick I have learned from Elsa. 'It's not really what you said about your mum. Maybe it's because of Kate being nice today.'

Kay swallowed, lost for words for once.

'Sorry,' I said.

Kay put down the hosepipe, then she got hold of Gerta's lead and tied it through a metal loop embedded in the quay wall. She stood up and looked down at the dog. 'Stay, Gerta!' she said. 'Good girl.' Then she wobbled slightly over the gangplank and plonked herself down next to me.

'I'm OK,' I said. 'Don't worry.'

Kay linked her arm through mine. 'Course you're OK,' she said, bumping my shoulder with hers. 'What do you reckon your mum would've thought of your hair?'

'She'd have hated it,' I said. 'Never mind the hairdresser, Mum would have chopped it all off herself and made me put up with the lurid ginger.'

'She sounds a bit like your sister,' said Kay, laughing.

'Yes,' I agreed, cheered and sad at the same time. 'Elsa got most of Mum's fiery nature. I'm more like Dad, I suppose.'

'Could do a lot worse than that,' Kay said. She looked at me and smiled.

In front of us, Gerta had taken advantage of our conversation and had chewed off some of the hosepipe. She was spitting out bits of rubber on the quayside.

'Gerta . . .' Kay groaned. 'Why do you have to destroy everything? It's like looking after a bloody dragon.'

It was just beginning to seem like a good end to a day that had started very badly, and then Sam arrived home from having a swim and annoyed me by sitting down next to Kay and talking to us. I felt agitated all over again, even though I knew on Kay's part that she was only being polite.

Sam's hair was wet and sticking up all over the place and he was wearing a T-shirt with a great big hole in the neck and baggy old army shorts and I could see a red spot emerging on his chin, but he didn't seem to care about that at all. Even Bob, who had crept up on deck and had been glaring and quivering at Gerta tied up on the quay, looked over at Sam as though he was disappointed in him.

'Did Lydia tell you about her tantrum this morning, Kay?' said Sam, nodding at my hair.

'It wasn't a tantrum,' I said coldly.

'Well, one of your self-induced disasters then.' Sam shook his head, lightly spraying me, Kay and Bob with saltwater.

'We live and learn,' said Kay. She looked Sam up and down. 'Anyway, you could do with a hair transplant yourself. You look a bit like that Catweazle.'

Catweazle was a favourite TV programme of mine and Sam's when we were much younger. Catweazle is a time-travelling wizard from the eleventh century who arrives in the future in 1971 and who hides behind trees a lot while he tries to work out the mysteries of the twentieth century, and how he will get back to his own time. Catweazle had the appearance of an eccentric scruffy old tramp and scared people with his looks.

I laughed silently with my mouth open, fully expecting Sam to try and hit me, but instead he laughed too, though I noticed he went slightly red at the same time.

'I did love that programme though,' Kay went on. 'Me and my dad did. In fact, Dad used to joke about how he wouldn't mind stepping into Catweazle's shoes every so often and time-travelling away from Mother's nagging.'

Sam grinned at her. 'Catweazle is a hero of our times,' he said.

'*His* times, you mean,' said Kay. She and Sam laughed together at this.

'Anyway. I don't really care what I look like,' said Sam after a bit. 'I can't see what all the fuss is about. What does it matter?'

This is obviously only Sam's view. Everyone else knows it matters very much what you look like. Jake knows. He spends most of his money on clothes and things to put in his hair and even polishes his Doctor Martens. Jake says that girls really appreciate it if you make an effort.

Sam sat with us for ages, making Kay laugh for some reason, and even though I gave out a few death stares, he didn't take the hint. In the end, I sat and glared down at the mud, imagining Sam's face gradually getting sucked under.

Kay went off home about six and I picked up Sally's mirror and was just about to go down the hatch when I spotted Dad, who was sitting over by the bow of *Lady Beatrice*, looking out at the estuary, watching the tide coming up. He seemed quite alone and lost in thought. A part of me felt guilty and wanted to go over and cheer him up. But another part of me felt quite resentful that everything ends up being about him somehow.

Today, before he went to work, Dad was reading a letter at the table in the saloon. There was a torrential rainstorm last night and two buckets were sitting underneath the big skylight, catching the large drops of water. We sat listening to Radio 4 to the background sound of ominous plopping, and a little pool gathered underneath one of the buckets where the drips had missed. I stepped round it all, noticing a new orange stain on my white school shirt and thinking I'd have to wear my cardigan all day again.

Kate was in the galley, arguing with Sally over her P.E. kit, which Sally hadn't given her to wash in time and because Harry had gone off to the boatyard early, and Sam had already gone to get his bus, it was just me and Jake and Dad having our breakfast.

'Who's that from?' I said, as Dad was reading the letter with a lot of interest.

'It's from your Aunt Lorna,' he said. 'She's been on a cookery retreat in Italy for the past two weeks. She says she's made a perfect cheese soufflé and your mother would have been proud.' He took his glasses off. 'Your mother's soufflés were very good,' he added.

'Do you remember when Mum made a lemon soufflé on my birthday?' I said. 'It was like eating lemon air.'

'Exactly; it was,' Dad agreed. 'Quite a lot of skill goes into making edible air.'

We exchanged one of our old satisfied, conspiring looks, which we haven't done for a long time.

159

Jake was spooning cereal into his mouth, shaking his head at us. 'You two . . .' he murmured.

'Does Lorna mention me, or say anything about me visiting?' I said. I had a lovely vision of Lorna's nice Persian rugs and the central heating, and tea and Jamaican ginger cake.

'I'm sure you're always welcome at her cottage,' said Dad. 'As she is here. Though perhaps we're not ready for visitors just yet.'

'Do you think she'd be shocked by our habitation?' I looked pointedly at the buckets on the floor.

'Lorna drove an ambulance in the war,' Dad said. 'Not much shocks you after you've experienced that. She's a tough cookie.'

Lorna is much older than Mum, who claimed that she was 'an accident' in her family. Mum said that Lorna was more like a mother than a sister.

'Wow,' said Jake. 'She really did that? That must have been terrifying.'

'Indeed.' Dad folded the letter up and put it in his top pocket. 'Driving through the London streets at night, not knowing if you'd be blown up. Terrifying is the right word.'

Jake was studying Dad as though he was somebody he'd never met before. I must admit, because I was born quite a long time after the war ended, I never think about Dad being part of all that. He was in the Navy when he was very young, though he never ever talks about it. Now I thought he might have seen awful things, different to what I would think of as awful. People you know being killed, bombs exploding.

'Lorna sounds amazing,' said Jake. 'A real hero. I bet she's got lots of stories about the Blitz.'

'Who has?' said Kate, finally coming out of the galley and putting Sally's coat on for her.

'Aunt Lorna,' I told her. 'Dad's just got a letter from Italy, where she's doing a cooking course.'

'She drove an ambulance in the war, Mum,' added Jake. 'Did you know that?'

'I didn't know that, no.' Kate's expression was hard to make out. 'Well, how nice to be in Italy. I've almost forgotten about luxuries like going abroad.'

Dad frowned and put his glasses in their case.

'Charlie, have you remembered to ask the carpenter for a quote for shelves for Sally?' Kate went on. 'She's still got most of her things in cardboard boxes by her bunk.'

'Quote?' said Dad, looking up. 'Ah, yes. I'll get on to that today . . . or tomorrow.' He suddenly looked in a hurry. 'I'd better get my train actually. I'm very late as it is.'

Kate glanced at him suspiciously while Sally looked anxiously between them.

'I can probably do Sally's shelves,' said Jake. 'It can't be that hard.'

'Thanks, my love,' said Kate. 'But they need to be proper.'

'I've sold some of my vinyl at the record and tape exchange,' Jake went on. 'So maybe I could help out with the money?'

Dad, who was putting his coat on, gave Jake a look that wasn't exactly grateful. 'No need for that,' he said shortly.

Kate bit her lip, and she had angry frown lines. 'Let's hope there isn't,' she said. 'Anyway. I've got to get the girls to school.' She went off to collect Erica, with Sally trailing miserably behind her.

'My mate Dean at school . . . his uncle's a carpenter,' said Jake when she'd gone. 'I could ask him for a quote. We might get some money off.'

'We don't need to get any money off,' Dad snapped. 'I shall sort it out.'

'I was only trying to help,' Jake said quietly.

'Well, don't. I hardly need another member of your family reminding me of my utter failure to provide for them,' Dad snapped.

Jake's expression was hurt and annoyed at the same time, and Dad didn't look at either of us as he picked up his briefcase and walked out of the saloon.

'Dad's just in a bad mood, I think,' I told Jake.

He shook his head, and seemed as though he was really trying not to say something.

'Anyway, I suppose we'd better go to school now.' I felt awkward and worried. It was not like Dad to be moody and rude. And he had been quite rude.

'I'll cycle there,' said Jake without looking at me. 'You go on ahead.'

At school later, Kay had the brainwave of putting toothpaste over the rust mark on my school shirt, and we locked ourselves in a cubicle, while Kay did the application.

'Mother's paranoid about my teeth falling out so she makes me take my toothbrush and stuff to school,' said Kay, breaking open a fresh tube. 'I've got loads to spare.'

I smiled in gratitude as Kay dabbed at my shirt.

'I'm just wondering why we're hiding in the cubicle, though?' I said.

'It's in case of Ruth Porter,' said Kay. 'She does all her worst crimes in the girls' toilets. In the First Year, she used to take everyone's sandwich boxes out of their bags and drop them into the loos. It's like the toilets are Ruth's portal into the deadly underworld.'

'Thank goodness she hasn't singled me out yet,' I said. 'I don't think I could cope with Ruth along with everything else.'

'Poor Ruth never stood a chance,' said Kay. 'Apparently, she has relatives in Broadmoor prison – which is a kind of a loony bin for criminals – and a couple of years back her mum was up in court for trying to strangle her dad. She got let off, but I'm sure she did try and strangle him as he talks like a parrot these days. Best thing with Ruth is to act like you don't care. In my case, it's handy too that I've got Gerta and I've already implied that Gerta is a killer so she steers well clear of me.'

'How many people has Gerta actually killed?' I asked, only slightly joking as Gerta is so huge with a massive jaw.

'None,' said Kay, smirking. 'My Gerta wouldn't hurt a fly. But Ruth's not to know that.' She blew on the toothpaste to help it dry.

'I'm sure Sally's being bullied at school,' I blurted then. 'She's not saying anything though, she's suffering in silence.' I sighed. 'Something's going on, anyway. Shall I tell Kate? I don't want Sally to get worried about everyone knowing. But someone's got to say something.'

Kay thought. 'You should tell Kate,' she said. 'Some people aren't strong enough to stand up to bullies and they need help.'

As I think I am one of those people, this seemed to decide the matter for me. 'You're right,' I said. 'The thing is, there's also a bad atmosphere between Kate and Dad at the moment. Dad got a postcard from my Aunt Lorna this morning and Kate didn't seem too pleased about it.'

'Is that Jamaican ginger cake Aunt Lorna?' asked Kay.

I've told Kay about Lorna's tradition of tea and Jamaican ginger cake, and Kay agrees that along with Lorna's little terrier, it sounds idyllic.

'Yes,' I said. 'And Kate was a bit frosty about the letter.'

'Maybe it's because of Aunt Lorna being your mum's sister?' said Kay. 'She feels left out?'

'Maybe,' I said, suspecting it might be more than that. Relations between Kate and Dad have definitely been deteriorating since the dangerous driving incident.

'Why do you think Kate married your dad?' asked Kay, tuning into my inner thoughts.

'I think she must have thought he was someone else,' I said. 'I love Dad, but he's never been a practical person. It must be quite disappointing for her.'

Kay sighed and then peered at the hardening blob of toothpaste on my shirt. 'I think I've overdone the toothpaste, Lyds. It might look a bit like dried bird's poo.'

After school, Kate was unloading shopping and putting it in the galley cupboards very noisily, and I hovered in the doorway, determined not to let her obvious bad mood put me off my mission. I knew Sally and Erica were doing homework in their cabin.

'Kate,' I said quietly when she'd finished and had put the kettle on.

She turned and I nearly changed my mind because her face was so stony. 'What is it?' she said.

'Well . . . I think Sally's got something going on at school,' I said. 'I think she might be being bullied . . . maybe.'

Kate opened her mouth, just as the kettle was reaching boiling point and making a racket. She switched it off. 'Oh . . . God,' she said then, and put her head in hands. 'Of course she is.'

'I just think she feels ashamed to tell anyone . . .' I went on.

Kate's face softened. 'But she's told you?'

'Not really,' I said. 'I mean, mostly Sally just talks to Erica, but I noticed she was a bit off and I put two and two together sort of thing.'

'Her stomach,' Kate nodded. 'I thought she was just trying to bunk off school. I didn't think it was for anything serious.'

'Sorry,' I said. 'Maybe you can speak to her teacher.'

Kate looked at me and now her expression was much softer. 'Thank you,' she said. 'You're a kind girl, Lydia.'

I shrugged. 'I know what it's like.'

Then Kate came over and hugged me. For the first time ever. 'I'm so sorry for everything that has happened to you,' she said.

It felt so nice to be hugged and talked to like someone's

child, I'd forgotten what it was like. But it was also a bit confusing. I was scared to think of Kate as my new mother.

'I'll go in with her tomorrow,' said Kate. 'Thank you for telling me, Lydia.'

Now that it's spring, Kay and I sometimes go down to the sea wall after school and today she said that she was too annoyed with her dad to go straight home, and why don't we hang around Woolworths and then go and get some sausage rolls from the bakers and watch the sun and the tide going down instead? Since Wednesday is 'Cauliflower Cheese' on the dinner rota, Kay's suggestion was a godsend. I asked Jake to let Kate know I was eating out, and not to save me any cauliflower cheese at all.

At 5.30 p.m., Kay and I hiked in our school uniforms over the Maling bridge and all the way round to the other side of the estuary.

Once we'd put our inside-out blazers down for sitting on, Kay got out the giant bag of still-warm sausage rolls, and a bottle of lemonade. We watched a man and woman in a white plastic dinghy sail straight into one of the marsh banks and start arguing, and we sat and laughed with our mouths full.

'Should we let them know the tide will be out in fifteen minutes?' said Kay, already on her second sausage roll. 'They're never going to get back across the estuary.'

'That man is being henpecked to death,' I said.

'Reminds me of my dad.' Kay chucked her food at a seagull.

'Why are you so annoyed with your dad anyway?'

Kay sighed. 'It's not really his fault,' she said. 'But we were going to drive to the greyhound tracks in Walthamstow this

Friday night after school. I love going to the dogs, and last time I won twenty pounds. Dad's different when it's just us and Mum's not going on at him all the time. It's like our special thing.'

'So you aren't going now?' I asked.

'No, because Mum's insisting we all go round to our old neighbour Val Jones, as she's a divorcee and Mum thinks she must be lonely. Apparently she saw her looking sad in the Co-op. Next thing, Mum's inviting us all round hers for a get-together on Friday night, and Dad just said, "OK, love." He didn't even try and get out of it.' Kay rolled her eyes. 'I wish Mum would stop interfering in people's lives. Val has been divorced for a while now, and she seems quite happy about it to me.'

'But still she means well, your mum,' I said. 'Despite her being a busybody.'

Kay grinned when I said busybody.

'But why do *you* have to go?' I said.

'I've got to go because of Jimmy,' said Kay.

'Who's Jimmy?'

'He's Val's kid. He's our age, and he's been living with his dad in Cornwall since Val and Pete got divorced, but he's back for a few days, and Val says he hasn't got any friends round here any more.' She sighed. 'Why do parents always think you can suddenly make friends with people, just because you're the same age? Don't they remember being young?'

'What a terrible bore,' I said in my Lady Penelope voice. I rested back on my elbows. 'But maybe Jimmy will be nice.'

'I haven't seen Jimmy for years. Last time I saw him he was shorter than me and I think he had a squint,' said Kay. 'I can't remember if he was nice or not.'

'He's most likely had the squint corrected by now,' I said, remembering Elsa's friend Andrea, who had hers operated on when she was young. 'And he might have got taller and maybe more interesting.'

Kay made a face. 'Maybe.'

For some reason I was imagining Jimmy as the Milky Bar Kid. 'I've got an idea,' I said, feeling bad for him. 'Why don't you bring Jimmy down to *Lady Beatrice*? Then you wouldn't have to talk to him on your own all the time and we could go over to the prom and have doughnuts at Danny's Donuts kiosk.'

Kay looked at me. 'That would be a million times better than sitting round at Val's with fish-paste sarnies. Jimmy will no doubt like all the ropes and stuff.'

'All boys seem to love ropes for some reason,' I said. 'Sam can stare at ropes and knots for hours. I don't get it.'

'Aren't we humans strange?' said Kay, staring at the sun sinking in the sky.

Friday 9th May

This afternoon I was starting to regret inviting Kay to bring Jimmy to *Lady Beatrice*, as after school Sam and Jake got into a petty argument over Jake's second-hand bikes taking over on deck.

Jake's started buying old bikes and doing them up and then selling them on for twice what he paid for them. He confided in me that he needs the money for his social life, and to keep his girlfriend, Dawn Burrows, in the manner to which she is accustomed. The way Jake talks about Dawn, she reminds me of Donna, as Dawn's parents have a massive house with a pool and a Jacuzzi from her dad's property development business. Apparently Jake is reminded every time he goes round that Mr Burrows started with nothing and has built his empire on hard graft.

'I admire your entrepreneurial spirit,' Sam told Jake, in a pompous way that implied he didn't at all, 'but it's like the Tour de France round here lately, and it's a safety hazard.'

'Huge exaggeration,' said Jake. 'There are three bikes up there and they're all tied up out of the way by the wheel-house.'

'I'd like to tie *you* up by the wheelhouse,' muttered Sam.

'What's that?' said Jake, who like me had heard perfectly well.

'Please don't argue,' I said, pained. 'I've got guests coming and I don't want an atmosphere.'

'Guests?' said Sam. '*Guests?*'

'Who is it?' Jake said, interested. 'A boy?'

I saw Sam frown at this.

'Kay,' I said, 'and this kid called Jimmy who I've never met.'

'Ooh, *Jimmy*,' Sam and Jake both said at the same time, then looked annoyed at being in harmony for once.

I looked at Sam. 'If Jimmy wants to know about ropes, please *please* don't be rude to him and show me up.'

Sam looked offended. 'I would never be rude,' he said haughtily.

Nobody said anything to this, but Jake and I did exchange a look of disbelief.

'Also,' I said, 'don't say anything else at all to make me look stupid.'

'Righto,' said Sam.

'Cool,' said Jake. 'Anyway, I'm going round to Dawn's.' He brushed at his denim jacket and picked a loose thread off his jeans. 'Actually, I'd better go and get ready, make sure my new Fred Perry isn't too creased.'

Sam looked as though Jake was speaking Martian as he himself has been wearing the same manky old sweatshirt for months. He scratched at his scruffy hair. I suddenly felt a wave of affection for him and his scarecrow image. It would be so weird if he was like Jake and took care of his appearance, I'm not sure I'd like it.

I was down below when Kay arrived. I had planned to be up on deck to intercept her, just in case Dad came home early in one of his morose moods. Luckily, everyone seemed to be somewhere else when she walked through the saloon door with a tall boy behind her. I was unprepared, and blushed the colour of a tomato as I sprang up from my place on the sofa.

'Caught you!' said Kay, laughing at my face. 'I would have knocked but you don't have a knocker, or a door, so . . .' She turned to the tall boy behind her. 'Jimmy, this is Lydia.'

Jimmy nodded and smiled at me, and I saw very blue eyes and a little mole like a beauty spot by his mouth, and his hair was extremely short. He looked nothing like the Milky Bar Kid.

I nodded and smiled back, trying not to stare at him too much. He was at least two inches taller than Kay, which meant he was four inches taller than me.

'This boat is nice,' said Jimmy, whose voice was quite deep. He looked around and I cringed inwardly at all our higgledy-piggledy furniture and the muddy boots and shoes by the stove and Kate's makeshift washing line with mine and Sally's knickers just hanging on it for all to see. To my added embarrassment, Bob had chosen this moment to clean himself thoroughly on the bench by the table. Seen through a stranger's eyes I thought our saloon must look a bit like Fagin's lair from *Oliver Twist*.

'It's OK,' I said, and then, 'What's your house like?'

Standing just behind Jimmy, Kay smirked at me and my attempts at small talk.

'Very ordinary,' said Jimmy. 'Well, my mum's flat is. My dad's house is a bit more characterful.' He smiled awkwardly and I felt a little shift in my stomach, because he was quite shy and I much prefer shy people on the whole. Most boys

172

our age are downright rude all the time to everyone, especially girls. I liked that Jimmy had used the word 'characterful' and I wondered if he was a reader like me.

'Well,' said Kay bluntly, breaking up my thoughts. 'This is fascinating, but are you going to offer us some tea and biscuits or shall we head off to the kiosk for Danny's doughnuts?'

Sometimes I'm surprised that Kay isn't the size of an elephant as she is either thinking about or eating food every minute of the day. But she isn't, she's 'rangy', which is a good word I have stolen from Elsa.

'Tea,' said Jimmy, smiling at me again. 'If Lydia doesn't mind.'

'Course not,' I said.

'Well, take a seat, Jimmy,' said Kay quite bossily. 'While I help Lydia in the kitchen.'

'Thanks,' he said, sitting on the sofa. I watched him bend down to stroke Bob, who rubbed his head against Jimmy's palm. Right on time, Eugene cantered in from the direction of the galley and leapt up on Jimmy's lap. 'This one's sweet, too,' said Jimmy, while Bob lashed out a clawed paw at Eugene's tail. I was very pleased to see that Jimmy is a cat person.

In the galley I took the dinner rota off the fridge as there was no way Jimmy was seeing that, and Kay washed up some mugs for us.

'I told you they would have fixed Jimmy's squint,' I whispered to her. 'And didn't I say he might be tall and interesting now?'

'All right, clever clogs,' Kay whispered back. 'It's obvious you've already taken a shine to him.'

'No I haven't,' I said, mortified.

'I must admit the moment he opened his mouth back at Val's, I knew he was one of those serious types like you,' she said. 'Uses lots of big words all the time. Val thinks he must be writing a novel, or poetry or something, as he's always got his head in a book and writes things down in a notebook.'

'What do you mean, "serious type"?' I said, as no one has said that about me before. 'Actually, I'm a bit jealous about Jimmy maybe writing a novel. I'd really like to write a whole book but I can't get further than a page. That's something we can have a conversation about later if everything else dries up.'

Kay laughed at me. 'See. *That's* what I mean by serious,' she said.

I opened the tin where Kate puts all the boring biscuits. 'Custard creams,' I said. 'They're a bit stale.'

'Oh well,' said Kay, grabbing one and biting it in half. 'It all goes down the same chute.'

Once we'd brought the tea out, leaving behind the stale custard creams, me, Jimmy and Kay sat in a line on the sofa, and Bob, in the hopes of Jimmy lavishing affection on him, bullied Eugene off his lap and sprawled himself across Jimmy's legs, his claws extended out to Kay's thighs, threatening her woolly tights.

'I like sailing,' Jimmy said then. 'My dad's got a little boat where we live. The sea's a bit rough around Penzance, but we go out in it in the summer. Well, we did before my dad's girlfriend got pregnant—'

'Your dad's going to have another kid? Isn't he quite old?' interrupted Kay.

Jimmy looked a bit uncomfortable. 'It's due just before Christmas. Dad's building an extension on the house, just for the baby. Everything's about the baby now.'

Kay sipped her tea.

'What's your dad's girlfriend like?' I asked Jimmy, both hoping and dreading that he would say 'lovely'.

'She's all right,' he said. 'I mean, she's not my mum, she's always been more like my dad's friend.'

'I've got a stepmother,' I said, safe in the knowledge that Kate was at an all-ages pottery workshop in town with Sally and Erica. 'But she's not exactly my dad's friend. Not at the moment anyway.'

Jimmy looked surprised. 'I didn't realise,' he said. 'What about your real mum? Do you see her much?'

'She died,' I said.

'Oh.' Jimmy looked horrified. 'Sorry. When was that?'

'A few years ago,' I said, keeping my voice steady. 'When I was ten.'

'That's really sad.'

'It's OK.' Not true, but what are you supposed to say. You can't explain all the feelings you have about something like that. It would take hours.

'Anyway . . .' Kay said, as the conversation was a bit depressing. She finished her tea quite noisily and me and Jimmy looked at each other over her head in a sort of relief.

Just then Sam came in with a plastic bag and a delicious aroma. 'Anyone want some Chinese?' he said. 'Won-Kei at the top of the hill closed early because the kitchen flooded, and I got all this takeaway for free. I only went to get prawn crackers!' He looked at the three of us. 'It might stretch to four, as long as you lot don't eat much.'

'Brilliant. Chinese is my favourite,' said Kay. She got up and stood like a vulture over its prey, watching Sam take out all the little foil boxes.

'I don't think we'll make it to the kiosk,' I said to Jimmy. 'We can go another time.'

'I'd like that,' he said, and then we sat and watched as, unbelievably, Sam allowed Kay to order him around with the food.

'Better get some plates and cutlery,' she told him. 'And tomato ketchup for the fried rice.'

'Ugh,' said Sam, disgusted. 'Worcester sauce for me.'

'Boys,' said Kay with a shudder. 'Heathens.'

'I think you mean Philistines?' Sam laughed.

'Whatever you say, Professor,' sighed Kay. 'Go on then, bring it all out.'

'Yes, ma'am,' said Sam, which made Jimmy laugh.

Even though I'm still not sure what I think about Kay and Sam being so friendly, I laughed too, as it's nice to see people getting on.

In fact, for a moment I felt quite happy that nothing excruciating had happened, and no one was angry with anyone. And that Jimmy had turned out nice.

It wasn't till we'd finished the Chinese, and Kay and I

were lying on the floor on our backs as we'd overeaten, that I remembered that Dad still wasn't home and it was nearly 8.30 p.m. I decided not to think about it and spoil the evening, but even when you're trying not to think about something, you are really underneath.

Jimmy looked at the big clock above the saloon door. 'I'd better get back to my mum's,' he said, but not very enthusiastically. 'She probably needs help with the washing-up.'

'Are you at Lydia's school?' Sam asked, still picking bits of chicken out of one of the boxes and eating them.

'No, I'm just here for the weekend,' said Jimmy. 'I live in Cornwall with my dad the rest of the time.'

'I went to Cornwall on a school trip once,' said Sam. 'We went to a place called Sennen Beach.'

'That's really near us,' said Jimmy. 'My dad goes surfing there. I prefer the cove though, as it's quieter and you can think . . .' He trailed off, embarrassed.

'I'd prefer that too,' I said, coming to his rescue. 'I like to be quiet.'

'You what?' Sam was laughing. 'You should see her trying to work out a square root,' he said to Jimmy. 'She's like a squealing piglet.'

Of course, I couldn't expect an entire evening to go by without Sam saying something like this, but then I caught Kay grinning at Sam out of the corner of my eye and I felt slightly furious. I gave Sam a look of thunder.

'I hate maths too,' said Jimmy. Then, 'I'm useless at it. It's never made much sense to me.'

Kay bit her lip in a smirk, but though I was quite irritated by her and Sam being in cahoots together, I did take small comfort in Jimmy hating maths.

'Are you going now then?' said Sam, looking at Kay. 'You eat my Chinese and then just run off?'

Kay laughed. 'Thanks for sharing your Chinese with us, Sam.'

'You're very welcome,' said Sam, looking quite pleased with himself.

I made another mental note to closely observe Sam and Kay's behaviour from now on.

'Come on then, Jimmy,' said Kay. 'Val's dishes are mounting up.'

Jimmy got to his feet and I noticed he had on those skateboarding plimsolls that the cool boys at school are wearing.

'I like your plimsolls,' I told him.

'Thanks,' said Jimmy.

'You're very welcome,' I said, giving Sam a flinty look, just to let him know I had noticed his behaviour.

'Nice meeting you, Lydia,' Jimmy said. 'Maybe see you next time.'

'Maybe.' I truly hoped I wasn't blushing at all as it felt like Kay's eyes were boring holes in the side of my face.

'Jeez,' she said. 'I haven't got all day. Gerta needs her bedtime cuddle. See you at school, Lyds. Bye, Sam.'

'Bye, Kay,' said Sam, and I could see he was trying to hold in a burp until they'd gone.

As soon as the saloon door shut behind them, Sam collapsed in the egg-chair and let out the huge burp.

'That's better,' he said.

'Oh my God, Sam, you are disgusting,' I told him, before putting a whole leftover sesame chicken wing in my mouth.

Thursday 5th June

Kay is determined to get a summer job at Danny's Donuts kiosk, so after school today we hung out on the prom by the freshwater pool, sitting at one of the plastic tables and chatting to Danny the owner, who doesn't exactly look rushed off his feet. Kay says that Danny owes her, because Kay's dad came out to fix the pipes in the kiosk at 8.00 p.m. one night and forgot to bill Danny for the work.

I'm not sure I could stick a job at Danny's Donuts. Just standing at the counter choosing which doughnut to have makes my hair feel greasy and sugary and my skin itch. But Kay somehow reckons she could earn more than £50 a week over the summer holidays, which is practically like a proper job.

Danny came out and started collecting greasy paper plates and shoving them in a black bin bag.

'All right, Danny?' said Kay.

Danny squinted at her. 'Oh, it's you . . . Terry's kid, isn't it? How's the old man?'

'Fine,' said Kay. 'You know, working all hours, for no money.'

Danny chewed on his lips. 'I owe him for a job. Tell him I'm good for it. Come the summer it'll be swarming. It's nonstop with those bloody kids.' He smiled. 'No offence.'

'None taken,' said Kay cheerily. 'Actually, Dad was wondering if there was any work going here . . . helping out with the doughnuts and that.'

'Terry?' Danny looked confused. 'He can't be that hard up?'

Kay laughed and sat back, her large boobs bobbing around. 'No, not for him, silly,' she said. 'For me.'

'Ah,' said Danny. 'You want a job on the kiosk?'

'Just for the summer,' said Kay. 'Helping out with all those bloody kids.'

Danny blushed and looked worried. 'Don't go telling your dad about my language.'

'Course not,' said Kay. 'If you give me a job, I swear I won't.'

Danny laughed. 'All right then. Come back soon and I'll give you a trial run and then we'll see.'

'Nice one,' said Kay. 'I'm fifteen pounds a day. Seven pound fifty for a half day. If you decide to take me on.'

'You what?' said Danny.

'Those are my rates, Danny. Take it or leave it.'

'How about ten quid a day, no tea breaks and no half days,' said Danny, shaking his head at Kay. 'Little tea leaf.'

'Fair enough,' said Kay immediately. She stuck out her hand. 'Shake on it then.'

'That was brilliant,' I said to Kay when Danny had gone back inside. 'Fifty pounds a week in the holidays!'

'Stick with me, kid,' said Kay, picking up a custard doughnut. 'It's all about pretending you know what you're doing, if you get my drift.'

I arrived back home and once again nearly tripped over the Hoover lead ranged across the saloon. Kate has started doing the housework at around six-ish. Which is odd as she has the whole day to do it. It's like she is making some kind of point.

The noise of the vacuum cleaner was deafening, and on top of that Kate was humming quite threateningly.

Harry was pretending to read a book on the sofa. He must have been pretending – he couldn't possibly have been able to concentrate. He looked up and winked at me. I have never been able to wink so I didn't attempt to do it back.

The table was already set for dinner. It was a Wednesday, so according to this month's rota that meant pork pie and salad. I'm not keen on pork pie, because of the jelly lining, which not even Eugene will eat when I slip it to him under the table. 'Where's Dad?' I shouted over the noise Kate was making. I looked at Harry.

He shrugged. 'On his way back from work?'

Kate, who must have sonic hearing, switched off the Hoover and said coldly, 'Let's hope not.'

Even Harry looked shocked. I opened my mouth to say something but Kate's face was hard with annoyance and I decided against it.

'Pork pie for dinner?' I asked cheerfully, trying to lighten the atmosphere.

'If you don't want it, make yourself some toast,' said Kate, unplugging the vacuum cleaner and winding the lead round her wrist. 'I'm afraid I haven't got the time or the inclination to be imaginative with meals.'

Harry gave me a look, and I willed a magic carpet to come sailing down the hatch and whisk me away.

We ate the pork pie in silence. Dad did not appear and Kate seemed quite relieved. I didn't dare enquire where he was. Sam was kicking me under the table while slowly churning pork pie around his mouth, but I realised that this was some kind of nervous tic and he didn't even know he was doing it. He swallowed and immediately tried to climb over the bench and away.

'Where are you going?' Kate said icily.

'Got to go and help Ben next door,' said Sam, who has taken to spending a lot of time with Ben, who is a bit older than Harry and looks after all the maintenance on *Philomena*, the barge moored next to ours. Ben is half-Indian, and very handsome and muscular and tall, but also quite gentle and kind. He has rescued Bob and Eugene from the mud on many occasions when they've accidentally slipped overboard. If it weren't so pointless I would definitely be in love with Ben.

I quickly stuffed in the last bit of pork pie, revolting jelly and all. 'I'll come too,' I said, getting up.

'No you won't,' said Kate. 'You'll wait until everyone has finished eating.'

As neither Erica nor Sally had touched their food, and Harry – who seems to be exempt from Kate's orders – was rolling a cigarette instead of eating, this meant that we might be sitting at the table in interminable silence all night.

But I sat back down. Sam, on the other hand, ignored Kate and walked off whistling.

'Sam,' said Kate, and her voice was the kind of quiet-angry

that gives you goose bumps. 'Come back and sit at the table, please. Do as you're told.'

Harry raised one eyebrow, and put the roll-up in his mouth. He and Sam never stick up for each other, which depresses me slightly.

'But why?' I asked. 'He's finished his food.'

'*You* may have been brought up with no manners,' said Kate, looking at me with impatience, 'but I demand manners and you will all do as you're told.'

'Where's Charlie?' said Erica. 'Do we have to wait till he comes home?'

Kate shut her eyes, put down her knife and fork and sat there without answering.

'Mum?' said Sally, her hand gripping mine under the table. I gripped back as it was quite nice to have someone hold my hand just then.

'I have no idea where Charlie is,' Kate spoke at last. Her voice was very flat and cold.

Sam, who had been loitering on the point of leaving by the door, turned at this and his face was thunderous. 'He probably can't face your nagging and moaning,' he snapped.

'That's enough!' Kate stood up so quickly that her plate containing bits of broken pastry flew off the table and smashed on the floor.

Sam looked quite alarmed but he stayed put. Harry had his head in his hands, his fag smoking quietly on its own between his fingers.

'Let's all calm down, shall we,' I said, unwisely.

'And you can shut up!' said Kate. 'You have no idea what it's like to live with your father.'

'Well, actually I do live with him,' I said. 'So—'

'Don't be a smart arse,' snapped Kate. 'There are things I could tell you about your dad—'

She stopped abruptly before she could come out with all sorts of stuff about Dad that I didn't want to hear. I realised I was vibrating a bit, and the bench was wobbling.

'Lydia,' said Harry, noticing. 'It's OK.'

'Oh, Christ,' said Kate. But she looked more guilty than cross.

Harry held onto my hand, though he was still smoking his roll-up. Sally was held prisoner by his arm across her. It was a funny sight, if it hadn't been so miserable.

I looked at Kate then, the dark circles under her eyes and the way her hair was scraped back and her baggy jumper and her thinner face. How had this happened? Was Dad really so awful that she had stopped caring about everything? The manic housework must be her way of dealing with it, I thought. I felt a bit sorry for her, because even though she is mostly snappy with me, she isn't a horrible person either. I thought of her taking me to get my hair cut and hugging me when I'd told her about Sally, but this somehow made what was happening now even worse.

'Listen. You children think you can do what you like, but you can't,' said Kate, a bit more calmly. 'I'm trying to make this some kind of civilised home. God knows that is an impossible task. I need your help.'

Harry nodded.

Sam still looked murderous but he couldn't really argue now that Kate was being reasonable. I was torn. I knew exactly how Sam felt, how enraging it is to have someone who isn't our mother talk to us like this. But when I looked at Kate, I saw someone so miserable she might as well have been wearing one of those sandwich boards around her neck with I'M VERY UNHAPPY written on it in large capital letters.

Later on, Sally knocked on my cabin door. She had her nightie on and damp hair from her bath. I was trying to tune the transistor radio in to Radio Luxembourg again, as Eugene had been playing with the dial and messed it all up. I was looking forward to the phone-in show on relationship and emotional problems and wasn't really in the mood for a visitor.

'What is it?' I said, trying not to sound irritated.

'I just wanted to say . . .' Sally said. 'Thanks for talking to Mum about school and everything.'

I put the radio down. 'Is everything OK now?'

Sally nodded. 'My form teacher sorted it out and everyone's been a lot nicer this term. I feel much better.'

'Well,' I said. 'That's brilliant news, Sally.'

'Just wanted to say thanks anyway.' She fiddled with her damp hair.

'Glad to be of help,' I told her, which is what the radio agony aunt says at the end of every call. 'Night, Sally.'

After Sally went off to bed, instead of tuning in to Radio Luxembourg, I lay in the dark wondering if being a professional

Agony Aunt could be my future career, rather than being a professional psychic, as helping people with their everyday problems is clearly one of my gifts. Except for Kate's and my father's problems, of course, which are completely beyond me.

Dad still isn't home.

Tuesday 24th June

It's only weeks till we break up for summer, and very nearly my birthday; two things that used to fill me with tremendous excitement. But this year it means six weeks with nowhere to go every day to get away from Kate and Dad, even if school in general is wasted on me and no one there seems bothered enough to help me get better at the whole tests and exams thing. I don't know what's to become of me.

Elsa said she isn't going abroad this summer and she's staying on in Cambridge as she's got herself a job in a fancy clothes shop and is living with someone's parents in a place called Barton, which is just outside Cambridge. She wrote this on a postcard and I read it quite a few times and still thought it was a bit flat and not like Elsa.

Of course, a part of me was hurt that she doesn't want to be with us, even though I don't blame her. When she's back at college in the autumn, I am definitely going to visit her. Apart from anything else, maybe it will inspire me to do better in my subjects, though I fear that only a brain transplant would work for that.

After school me and Kay went to have a Coke outside this little pub behind the quayside called The Smugglers' Tavern, which looks like a real-life gingerbread house and has a large beer garden in the front with a trellis and fake ivy weaving in and out of it. I know it's fake, because once we experimented by lighting one of the leaves with a match and it set it on fire and smelled of burning plastic. Anyway,

Kay and I sometimes have a Coke sitting outside, as Rich, who is the manager, loves Gerta so he overlooks the fact that Kay and I are underage as long as we sit on the benches at the far end of the patio in case any police walk by. Kay looks older anyway, because of how well developed she is, so we've got away with it so far. We feel a bit bad about setting fire to the plastic ivy, especially as Rich's wife Denise has moaned about vandalism in front of us.

Today Rich came out and spotted us and was having a tussle with Gerta when Denise stomped out of the back door, flapping a tea towel around in a temper. She was wearing a sort of turban-style hat on her head.

'Carla's walked out,' she snapped at Rich, who stopped playing with Gerta and looked up.

'In the middle of lunches?' he said. 'What about tonight? We've got eight tables booked in the restaurant!'

'I know that!' Denise sank down next to Kay on the bench and scratched at her turban. 'Little madam said she wanted extra because of her hands. Silly thing thinks she's going to be a model, and all the washing-up is going to affect her chances.'

'Bugger,' said Rich, putting his hand on Denise's leg. 'We'll have to call the agency.'

'Sweetheart, they're useless,' said Denise. 'They sent us Carla, remember?'

'Hmmm,' said Rich.

'What's the hours?' said Kay, stabbing at the ice in her Coke with her straw.

'Lunches, eleven thirty to three. Dinners seven to eleven.

And it's weekends only,' said Denise. 'I just want someone who's not a dolly bird this time.'

Kay looked at me. 'What about you?' she said. 'Then we'd both have jobs?'

Before I could answer, Denise threw a flinty stare at me, assessing how much of a dolly bird I was. 'One pound fifty an hour, sweetheart,' she said, as I had obviously passed the test. 'Extra if we go past eleven p.m. and double on Sunday lunch times.'

'Go on . . . it's only a few hours at the weekends,' said Kay, 'and if you do all three sessions you'll get about fifteen quid.'

'Maybe,' I said, thinking how I wouldn't mind the money but hated washing-up.

'Think about it love,' said Denise. 'I think I can sort something for the next week or so, but we'll definitely need someone after that. Right I'm off for a nap. I'm not firing on all cylinders right now since the chemo.'

'What's the matter with you?' asked Kay, a bit bluntly.

'Breast cancer, sweetheart,' sighed Denise. 'The doctors say I should really take it easy . . .'

Kay gave me a look like Bambi in the forest.

'OK then,' I said. 'Why not.'

'Sorted,' said Rich, winking at Kay. 'We're a nice bunch, aren't we, Denise? We have a bit of a laugh.'

Denise says that her sister-in-law is going to help out for a couple of weeks but I can start washing up at The Smugglers' Tavern in July if I want.

Soon I will have more money to put in my post office savings for emergency running away or books. This makes me much happier than the thought of passing my maths O-level, even though that is very unlikely. Sam has pointed out already that this is not the point and that concentrating at school will increase my future earning power way beyond cleaning out a chip-fryer every Saturday night, but Sam and I are cut from different cloth.

As far as I'm concerned short-term gain is everything, and I am becoming an expert in living from one day to the next.

Saturday 28th June

Kay and I went to Southend today as Kay had planned an early birthday treat, ordering me to get to the bus station at 8.30 a.m. to get a bus to the train. She kept the rest of the day under wraps until I was safely on board. I don't know why, maybe she thought I would be disappointed by elevenses on the seafront, followed by three hours on the Waltzer, Big Wheel and Dodgems on the pier at Southend.

The fact is that I love the funfair and everything that goes with it – candyfloss till you feel like throwing up, being spun and spun by the men with tattoos on the Waltzer, and shooting for goldfish. Much as I've tried, I've never actually won a goldfish, and to be honest if I did it would get eaten within hours by Bob who is a cold-blooded murderer when he puts his mind to it.

Kay bought me an enormous bacon butty and tea in the café we went to by the pier. We were the only people in there, and one of the ladies who ran it kept giving us suspicious looks, probably thinking we were going to do a runner, but Kay ignored this and ordered our food as though she was twenty-five and used to ordering adults about.

'What are you getting for your birthday, then?' asked Kay when we'd finished our butties.

'Dad said a book token and a new transistor radio,' I told her, without enthusiasm. 'And I'm sure I'm only getting the radio because Dad's fed up of me borrowing his all the time.'

'Oh well,' said Kay. 'At least it isn't lavender sachets and coat hangers. That's what Mum got *me* this year. I've given up expecting anything good. I reckon you only get the good stuff when you're a proper kid. My mum prefers to spend Dad's money on herself these days.'

'I don't really care anyway.' I put two teaspoons of sugar in my tea and stirred. 'I used to care so much, Kay, but last year I kind of went off the whole birthday thing, when my dad pawned my silver Christening mug for money.'

'He did what?' said Kay, putting down her tea.

'He never did get the mug back either. Not that he's told me anyway. I've given up.'

'Well,' said Kay. 'He has got five hundred and thirty-three children living in a shoe. He can't get much spare change out of that.' She stared down at her tea and then reached and grabbed my hand. 'Parents should be banned by Child Protection or something,' she said seriously. 'They're a menace to society.'

A couple of bubbles of tea came up through my nose as I laughed.

'Imagine,' I said, 'spending a birthday worrying about parents?'

'Well, we're not going to,' said Kay. 'Definitely not today, anyway.' She wiped her mouth with a napkin and burped. 'Shall we crack on with the funfair, Lydia?'

We paid up, watched hawk-like by the lady who'd served us, and then ran down to the pier. It was a brilliant, sunny day and we had a few hours of holding down our bacon butties in store.

Luck was finally on my side, and though I didn't win a goldfish I did win a huge cuddly bear with HUGS embroidered on its stomach.

'Jesus,' said Kay, goggling at the size of it. 'Where's it going to sleep?'

We'd exhausted all the rides and Kay had given me fifty pence to shoot for the bear; now it was nearly time to get the train back to Reality Town.

'Thanks for everything,' I told Kay. 'I've had a brilliant day.'

'It was only a bacon butty and a stupid funfair,' she said gruffly. 'But you're welcome.'

'It's just nice that someone cares,' I said, a bit pathetically.

'They do care. They're just being selfish right now. You're lucky, you know. Your brothers love the bones of you. I've not met your sister, but she probably does too.' Kay held out the bear in front of her, grimacing.

'You can have that if you want,' I told her. 'Give it to your mum.'

'Cheers, it might buy me a bit more time off from being shouted at.' Kay stroked one of the bear's ears.

I really wanted to tell Kay that her mum and dad loved the bones of her too, but I couldn't be sure. They must, deep down, because Kay is wonderful. But she was right about the selfishness.

'We need something good to happen,' I said. 'To bring back our faith in humankind.'

Kay nodded. 'Actually, Jimmy Jones might be coming to Val's for the summer. I think it's something to do with his dad's girlfriend's morning sickness and it's a bit of a downer for him. Val told Mum that she wishes she could have Jimmy all the time, but it's a bit complicated apparently.'

'I wonder what that means,' I said. 'Is Val's house too small for two people maybe?'

'It's a flat,' said Kay. 'But he has got his own bedroom.'

'Hmmm,' I said. At the same time I was trying not to have a secret fantasy about Jimmy arriving and then somehow falling in love with me. 'I feel sorry for Jimmy,' I added, to throw Kay off the scent of my inner thoughts.

'You two really do have a lot in common,' Kay said, nonetheless tuning into them. 'He's troubled and deep, and he has a sort-of stepmother. And he hates maths!'

'Loads of people hate maths,' I said. 'That doesn't mean anything.'

Kay sighed. 'Well, he was definitely looking at you when we came to *Lady Beatrice*.'

'Do you think so?' I asked, forgetting not to look pleased.

Kay nodded. 'However,' she said, 'my cousin told me that you should never make your first boyfriend one you really like. First you should go out with someone you're not bothered about, so that you can practise kissing them and flirting. Then when you've got really good at it, you can show off your expertise.'

I laughed. 'That's so daft and complicated,' I said. 'I can't help thinking that it's a lot of hard work liking people. However do people find each other in the end?'

'No idea,' said Kay. 'Probably better if you don't think about it all too much.'

Monday 30th June

When I got back to *Lady Beatrice* after school today, Kate had made a Victoria Sandwich and Harry had been to London and bought me a Fiorucci T-shirt with a bit of glitter on it. On the table in the saloon there was a battered package addressed in familiar handwriting: a gift from Elsa – a pair of red ballet slippers. And Jake had put a ribbon round his old racer bike – as he's just got a new one. It had been waiting for me when I came aboard.

'Happy birthday, Lydia,' said Sally. She and Erica presented me with a troll keyring, which was very sweet as they must have investigated to know about the trolls. I stroked its bushy, fluorescent-green hair, before noticing Jake wrinkling his nose at me in amusement.

Sam, who was loitering next to me, gave me a guilty smile. 'I'm saving up for your present,' he said. 'I haven't forgotten.'

'Thanks, everyone,' I said, looking around for Dad, who wasn't there. 'I wasn't expecting anything.'

'Not much you weren't.' Sam rolled his eyes good-naturedly.

'Lasagne for dinner,' said Kate as she bustled past with some cardboard boxes. 'I've got to pop out for an hour, but if one of you wouldn't mind turning on the oven in forty-five minutes . . .'

'Where are you going?' I asked, never one to mind my own business.

For a second, Kate's expression dropped. She looked like

someone who's been caught eating a delicious sherry trifle straight out of the bowl.

'I won't be long,' she said, trying to smile. 'Happy birthday, Lydia.'

Dad didn't come home for lasagne, and by that time a bit of an atmosphere had brewed up again and Kate didn't even mention it, or where he might be. Harry and Sam tried to distract me by making jokes, but by ten o'clock I escaped into my cabin and turned on my new radio, tuning it in to Radio Luxemburg.

I was in bed with both cats snoozing by my feet when an advert came on for the Samaritans, who are there to help you through 'all life's ups and downs, including depression, bereavement and alcoholism in the family'.

Saturday 5th July

Today *Lady Beatrice* set sail for Brightling-on-Sea, which is on the coast near Southend and Clacton. Over the past year, Harry and Sam have been preparing *Lady Beatrice* for seafaring, filling in holes and painting her and getting the sails mended so that she is less likely to sink.

Dad looked at the weather in the week and said the weekend was going to be 'partly sunny with a variable wind' and it was time *Lady Beatrice* properly got her 'bottom wet', which might be a sailing term but filled me with anxiety at the thought of us sinking in the middle of the North Sea and getting all of our bottoms wet and more. Sam, Harry and Dad found my face of horror very funny but they didn't actually say that *wouldn't* happen. I suppose I don't have a choice anyway, seeing as I live on *Lady Beatrice*, and at least I will have all my things around me if we go down at sea.

Kate very quickly said she was taking *her* children to see their grandparents in Wales for the weekend, and although Dad said, 'Oh, that's a shame,' he looked quite relieved and seemed to be in the best mood he's been in for the whole year practically.

'I'll pop to the shops for some supplies,' he said after Kate had driven off yesterday evening, practically rubbing his hands together with glee.

'What about life jackets for the cats?' I said, thinking of Bob and Eugene.

'Nonsense, Lydia,' said Dad. 'Have you never heard of "ship's cats"?'

Bob, who was cleaning his paws by the sofa, looked up then and gave Dad a look of utter contempt.

'Well, can I ask Kay to come?' I said, not wanting to be the only girl on board.

'Yes, of course!' said Dad. 'The more the merrier!'

This was better news. I hoped Kay could get time off from the kiosk.

'Perhaps you girls can be the ship's cooks,' added Dad. 'It will be an adventure.'

I had a feeling that Dad's suggestion might be what's known as sexist in the world, but I did want to do my bit. As I've said before though, cooking is not one of my strong points. I wondered if Kay was any good at shepherd's pie.

Kay had been very keen when I told her about Brightling-on-Sea. She phoned Danny to tell him she was coming down with something and it was best if she didn't come in this weekend and risk infecting the doughnut batter and a whole load of kids besides and get Danny investigated by health and safety inspectors. She went on so long about this that apparently Danny started laughing in the end and told her she needed to work on her skiving technique, but top marks for trying.

'I think Danny likes having me around,' said Kay. 'He keeps telling me I'm wasted on the kiosk and should consider a career as a stand-up comedian.'

Kay said she wasn't brilliant at cooking either, but seeing as we were being put in charge of food she could bring some Mrs Field's Cookie Mix and some cup-a-soups and tins, and maybe steal some of her mum's Chicken Kievs from the freezer.

'She won't notice, probably,' said Kay. 'Mum's been a bit forgetful lately. I'm sure some things in our freezer have been there since before I was born.'

'Thanks, Kay,' I said, feeling a bit queasy.

Kay arrived at 8.00 a.m. in the morning, as the tide was going to be full at 9.00 a.m. and Dad said we'd need to set sail sharpish then. She was very prepared and had brought her wellington boots and blankets and an extra-strength bag from Tesco full of tins and things wrapped in foil.

'Welcome aboard, Kay,' said Dad, saluting her.

'Aye aye, captain,' said Kay, saluting back.

Harry gave me a big grin at this, and then smiled at Kay, who got a bit embarrassed and hurried down below with her Tesco bag.

Once Bob and Eugene had overcome the smell of Gerta on Kay, they took a shine. I've always known cats have good instincts and of course Kay was an extra person to pay them attention. We lined up all the tins on the kitchen counter, and I had a bit of laugh to myself over the thought of Dad eating Alphabetti Spaghetti, and then Kay went to unpack. She put another pair of jeans over the ones she'd already got on then laid out her pyjamas on the bottom bunk of Erica and Sally's cabin. Finally she took a small stuffed bear out and put it on her pillow.

'What?' she said, seeing my face. 'Never go anywhere without Mr Bear.'

'I'm going on the top bunk if you don't mind,' I said. 'So if the worst happens I will go down at sea with you by my side, or at least underneath me.'

'Charming. But that's not likely though, is it?' said Kay, looking a bit alarmed. 'That the boat will sink?'

'Probably not,' I said in a voice of doom. 'But you never know.'

'We'll have the engine on until we're out of the estuary,' said Dad when we were all up on deck, waiting to go. 'Once we're at sea we can use the wind in the sails.' He sighed very contentedly, and looked like his old self again.

Dad has been sailing his whole life – it's one of his passions, like cars used to be – and he's told us about his adventures as a boy, sailing with his school friends. 'In many ways, the happiest times of my life,' he would say, a faraway smile on his face.

It was nice to see Dad looking happy again. I'd almost forgotten that he used to be quite a contented person. I wondered whether it was just the thought of the trip or also the fact that Kate wasn't here to remind him of life's failings.

As we cast off from land, and Harry and Sam had to put their feet against the quay wall to push *Lady Beatrice* off, Dad stood in the wheelhouse to turn the boat around. The sky had been covered in clouds first thing this morning, but as *Lady Beatrice* finally pointed her nose in the right direction, a beam of sunlight shot through, nearly blinding Kay and me, as we'd been watching the sky like hawks in case it rained and we needed emergency hair cover.

'Blimey, they all look like they know what they're doing,' said Kay, who was watching the boys running around tying ropes up. 'They're like professional sailors.'

'Suppose,' I said. I passed her a bit of cold toast and peanut butter as I'd made a huge pile on the grill, just before the electricity was disconnected. 'I think I've just taken it all for granted. My dad is in his element when he's at sea. Harry and Sam too.'

'That's nice,' she said, smiling. 'It's so romantic, Lydia.'

'You wait till it starts raining and getting stormy,' I said, ruining the moment. 'Then it'll be more like the sinking of the *Titanic*.' I bit off a huge chunk of toast, while Kay rolled her eyes and started on hers.

Soon we were chugging out of the estuary, past all the muddy marshes. People walking along the sea wall and the prom were waving at us as though we were famous.

'I love this,' said Kay, waving back. 'I feel really important.' She stood up and did a little bow at a couple who were watching us through binoculars.

'Kay,' I said, laughing, 'you look like you're out on day release from an asylum.' I must admit though, I did feel a bit like a member of the Royal Family on one of their parades outside Buckingham Palace. But I knew all these people waving were going back to their nice cosy dry houses, where the telly works all the time and baths are hot, and none of them would want to actually live on a place like

Lady Beatrice. Not all the time. For a second, I ached for my old bedroom, but I pushed it away.

'We can start lunch soon,' I said, having a surge of productivity.

Kay brushed toast crumbs off her jumper and then gave me a sidelong look.

'It's not even nine fifteen in the morning, Lyds,' she said. 'We don't need to start heating up the tomato soup for at least three hours.'

By midday we were sailing in the North Sea, gliding past the big power station. In front of us there was nothing but the greenish-blue sea. No buildings, not even any marshes, just like we were heading to the edge of the world. It was breezy enough to move us along and the smell of the salt from the sea tingled in my nose. I tried not to think about what my hair looked like, as salty air is like dunking your hair in a bucket of melted sugar and then leaving it to dry.

Dad had brought the radio up and turned on Radio 4, and Kay and I lay back on the deck, staring up at the huge brown sail, flapping a bit in the breeze, listening to Sam and Harry shouting instructions to each other. For the first time ever I could see why Dad loved it all so much. There was something about just air and sky and sea that made your worries seem small and unimportant, and *Lady Beatrice* felt like she was rocking us, like babies in a cradle.

'I'm not even missing Gerta yet,' said Kay as we drifted off to sleep.

I had a fleeting picture of Jimmy in my head, and I felt a kind of pleasant dreamy feeling and then everything faded.

'Lydia!' Kay was saying to me next thing I knew, and I opened my eyes. 'It's nearly two p.m. and time to feed the crew.'

I sat up feeling rather disorientated. I'd had a lovely dream, though as usual I couldn't remember a thing about it.

'Dreaming about someone, were you?' said Kay slyly.

'Me? No,' I said, trying to sound off-hand.

Kay and I got down into the galley and put together an assortment of food. Three mugs of chicken cup-a-soup, some bowls of Heinz tomato soup and half a large cold steak pie that was left over from Kay's dinner last night. We would have heated it up, but I wasn't sure about the oven running on the generator as it probably takes hours – seeing as the kettle took at least fifteen minutes to boil, and heating the pan of tomato soup.

Sam peered warily into his cup-a-soup when we brought everything up outside. 'What are those things floating in it?' he said. 'Like bits of twigs.'

I drank some of mine and crunched down on what felt like dirt.

'Kay,' I whispered, as Sam held his nose and downed his soup in one. 'I don't think the water boiled properly and none of the gunk has melted.'

Kay's shoulders shook a bit at the word 'gunk' and we both watched Sam's face as he tried not to taste what he was eating.

'I've never tried nuclear debris before, Kay,' he said. 'Thank you for introducing me to it.' He then took a bit of cold pie and stuffed it in to smother the taste.

'Pleasure, Professor Yaffle,' Kay said, and then we couldn't hold in our laughter any longer and my soup dribbled all down my jumper. Sam *was* exactly like Professor Yaffle from *Bagpuss* sometimes. How had I not seen it before?

'Hilarious,' said Sam, but I could see he was trying not to laugh too. 'Pie's not bad though, I must admit.'

'Delicious meal, girls,' Dad said enthusiastically, coming towards us and dumping his empty bowl of Heinz tomato soup on deck. 'I'm looking forward to seeing what you've planned for dinner tonight.'

Kay and I looked at each other, as of course we hadn't thought that far ahead.

Dad adjusted his glasses, watching us. 'Though as an alternative we could anchor offshore and take the ship's dinghy in to Brightling-on-Sea,' he said. 'Get some fish and chips.'

'Oh yes!' said Kay and I together. 'Brilliant!'

'Thought you might like that idea,' said Dad, winking at Sam.

'I love your dad, Lydia,' said Kay when Dad wandered off again. 'What a gentleman.'

By 6.00 p.m., Kay and I were under blankets on the sofa in the saloon. The clouds had returned in the afternoon and the wind had properly picked up. Right out in the middle of the sea, *Lady Beatrice* was rocking a bit precariously from side to side, and Dad had instructed the boys to take down the sails so that we would continue on with just the engine until everything calmed down. We'd all looked up at the sky and watched as it turned from pale grey to charcoal, and then big blobs of rain came down.

'Why don't you two go downstairs,' said Dad, noticing Kay's colouring had turned a bit green. 'I expect those cats need keeping an eye on.'

Eugene and Bob were perched on the keelson, which is the long metal bar that runs through the middle of the barge, like an upside-down rudder. They had that wild-eyed look of fight or flight that cats have in times of peril, when survival is at the forefront of their minds. Eugene's little body was trembling and Kay picked him up and settled him in her lap. Bob, who should have been setting an example, glared at Kay and then started retching. He produced a mixture of hairball and sick.

'Did you see that film *The Poseidon Adventure*?' asked Kay, wrinkling her nose at Bob. 'About all those people trapped in the bottom of a cruise ship?'

'Kay,' I said, having fetched some toilet roll to clean up Bob's sick. 'I was only joking about the *Titanic*. It's just a bit of heavy weather, that's all.'

'I suppose at least we've got that little boat to escape in,' she said. 'If push comes to shove.'

At this point *Lady Beatrice* lurched violently to one side and we heard a gigantic crash coming from the galley, and from up above came the sound of Harry, Sam and Dad all shouting at once.

A lot of the china crockery that we use for special occasions had fallen out of the cupboards and was lying smashed on the floor of the galley. Kay and I just stared at it.

'I'm sure the storm will pass soon,' I said anxiously. 'And before we know it, we'll be enjoying our fish and chips on dry land.'

Kay groaned. 'Not sure I fancy it now,' she said. 'I'm still tasting cup-a-soup and pie.'

Dad appeared in the saloon doorway. 'You girls should put on your life jackets,' he said. 'Just as a precaution . . .'

'Or . . . we could get off now, Dad?' I suggested. 'And not wait for the worst to happen?'

'I can't swim,' murmured Kay. 'Not properly anyway.'

Dad laughed. 'Oh, I've been in much worse than this!' he said. 'This is absolutely nothing to worry about.' He went over to the cabinet at the far end of the saloon and got out a bottle of whisky.

Kay and I watched as he poured some into a plastic tumbler and took a large glug.

'It'll all be over soon,' said Dad. 'We're only a mile or so from Brightling-on-Sea, and then we can all pile into the dinghy and go ashore.' He took another glug and then added a bit more whisky before putting the bottle back in the cupboard.

'And if that doesn't work out, there's loads more tins,' said Kay, trying to sound positive. Dad gave her another little salute and then disappeared back upstairs with his tumbler.

I was worried about meeting Kay's eye. It was suddenly really important to me that she didn't think badly of Dad.

But there were no signs of disapproval on her face when I looked, just a quite matter-of-fact expression.

'Your dad's still a proper gentleman,' she said, stroking Eugene's ears. 'Anyone can see that.'

I relaxed a bit and smiled at her, just as Bob extended a paw onto my lap and tried to rub his face against mine, which was comforting for a second, before I remembered he'd only recently been sick.

Kay and I have agreed that this weekend will be something we will remember for years to come, and that even if we realise one day that our lives have been mostly uneventful and dull, at least we can tell our grandchildren about the night that Kay became one of the world's most heroic rowers.

At about 7.00 p.m., as Dad had predicted, the clouds got paler and the rain stopped and the sea changed from stormy to just choppy. Dad seized the opportunity to rally us all to get our life jackets on, ready to motor ashore as Sam and Harry dropped anchor on the barge. I'd seen him peering at the rest of Kay's tins in the galley, and am sure that this had something to do with his decisiveness and sense of urgency.

We all got into the dinghy, leaving the cats behind. I glanced back and saw Eugene at the top of the hatch: ears erect and eyes gleaming in terror. I was leaving him alone with his nemesis Bob. I could only hope that Bob was feeling too ill to take advantage of the situation.

'Cat stew for lunch tomorrow,' said Sam, quite evilly, and I thumped him on the back.

Everything seemed fine at first. Harry pulled the cord on the outboard motor and we buzzed forward, heading for the lights of Brightling-on-Sea.

But about halfway there the motor started making sputtering sounds, and I saw Harry and Sam exchange a look. Dad, who had put a bit more whisky in a little metal flask, was sipping at it, oblivious.

'What does that sound mean?' said Kay suspiciously, hugging her knees as the sputtering carried on and the dinghy stopped moving quite so fast. Then the engine cut out altogether.

Harry pulled the cord again, but this just made more sputtering which stopped almost immediately, so there was silence. He tried again, but nothing happened.

'Uh-oh,' said Kay, trying to sound buoyant but shivering a bit.

I patted her knee. 'Just a bit of engine trouble,' I said. 'Harry will fix it, won't you, Harry?'

Harry frowned and looked over at Dad, who was still quite calmly taking sips from his flask, seemingly not bothered at all.

'Did anyone top up the fuel in this before we left?' Harry asked him.

Dad thought. 'I'm afraid not,' he said. 'I hoped there would be enough for a couple of short trips.'

Sam and Harry took very deep breaths and Harry gave the cord one last pull. He pulled so hard that his arm shot back and whacked against the side of the dinghy. 'Damn!' he said, wincing in pain and clutching at his wrist.

'Oh, Harry!' said me and Kay together.

'Lydia.' Harry looked at me and nodded at Dad who was looking less and less alert. 'Can you go and sit with him.'

'Do I have to?' I said, not wanting to move away from Kay. 'Can't Sam do it?'

'Go on.' Harry smiled at me. 'Sam needs to row.'

This meant Sam would be sitting next to Kay, which I didn't want, but obviously saying that would make me appear difficult and cast me in an unfavourable light.

'OK then.' I tried not to look long-suffering and moved, wobbling about all over the place, to sit next to my father, who barely noticed. I thought how easy it would be just to push him overboard.

Of course Sam immediately shot over to sit in my place and I glared at the tuft of hair that always sticks up on the back of his stupid head.

'You take one oar and I'll take the other,' he instructed Kay, just as the heavens opened wider and we were all pelted with torrential rain.

It's amazing how quickly somebody gets the hang of something in emergencies, and I must admit I was quite impressed with Kay's beginner's technique. When Sam grabbed hold of his oar, she got hold of hers, and the two of them rowed so hard that Dad nearly did topple overboard and I had to hold onto his jumper to keep him steady.

'Go on, Kay!' said Sam, laughing a bit breathlessly. 'Quite impressive, for a girl.'

'Bog off,' shouted Kay, which only made Sam laugh more.

By this time the wind had picked up again, and everyone's hair was soaked and mine kept sticking in my eyes, but I could see we were getting closer and closer to land. And then finally we felt the bump as we ran aground, and Sam and Kay let out a cheer of camaraderie and even Dad raised his little flask in their direction.

'Oh, well done, you two!' he said. 'You've saved the day!'

I fought off the urge to kick Sam in the back.

'I quite enjoyed that.' My brother was looking around at everyone like we should give him a medal.

'I didn't,' I muttered.

Harry heard, and gave me a look and a wink. 'Your turn next time,' he said. 'You need your arm strength for all the writing you do in that diary.'

'You write a diary?' said Kay as Harry tied the boat up. 'Blimey, am I in it?'

'A bit,' I said nonchalantly.

'She probably just writes about the cats,' said Sam annoyingly. 'Or her hair.'

You'll see, I thought.

The rest of us clambered off, and then Kay and I sat slumped on the little jetty that led to the quayside.

'Jesus and all the saints,' said Kay, breathing hard in and out. 'I never want to do that again as long as I live. I think my arm's going to fall off.'

We got our fish and chips, and everyone agreed that we had never tasted anything so good in all our lives and I felt a bit better about being left out earlier, because now that it was over it did seem quite exciting and triumphant. The five of us all sat sheltering in a little hut opposite the dinghy, wolfing our food down, and I wondered if this was actually part of the point of being alive. Tremendous struggle followed by tremendous gratitude for little things, like a fish supper.

And then something really weird happened, that I've been thinking about afterwards and that maybe I imagined.

Sam was laughing with Kay about something. And when I turned to join in, I'm sure his face was much too close to hers, but in a second it wasn't and Sam was staring over at a row of beach huts.

I looked at Sam and then I looked at Kay, but Kay was pointing at the top of the hut, which was nearly being blown off because of the wind, and still laughing.

I turned round again and looked at the sea and thought maybe I was going a bit mad.

Harry went off to get a can of fuel for the outboard and at 9.00 p.m. we motored back to *Lady Beatrice*, full and exhausted.

Kay and I went straight to our bunks and I couldn't sleep for ages because I had a tight feeling in my stomach again, and neither of us woke up until noon on Sunday. Meanwhile, Dad, Harry and Sam had got up at 5.00 a.m. – to get us all back in time for Kay's Sunday roast with her mum and dad, as Kay had mentioned her mum's roasts in a loud voice of longing several times while we'd been queuing up for our fish and chips last night.

'I'll totally understand if you never want to see me or any

member of my family again,' I told her, when we'd finally got up and dressed, and Kay was ready to disembark.

Kay laughed, and I saw that her face looked all rosy and her eyes were sparkling a bit.

'Don't be daft, Lydia,' she said happily. 'I've had an absolutely brilliant time!'

Sunday 13th July

Yesterday I did my first evening shift at The Smugglers' Tavern. I had to stand for four hours with not even one sit-down and I didn't finish till 11.30 p.m., as a big wedding anniversary party of fifteen were having all three courses, and then liqueurs, and I had to wait for all the pudding plates and glasses to be done with.

Denise is very bossy, and overly fussy about rinsing plates and seems to have X-ray vision about it, judging by how much she ordered me to wash crockery again. By the end of it all, I never wanted to see another plate or cup ever again and I've gone right off prawn cocktails, as Denise just gets bags of frozen prawns and leaves them next to the baking oven to defrost, which I'm sure is not right, and the cocktail sauce isn't mysterious at all it turns out – it's just ketchup and salad cream mixed together.

But the oddest thing is Denise's 'Sorbet Surprise', which is hollowed out oranges that I had to rush to get out of the big freezer and then Denise put scoops of sorbet in them. When the Sorbet Surprise shells came back from the restaurant, She made me wash them up and cut off any unattractive bits and then put them back in the freezer for next time! I didn't say anything because of Denise's chemo and her not being well, but I honestly can't think of anything more horrible than eating her Sorbet Surprise. Something tells me that Denise and Rich wouldn't want me to tell anyone else about it either. Especially not anyone who comes to dine at The Smugglers' Tavern.

I am envious of Kay as all she does at Danny's Donuts is mix up batter and press buttons for the Slush Puppie machine, then chuck paper plates and plastic cups into the bin. On the bright side, Denise gave me a little envelope with eight pounds fifty in it. She said she'd put a bit extra in as it had been unusually hectic tonight. I must remember not to spend it all in Woolworths and put it in my post office account instead as there is still a distinct possibility that I will need running away money at some point.

But I forgot all about my wages when I got home, as back at *Lady Beatrice* Jake had friends round. Dad and Kate aren't here as Dad's old friend Bill in London is ill with Parkinson's disease and they are visiting and helping out Bill's wife Zelda. Sally and Erica have gone along too, and Jake has taken full advantage of this.

I was curious about Jake's friends, as I've only ever seen them at a distance at school and they always seem a bit gormless. The only one that sticks out is a boy called Dean Carter, and Kay and I have discussed how Dean is quite magnetic in a way that we can't really explain.

Jake says Dean is a 'nouveau punk' because he has black spiky hair, and over his school uniform he wears a leather jacket with SHAM 69 in white writing on the back. He always has on big black Doctor Marten boots and – Kay swears – he wears eyeliner, even though not even the girls are allowed to do that at school. Dean once sort of looked at us in the canteen and Kay and I wondered if this might be significant in some way.

I hovered for a bit outside the saloon door, inhaling the

smell of chips on myself and craning to hear if Dean's voice could be heard above the music, but it was all just a blur of voices. Then I rushed into my cabin and lavishly applied Mum deodorant and searched in my drawer for something to wear that didn't smell like the deep-fryer. I pulled out a frilly white shirt that I'd got from the Oxfam shop for the school disco at the end of last term, which was a 'Come as a Pirate' theme.

Inside the saloon, Jake and his other friend Pete were having an argument about who got spat on the most at a recent gig. Unbelievably, the winner *is actually* the one who got spat on the most. Pete has long black hair and never seems to take off his charity shop overcoat, even at school. Dean was sketching something on the back of one of my school exercise books. It was the perfect moment to engage him in conversation.

I just stood there in my frilly shirt.

Luckily Dean looked up and gave me his wolf smile. He also raised a hand in greeting. No words.

'Lydia,' Jake said. 'I thought you were in bed!'

'I've just got back from my job at The Smugglers' Tavern,' I said importantly, a little annoyed that in front of Dean he was making me out to be a child who goes to bed early on a Saturday night.

'That pub up the road?' asked Dean out of the blue. 'I'm barred from there.'

Jake snorted. 'You weren't barred, Dean, you were thrown out for being underage.'

Dean shrugged. 'Same thing.'

'Where's Sam and Harry?' I said, as there were no signs of them and it was nearly midnight.

'Harry's having a thing with the girl who works behind the bar at the Admiral,' said Jake. 'He's probably with her somewhere. And Sam's gone out with Ben on *Philomena*. They're going up to Suffolk. They're probably there by now.'

'Oh.' I felt slightly put out that Jake knew more about my brothers' whereabouts than I did. And particularly about Harry and a barmaid. I suppose boys tell each other these things and I'd never have known if Jake hadn't said. I don't like to think about either Harry or Sam having lives that don't involve me in some way.

Dean had a fag on and was blowing smoke rings. I watched him, which Pete must have noticed because he took a pack of Benson & Hedges out of his jeans' pocket and offered me one.

'Fancy a cigarette?'

'Of course she doesn't,' said Jake, before I could reply. Then he moved a bottle of wine on the table so that it was out of my reach.

I rolled my eyes. 'I've tried alcohol before, you know, Jake.'

I've also had a fag, with Donna – in the alleyway by the Woolpack Pub in Cottlesham a year or so ago. She'd nicked a packet of John Players cigarettes from her cousin and was determined we should experiment. I'd not inhaled, though I'd pretended to, and the whole experience had been a non-event that made me cough.

Jake frowned at me, and I couldn't understand why he was so annoyed.

Then Pete said to Jake, 'There's a party next Friday at Arnold Terry's house over the bridge in Hatton. You're coming to that, aren't you?'

'Probably,' said Jake, a bit stiffly for him. 'I'll have to check with Dawn.'

Pete looked contemptuous, then swivelled in Dean's direction. 'You're both coming then, yeah?'

Dean blew out a perfect smoke ring before replying. 'Reckon so.' He looked over at me. 'What about you?'

I was stunned. Dean had practically just invited me to a party!

'Um . . . yes, OK,' I said. 'I think I'm free actually.'

'No way José,' said Jake quickly. 'She can't come.'

I didn't know why Jake was being so stuffy about it.

'Can I bring my friend Kay?' I asked Pete, ignoring Jake.

'Don't ask me,' said Pete. 'We haven't been officially invited either. Bring who you like.'

'She's only fourteen,' Jake went on. 'I'm not spending the whole evening babysitting fourteen-year-olds.'

'No one says you have to,' I snapped.

Pete and Dean laughed and Jake looked even more annoyed.

'Fine,' he said. He looked like he was going to say something else, but he didn't. He went over to the record player and started shuffling records about.

Pete and Dean exchanged a glance and then Dean took another drag of his fag and smiled at me. 'I like your shirt,' he said. 'Cool.'

'Thanks,' I said, grateful of the dim light.

At this point I felt desperate to go to bed and start fantasising, and also so as not to risk saying or doing anything that might make Dean regret his invitation. 'Well,' I said. 'I'm tired. It's been such a long night.' I yawned, careful not open my mouth fully and appear ungainly in front of Dean.

'Night, Lydia,' said Dean, flashing me his wolf smile again.

I fled from the saloon before Jake could say anything more about the party, and was soon in my bunk, wedging the duvet against the damp bit and putting my earplugs in.

I've been awake for hours in bed with both the cats sound asleep by my feet. Why did Dean say he liked my shirt? Does it mean he has taken a fancy to me? Why is Jake trying to spoil it? I thought Jake liked fun and parties. I thought we were the same. He's only a year older than me, and as Kay says girls are always more mature than boys then that makes me and Jake the same age when you think about it. Thoughts are whirring in my head, but most importantly, me and Kay are going to an actual party and now we will be normal.

I can't wait to tell Kay all about it.

Wednesday 16th July

It's the last week of school, and on Monday it was very satisfying telling Kay about Saturday night, and that we had both been invited to Arnold's party on Friday.

'Well, Arnold hasn't actually invited us,' I confessed. 'But Jake's friend Pete was quite encouraging.'

'So we're gate-crashers,' Kay said, peeling a banana by her locker. 'In a way that's more glamorous than being invited.'

'I agree,' I said eagerly. 'And also, Dean said he thought my frilly shirt was cool. He was very talkative. What do you think that means?'

'Had he been drinking?' said Kay.

'I think so,' I said.

'Hmm,' said Kay.

'Maybe Pete will like you,' I said, trying to be helpful.

Kay's nostrils flared. 'I don't care if he does or he doesn't,' she said. 'Why are you boy-mad all of a sudden? And what about Jimmy?'

'But Jimmy's not here, is he?' I said.

'That's true,' she said, breaking her banana in two and giving me half.

'What kind of outfit do you wear to a party like Arnold's?' I asked.

Kay was chomping on her banana and shrugged.

'I've only got the frilly shirt really,' I said. 'And Dean's already seen that.'

'I'm not dressing up,' said Kay, 'even if I had anything to

dress up in. We don't want to look too keen. I mean, look at that Dawn thingy Jake goes out with. She's all done up like a dog's breakfast every day, looks well uncomfortable.'

'She really does,' I said. I thought of Addie Loggins and her boys' clothes, and smiled. And then I thought about Jake again and felt disgruntled.

Kay had stopped eating and had a thoughtful look on her face. 'I bet they're going to be smoking marijuana and there'll be loads of booze at Arnold's,' she said. 'I'm going to have to make up a lie for my mum. She hates the thought of me enjoying myself at the best of times, and my dad won't be too pleased probably.' Kay paused. 'Have you told your dad . . . or Harry, or Sam or anything?'

'Dad won't mind,' I said. 'Or Harry. Sam wouldn't understand because he's not normal.'

'He's all right,' said Kay. 'You're quite horrible about Sam sometimes.'

I chewed on my lip, determined not to fall out with Kay but irritated that she was sticking up for Sam.

'Helping you with your maths and stuff, that's all,' Kay went on. 'I mean, that's quite kind when you think about it.'

'Yes, you mentioned that before, Kay,' was all I could get out. It was hard to argue with her on that.

She gave me a funny look. 'At least you've got Jake there to look out for you anyway. Just in case,' she said.

I didn't tell Kay how sour Jake had been about the whole thing. Arnold's party was beginning to look like a bad idea now. I'd have to focus on the Dean part of it to make it all right.

Friday 18th July

It was very convenient that Kate roped Dad into visiting her parents with her in Wales again this weekend. Kay came over to *Lady Beatrice* before Arnold's, to get ready in my cabin, and I said we could share the bring-your-own-bottle. Obviously we weren't buying alcohol, but Harry keeps a supply of booze in the drawer under his bunk, which I discovered when I was investigating one day. Also, Kay and I had a light meal of frozen mini-pizzas on toast, which is our amazing new recipe. If Kate had been here she would never have allowed it, especially as we ate the last of her emergency mini-pizzas in the freezer compartment. I must remember to replace them.

'What's going on,' said Sam, who appeared in the saloon just as we were polishing off our snack. Sam is helping Ben from *Philomena* with more maintenance work after school, and was wearing overalls and had flecks of white paint in his hair.

'Nothing,' I said.

'We're going to a party, Sam,' Kay said.

'What party? Who?' Sam stepped out of his overalls to reveal his scrappy old T-shirt and falling-apart jeans.

Nobody,' I trilled, trying to eye-signal to Kay to shut up about it.

'It's just somebody at school,' she went on regardless. 'It'll be mostly people's parents and Musical Chairs probably. Nothing special.'

'Oh.' Sam looked relieved. 'That's why you're not dressed up then.'

Both Kay and me were casual. This meant we were wearing our best sweatshirts and our best bottom halves, which were jeans.

'Well, that's nice,' Kay said to Sam. 'After all the effort I've gone to.'

He grinned and then snatched up a forgotten piece of pizza on my plate. 'Enjoy yourselves,' he said, then thankfully went off to the bathroom to clean the paint out of his hair.

Kay and I arrived at Arnold's at 8.00 p.m. – half an hour late so as not to appear too keen – and rang the bell. The front door was opened by Rat, who was dressed all in black clothes. Her hair was almost the size of her whole body as she'd gelled it into three big spikes going off at different angles, which must have taken all day. Rat had very white make-up on and red lipstick and her eyes were just large black blobs – you could hardly see them for all the eyeliner and mascara. She looked like a raccoon.

Rat held the door open. 'All right, Lydia, all right, Kay,' she said, squinting at our clothes, as though all the make-up had affected her eyesight.

'I'm in agony,' Kay whispered beside me. She had borrowed her mum's court shoes without asking, and had moaned most of the way to the party that her feet were killing her, and in the end she took them off on the doorstep.

'Nice outfits,' said Rat, and it was hard to see through all the make-up if this was meant as a sarcastic joke.

'Hello, Rat,' I said. 'Are we really late?'

Rat laughed, which made her look like The Joker out of Batman, only miniature.

'There's about ten people here,' she said. 'I'm only here cause Arn's my stepdad's nephew.'

'Where is Arnold?' I asked, a bit worried he might throw us out before we'd got in.

'Upstairs with his horrible friends, I think,' said Rat. She patted one of her spikes.

'Oh,' I said, trying not to sound too relieved. I held out a bottle of sparkling wine I'd nicked from Harry's cabin. 'Shall I put this in the fridge?'

Rat shrugged. 'Can do,' she said.

Rat led us through to the kitchen, past the living room where a ghettoblaster on top of the telly was playing loud and distorted punk, or heavy metal – I couldn't tell. Either way it was a racket.

'Oh, by the way,' Kay whispered to me, 'Jimmy's arrived back at Val's now for the summer. Mum said to Val that we were going to a "nice" party tonight and Jimmy should come if he wants.' She gave me a look. 'I didn't say earlier because I thought it might send you into a tailspin.'

'Jimmy?' said Rat, forgetting to be nonchalant for a second. 'Who's Jimmy?'

'Just a friend of ours,' said Kay. 'A boy.'

'Yeah, I gathered,' said Rat, and rolled her eyes.

'Anyway,' Kay went on, 'he might turn up in a bit, though I deliberately told Mum the party was going to be boring so she didn't go off on one about it.'

'I don't mind,' I managed to say, even though this was an

utter lie and my plans had been thrown into disarray. I half hoped Jimmy would come and I half hoped he wouldn't.

In the kitchen there were four people, and two of them were adults – Arnold's mum and dad probably. One of them, the woman wearing an evening dress who looked a bit out of place, was standing with her arms crossed, scrutinising the other two people in the room – two girls who were dressed similarly to Rat, only they were taller.

'My cousins,' said Rat. 'Kelly and Maria.'

The girls looked over at us. 'You mates of Arnold's?' asked one.

'Kind of,' I said.

'In a way,' Kay added.

They exchanged a doubtful look. 'Have you let God squads in again, Rat?' the other one said.

'Don't worry about Maria,' said Rat, smirking. 'She's just jealous.'

Kelly and Maria tittered, and I was left wondering whether or not Kay and I had just been insulted. I couldn't wait for the party to fill up, then we could lose Rat and I could try and compose myself for seeing Dean.

I found the fridge and put the sparkling wine in.

'At last some respectable girls have turned up,' said the woman with the evening dress on as I turned round from the fridge. She looked a bit merry. I smiled at her, though 'respectable' didn't sound much like a compliment. I had obviously made a big mistake with my outfit and did look like a God squad.

'Do we look really square, Kay?' I said.

225

'No. Those girls look like they're off out for Halloween.' Kay helped herself from a bottle of lemonade on the counter.

There was a glass bowl of something that looked like a kind of strawberry squash with bits of lemon and orange in it and a huge ladle. Kelly and Maria were helping themselves and I nudged Kay.

'I'm having some of that,' I said. 'I love fruit squash.'

'Hmm.' Kay had a doubtful look on her face.

I ladled some into a paper cup, and caught Maria smirking at me for some reason. It was sweet with a sort of tang to it, sort of tropical and syrupy and rich and it was absolutely delicious. I finished my cup just as the doorbell rang, and then I had a sudden surge of confidence. Despite Kay being reassuring about our outfits, I couldn't help thinking that I could look slightly less boring.

Kay had disappeared, to nose around Arnold's house probably, and the music suddenly got a lot louder.

I spotted some scissors on the table. I ladled myself another cup of squash, then I put the scissors in my back pocket and went to find the toilet. I didn't feel quite myself; I felt like I used to when I was overcome with Christmas fever and wanted to open all the presents under the tree. I felt a bit giddy.

In the toilets I took off my sweatshirt and faced the mirror with my old black T-shirt on. I snipped a big gash around the neckline and dragged it down with my fingers, then cut another hole just below my boobs, so that you could see a bit of my skin, but not too much, then I took it off and got rid of the arms completely. When I put it back on I knew I'd done the right thing. My head was swimming a little bit and my cheeks were very flushed, but I was satisfied that I no longer looked 'respectable'. I sat on the toilet seat and drank the whole of the second cup of whatever it was, and then my head really rushed. I had to lean back for a minute.

Outside, the doorbell had rung a few times and more people had arrived. Someone was also trying the handle of the toilet door so I got to my feet and tied my sweatshirt round my waist. Suddenly I felt very woozy, as though I had got up too quickly, everything was slightly hazy. I checked myself again in the mirror and felt a kind of euphoria. I was sure that this evening something really important would happen.

Kay was standing right by the toilets when I came out, and Jimmy Jones was next to her with a can of ginger beer in his hand. Jimmy looked really nice I couldn't help noticing. He had on a black button-down T-shirt with small collars, and smart trousers that shimmered blue and green at the same time, and suede shoes, like Teddy Boy shoes. Jimmy's hair was super-short, and I felt an urge to run the palm of my hand over it, like it was grass that'd just been cut.

'Hello, Jimmy,' I said. 'You look really nice in your clothes.'

'Hello, Lydia,' Jimmy said, smiling, and his face looked so clean and scrubbed and safe. He then looked at my T-shirt with all the snips in it and said a bit uncertainly, 'So do you.'

Kay on the other hand, looked quite aghast. 'You've ruined

that T-shirt,' she said, gawping at it. 'You didn't have any more of that squash, did you?' she asked. 'Because I think it's—'

'Do stop fussing, Kay,' I interrupted her, irritated that she was acting like a teacher all of a sudden. Normally Kay's concern is appreciated, but I felt full of optimism and as though I might actually not be unattractive. Why do people pretend to be looking after your best interests, I thought, when what they really want to do is spoil things for you?

Kay frowned. 'All right, keep your wig on,' she said. 'You're being quite loud.'

'No I'm not,' I shouted, and pushed past them to the living room before my confidence disappeared.

I saw Dean straightaway. He was with Pete on the sofa, smoking. Dean had his leather jacket on and his drainpipe jeans, and his hair looked even blacker than normal. I noticed he was wearing stripy socks though, which was quite reassuring.

As I'd finished my drink and needed something to do I picked up a can of beer and opened it. Unlike the lovely tropical drink, the beer tasted vile. Like washing-up water, which I've not actually tasted, but who knows, I may be reduced to it in the near future.

I took another gulp of beer and pretended to be interested in the wallpaper, which in a way I was, as it was a nice bird pattern and I still miss my swallows wallpaper.

A boy I didn't know walked past me, looked me up and down and winked at me, and I felt a nervous flutter, a feeling of strange new excitement. I leaned back against the wall and then slowly turned to look at Dean and Pete. Dean was leaning forward taking a glug of beer, his fag smoking away in his fingers, but then he looked up and saw me.

And he frowned.

And then he did a little wave at me.

'Blimey, it's Lydia,' called Pete, who had spotted me too. He blew out a plume of smoke. 'I was wondering who the mysterious blonde in the corner was.'

Thank God it was dark and my cheeks had hopefully only gone a couple of shades darker pink. Also, I heard his words like he was talking through a brick wall.

Rat wandered past me carrying a big bottle and swigging out of it. She belched and closed her eyes, swaying. When she opened her eyes again she saw me and took in my changed appearance.

'Have you been attacked?' she asked, peering at my customised T-shirt.

'Just taken my sweatshirt off,' I said casually.

'I'm going over the road,' said Rat. 'To my nan's.'

'OK then.' I wondered if the party was really rubbish and I didn't realise.

At this point a huge boy-version of Rat walked into the living room and Rat's face lit up. She stood on tiptoe and started snogging him, which looked really odd since she was at least half his size if not shorter.

It seemed like she wasn't going over to her nan's after all, but now I had no one to talk to and I couldn't see Jimmy or Kay. I picked up another beer and drank some more. Once you've had quite a few swigs of beer, you get used to the smell of drains and the taste isn't so bad.

I took my beer and tried to saunter over to Dean and Pete, but a crate of beer sticking out from under the coffee table meant I tripped instead and fell onto them, my eyes ending up level with the bottom of Dean's T-shirt.

Dean stubbed out his fag and used both hands to lift me upright. 'Steady,' he said.

I lifted my head up and stared straight at his mouth and his eyes and his neck. And then Dean's face turned into Jimmy's for a second, before becoming Dean's again. I was very close to him and could see he had one of his ears pierced and another earring in his eyebrow, and he seemed a bit frightening this close up.

'Have you had a bit to drink?' Dean said, and he smiled a nice wolf smile and I rested my head on his chest and rubbed my face against it, like Bob does to me sometimes.

And then suddenly I felt an iron-like grip around my waist and I was wrenched away from Dean, and Jake's face was looming at mine.

'What on earth are you doing?' he said, quite pale with a little pulse hammering away in his cheek.

'She's all right,' said Dean.

'Shut up,' said Jake, glaring at him.

'I'm *all right*,' I said, shoving Jake off me. But then I tasted something horrible at the back of my throat, like tropical sick. It didn't come up, but it was bitter and, to be honest, I did feel quite ill.

'Calm down, Jake,' said Dean. 'She's only a kid.'

'Yeah, that's the point,' said Jake. He glared at me. 'She shouldn't be here.'

'Mind your own business,' I said. 'You're not my dad!'

'Thank God,' said Jake. 'Because he's a proper drunk.'

And then the whole room went quiet, and all I could see were faces, just gawping at me, and my euphoria and confidence disappeared.

'Well, *your* dad must have hated you,' I heard myself say. 'That's why he left and never came back. He doesn't care!'

I stopped then, because Jake's face had gone bigger and angrier – like The Incredible Hulk's when he's halfway through transitioning into a monster.

'Not like Charlie then?' he said sarcastically. 'He doesn't care much about you, either. You must realise that. Or are you more stupid than I thought?'

He shut his eyes as soon as he'd said it. But all the bravado fizzled out of me and I had to swallow down some tropical sick again. I felt tears pricking at my eyes, because of what I'd said to Jake about his dad, but also as Jake had just told me things I feared might really be true about mine.

And I *am* stupid, I thought. I am full of fog. Not even Elsa likes me really. She just has to put up with me because I'm her flesh and blood. Why would she like me? I'm so dim.

While all this was going around in my head, I saw that Jake's shirt, which had been very white and clean, was now covered with squash and bits of soggy lemon peel and some mini-pizza from earlier. I had been sick on him and I had barely noticed.

I was trying to wipe my mouth with the bottom of my

T-shirt, and I realised that I was properly crying too. My whole face was awash with sick and tears.

'Oh, Jesus,' said Jake.

'Oh, I don't feel well,' was all I could say. I didn't dare look up at his face. I just turned round so that I could run away and hide from everyone.

'Lydia . . .' I heard him call, but all muffled. 'Don't . . .'

'Please go away,' I said, and then I somehow made my way through all the staring people, and I could see Kay and Jimmy out in the hall, and Kay's expression was distraught. I had no wish to see Jimmy's expression. Everything in my life is now properly terrible, I thought, and I am a stupid ugly idiot. How could I have ever thought I wasn't?

Kay put both hands out to try and stop me in my tracks.

'I have to phone Harry to come and get me,' I said, thinking: Harry doesn't think I am ridiculous. Harry would never make me feel awful like that.

'But we'll take you home, won't we, Jimmy?' said Kay, who looked a bit tearful herself, which is not like Kay at all.

'Of course we will,' said Jimmy.

But the thought of being in a car with Jimmy was so dreadful that I shook my head very feverishly.

'No, it's OK.' I tasted salt in my mouth and wiped my face with the back of my hand.

Jimmy quickly rummaged in his pocket and brought out a clean tissue, which somehow made me feel even more of a wretch. I was so grubby and must have smelled horrible, while Jimmy was all scrubbed-looking and had a nice clean tissue.

'Here,' he said quite gently. 'Please don't cry. It will be all right.'

'Thanks.' I looked at his worried blue eyes, and then looked away again.

'It doesn't matter anyway,' I said, as it was extremely important that I didn't show how I really felt. 'I don't care if everyone hates me.'

'Well, I don't hate you,' said Kay. 'And I'm pretty much the only one who matters.'

I couldn't help smiling then, and she put her arm around me so that I was sort of nestled on the side of her boob.

'Let's go and phone Harry then,' she said, rubbing my arm.

Luckily, when we got through to the telephone in the Admiral, Harry was in there having a beer, so the barman went and got him. I only got to explain for about thirty seconds before he said, 'Stay there, I'm coming in a taxi. What's the address?'

And then I put the phone down and went to wait outside with Kay, as Jimmy had disappeared somewhere and we couldn't find him. Not that I minded about that. I was a hundred per cent sure now that Jimmy would never view me as anything but a teenage alcoholic with emotional problems.

As we stood on the path, something rustled in one of the flower beds and a head emerged. It was Rat, looking very pale and worse for wear. One of the spikes on her head had collapsed.

'All right,' she said, weaving around a bit in the bushes. 'Do excuse me.' Then she bent over and chucked up all over the flowers. When she'd finished, she wiped her mouth with some leaves off a bush. I must admit, Rat being inebriated did make me feel a bit less alone.

Rat staggered unsteadily back up on her feet again, and a shudder went through me that I might have looked like that to Jake and Dean, and Jimmy, and everyone. I didn't know what to do with the horror of it all.

'You going already?' Rat said. 'That boy was well out of order. Isn't he your brother?'

'No,' I said firmly. 'He's not.'

'Well, he came off worse if you ask me,' Rat said. Then she climbed out of the flower bed and zigzagged back into the house.

Then Harry arrived in the taxi, and I got in and he looked at me and sighed and rubbed my back. I turned round to wave at Kay, but she was busy trying to help Rat up off the doorstep where she must have keeled over again. There was no sign of Jimmy at all.

I closed my eyes and leaned against Harry's shoulder and wished I could go to sleep for ever.

Yesterday I phoned The Smugglers' Tavern to tell Denise that I didn't feel well, and couldn't come in for my shift last night – and then was terrified that she might come outside to clear all the rubbish off the benches outside and see me on *Lady Beatrice* so I had to hide down below most of the day. Harry said on Friday that he wouldn't say anything to anyone about coming to get me from Arnold's, and I just crawled into bed without Sam seeing, so I think I got away with it. But Sam's funny like that. He has an acute radar for oddities of my behaviour. Even if he doesn't understand what's going on. He senses abnormalities.

'Are you ill?' he said this morning. 'You're unnaturally quiet.'

'I'm allowed to be quiet,' I snapped at him. 'I can't win, can I? Most of the time you're wanting me to shut up and saying I'm too dramatic.'

Sam flinched. 'You're being quite dramatic right now,' he said. 'I only asked if you were ill.'

'Go away,' I said, and tried to turn on the telly.

'It's broken,' Sam told me. 'Bob chewed through the aerial lead.'

'Brilliant.'

Jake came into the saloon then, and for a second we made eye contact, but he looked away and got his bag. 'I'm going over to Dawn's,' he said, even though I didn't care and Sam certainly wasn't interested.

'Right you are,' said Sam sarcastically.

Jake slammed the saloon door shut behind him and I could feel my brother giving me a sidelong look.

'What?'

'Something very strange is going on,' said Sam. 'I can't quite put my finger on it.'

'Hmm, well, if the telly isn't working, I'm going out to see Kay,' I said, not wanting to have to answer any more questions.

'Does Kay still work in that doughnut kiosk?' said Sam, staring at the black screen of the telly. 'Can she get me free doughnuts?'

'Probably,' I said. 'I'll ask.'

I thought then that maybe Sam's request was actually a code for I really like Kay and I'm only asking about the doughnuts to cover it up. Or maybe it was really just about the doughnuts and I was imagining things?

At this point Kate and Dad arrived back from Wales with Sally and Erica, and Dad actually didn't look miserable. In fact, he and Kate were sharing a little joke about an eccentric cashier in the service station where they'd stopped off on the motorway home. They were laughing and seemed happy.

It was quite discombobulating, and I wondered what on earth might have occurred for Kate and Dad suddenly to be on these terms again.

Sam didn't seem too pleased at this turn of events, and was very monosyllabic when Dad spoke to him. I almost thought I should ask Sam if he wanted to come over to the prom with me to see Kay, but I thought better of it. This was not a time for being unselfish.

'All right, sleepyhead,' said Kay as I walked in a daze towards her. She was sat on one of the green benches opposite a group of toddlers being taught to swim in the shallow end.

I flopped down next to her.

Kay peered at my face. 'You're not still poorly?'

'I'm just sad and depressed,' I said.

Kay heaved a sigh. 'Arnold's party?' she said. 'It probably seems worse than it was. I mean, everyone at Arnold's was a bit merry. I doubt they noticed.'

'You weren't though,' I said. 'Or Jimmy.'

'True,' Kay said. 'But that's only because my mum would have gone mental about it.'

'Whereas my dad couldn't care less.'

Kay looked excruciated. 'Me and my big mouth,' she said. 'One thing my mother might possibly be right about.'

I smiled in spite of the weight of melancholy upon me.

'Jake didn't half have a go at you though,' Kay went on. 'Me and Jimmy were quite shocked. I thought you two got on?'

'We do ... I don't know. Maybe all this time he's just pretended not to notice I'm as thick as two short planks.'

'Here we go,' said Kay.

'What?'

'Well. That's obviously a load of rubbish. Anyone with half a brain could tell you're not thick.'

'But he did say it. He used it as a stick to beat me with.'

'A stick *with which* to beat me,' Kay shot back.

I guffawed.

'Anyway.' Kay composed herself. 'Let's have a plan.'

'A plan?'

'Well, you need something to look forward to, or think about. What about thingy?'

'Dean Carter. Are you joking, Kay?' I said. 'Dean saw me being sick on Jake's shirt. I think I might have to change schools again.'

'Well,' said Kay, crossing her arms over her boobs. 'After me and Jimmy phoned Val to come and get us, we went out the front to wait, and Dean was smoking marijuana by the bins. He made a special point of coming over and saying were you all right and he hoped you got home OK.'

'Is that true, Kay?'

'Swear on Gerta's life,' she said. 'See?'

'But if only I got noticed for other things than embarrassing ones,' I said. 'For once in my life I want to be special.'

'Oh, you're special, all right,' said Kay. 'Of that I can assure you.'

I walloped her lightly on the arm, laughing, and Kay walloped me lightly back.

'Sam has asked if you can get him free doughnuts,' I said once we'd stopped hitting each other. 'I told him I'd ask.'

'Well, not free,' said Kay. 'But I can get money off, maybe. Tell him he'll have to come and get them though. We don't do home deliveries.'

'It's OK, I'll collect them,' I said. 'You don't want Sam hanging round here – he'll frighten the customers.'

Kay laughed, but not like I thought she would. 'I don't mind,' she said. 'He amuses me in a way.'

'That's nice,' I said, as though Kay's remark did not threaten me. 'Anyway,' I said, changing the subject. 'My dad and Kate got home from Wales today. They're pretending to like each other again. It's weird.'

'Maybe they do?' said Kay. 'Maybe they've fallen in love again? Is it their wedding anniversary or something?'

'That is actually a very good point, Kay. . .' I said, suddenly remembering that it was more or less a year ago that Dad married Kate. 'But how can they hate each other one minute then be all lovey-dovey the next minute.'

She shrugged. 'I think when you get married you mostly just make the best of it because it's too much bother to split up.'

'That's rubbish,' I said. 'Marriage is weird.'

'You're right there,' said Kay. 'I'm never getting married.'

'Me neither,' I said, trying out the name *Lydia Carter* in my head.

'Want to go on the Waltzer?' said Kay, after a bit. 'I'll let you scream down my earhole again, if you like?'

Tonight when I was in bed at 10.00 p.m., trying to go to sleep, I heard Harry arguing with Dad outside his cabin, and I heard my name mentioned. I didn't want to hear anything bad so I switched on Radio Luxembourg and listened to recurring adverts about tampons and women's products instead.

Saturday 2nd August

Sam has gone away to stay with Dad's old school friend Johnny and his wife, in Devon. Johnny is like a much older version of Sam really. He lives in a tiny cottage by the water and has a little sailing boat, and he's Sam's godfather. Sam goes most years and says that he helps Johnny make home-made cider and do jobs on the boat, and they mostly eat sandwiches and sail around and don't really talk to each other, but apparently that doesn't matter. This sounds very weird to me as I can't imagine being silent for long, but Sam loves it.

I miss Sam a bit though, especially as Jake and I don't talk to each other and never will again. I've not told Sam about what Jake said at Arnold's party, and I have sworn Kay to secrecy too. I know Sam wouldn't understand, and would possibly make things worse without meaning to. And things couldn't get much worse, not after what happened tonight.

Tonight it was the busiest night of the year at The Smugglers' Tavern, according to Denise, as it's the Maling Regatta and people get very merry and then decide to have a meal, so Denise has to create extra space in the bar area for dining. Rich's brother Mick came in to help with any rowdy customers because the bar staff have their hands full. Denise says that if she's being honest the Regatta week is a night-mare and only worthwhile for this year's holiday in Florida, that her and Rich can afford to have because of all the takings.

'Nice little treat for us now that I'm on the mend,' said Denise, handing me an apron and a pair of Marigolds when I turned up promptly at 6.30 p.m. 'If it was like this every weekend then Rich and I could cash in our timeshare in Tenerife and buy a nice little property in Malta and retire next year.' Denise sighed then and a wistful look came over her face. 'We've been running this place for twenty years,' she said. 'Sometimes that property in Malta is the only thing that keeps me going.'

'That sounds really nice,' I said politely, though I'm not exactly sure where Malta is. I think it might be famous for bird wildlife, as people often refer to the Maltese Falcon. And it's probably hot all year round, as Denise is a Sun Worshipper. Her skin is very brown and crinkly and below her neck it looks a bit like salami that has gone off.

'Well,' she said, switching on the fryers and wiping over a greasy saucepan with a J-cloth. 'Just be prepared for a long night. This fryer will be going nonstop. After a few pints, all anyone wants is chips, or scampi in a basket.'

At 9.00 p.m. Rich came in with a trolley-load of dirty plates and gave me a funny look, and then he went over to Denise and stood next to her as she was prodding a steak in a pan and whispered something in her ear, and I got a horrible feeling in my stomach, a feeling of intuition, which was most probably my gift of the sixth sense.

Denise looked over at me and smiled strangely, and then Rich went back out into the bar area and she went back to prodding her steak.

And then for a short while there was quiet in The Smugglers' Tavern kitchen – except for the sounds of me scrubbing at dried tomato ketchup and gravy on plates and the spitting of the oil in Denise's pan.

Suddenly there was a huge crashing sound coming from the bar and a shriek from Annette the Saturday evening barmaid, and then Mick shouted, 'All right, folks, carry on enjoying yourselves, everything's under control.'

At this point I had just started cleaning a Sorbet Surprise shell, but I stopped and looked at Denise, who moved her steak off the heat and put a waiting plate full of chicken and rice in the oven and slammed the oven door shut and said, 'Oh, for heaven's sake!' Then she took off her apron and shoved it on the counter and stomped out to see what was going on. And I just stood there at the sink with my Marigolds on, staring down at a crusty old orange shell without really seeing it.

'I ordered a whisky!' I heard someone say loudly. 'And I've paid for it, so I'm bloody well going to have it!'

It was Dad.

Dad was shouting in the bar of The Smugglers' Tavern. And I knew that was why Rich had come in and whispered to Denise and she had smiled weirdly at me. Because my father was causing trouble.

I took off my Marigolds and thought about just running off to save embarrassment, but instead I went to the doorway and hid behind the bell that Rich rings for last orders.

And there was Dad on the floor, propped up against one

of the banquettes by the window, with his legs splayed out underneath a table and the front of his shirt covered in liquid.

A huge man was standing over him, with a woman who was glaring at Dad. Denise was rubbing the woman's shoulder, and saying, 'I do apologise, Bernie.'

'You're upsetting my wife,' I heard the huge man say to my father.

'Well, I'm sorry about that,' said Dad wearily. 'But all I ask for is a drink and I am being unreasonably refused.'

'I think you've had enough, Mr Thomson, love,' said Denise, looking down at Dad. And then I saw that the zip on his trousers was slightly undone, probably because he'd fallen down. I stared at his wet shirt and his trousers and I felt cold all over, even though it was boiling hot in the bar area.

'That's for me to judge, madam,' Dad told Denise blearily. 'Since this is a pub, I would have thought that supplying alcohol was somewhat *de rigueur.*'

'Come on, mate,' said Rich, who was picking up some glasses from the floor. 'You don't need another drink. Wouldn't you rather have a nice cup of tea at home now?'

'Tea?' said Dad, and he groped on the floor next to him and found his glasses and put them on. 'No, I wouldn't. Tea doesn't quite have the same effect as a stiff whisky, you see. Not the same at all.'

Dad's voice seemed to chime out like the lord of the manor, but at the same time he looked tired and quite old. He sighed and then somehow, with his glasses on, his gaze settled on me, where I was still trying to hide behind the bell.

'Is that you?' he called, and he looked round at the huge man – Bernie – his wife, Rich and Denise. 'That's my little girl,' he said. 'Lydia. She'll get me another drink . . . won't you, my love? She's a good girl.'

And then everyone in the whole pub turned and looked at me.

Annette was taking glasses out of the washer next to me, but she stopped and put her hand out and held my arm. 'Go back in the kitchen, Lydia,' she whispered. 'Rich and Mick will look after him.'

'Lydia!' Dad was shouting. 'Tell them. I only want a glass of whisky.'

I wanted to move, but couldn't. 'Why is he on the floor?' I asked Annette. 'How did that happen?'

'Bit of a kerfuffle with Mick,' said Annette. 'Mick's a big bloke. He was just trying to settle him down.'

Denise came over. 'Table over there needs clearing, Annette,' she told her, sounding exhausted. Then Denise looked at me and sighed. 'I think you'd better go and get your mum, love,' she said. 'Your dad needs to sleep it off.'

Everyone in The Smugglers' seems to know that Charlie Thomson is my dad. And everyone knows he drinks too much. It is excruciating.

'She's not my mum,' I told Denise, even though this was beside the point.

'Oh, well. Someone else then . . .' Denise said. 'One of those boys . . . your brothers?'

Before I could reply, the pub door opened and Kate walked in, followed by Jake.

'Oh, for Christ's sake, Charlie,' Kate said, standing over Dad. 'I knew you weren't going for a walk. You've been gone three hours.'

Dad hiccupped. 'My lovely wife,' he told anyone who was listening. 'My lovely patient wife.'

Kate looked as though she was beyond embarrassment. 'You've got *that* right,' she said. 'Now please get up.'

Jake had his head down behind Kate, and I knew I should go back into the kitchen now, or he might see me and feel even more that we were a family of disasters.

But I still didn't move, and Denise's eyes were boring into me.

'Charles,' Kate said again. 'Get up.'

'Oh God,' said Dad, and he rubbed his beard. 'I don't have this kind of censorious rubbish from my daughter.' He nodded his head in my direction. 'Lydia understands. Don't you, my love?'

And now Kate and Jake were looking over at me too.

I was mute, just staring back at them all.

'Oh, love.' Denise tucked one of my horrible curls behind my ear. 'Is your dad having a hard time?'

I opened my mouth to say, 'What does it look like?' but shut it again, as Denise was only trying to be kind.

Eventually Kate and Jake managed to help Dad up onto his feet and took him back to *Lady Beatrice*, but not before he cast me a very disappointed look. He must have been

245

hoping I would charge over and stand up for him, but the more I think about that the more I think it is unfair and even horrible of him. Also it means he has completely forgotten I have a job washing up in The Smugglers' Tavern kitchen and doesn't care that he made me look like the daughter of a drunkard.

Mum's face keeps flashing into my head and I am glad that she can't see Dad. But maybe she can, and there is a heaven and it isn't just made up. I wish that was true and that I will see her again, but then I don't really believe it. If dead people do watch over us, then how can they just stand up there while awful things are happening? Why don't they swoop down and help?

Denise said I should go home and not to worry as she would make up my wages anyway, and then she said something quite un-Denise-like.

'Don't worry too much, sweetheart,' she said. 'Don't let it spoil your life.' And then she gave me a hug that was awkward, because her arm's still a bit funny from the chemo and she's not got much strength, and my face was buried in her salami chest.

'See you tomorrow lunch, lovey,' she said briskly then. 'Eleven thirty sharp.'

When I got back to *Lady Beatrice*, Dad was asleep on the saloon sofa, with his mouth open and in a state of disarray, while Jake and Kate were sitting at the table. Kate was staring down at a mug of tea with a very stony expression. I felt ashamed on behalf of Dad, so I scurried past them and went to drink a glass of water from the galley. When I came back through again, Kate was writing something down in a little notebook and I wondered if she had a diary too, and maybe like me it helped her to write down noteworthy events.

Jake had got the ironing board out and was going over a shirt, which was quite a weird thing to do, but thinking about it might be Jake's way of staying calm and in control.

'Is Dad OK?' I said.

Kate shut her notebook and put it in her bag. 'No,' she said stiffly. 'He's not.'

Kate doesn't bother at all lately to pretend to be reassuring or anything I've noticed.

'He'll be fine,' Jake piped up, finishing his shirt and putting it on a hanger. 'He'll just feel a bit rough in the morning. Don't worry about it.' He and Kate gave each other a look.

'But *will* he be fine though? I mean, there's obviously something not right with him?'

Kate's breathing was quite loud, as though she was really trying to stop herself saying something mean about Dad. 'Yes,' she said eventually. 'Well, he's not well.'

I thought of Mum and panicked. 'He's not going to die, is he?' I said. 'He hasn't got a fatal illness?'

'It depends what you mean by that,' said Kate. 'If he doesn't stop what he's doing, you could describe it as fatal, I suppose.'

'Mum . . .' said Jake, glancing at me.

She gave her head a little shake. 'It's not that, Lydia. He's not physically ill.'

My heartbeat, which had sped up, started slowing down again.

'How would you know?' came a loud, peevish voice from the sofa, and we turned to see Dad sitting upright with a glassy, cold look in his eyes. He was looking at me, but I knew he couldn't properly see me.

'Because your problems are psychological, Charlie,' Kate said, quiet but angry. 'You're in a bit of a mess.'

'Well, that's very nice.' Dad's voice was flat. 'A mess who has tried his best, despite constant criticism.'

'Hang on a minute,' said Jake. 'Mum's trying her best too.'

'Ha!' said Dad, and a big nasty grin appeared on his face. 'Well, I suppose you would say that. You lot are all the same.'

'Meaning?' said Kate.

'Meaning you're a family of narrow-minded prigs. No imagination. Sour and superficial.'

'Dad, stop,' I said. 'Stop!'

Nobody took any notice.

'You do nothing, Charlie!' Kate shouted. 'I cook, I do the laundry, I feed your children. I come and fetch you from endless undignified scenes. All you do is sit around and pity yourself.' She shot a look in my direction. 'Who is looking after your daughter? You hardly show any interest in her. Except when you use her to bolster your pathetic ego.'

'Oh, go away.' Dad put his head in his hands. 'You have no idea, none of you . . .'

No idea about what? I thought.

The saloon door opened then, and Sally's face appeared

round it. 'Mum,' she said in a timid little voice. 'What's happening?'

Kate shut her eyes and then opened them again. 'Nothing, Sally. Go back to bed. Everything's all right. I'll be through in a minute.'

I'm not being funny, but Sally's not stupid. I wish adults wouldn't tell such blatant lies. They never make you feel better. They only make you feel more unsafe. But Sally just nodded and then shut the door. It's easier to go along with things sometimes.

I had no words, but I suddenly felt freezing cold, and one of my legs was twitching, from anxiety. I felt like I was all alone, like an orphan. Kate isn't my real mother, and Dad is lost. I didn't want to believe Kate was right, and all the things Jake said, but it was really hard not to.

'I'm sleeping in the girls' cabin tonight,' said Kate. 'And on Monday morning I am taking you to the doctor.'

'You're bloody well not,' said Dad, trying to get up but unable to.

'Do you really want everything taken away from you?' Kate said. 'It doesn't matter about me, but think what you have to lose.'

And then she gave Jake a meaningful look, and touched my arm and left the saloon, closing the door quietly behind her.

Dad, meanwhile, had already fallen asleep again.

While I carried on standing there feeling wide awake Jake carefully folded up the ironing board. Then he came over to me, and I was sure he was going to start on again about Dad and how tonight just proved that he was right about what he'd said at Arnold's.

'Night then,' I said, and started for the saloon door.

'Lydia,' Jake said quietly. 'Don't go yet.'

But I ignored him. Instead I went past my cabin and up the stairs to go and sit on deck. Bob and Eugene were up there, gazing at the moon, and I dragged them over to me so that I could stroke them.

The three of us sat in peaceful silence for a few minutes until I heard footsteps and my heart sank. It was Jake coming up the stairs. I clutched the cats tighter and Bob bit me, though I hardly felt it.

'I brought you some tea,' he said.

I didn't turn round. 'I don't want to hear another one of your rants, Jake,' I said. 'Like your mum is better than my dad and all that.'

'I'm sorry, Lydia.' I heard him putting the tea on top of the hatch and Bob of course immediately wriggled out of my grip to investigate. 'I'm sorry about what I said at that party.'

I hesitated for a moment, then I reached out and took the tea and had a sip, and it was lovely. Just how I like it.

'I was maybe a bit of a prat though,' I said then. 'And I didn't mean it about why your dad left. I just said it to upset you.'

'I understand,' Jake said. 'And you're not stupid, not at all.'

'I think I might be in a way,' I said. 'I'm rubbish at school.'

Jake shook his head in a nice but slightly exasperated way.

'Charlie does care about you, you know,' he said. 'He just seems to have a lot of problems at the moment.'

'I know he's a worry,' I said. 'I worry all the time about him.'

Jake said, 'Do you remember when we had that conversation and I told you I worried about my mum, so I knew how you felt?'

I nodded. 'That seems like so long ago.'

'I don't know what's going to happen with Charlie and Mum,' said Jake. 'But I don't want to fight with you of all people.'

I felt such a whoosh of relief.

'I don't understand. I thought Dad was getting on with your mum,' I said. 'When they came back from Wales. It seemed like they liked each other again.'

Jake shrugged. 'I don't know,' he said. 'Sometimes they do. But most of the time they don't seem to, do they?'

'I know Dad's not perfect. But he's nice really. He used to be quite a happy person. It's just the drinking that makes him horrible.'

'Yeah,' said Jake. 'I know.'

I felt so sad about Dad.

Jake sat there for a minute and then he said completely out of the blue. 'That kid. Jimmy . . . ? Is he soft on you or something?'

I was very unprepared. Mostly because it felt so weird in the middle of our conversation for Jake to say Jimmy's name.

'Jimmy?' I said, deciding to reply as though the idea had not once occurred to me. 'No way. I hardly know him.' I stared at Jake. 'Why?'

Jake shrugged. 'He had a bit of a go at me, that's all. After you'd left the party. He came over and said I should be ashamed of myself.'

For once I rejected Bob's approach for affection and pushed him away. 'But he can't have. Are you sure it was Jimmy Jones?'

'The kid with the two-tone trousers and the prison buzzcut?' Jake said. 'I remember his shoes. They were way cool. Wouldn't mind some of those myself.'

'Yes, that's him.' Now that I had digested it, I allowed myself a secret bit of pleasure, though making sure this was not at all evident in my facial expression. 'How weird.'

'I mean, he had a nerve,' Jake went on. 'But, you know . . . he was right. I *was* out of order.'

I couldn't hide the smile now. 'That actually means a lot to me, Jake. That you said sorry.'

'Well, don't get used to it.' Jake got up and brushed down his jeans. 'It's not my style.'

But he flashed me a friendly grin all the same.

Jake went back down below and I sat up on deck with the cats for ages, thinking. First about what Jimmy had done, which explained why he disappeared while Kay and me were waiting for Harry. How odd boys are. Do they never say it to your face if they particularly like you? Or is Jimmy just super-nice and that's all?

Then I thought about Jake, and how it all made sense – him being so angry at Arnold's party. I must have seemed like a different person. I remember in school in Personal Guidance, the teacher Miss Boon saying that some people are born with addictive personalities and can easily take a habit too far. Also, that addictive personalities run in families. What if in years to come I end up being a drunkard like Dad? Will Kay have to pick me up off the floor in some pub when we're living in the shared flat in London as I have planned? Miss Boon also said that people often hide behind alcohol – and of course a few of the boys in our year made jokes about giant bottles of wine that you hide behind. But now I know exactly what Miss Boon was talking about, because I think it's what my father is doing right now. He's hiding.

Eventually I saw Harry coming home from the pub, and I'm not sure if he had found out about Dad somehow, but he came on board *Lady Beatrice* and then sat down next to me. He took off his leather jacket and put it round my shoulders. Harry and I sat there, while the masts clinked and the smell of sulphur rose from the mud, and I had one of those intervals where everything seems better, even if it won't last for ever.

Friday 8th August

Life on *Lady Beatrice* continues to be in turmoil, but at least Jake and me are no longer enemies. I didn't realise till now how important that is.

After the incident at The Smuggler's, Kate's face has had the appearance of one of those gargoyles that are hidden outside church buildings and frighten the life out of you when you spot one. She has not forgiven Dad, even though he apologised to her the day after and brought home some flowers on Monday. I've noticed that Kate has been quite busy writing in her notebook, but since she keeps it in her handbag, which just lately is welded to her shoulder at all times, I can't sneak a look at what she's writing down.

I am beginning to wonder though if it's always women who have to be unpopular and point out bad behaviour and get called nags. Mum would have been angry with Dad, too, if she was still here. Kate is only doing what Mum would have done.

'I know what you mean,' Kay said this afternoon at 4.00 p.m. when she was having a break at the kiosk. 'Except in my mum's case she makes up bad behaviour that doesn't exist most of the time. Dad can't win. Every time he tries she just starts on about childbirth and how Dad wouldn't know proper pain if it slapped him in the face.'

'Childbirth does sound awful though,' I said. 'You'd think they'd have invented something by now that means you don't have to endure it. I keep waiting for it on *Tomorrow's World*.'

'They have, though,' said Kay. 'It's called a Caesarean. Possibly they suck the kid out through your belly button.'

'Yuck,' I said, pushing away my Slush Puppie.

'If life is all about testing how much pain you can withstand,' Kay pondered, 'd'you reckon you get your reward at the end of it? Like an OBE or something?'

'Maybe, but I think only certain people get chosen for the test,' I said. 'People like us.'

Danny was outside writing a special offer on the kiosk blackboard, but he turned round and shook his head at us. 'You two,' he said. 'Right pair of miseries.'

'You would say that,' Kay told him. 'You're a man.'

'Give over.' Danny grinned. 'You've got your whole lives ahead of you, you lucky beggars.' Then he stood up and rubbed his back and returned to the kiosk.

'I wish I worked here,' I said. 'Honestly, Kay, I never thought I'd say this, but I'm almost looking forward to going back to school soon.'

'Well, if you're after something to do, Jimmy's at a loose end since I can't be his friend so much. Not now that I'm here most days at Danny's.'

I thought again of what Jimmy had said to Jake at the party, and then I thought about how I had looked at the party and I couldn't quite believe that Jimmy had felt anything else but sorry for me.

'Hmmm,' I said. 'Last time I saw Jimmy I was covered in sick, Kay.' I felt depressed that both Dean and Jimmy had now seen me at my absolute worst and therefore romance is a ridiculous idea.

Kay rolled her eyes. 'Who cares anyway? It's not like Jimmy's perfect.'

'What do you mean?' I said.

'Mother said that a while ago Val mentioned that Jimmy's got a girlfriend back in Cornwall—' Kay began.

'A girlfriend!' I half shrieked.

'Anyway, Mum said he also confided in Val that he likes someone else, some other girl, but he didn't go into details.'

'That's absolutely outrageous,' I said, thinking Jimmy was a sly dark horse.

'Hang on . . .' Kay stared at me. 'It's not like I've just said Jimmy murdered someone. I thought you didn't like him that much.'

'I don't. It's just annoying that he has a love dilemma when I haven't.'

Kay laughed. 'Only you would be jealous of a thing like that,' she said. 'That's the funniest thing I've ever heard. Actually, Jimmy asks about you quite a lot; he seems quite interested in you and your family, in fact.'

'What does he say?' I asked, a bit too eagerly.

'Not that you care or anything,' Kay said.

I knew Kay was baiting me, so I turned my face away to look at all the boats resting on top of the mud.

'About your dad . . .' said Kay after a bit. 'Maybe you should tell your sister about what happened last Saturday?'

'She's got all her studies and parties,' I said, turning back. 'I don't want to bother her.'

Kay gave me a long look. 'But your dad is her dad too. If I was Elsa, I'd want to know.'

'Maybe,' I said. 'I might write her a postcard and just mention it right at the end. I don't want to look like a crybaby to Elsa.'

Kay got up and fiddled with her Slush Puppie carton and then sat down again. 'Lydia. I know I often take the mickey out of you, but . . . sometimes when I'm at home and Mum is nagging me at the same time as putting my dinner in front of me, I stop myself from answering her back because of you.'

'What do you mean?'

'I think of how nobody is doing that for you. Not really. I know my mum and dad are weirdos, but they've always been weirdos. Regular as clockwork. You don't know if you're coming or going with your dad. And you still find the time to be almost normal . . . as well as a drama queen who's pretending you don't care about Jimmy Jones . . .' She paused. 'I'm saying you're definitely not a crybaby, that's all.'

I overlooked the comment about Jimmy because of what Kay had just said, and also, what was the point? Nothing ever gets past Kay!

'Is that what you really think?'

'Yep.' Kay got up and emptied the last of her ice onto her feet. 'Oh, that's better,' she said, a look of rapture on her face. 'I've been wanting to do that all day.'

'Kay!' Danny yelled at her. 'Break's over.'

'A woman's work is never done.' Kay chucked both our cups into the bin. 'I'll tell Jimmy you're busy then, shall I?' she added, and limped back over to the kiosk before I could properly react.

As it turned out though, I did see Jimmy later this afternoon. It was when I was buying a postcard to send to Elsa from a little junk shop in town that sells knick-knacks and ancient radios and furniture, along with broken jewellery from years ago.

Elsa likes old cards. In her bedroom in our house she had loads pinned to her walls of film stars from the 1940s and 50s. I chose the famous one of Marilyn Monroe where her skirt is billowing up all around her waist and you can almost see her knickers. I was just paying for it when the junk-shop doorbell jangled and the man who runs the shop nodded at whoever had come in.

'Go and say hello then,' I heard some woman say, and I turned round with my paper bag and Jimmy was standing by the door with a woman in a pink sundress. He was wearing a white T-shirt and his skin was quite brown from the sun. It was annoying as he did look very handsome and it would be hard to pretend I was indifferent.

'Hi . . . hello,' said Jimmy awkwardly. 'How are you?'

'Fine,' I said quite loudly, and Jimmy looked more awkward.

'This is my mum,' he said. 'Mum, this is Lydia.'

'Hello, Lydia,' said the woman. 'You're the one who lives on one of those lovely old barges, aren't you? Jimmy's told me all about you.'

I darted a look at Jimmy, who smiled. 'Not everything,' he said. 'She likes to exaggerate, don't you, Mum?'

'Are you this cheeky to your parents?' Mrs Jones asked me.

Jimmy looked suddenly worried, as if his mum might put her foot in it, as my mum is dead and everything, and then it was me who felt sorry for him. No, it wasn't pity I felt a bit of a pang for him.

'I'm worse, probably,' I said, and decided to change the subject. 'What are you going to buy?'

'Oh . . . a desk for brainbox here,' said Mrs Jones. 'Now that he's going to be in Maling for the time being, he needs something to do all the endless homework on. I want something with a bit of character and I love this place – I could spend hours in here.'

'Aren't you just here for the summer?' I said to Jimmy.

'Not sure,' interrupted Val. 'It might have to be a bit longer than that.'

Jimmy gave me an awkward smile. He probably feels really annoyed to be dragged away from his new love interest in Cornwall and having to make conversation with me, I thought, trying not to look at the little beauty-spot mole near his mouth.

'I might be at your school for the autumn term,' Jimmy said then. 'Dad's girlfriend's having a few complications with her pregnancy.'

Before I could say anything back, Val had a bit of a coughing fit and then she started studying a chipped enamel jug with great interest.

'Anyway, I've just bought a card for my sister,' I said then.

'Lovely,' said Mrs Jones, looking up at me.

'Is she like you?' said Jimmy then. 'Your sister?'

'No. She's much more sophisticated.' I realised how that

had come out and that it seemed like I was drawing atten-
tion to myself being so unsophisticated recently. 'Anyway,
I'd better go as I want to put this in the post tonight before
I forget.'

'Oh, OK,' said Mrs Jones. 'Lovely to meet you, Lydia. I
hope you'll come to see us in the flat. We're not that far
from you.'

Jimmy looked mortified, I'm sure because I'm the last
person he wants round for tea. He probably thinks I'd try
and steal his mum's gin out of her drinks cabinet, I thought.
I tried to smile and be polite though, as Mrs Jones did seem
nice, and warm and friendly.

'Thanks, that's really kind,' I said, almost at the door now.
'Bye, Mrs Jones. See you, Jimmy.'

And I left with the bell jangling very noisily before either
of them could say goodbye back.

Tuesday 12th August

Dad came back early from work again yesterday with a big carrier bag under his arm and asked me if I wouldn't mind making him a cup of tea so that we could have a sit-down together. Firstly this made me startled and then nervous that he was about to tell me something terrible again, like Kate was having a baby. Though as I was making the tea – which takes twice the time it takes normal people to make because the electric kettle keeps making the fuse box blow and we now have to put an old-fashioned kettle on the hob to heat water – I reasoned that since Kate is disgusted by Dad more often than not lately, her having a baby probably isn't very likely.

Anyway, when I came out with the tea, Dad had put the big carrier bag on the table and had a sort of satisfied look on his face.

First he took a slurp of his tea, and then he added two heaped spoonfuls of sugar.

'You don't have sugar in tea, Dad,' I told him, despite the evidence before my eyes.

'Not usually,' said Dad, giving it a good stir. 'But my sweet tooth has reappeared – I'm trying to cut back on other things . . .'

As Dad has not smoked for months, this must mean that he's cutting back on alcohol consumption.

'That's very good news.' I hoped I was being encouraging and mature.

'Thank you, my love,' he said. Then he reached for the carrier bag next to him. 'I got you a little something.'

Of course, then I forgot about being mature and snatched the carrier bag away from him. 'What is it?' I said, frantically dragging out a box from inside it. 'What can it be?'

'It's a portable record player,' said Dad, and as I looked up I saw the expression of pleasure on his face as he watched me attack the box with such gusto.

'A real one?' I used to have a record player when I was a child, but it was a toy one on which I played tunes like 'The Runaway Train' and 'There Once Was an Ugly Duckling'. It was quite tinny and you had to be right near it to properly hear the songs.

'Yes,' said my father. 'I know you young ones like your music and those seven-inch singles. I thought you'd like something of your own to play them on.'

'Thanks,' I said, having finally got the record player out of its box. It was red, with a leather-type case with the word *Rumbelows* on the lid.

'Do you like it?' Dad asked. 'I thought you might.'

'I do,' I told him truthfully, but it was hard to know exactly how I was feeling. It's hard when you feel angry at someone, and then they give you something you didn't know you wanted until you saw it. It's hard to let go of one feeling and have another so quickly.

Dad cleared his throat, while I inspected the record player from top to bottom.

'Lydia . . .' he began. 'I am sorry if I've embarrassed you . . . I'm not—'

'It's OK,' I said quickly, cutting him off. I wasn't ready for his explanation. In fact, I dreaded it. Dad's got a kind heart, but sometimes I wish he would *do* something, instead of explaining. If he explains, then I am lumbered with his explanation, and I feel bad for him but also helpless, as how can I help him? I have no idea.

'Well, good.' Dad picked up his mug of tea and drank some of it.

'Actually,' I said, shutting the lid of the record player. 'In a way, it's quite crafty of you to buy me a present after what happened. It feels a bit like a bribe or something.'

Dad sighed and rubbed his beard. 'I can see why it might appear like that. But . . . I just want you to know that I haven't forgotten.'

'Forgotten what?'

'That you're my daughter. You're growing up very fast, and I am not very good at being your father at the moment.'

I knew I was supposed to say something like, 'Yes you are,' but that was not really true. What could I say that would be the truth but not hurtful?

After some thinking I said, 'I know you're doing your best.'

Dad smiled a very weak smile. I felt bad then, for not giving Dad a chance to talk to me when it seemed like he'd wanted to.

'Is there something else wrong?' I asked him.

Dad was now reading the instructions leaflet. 'What do you mean?' he said, without taking his eyes from it.

'You said something that night when you . . . you know,

after The Smugglers' Tavern . . . You said "none of us have any idea". What don't we have any idea about?'

Dad folded up the instructions and put them back in the record player box, then he took his glasses off and rubbed at the lenses with the bottom of his shirt.

'I actually cannot remember saying that, you know,' he said in a strangely calm voice. 'Probably nonsense.'

It's just that it hadn't seemed like nonsense. The way he said it. But I could tell Dad wasn't going to say, even if I was right.

'OK.' I stroked the record player.

'Don't you worry.' He got up and stretched. 'Nothing to worry about.'

'Cool!' said Jake, when he saw the record player Dad had bought me. 'Where did you get that?'

I had been sitting for hours on the sofa just touching it. 'Dad bought it for me,' I said, embarrassed for some reason.

'Nice.' Jake sat down on the sofa and examined it in exactly the same way that I had. 'You can borrow some of my records if you want, to play on it. As long as you don't scratch them.'

'Thanks,' I said. 'I'm going to get my own though, probably, as I'm not sure about your taste in music.'

'Cheeky little sod,' said Jake, grinning.

'I can't help thinking there is something going on with Dad,' I said after a bit.

'There is, you daft git.' Jake bent down and made sure his socks were sitting at an identical level on his ankles. I noticed again how polished his DMs were. He must spend hours on them.

'I mean, apart from . . . the obvious thing,' I explained.

Jake sat up again. 'Like?'

'Dunno.'

'You're too sensitive,' he said, but trying to be kind. 'Sometimes there isn't anything wrong, you know.'

'Uh-huh.' I hoped Jake was right. 'But then again, I do think I am sort of gifted in that way,' I went on. 'You know. A sixth sense.'

Jake looked at me straight-faced for two seconds before he burst out laughing.

'What?'

'You might laugh, Jake, but it is actually a bit of a poisoned chalice.'

'Sorry,' he said, trying to control himself. 'It's just I think all that stuff is complete rubbish.'

I sighed. 'Jesus had the same reaction when he tried to tell people about his special powers,' I said. 'And look what happened there?'

'Jesus?' Jake practically bent over double at my observation. '*Jesus?*'

'That's right,' I said. 'Laugh away. It's not my fault if I am cursed with Second Sight.'

Saturday 16th August

I have been in Maling and living on *Lady Beatrice* for over a year. I feel a hundred years old, but at the same time seem hardly to have matured at all.

Elsa got my postcard and sent a reply back on a card of the Muppets, which made me laugh, though my efforts at being sophisticated with my Marilyn Monroe one have obviously gone unnoticed. In the end I hadn't written much about Dad, just that he seemed quite unhappy. I didn't want to write about the pub incident on the back of a postcard for everyone to read and embarrass my sister, but also, a part of me wants Elsa not to have to be concerned about it. What's the point of all of us worrying about it? Anyway, Dad is trying now.

Elsa said that her summer job in Cambridge is fine, but that she's having a bit of a 'funny time' in general, and that she can't wait to go back to her studies again and maybe I could come and visit her soon in the autumn. This last bit was music to my ears as I didn't dare ask before in case she said no. I must remind Elsa that she invited me so she can't take it back.

I met Kay in the high street today. Danny's kiosk is closed because it's his wedding anniversary and he's taken Mrs Danny to Leigh-on-Sea for a day out. Kay said, why don't we just hang around town and go to the shops?

We went to Tesco, as Kay and I are both passionate about Arctic Roll, and headed straight for the freezer section. Then

Kay revealed that she has another motive for visiting Tesco as she is having a flirtation with a boy from the sixth form, a Saturday shelf-stacker called Ray. He apparently came to Kay's rescue a while ago when she slipped over on some spilt cocktail sauce and then fell over himself. Now Ray and Kay laugh about it every time she goes in on a Saturday morning to get supplies for Danny. Kay has never said anything about Ray before, and I wondered if that was because my dramas have got in the way. I felt a bit bad.

But I am also very relieved that any romance between Sam and Kay has been a figment of my imagination.

Ray is tall like Kay, and he's got a few spots and a few bristly dark hairs on his chin and laughs a lot. I saw him looking admiringly at Kay's legs and boobs. I was beginning to feel a bit left out, to be honest, but I did marvel at Kay's ability not to act like an idiot in these situations.

Kay and I walked over to the benches outside the church afterwards, to eat our Arctic Roll, which was melted in the middle by the time we got there, so we quickly had half of it each.

'I bumped into Jimmy,' I said, having cogitated since on the encounter in the junk shop. 'And it's quite obvious he sees me as a teenage renegade.'

Kay laughed. 'A what?'

I shuddered, remembering. 'It was quite awkward, that's all, Kay. But Jimmy said he might be coming to Oaks for the autumn term. Did you know that?'

'Hmmm. The pregnancy is proving "quite problematic", according to Mother. Also, Val is a bit funny about it all.

She told Mum she doesn't want Jimmy being neglected because of the new baby, even though his dad's got more money than Val, and Jimmy wants for nothing in many ways.'

'Not very nice for Jimmy, I suppose, is it?' I said.

'See,' said Kay. 'You do care about Jimmy.'

I sighed, as Kay doesn't mince her words, and that can be quite inconvenient at times.

'I don't know. I wish I was more like you,' I told her, wiping some ice cream goo off my skirt. 'I just don't understand about boys really.'

'Remember when I got Danny to give me the job at the kiosk?' Kay said then. 'It's all about pretending you know what you're on about.'

'Yes,' I said. 'I remember.'

'Well, with boys it's the same thing. You've got to make them believe you are simply irresistible. No blushing, no being tongue-tied, just front it out.'

'So, pretend,' I said. 'Like acting.'

'Exactly,' said Kay. 'Funny thing is, once it works, it's not pretending any more. It's true!'

'Yes,' I said. 'But my emotions take over and I start worrying about what I look like and just thinking too much about it all.'

Kay shook her head, screwing up the packaging for the Arctic Roll and then putting it in the bin next to us. 'Maybe we're just different then,' she said. 'But do you always want to be the one who doesn't get what they want?'

Kay might soon have an actual boyfriend, while I will be lying awake at night analysing everything I've ever said to boys and how I've said it.

But I've been sorting through feelings in my head this afternoon and I have realised something. Even though Dean Carter is like one of those prizes in the booths on Clacton Pier – the one you can never win, however hard you try – it's not Dean that makes me feel confused at all. It's Jimmy.

Wednesday 20th August

Jake told me yesterday that Kate and Dad are thinking of going to marriage guidance counselling. Kate confided in Jake that the situation is at breaking point, and she is at her wits' end.

Sam, who is still properly grudge-bearing when it comes to Kate, says that Dad is not behaving *that* badly in his opinion, and that Kate is just a pernickety type. I have written to Elsa about all of this and also to accept her invitation to visit her and can we fix a date. Elsa wrote back to say that Sam misses our mother more than he lets on, and Kate is getting the brunt of it.

'Not that she isn't a cow,' Elsa was careful to add, as she is something of a grudge-bearer too.

It's true that Kate does have a very short temper these days. The other day Bob jumped up and ate some raw hamburgers Kate had made and then left on the counter in the galley while she went to the bathroom. Of course, Bob was violently sick straight afterwards because of the raw mince, and Kate returned to find a horrible mess on the galley floor.

'Even that cat . . .' she said, breathing heavily. 'Even that wretched *cat* hates me.'

This was not entirely fair, as Bob is and always has been self-obsessed and out for himself, so it's not personal. Still, it feels like Kate is fighting a losing battle and Dad is not helping her at all. He just wanders around with a paper under his arm and doesn't talk to anyone.

I think Dad is very depressed.

To try and make myself drift off tonight, I am fantasising about me and Kay winning the pools, even if we aren't old enough to enter. Imagine if we won the pools? We could buy a huge mansion together and hire servants and buy all our own food and clothes and books, and neither of us would have to see our parents ever again.

Thursday 4th September

Kay and Ray are officially going out together, though they mostly seem to hang around in the rec near Kay's house. Ray's got one of those spindly little mopeds that make a high-pitched buzzing sound when it speeds up. Kay says the moped embarrasses her, but other than that Ray's all right. He's left school now and he's doing an apprenticeship in retail management. Apparently Ray is wittier than he first appears.

Kay and I were on the swings in the kids' playground at the top of the prom after school, while Gerta gambolled around and barked at the slide for some reason.

'Gerta!' Kay kept yelling. 'Sit!'

Gerta always stopped immediately and sat down and started yawning. I'm quite impressed by Kay's authority over Gerta. I have no authority over Bob or Eugene. If anything, it's the other way round.

'Has Ray come over to yours then?' I asked. 'Has he met Gerta?'

'He's met Gerta, all right,' said Kay. 'That's what we do, walk the dog around. But no way is he meeting my mum. She'd make a total show of me. She flirts with everybody.'

'Even someone our age?' I found the thought of Kay's mum flirting quite disturbing in general, let alone with someone young enough to be her son.

'She's incorrigible,' said Kay. 'That's what Dad says, and he's right.'

'So, have you and Ray kissed?' I asked.

'Course we have.' Kay sounded almost bored. 'Loads.'

I tried not to feel jealous, but it was hard not to worry that Kay might grow apart from me now.

'So if Jimmy's a washout,' said Kay, 'what about Dean Carter?'

'That's all too silly for words, Kay. Just thinking about it makes me want to cringe.'

But Kay's attention had wandered. 'Don't look round,' she said then. 'But Dean's over by the war memorial *right* now.'

I somehow stopped myself from turning round. 'What's he doing?' I said. 'Maybe he thinks I'm spying on him. Can he see us? Is he looking over?'

'Not exactly,' said Kay carefully. 'He's . . . with a friend.'

'Who? Is it a girl?'

She hesitated. 'I'm not sure if it is a girl to be honest. They've got all this black backcombed hair and really tight jeans on . . . with rips and chains hanging off them.' She angled her head to see better. 'And those boots with spikes coming out of the heels.'

I couldn't hold out any longer and turned round. Dean was standing with someone laughing, and then the someone turned her face a bit and I recognised her as a girl called Michelle from the sixth form who everyone says is the spitting image of Kate Bush.

'Oh, it's thingy from the sixth form. She looks looks well old,' said Kay, blatantly ogling them, just as Gerta took up barking really loudly. Before we could stop her, she was off, galloping over to Dean and Michelle.

'Gerta!' shouted Kay too late. 'No, Gerta! Sit! Sit!'

But it was too late. Gerta's jaw had clamped round one of the chains on Michelle's jeans and she was dragging her over the grass.

'Bloody hell. Gerta's got a thing about chains,' muttered Kay. 'When we got her at the dogs' home, they told us it was something to do with her past life. Chains make her very angry.'

Kay ran over and somehow dragged Gerta off. But the whole of one leg of Michelle's jeans had been torn away and she was screeching and shouting at Kay. Dean just stood there, a bit useless, but at least he couldn't see me as I had hidden myself inside the kiddie castle and was watching through a little hole in a turret.

Finally, Kay wrestled Gerta away and they came back over. I saw Dean and Michelle walking off, and him trying to put his arm round her but she kept shoving it off.

'Jeez, what were the chances?' said Kay, coming towards me a bit breathless. 'Gerta attacking Dean's new girlfriend.' She frowned at Gerta. 'Bad Gerta!'

'I feel a bit shellshocked,' I said. 'It's as if Gerta was listening to our conversation or something . . .'

Kay looked at me then, and a little smirk appeared on her face. 'To be honest though,' she said. 'If you must wear chains hanging off your jeans, what do you expect. Accident waiting to happen, if you ask me.'

'Exactly,' I said, feeling a lot cheerier now. 'Stupid chains.'

I told Jake about the incident with Dean and Michelle and Gerta and, though he did find it very funny, I had to make him swear he wouldn't let on he knew or Dean would think I was a weird stalker. Jake said Dean's a bit of berk anyway and a dozy sod, and that I could do better, which is a lie, but Jake meant well.

'If you are intent on having a boyfriend, you should go out with someone more like you,' Jake went on. 'That Jimmy, for instance? He's at Oaks now, isn't he? I'm sure I saw him in the canteen.'

I've managed to avoid Jimmy since we've been back, and although he's in my year he's not in any of my lessons, probably because he's clever, which makes it easier, really. Kay has also hinted that his love problem is ongoing so I'm doubly glad I've not encouraged our friendship further.

'I think so,' I said, as though I didn't care. 'I don't get how all that stuff works, so I'm not sure I'm that keen on the idea of a boyfriend now anyway.'

Jake looked slightly relieved when I said that. 'Maybe that's for the best,' he said, which unbeknownst to him was aggravating and made me slightly change my mind about what I had just said.

I've decided to concentrate more this year and make more effort to actually think about the lessons I am in, rather than count the minutes until they're over, and it's only after the last bell rings that I allow myself to mope over the fact that I may always be alone for ever.

Everyone seems to have someone: Jake has Dawn, Kay has Ray, Dean has Michelle, and now Sam is being very secretive and washing his hair more, so I am quite suspicious of his motives. But when I conferred with Kay about that she was quite dismissive of it, and said that unless Sam enrols in a monastery, sooner or later he is going to have a romance, and I might have to come to terms with it.

'Look, you're always going to be Sam's sister,' said Kay. 'Anyway, no one ever stays with their first love, except in the old days or in films. I doubt most girls would put up with all that stuff about scientific equations or when the tide's coming in or going out or whatever. Doesn't matter how many times a boy washes his hair.'

I laughed, feeling better, and started on the tuna sandwich I'd bought for lunch, even though it was only 11.00 a.m., and Kay got out some bread pudding and we sat eating on the chairs by the lockers in silence. But the thing is, Kay has this habit of catching you unawares and asking you about things when you haven't had time to prepare an answer – usually when you're in the middle of a sandwich or a bit of cake.

'I've got a question,' she said, having quickly finished the last morsel of her bread pudding. 'If Jimmy and Dean were together in a house on fire, which one would you want dragged out alive?'

'Jimmy,' I said immediately, dropping half my tuna sandwich on the floor.

Kay looked smug. 'I knew it.'

'But anyway, so what?' I said, flustered. 'That's so unlikely, and it's not as if I'd be the one to visit him in the Burns Unit, as one of his hundreds of love interests would do that.' I stared down at my sandwich as I didn't want to look at Kay, who was rolling her eyes and guffawing at the same time.

'You're funny,' she said. 'But you've missed the point.'

'Really, Kay,' I said grumpily. 'I haven't. Anyway, I am quite happy now just trying not to fail all my tests and having nothing humiliating occur in my life.'

I was determined not to say anything more about my confused feelings for Jimmy. I am no longer going to be a drama queen about these things.

'If you say so.' Kay picked up her school bag just as the bell rang for the end of break. 'I've got art now. I'll see you later.'

I went to my locker and put in the rest of my packed lunch for later. I had maths next and I was in no hurry at all to get there, walking very slowly down the corridor when the double doors at the end opened and Jimmy Jones came through them with his arm in plaster, supported by a sling.

'Jimmy! What've you done to your arm?' I said, forgetting to be indifferent.

He looked down at his sling. 'Fell off my bike.' He looked up at me and said quickly, 'I thought you were avoiding me or something.'

'Oh no, not at all,' I said, as though it was a matter I had given no thought to whatsoever. 'I've just been quite busy . . .'

'Oh, that's good,' Jimmy said. 'So, what have you been doing?'

I shrugged. 'Loads. Can't really remember now. How about you?'

'Nothing much,' said Jimmy, 'Actually, I—'

But at that moment Mr Turing poked his head through the double doors and frowned. 'Lydia,' he said crossly. 'We're all waiting for you. You're late.'

'Better be off,' I said cheerily to Jimmy. 'Sorry about your arm.'

'Thank you.' He smiled. 'Sorry about maths.'

I couldn't help laughing, despite my vow to be cool and aloof. 'See you then,' I said.

'See you,' he said, smiling.

I sat in maths feeling churned up, as once again I didn't know what to think. In the unlikely event that Jimmy is keen on me, I thought, then he'll have to tell me in exact words to my face so I am one hundred per cent sure.

Monday 8th September

Dad announced this evening that he is going away for work. When I was a lot younger he often used to go to America for work and come back with exotic presents – like Indian moccasins and Kicker boots in colours that you can't get in this country.

But he's not going to America this time, he said. He's going to South Shields, which is near Newcastle, for a training course. This seems strange as Dad's been doing the same job for years and I would have thought he'd be able to do it by now and wouldn't need training. But when I started prying as to the exact nature of the training course, Dad shut me down quite quickly by saying it was 'a dull management thing'. This explained his depressed face.

Kate seems pleased that he'll be out of the way as whatever they're talking about in Marriage Guidance hasn't stopped Dad coming home from the off-licence with bottles wrapped in paper. For the first time in ages though, he asked me about school.

'How are you getting on there?' he said. 'Must be your O-levels soon.'

'They're not till I'm sixteen,' I said, pleased that he had asked, but dismayed that he couldn't remember how old I am.

'Oh, are they? I can't keep up with these modern exams,' he said quite jovially. He'd just come in with one of his bottles and unscrewed it, pouring some clear liquid into a glass.

Sam, who was doing some homework of his own, glanced up and gave Dad a look, but he didn't say anything.

'And what do you want to be?' Dad went on, after he'd taken a swig of his drink. 'What job would you like?'

I thought, allowing the many versions of my future to flit through my brain: air hostess, professional cat carer, café owner – or someone who reads all the time, like an editor of novels or a librarian. The last one would be perfect as it wouldn't actually be a job, just a brilliant thing to do that you get paid for.

'Dunno,' I said.

'I think you'd make a marvellous actress!' Dad declared. He looked over at Sam, waving his glass around. 'Don't you think, Sammy? She'd be a wonderful comedy actress. All that flouncing around and the amateur dramatics!' He laughed to himself.

Sam, who not so long ago would have found this funny and agreed with Dad, just looked at him as though he was insane.

'I really don't want to be an actress,' I snapped, as I am far too shy, though I am quite good at voices.

'I think she should work with books,' Sam said, deadly serious. 'You know for a publishers . . . or maybe working in a library.'

'Oh my God, Sam!' I goggled at him. 'I was thinking that too!'

Sam half smiled. 'Well, better crack on and start doing your homework more often then,' he said.

'Yes, yes,' I said, thinking that I already did the homework for that particular job.

'You do need a degree for jobs like that,' Sam added. 'Seriously.'

I knew that, but I couldn't see why. Why, when you're perfectly able to read anyway, do you need to do an exam in it?

'But really. All a librarian does is stamp dates in the backs of the books and then put them away in alphabetical order,' I said. 'That's something I could do right now.'

'I think there's a bit more to it than that.' Sam rolled his eyes.

'Oh, for goodness sake,' said Dad, who was topping up his drink. 'All the people I have ever worked with have absurd levels of qualifications, and many of them are imbeciles. It's obvious that Lydia has a very high IQ. She's terribly clever.' He turned to me. 'I wouldn't worry too much if I were you.'

Sam sighed loudly.

'Do you really think that?' I asked Dad quietly.

Dad stared at me, which was when I noticed his eyes were slightly bloodshot. 'What's that?'

'About me being clever,' I said.

'Yes, my love,' he said. 'Very clever indeed.' He leaned forward. 'Can you do me a favour and see if there's any wine left in the rack in the galley for dinner?'

Sam, who had heard this, shut his book with a snap and looked at me as though he wanted to burst into tears.

Wednesday 10th September

As I can't keep my mouth shut about anything, I have confided in Kay about my last encounter with Jimmy. Of course this made Kay feel quite pleased with herself about knowing what my feelings are even before I do, but then she made it clear that I should not make myself too obviously available and keen to be Jimmy's girlfriend, as boys like to do the chasing.

'Hang on though,' I said. 'Jimmy already has a girlfriend *and* another love interest, you said.'

Kay ignored this as though it was irrelevant. 'Don't be unfriendly,' she went on, 'but always be the one to end a conversation first and walk away.'

'So it's a bit like chess, or Gin Rummy?' I said. 'And the trick is becoming a master of the game.'

'Mistress,' corrected Kay. 'But exactly.'

'Is that how it is with you and Ray?' I asked.

'Sort of,' she said. 'But me and Ray are over.'

'Oh, Kay! Are you all right?'

'I finished with him,' she said. 'To be honest, he was a bit boring and that stupid moped got on my wick. He was good for a trial run though.'

Trial run for who and what? I was going to ask, but Kay was hastily packing up her bag to go to a history lesson, so I didn't get a chance to.

At lunch time I went to the school library to get out a book about the Industrial Revolution as we had a test this afternoon.

It was deserted in there as Wednesdays are Burger and Chips day in the canteen, and even the packed-lunchers eat that on a Wednesday.

Except Jimmy was there.

He was sitting trying to write with his right hand, as his left arm is still in plaster. The cast is covered with messages and signatures, even though he only started this term. I got my book and snuck back past Jimmy, finding a seat where I could sneak a look at him but not too obviously.

I managed to read the bit of the book that I needed to and I even wrote some notes, determined not to look at Jimmy once. But I have very little will power, so I looked up after five minutes, and he was staring right at me, and then he smiled and I couldn't help smiling back.

Jimmy held up his plastered arm. 'You're the only one who hasn't signed my arm,' he said.

'Please be quiet,' the teacher on duty told him, frowning, even though there was no need as the library only had us three in it.

Jimmy got up, wrestled his books into his bag with his un-plastered arm and came over to my table. I tried not to look too pleased.

'Will you sign my arm, Lydia?' he said quietly, sitting down in the chair next to mine and pointing at a spare patch of white on the cast.

I looked at what other people had written. Mostly things from boys like: *When are you having it off?* But loads of girls had signed too, things like: *Get Well Soon, love Cherry.* I wasn't going to put something as dull as that.

In an act of impulse I wrote: *To Jimmy, My Knight in White Plaster*. I did not put any kisses or love or any of that stuff. I thought I'd been witty and vivacious, but then I remembered what Jimmy had done for me at Arnold's party and I wondered if he'd think I meant that.

Jimmy angled his head so that he could see what I'd written, and I had a five-second period of wishing I had just put *Get Well Soon*.

But I could see Jimmy smiling, and felt a pinch of pleasure.

'That is really very good,' said Jimmy, reading it again. 'Did you just think of that?' He looked back up at me. 'You're welcome, by the way.'

I went very pink. I hadn't expected him to realise straight-away. I tried to think of something indifferent to say in return, but Jimmy had such a sweet expression on his face that I just sat there, mute.

'Is everything all right,' he said carefully. 'With your family . . . I mean?'

'Um . . . it's quite complicated,' I said.

Jimmy nodded. 'It's weird seeing your parents with other people. My dad and his girlfriend have huge rows all the time. There's a big age difference. Dad's trying to be Mr Cool Guy, but it isn't him.'

'What does he do to be cool?' I said, intrigued.

Jimmy laughed. 'His clothes, mainly. He thinks he's younger than he is.'

'Thank goodness my dad doesn't dress like a young person,' I said. 'That's one blessing to count.'

Jimmy smiled. 'You're funny, you know.'

'Thanks,' I said, though I didn't think I'd made a joke. 'Is your girlfriend funny too?' I blurted before I could stop myself.

'Who told you about that?' Jimmy said a bit sharply, and it was like someone had pricked the atmosphere with a pin and all the nice bit had rushed out.

'Oh . . . just Kay mentioned,' I said, flustered. 'She only mentioned.'

'Well, I don't have a girlfriend now,' he said. 'We broke up just before the summer.'

'Oh. Sorry,' I said, not very sorry at all.

'It's OK.' Jimmy smiled again. 'I didn't mean to snap.'

I wanted to change the subject, so I nodded at his cast. 'When's that coming off?' I said.

'In a few weeks,' said Jimmy. 'Just before the autumn half term.' He hesitated for a second, then he said, 'What are you up to at half term?'

'I'm hoping to go and stay with my sister,' I said. 'She lives in rooms at Cambridge University.'

'Very nice,' said Jimmy. 'Are you going all week then?'

'Probably not,' I said. To be honest, I haven't yet got an answer out of Elsa, despite my regular reminders of her invite. 'Maybe just a couple of days.'

'OK.' Jimmy sort of bit his lips then. 'Well, maybe one weekend we can go to the sea wall or something . . . with Kay, or maybe not with Kay.'

Maybe not with Kay. Did that mean Jimmy wanted to be on his own with me?

Then I reminded myself of Kay's rules about not showing

you're keen to boys. 'Perhaps,' I said. 'Anyway, I'd better go.' I stood up and shoved my notebook and pen into my bag. 'I hope it all goes well with your arm.'

'Thanks . . .' Jimmy looked as though he was going to say something else, but he didn't and I went to put back the book I'd borrowed. I only allowed myself to look round at him when I was out of the library.

He was staring down at the writing on his arm, smiling.

Elsa finally confirmed a date for a visit from me during half term at the beginning of next month. She made it clear in her last letter that she has a lot of work to do, and parties and events and the odd lecture to attend, but she doesn't mind me sleeping on the sofa in her rooms, as long as I don't talk too much rubbish to her friends and keep out of the way of the woman who comes to clean her rooms, a woman who is known as a 'Bedder'.

Dad, who has spent a lot of time looking anxious and being distant lately, said he thought it was a very good idea and that now that he's got his driving ban lifted, he could take me all the way there in the car, and we could take Elsa out for dinner too.

As much as I used to love being in the car alone with Dad, I had some concerns about his offer, as he has always seen me as a fellow sensitive type and I suspected he might confide in me during the car journey – things that I didn't want to know about Kate, or about his life.

'The thing is Dad,' I said, 'I'm not really a child any more, and Elsa can meet me off the train.'

Dad peered at me through filmy eyes for ages and then picked up a tumbler from the table. I couldn't help noticing his hand, unsteadily clasped around the glass.

'Good idea,' he said eventually, and drained his drink. 'Car's on the blink anyway. That's another bloody fortune to spend.'

Determined to leave things on a sort of agreeable note, I fled from the saloon before we could have a conversation about how grossly expensive life was.

Wednesday 5th November

Cambridge is a bit bleak, I decided as I waited outside the station for Elsa at 4.00 p.m. today. It was sleet-raining, and chocka with a lot of student types in glasses and carrying backpacks, all wearing uninteresting-looking clothes. 'Boffins', as Kay would call them.

I had dressed up in a fake-fur leopardskin jacket and a navy-blue sailor dress – both of which I had got from The Salvation Army charity shop in the high street, and my new Doctor Marten shoes, with pink laces. I had thought long and hard about my wardrobe for this visit and knew with certainty that my regular slapdash T-shirt and jeans would not be suitable, so I had gone for an interesting look, which I thought was bound to be.

Elsa arrived ten minutes after she'd promised on a heavy, cranky-looking bike with a huge basket on the front. She had her dark curly hair in bunches, which were sopping wet from the rain, and a very long checked scarf was wrapped around her neck.

'Quick,' she said, braking and putting one leg on the ground, then squeezing the rain from her bunches. 'Get on!'

'Oh, hello, Elsa!' I said with deliberate enthusiasm.

'Hello,' she said, smiling very quickly. 'Now, get on, will you.'

'On the back of that?' I said warily. 'How far are we going?'

'Only a mile or so,' she said breezily, looking me up and down. 'What's that you're wearing?'

Typical that within a minute Elsa had made me feel daft and wrongly attired. I ignored the question, placed my holdall bag in her basket, and climbed onto the back of the bike. As we set off I put my arms around Elsa's dwindled waist, and worried about snapping her in half if we went fast round a corner.

But like most of my family, Elsa is robust and she has a good grasp of road safety, so I allowed myself to relax slightly and breathe in her Opium perfume as well as the other, more comforting, smell she always seems to have of home-made biscuits – though I am not sure she eats many biscuits these days.

Thankfully the rain had stopped, and the journey was well worth it for the eventual sight of what looked like a stately home with a vast lush lawn in front and a swanky looking doorway and a porter's lodge. Elsa chained up her bike and went to collect something out of a pigeon hole in the lodge. Then she took a Bluebeard's keychain out of her pocket and jangled it.

'Home sweet home,' she said. 'Welcome to Magdalene College.'

A man in a uniform with a small hat on nodded at us as we went past and smiled at me. 'Afternoon, miss,' he said, as though Elsa and I were young aristocrats, gadding about in an old-times film.

There were endless stairs up to Elsa's rooms, the ancient stone kind that make your footsteps echo, though Elsa was bounding up them two at a time in bare feet – having taken off her soaked plimsolls on the ground floor. In my heavy DMs I felt a bit like a small elephant lumbering up after a gazelle.

A girl was sitting cross-legged outside Elsa's door, weeping.

'Cressida?' Elsa said, dropping her plimsolls and kneeling down to embrace the girl quite passionately. 'What's the matter, darling?'

'Oliver was out *all* night after the Swine's birthday do,' wailed Cressida, who has one of those faces that looks extremely pretty while crying. Cartoon tears were literally plopping out of her eyes and rolling like teeny glass beads down her face.

'No!' Elsa darted a quick look at me, before pulling Cressida's head forcefully to her bosom. 'What a pig. Where did he go, do you think?'

'Oh, that awful Clare College cow, Prue . . .' said Cressida, wiping her nose with the sleeve of her jumper. 'Plain as a pikestaff. Why, oh why??'

'Let's have a nice cup of cocoa,' said Elsa soothingly, and she got to her feet.

Cressida noticed me. 'Who's this?' she said, a bit sulkily.

'Oh, just my sister Lydia,' said Elsa, waving a hand in my direction. 'Don't worry about her.'

Had I not been intrigued by Cressida's drama, I would have felt more offended by this. Also I am well used to being dismissed by Elsa, especially when other more glamorous people are present.

Inside Elsa's rooms, I was desperate to investigate each

part of what looked to me like a kind of once-grand hotel suite slightly gone shabby, but most definitely with a lot of character. There was a large sofa covered with a striped blanket, and wooden floors on which lay a familiar-looking Turkish rug. A huge old fireplace in which some logs were still smoking slightly, and above it a mantelpiece with a smeared gilt-edged mirror and photographs of people in black ties and white shirts and ball dresses, holding champagne glasses. On the floor by the sofa, a half-drunk bottle of red wine stood next to two tumblers and an ashtray brimming with cigarette butts. Behind the sofa was a huge window, with a window seat and piles of papers, and mugs and a plate with crumbs on it.

'Sit down!' ordered Elsa, removing her jumper and giving me a glimpse of her ribs.

Both Cressida and I did as we were told, though Cressida curled up comfortably on the sofa, leaving not very much space for me. In the end I slid down onto the floor, while her feet in socks hovered by my face.

Elsa had disappeared through a door off the sitting room, which left me alone with Cressida.

'How old are you?' she asked. 'Twelve, thirteen?'

'I'm fourteen,' I said, pulling my leopardskin coat around me as there was a chill in the room, despite the smoking logs in the grate.

'Hmmm.' Cressida didn't seem very interested in that. 'Isn't Elsa wonderful?'

'Yes,' I said, as saying anything else didn't seem worthwhile to a stranger.

'Boys are vile,' went on Cressida. 'Don't ever get romantically embroiled with one. I wish I were a lesbian. Girls are so lovely.'

I thought of Jimmy, and suspected that Cressida was a drama queen.

Finally Elsa appeared with a tray bearing mugs of cocoa and a lardy-looking fruitcake on a plate.

'Stollen,' she said. 'Larissa has had a visit from her Austrian cousin again.'

'Indigestible,' said Cressida, breaking off a large bit of stollen and cramming it into her mouth as though she hadn't eaten for a year.

I took a mug of cocoa, which of course was exactly the right temperature and consistency, as Elsa is a perfectionist. It was delicious, sugar-syrupy and made with gold top milk, which is how she always makes it. I was relieved that she was at least getting some fat into her body and hadn't lowered herself to skimmed milk, which is disgustingly watery.

'So what are we going to do about Oliver?' said Elsa, inhaling her cocoa.

'The trouble is this whole engagement thing,' said Cressida. 'It won't be easy to disentangle myself from that.'

'But that was when he was drunk, Cress,' said Elsa. 'Doesn't really count. And you are a bit young to get married.'

'Yes . . . but he didn't take it back the next day, did he?' Cressida persisted. 'He meant it, even though he was sozzled. He must love me, deep down.'

Elsa shot me a look, warning me not to butt in. A good thing, as I had been about to. Cressida was seeming to me more and more pathetic and grasping at straws as far as this Oliver was concerned.

'Well . . . but *you* could always break it off then,' said Elsa, who was also sitting on the floor, resting her head against the end bit of the sofa. 'Then you'd see.'

'Oh, I don't know!' cried Cressida, who didn't seem pleased by obvious solutions, wanting to wallow in her problem for as long as possible. 'It's so hard!'

Elsa didn't answer, but looked down at her cocoa a bit impatiently.

'Who's the Swine?' I asked at this point; it was the one bit of Cressida's story that interested me.

Elsa, in the midst of a mouthful of her drink, started to laugh and choke a bit, and even Cressida cheered up with a high-pitched shriek of amusement.

'Oh, Lydia,' said Elsa, once she had recovered from her coughing fit. 'You *are* funny sometimes.'

As pleased as I was to be considered funny, I noticed that they didn't actually explain about the Swine, and I was left with visions of a pig wearing a bow tie, which actually is quite funny.

I am now settled down on Elsa's sofa underneath her spare duvet, enjoying the smell of Elsa's Opium-biscuit mix. Bits of old breadcrumbs are digging into me, and I discovered on rummaging down the sides of the sofa – safely after she had gone to bed – an invitation to an Arts Club Review, and a note to someone called Bash, which is blurry as she has spilt something on it, asking him to meet her in the

Copper Kettle at 4.00 p.m. I am devouring these snippets of Elsa's life as they might give me a clue as to who she is here. Or in fact, who she is at all.

Thursday 6th November

This morning, Elsa ran through her entire circle of friends, which seems to be huge.

'How do you make that many friends?' I asked. 'Do you just go up and talk to people and then become friends?'

Elsa laughed. 'I don't know really. I dislike quite a lot of them. I think you start off with a lot of people and then eliminate the ones who are pointless.'

'What about Cressida?' I asked, cautiously, as after Cressida left last night Elsa had not discussed her.

'Oh, she's a nightmare,' said Elsa without hesitation. 'I liked her at first – she seemed very confident and fun – but she's insane. She and that Oliver idiot are constantly breaking up and then reuniting, and he's a complete rat. He's sleeping with a brainiac from another college, a girl called Prue. Everyone knows this, but Cressida keeps forgiving him. I am so bored of the whole thing.'

'What about you?' I said. 'Have you got a man or something?'

'Or something,' said Elsa quickly. 'Nothing to write home about.'

She stalked off into the kitchen, leaving me with a few urgent questions, which obviously wouldn't be answered.

'Now,' she said, coming back into the sitting room. 'I've cleared the day for you, even though I should do some work on an essay, and we're going to the shops, and then the café in town where a few people usually gather. This evening, my friend Carlos is having birthday drinks in his digs near Trinity. He's invited about three hundred people so it might be a nightmare. But you must meet Carlos, he is so lovely and handsome and sweet.'

I was smiling at her, trying to arrange my face. She was hurling a lot of information at me. 'Will there be food to eat at the party?' I said.

'What?' said Elsa.

'Food. Like dinner.'

'Oh, probably not. Maybe some crisps or something.'

'So when will we have an evening meal?' I persisted. I am not sure why, but I think it was to normalise everything. Food felt like a life raft.

'I'll make you some eggs on toast before we go, if you want,' said Elsa, then yawned. 'To be honest, I haven't had a proper dinner since I left home. I'd almost forgotten all about it.'

This made sense of her thinness, I supposed. It depressed me to think that you could just forget about something as crucial as proper meals, which are honestly the main high-light of my life.

'Don't worry, Lyds. You won't starve,' said Elsa, catching my expression, which might have been forlorn. 'I did promise Dad that I would look after you.'

'I'd better get dressed for our trip to town,' I said quickly, not wanting to think about Dad being protective, not when I had come here to forget about him.

Elsa disappeared into her room and I got dressed. I was just deciding whether to wear fresh tights, or rinse the gusset of yesterday's, when she appeared back in the room, holding her make-up bag.

'I meant to ask,' she said, sitting down on the sofa and getting out her mascara. 'How are things on the Good Ship Ghastly?'

'Getting worse,' I said, smelling my tights. 'Dad's OK when Kate isn't there, but miserable when she is.'

'Oh,' said Elsa. 'That bloody woman. No wonder he's drinking more.'

I decided not to point out to Elsa that Dad's drinking might be the root of all our problems at the moment, as for some reason she didn't seem to want to see that.

'Well . . .' I said at last. 'It's not all her fault.'

'Huh!' Elsa huffed.

'But seriously, Elsa. Dad is quite horrible to her.'

'He's not horrible to you, is he?'

I shook my head. 'He doesn't really say much to me any more.'

'Oh dear.' Elsa unscrewed her mascara. 'He's spiralling into a depression.'

'Yes, I know,' I said, a bit annoyed that Elsa, who didn't even live on *Lady Beatrice*, was stating the obvious.

I've changed my mind. Cambridge is the cutest place I've ever seen. Everything is so old and pretty and quite grand at the same time. There are lots of little alleyways with interesting shops and a big bookshop called Heffers. I had twenty pounds from Dad and a bit from The Smugglers' Tavern, and Elsa took me to an antique clothes shop just a bit out of town called 'Tiger Lily'. The shop was full of stuff from the 1930s and 40s and I bought a blue rayon dress with a pattern of packs of cards on it, which Elsa declared fitted me exactly.

'You've definitely changed shape,' she said, looking at my chest. 'You've actually got a figure now.'

I hadn't really given my body much thought lately, but when I looked down at myself, there was a definite hump in the chest area.

'Have you got a boyfriend?' Elsa asked unexpectedly, adjusting the neckline of the dress a bit.

'Of course not,' I said, thinking with a bit of a lurch about Jimmy, and our conversation in the school library.

'But you do like boys, don't you?' she asked.

I sighed. 'Yes. I'm just not sure they like me.'

'Who?' she said sharply. 'Who doesn't like you?'

I bit my lip. 'No one . . . Well, it's more that I can't tell if they do. How can you know?'

'Don't ask me,' she said. 'It is a bit confusing, isn't it?'

'There is a boy,' I said, now desperate to share. I told Elsa about Jimmy and his dad having a baby even though he's old, and how Jimmy had stuck up for me at Arnold's but how it was all so confusing and I expected Elsa to be dismissive.

'Well,' she said after a minute. 'I can't believe my little sister got drunk for a start.'

'I didn't mean to,' I said.

Elsa raised an eyebrow. 'Jake had no right to be horrible to you,' she said then. 'If I'd been there I would have punched him in the face.'

'Would you?' I said, quite thrilled that Elsa would have been so gallant on my behalf.

'Of course.' She stuck her pretty nose in the air. 'How dare he!'

I didn't answer, as Elsa wouldn't want to hear that Jake did have a point. It was better just to be quiet about it.

'But that Jimmy does sound nice, defending you like that,' Elsa went on. 'In my experience, boys generally don't do nice things for girls unless they like them.'

'But how do you behave with boys, Elsa?' I asked. 'How are you supposed to *be*?'

Elsa smiled. 'I suppose if they're the right one, then you don't have to try to *be* anything except yourself.'

'You have the same parents?' Carlos was holding a bottle of champagne, looking between me and Elsa, a little flabbergasted. 'But you are so different.'

'Nope, she's my flesh and blood,' said Elsa. I waited for her to add 'unfortunately' but she was smiling, which was confusing.

'You are both just lovely,' said Carlos diplomatically. He poured champagne into my glass up to the brim and then turned to Elsa. 'So. Is HE here?'

I had taken quite a few sips of my champagne, but my ears distinctly pricked up at this.

'Little ears,' said Elsa, in a sing-song voice, catching my eye.

'You don't need to worry about me,' I said, holding out my glass. 'I'm drinking champagne.'

'Carlos, show Lydia your roof terrace,' Elsa said quite firmly then. 'And get her some lime cordial. I don't want to get arrested for allowing a fourteen-year-old to become drunk and disorderly.'

Carlos looked delighted. 'Oh! My terrace, Lydia! You can see the stars!'

I didn't want to hurt his feelings by pointing out that I could see the stars most nights from the skylight in my cabin and they weren't a big deal. He looked so pleased at the thought of impressing me.

'Don't drink any of that,' Elsa whispered, nodding at the glass in my hand. 'I don't want to have to leave early to take you back to my rooms.'

She needn't have bothered. I had already decided that champagne was quite bitter and was giving me indigestion.

The fact is, the highpoint of the evening was Carlos's cat, Rodriguez – Carlos calls him Rigo for short. He's short-haired and pure black with amber eyes. A sort of Royal version of Eugene. Rigo – like most cats, I've noticed – recognised me as a friend and kept me company on the roof terrace, winding himself round and round my legs. It felt quite homely.

As I looked up at the stars with the hubbub of Carlos's party through the French doors, I thought about the possibility of being someone else, somewhere else. One day. Where would I be? Where would Kay?

And then I thought of Jimmy Jones and it was as though part of my stomach had fallen off a cliff. I knew I shouldn't think about Jimmy, but could he really like me? I resolved to continue with Kay's rules after half term, just in case.

I was deep in my thoughts when Carlos appeared at the windows.

'Lydia!' he called. 'You must come. It's the B-52s! We are all dancing!'

He pulled me off my seat, which was immediately taken by Rigo, and through the windows to a room full of candlelight and people jumping up and down on the spot, throwing their arms around and shouting, 'Rock Lobster!'

Elsa, who was swaying next to an extremely tall and fairhaired man with glasses, gave me a dizzy smile and even though it was all quite overwhelming, I felt joyful. It seemed as though I was on the edge of something better . . . something like that.

Elsa and I walked back to her rooms through rows of nice old houses, across big grassy lawns, through tall iron gateways, on cobbled streets. It was magical.

'Did HE come in the end?' I asked her as we arrived at her porter's lodge.

'HE came, he saw, he disappeared,' she said, and sighed, taking her keys out of her little velvet bag. 'Attraction is the devil, you know. You must be careful, Lydia.' Elsa lurched back a little into me, a bit tipsy.

I straightened her up, thinking it might be too late to be careful now. 'I've had a brilliant time,' I said. 'It's really taken me out of myself.'

Elsa paused and then gently pinched my cheek and gave me a kiss, which ended up on my ear. 'Lovely,' she said. 'You deserve to have a brilliant time.'

It's my last night here and I am already used to Elsa's biscuit sofa and the way the shadows cast in this room at night. I am trying to think of what coming to stay with Elsa has meant, and I think it means I can see a bit of the future, where I am grown up, when I only have my own life to worry about.

Thursday 13th November

I am having breakfast in the Wimpy today. It was not even 7.00 a.m. when I got here and now I'm sitting on a really high stool facing the high street and eating a custard doughnut, which I don't want, but you can't sit in and not order anything and I only had enough for one thing. I stood outside the door for ten minutes to wait for it to open and the woman who turns on all the lights and appliances gave me a look when she let me in, as if I was a runaway or a delinquent. That's because normally only people who have finished night shifts in their jobs are there before 7.00 a.m. Not schoolgirls with hair like Worzel Gummidge.

It's freezing, and it's hours till school starts, but I had to leave *Lady Beatrice* before anyone else got up today, because of what I heard last night that I wasn't meant to. And I can never UNHEAR it.

It happened when I had a bath. Normally you have to write down on a bit of paper and Sellotape it to the fridge if you want to have a bath on *Lady Beatrice* – about a week before you want one. That's because only one person per evening can have a proper bath as the tiny immersion heater takes hours to get the water hot enough. Most mornings I rush into the bathroom very quickly and rub lukewarm water all over my body whilst standing on a towel, and then rush out again and put on my uniform and go to school. But last night no one had Sellotaped notification on the fridge. Actually, there was no one at home at all for a change, and

I was cold and consumed by the thought of a nice big hot bath so I seized my opportunity.

I took my book in with me. It's by *Bestselling Horror Author* Stephen King (this is what the cover says, along with *Now a Major Motion Picture*) and it's called *Carrie*. It has a picture of a teenage girl with wild eyes and what seems like a whole bucket of blood poured over her head. I have been informed before by Elsa, whose book it is, that *Carrie* is certainly not for the faint-hearted and she didn't think I had the stamina for it. However, since living on *Lady Beatrice* I am used to horror stories and can't imagine that anything in *Carrie* is worse than an unexpected and large drop of icy water on your nose in the middle of the night. This is like being attacked in the dark by a stalactite.

I used the last of Sally's Matey bubblebath, which I didn't feel too guilty about as Sally has more baths than me so it actually evens out. I'd run it so hot that my flesh was quickly ruckled and ribbed like a prune stone and I felt extremely pleasant and woozy and shut my eyes, soon throwing *Carrie* down onto the floor. But then I heard voices through the cupboard in between the bathroom and the galley, and one of them was Kate's and it was slightly haranguing.

'Have you got the money for Sally's school trip to Avebury and Stonehenge?' she was asking.

There was the sound of clinking and then the fridge opening. 'No bloody ice again.' It was Dad, who seemed in a bad mood. The fridge door slammed shut again.

'Charlie,' Kate said quite firmly. 'Did you hear me?'

'Yes,' said Dad, stretching the word out to sound as bored and weary as possible.

'Well? The school needs it before the end of this week. Everyone in her class is going.'

'Right,' said Dad. 'That might be a bit tricky at the moment, Kate.'

'I'll just take some of out of our savings account, shall I?' Kate said matter-of-factly, ignoring this.

There was a short silence, and then Dad said, 'Good luck with that, darling.'

Another silence and then, 'Don't tell me you've spent it all.'

'OK, I won't tell you that if you like.' I heard Dad take a large slurp of whatever he was drinking with no ice.

'We had four thousand pounds in that account!' Kate went on. 'The money my parents gave us when we got married.'

'Yes,' said Dad. 'Gone, I'm afraid. We do have rather a lot of outgoings.'

'Well, when do you get paid?'

'Ah well, you see . . .' he said. 'I haven't been paid for two months now.'

'What?' said Kate. 'Why not?'

'One doesn't tend to get paid when one is unemployed.'

I sat up in the bath and the whole of my top half was freezing. Goose bumps ran all the way up my arms. I tried to breathe properly in the steamy damp of the windowless bathroom and thought I would faint from the effort.

'Charlie. Have you been sacked?' Kate's voice was panicky

and shrill and I felt everything she was feeling. I hated Dad in that moment.

A drop of water plopped out of the bath tap.

'Oh . . . I'd grown to loathe that job anyway,' Dad said, then. 'I'll get another one.'

'At your age?' Kate hissed. 'I don't think there's much demand for pensionable alcoholics these days. Particularly as most of your brain cells have clearly been destroyed.'

'That's actually rather witty for you, Kate,' Dad replied.

'Well, *you* can tell your children,' she said, deciding to rise above this. 'I'm certainly not going to.'

'I have no intention of telling them anything,' said Dad pompously. 'No need to worry them.'

'Worry them?' Now Kate laughed, a little hysterically. 'That child carries the weight of your bloody worries on her shoulders, and she still trusts you, you know that, don't you?'

What child? I thought. Did she mean me? How awful to be talked about in this way. I put my fingers over my eyes and my throat felt thick with trying to breathe. I imagined getting out of my bath and coming out with a towel on and having to walk past Kate and my father, and I did actually want to be sick.

'Right,' said Kate, as Dad had refused to answer her outburst. 'I'm taking the car and I'm picking up the girls from their piano lesson and I'd rather you weren't here when I get back. I don't care where you go, just *go*.'

I slightly cared where Dad went, even though I hated him right then, and at the same time I wanted him to go away too.

'Right you are,' said Dad, and then there was the sound of pouring again and Kate was muttering, a bit breathlessly. It sounded like she was putting on her coat.

I strained to hear, and then, '. . . continue killing yourself. Do what you like,' she said.

'Many thanks.' My father sounded as though he'd just been handed a pound of sausages by the butcher.

With a muffled sort of roar Kate stomped out of the galley. I waited and heard her footsteps on the deck above me, while I lay there with the water going colder and the bubbles evaporating. I stared for a long time down at the wrinkles on my toes, listening to Dad roaming about opening and shutting the fridge.

'Good boy,' I heard him say after a bit, followed by the sound of Bob mewling. 'You're a sweet boy, aren't you, underneath? Eh, Bob?'

I was determined not to soften, even though I could picture Bob's chin being tickled and the ecstasy on his sweet face.

Eventually I climbed shivering out of the bath, trying not to make any noise, and I went down the ladder. I rubbed myself dry with the towel. When I looked down and saw the book, and Carrie's head with the bucket of blood all over it, it seemed very ominous and I felt all the horror of what Dad had said, and that he'd said it as though it was nothing.

After a few more minutes the saloon door banged shut and then there was complete silence. I shot out of the bathroom in my towel, picked up both Bob and Eugene, who were just finishing up their bowls of Whiskas and dislike being touched straight after food, and I rushed with them to my cabin and locked the door before anyone else got home.

Then I put on practically all my clothes and climbed up into my bunk.

But I didn't sleep at all. I didn't even turn on Radio Luxembourg. All I could do was stare up through the icy skylight at the moon, while Bob and Eugene snored either side of me, and wonder why I couldn't even cry.

I'm so tired. My eyelids keep closing. The woman who opened the door to me earlier came and hovered next to me a little while ago, and I had to shut my diary quickly.

'Are you all right, dear?' she asked kindly.

'Yes, thank you.' I was very polite. I saw her frown slightly because I knew I didn't sound like the sort of girl who should be in the Wimpy at this hour.

'Here you are then.' She put a mug of something in front of me. 'Nice hot chocolate.' Then she patted me on the shoulder and went back behind the counter.

'Thank you very much,' I remembered to say, but she was too far away to hear.

Friday 14th November

I didn't even want any of Kay's mum's home-made Swiss Roll that she brought to school yesterday. This of course alerted Kay to a problem, as I have never been known to turn down free cakes.

'Tell me,' she said, while we were sat on the playing fields at break.

It's so nice to have a friend who notices things and asks you concerned questions. Just Kay asking made me feel a bit better.

'My dad's been sacked from his job, Kay.' I suddenly blushed.

'Oh, my Lord.' Her eyes went very wide.

'I'm not supposed to know,' I told her. 'I overheard him tell Kate.'

Kay wrapped up her Swiss Roll and put it in her bag. 'He doesn't know you know?' she said.

I shook my head. 'No one else knows either. Dad told Kate he didn't want to worry us.'

'Your poor dad.' Kay looked quite upset. 'He's such a gentleman and really kind. It's not fair.'

I thought of how ungentlemanly and unkind Dad had been to Kate.

'Sometimes Dad is a bastard,' I said then, and Kay's mouth dropped open.

'No!' she said. 'He's lovely, your dad.'

'Not when he's drunk.'

Kay looked a bit out of her depth for once.

'He's so nasty,' I said, distressed. 'But he isn't nasty really.'

'I know.' Kay took hold of my hand. 'It's the drink talking. My nan used to say that about my granddad when he'd had a few.'

'The thing is, he just doesn't stop,' I said. 'He pretends he has, or maybe he tries not to, but he can't seem to help it.'

'Tell Elsa,' Kay said, and gripped my hand. 'Or Harry. Let's face it. No one's going to have a bloody clue, but at least they're older, and a problem shared and all that.'

'Maybe,' I said. 'Maybe I will tell them.'

'And just remember,' added Kay, 'my mother talks to cuddly toys.'

I laughed. Kay is not a huggy type of person, but I nearly burst into tears with gratitude and the effort of not hugging her. 'I just don't know what will happen now,' I said. 'It's going to be ten times worse than it was.'

'Look, your dad will have another job in no time. He's clever, isn't he?' she went on. 'He just needs to pull himself together a bit. Don't always think the worst, Lyds. Think the best.'

I smiled, but not properly. I couldn't quite do it.

'He'd never let you starve. Nor would Harry. Or Sam,' Kay went on.

'Sam would enjoy letting me starve, probably,' I said. I was trying to make a joke as it seemed more normal to make a joke, but Kay didn't laugh.

'You're wrong,' she said. 'Sam would do anything for you.'

'Hmm,' I said, too glum to agree with her, and then Kay

started talking about Jimmy to change the subject to a nicer one, I suppose.

Jimmy hasn't been at school so much since his plaster came off, and Kay said she thought his mum wasn't too well and Jimmy might be taking some extra time off and the school knows all about it. It's almost a good thing I have so much else to worry about or I would be more crestfallen at Jimmy disappearing, but there's only so much I can fit into my brain to fret about these days.

'What's wrong with Val, d'you think?' I asked Kay.

She shrugged. 'I think she's a bit, you know . . .'

'A bit what?'

'Just . . . Mum says that Val gets a bit down every so often, that's all.'

'Are absolutely everyone's parents a bit strange?' I said. 'It's beginning to feel like it.'

'I know,' Kay said wearily. 'Join the club, Jimmy!'

I remembered Jimmy asking about my family and being interested, and I wondered if maybe I should pluck up the courage to go and do that for him. Val did invite me over that time in the junk shop, after all.

After school I went past the boatyard where Harry works, and dawdled outside the fence for a bit until I spotted him. He came out of the big shed where they mend boat parts with an older man who was wearing dirty overalls and they both leaned up against a boat that was lying on its side like a wooden whale. Harry was rolling a cigarette and the older man said something to him and Harry laughed. I realised

I didn't want to say anything about Dad to Harry, even though this is why I was dawdling outside, because Harry looked carefree in that moment. Maybe Dad will get another job soon, or they'll give him back his old one? I thought, and telling Harry, Sam or Elsa would just cause unnecessary worry.

And maybe this way, I can pretend I don't know either, and soon I will just have imagined it.

This way of thinking is called Denial. But there was a programme on TV about people with incurable diseases who were in denial, and some experts were saying that sometimes it can help these people get on with the lives they've got left because as far as they're concerned they're not that ill at all.

I know it's not quite the same, and that having no job isn't a disease, but that does sort of make sense to me.

Monday 17th November

Imagine if you knew exactly what was going to happen to you every day. Like Kate's dinner rota, and knowing that if tomorrow is Tuesday then it's Ham Salad. I suppose at least you'd have time to prepare yourself or come to terms with it, and this would be quite sensible if tomorrow was Wednesday and Cauliflower Cheese, which as I've mentioned before is vile. But anyway, I remember Elsa saying after Mum died how none of us had known it was going to happen and how even if we had known, we wouldn't have felt any differently afterwards, but we would have worried a lot more before.

Today was one of those days that you don't see coming, though maybe deep down, if I really think about it, maybe I should have.

I had a funny feeling after school, a bit scared, and I wondered if this was my sixth sense again. I asked Kay if she wanted to sit in the Wimpy and people-watch, but she said she had to get home to feed Gerta as her mum and dad were going over to her nan's care home again. So I walked home by myself, my feeling of dread getting stronger the closer I got.

Lady Beatrice was deserted and very quiet. And even before I set foot on deck I knew there was something wrong. Jake's bike was gone, and I know he doesn't cycle to school now as everyone's bikes get nicked when they do that . . . And the hatch opening was all closed up, which meant definitely that no one was home.

With a bit of effort I pushed the hatch open, as it gets stuck on its runners and you have to put all your body weight against it to get it moving again, during which you can often fall down the stairs or end up hanging in mid-air.

Down below, Kate must have done a frenzy of housework as everything was unusually spick and span. The sofa was cleared of all its clutter and the ratty Indian rug had been shaken, Hoovered and was lying straight. The trestle table was wiped spotless and the benches had been pushed underneath. The old record player on the sideboard was shut, with all Harry's and Dad's records lined neatly up next to it.

It was when I walked through to the kitchen that my stomach properly tightened. The mug tree was gone. The sandwich toaster too. And the Kenwood Chef. The small shelf containing recipe books was empty. I looked in the cupboard below the sink and saw that half the plates were missing. On the cork noticeboard, all the photographs of Kate and her kids were gone too, leaving only one of me and Sam as small children sitting on a sea wall somewhere, covered in mud. I stared at this photo and at us, completely unaware of what was in the future and just playing with mud. I was so small and happy, I thought.

I came out of the kitchen and went through the saloon to where mine, Erica and Sally's cabins are . . . and Kate and Dad's. At this point my heart was beating so loudly it made my ears block up. I gently pushed open the sliding door to Dad's cabin, just in case he was in there, passed out on the bed, and would wake up and start shouting. But when I put my head round the door, the bed was empty and made and the door to the makeshift wardrobe opposite was open. Inside it I saw a few of Dad's shirts on wire hangers, next to a row of empty hangers. All Kate's clothes had gone.

'Oh no,' I whispered, also seeing that her bottles and jars were gone from the shelf above the bed and the large photograph of her children too.

I didn't really need to look in Erica and Sally's cabin, but I did anyway. The whole cabin was stripped bare, except for two mildewed duvets and bare pillows. All trace of them had vanished. It had taken me a while to get to like Erica and Sally, but seeing their dolls and stuffed animals and Disney duvet covers all gone made me feel quite sick.

And then I went into my own cabin and I saw the note on my fold-down table, in Kate's handwriting:

SORRY, LYDIA

That was all. No explanation, no phone number to call, nothing.

Kate had gone. She'd waited till Dad had gone off to wherever he spent his days now, and till Sam and I were at school . . . and Harry? Harry was skippering a boat, he'd told us yesterday.

Kate had been so careful about it. She must have been planning it for ages. And now she had vanished.

The worst thing was going back up on deck and then down to Jake's cabin. I knew what I would find, but a tiny bit of me hoped that maybe his things would still be there, that he wouldn't have gone too.

But Jake's cabin was echoey and empty like the others.

Jake had been sort of my friend and sort of my brother. He was never going to be Sam or Harry but he was definitely a person in my life. Jake had helped me see things in a different way.

But he'd vanished too.

Back down in the saloon, I finally sat down in shock on the sofa, only registering Bob who was cantering down the stairs towards me, followed by Eugene, on his awkward back legs that make him look like he's limping.

I picked them both up and buried my face into their fur. They must have known it was an emergency as they didn't attack each other as they usually do. I held them to feel them purring and warm.

And then, suddenly, I knew I couldn't be here. For some reason I was sure that Dad didn't know and he would get home drunk and then just get drunker. For the first time I was properly scared of my father.

I put the cats down and stroked them, and with Kate's note still in my hand I left without really knowing where I was going.

First I walked to the phone box at the end of the quay and I dialled Kay's number, but her mum answered and said Kay couldn't come to the phone.

'Can I take a message?' she said a bit sharply.

'Just . . . say Lydia called, thank you,' I said, feeling a bit desperate and wondering where Kay was if she wasn't at home.

I stayed in the phone box for a bit, thinking I must telephone Elsa – she'd given me a special number to call if absolutely necessary. I thought, She'll know what to do. But I didn't phone. I couldn't bear for someone to say she was busy too.

I just wanted to walk and walk until I was grown up and this was no longer happening.

I started going down the promenade and to the park. In the distance I could see one person sitting on a bench looking out to the end of the estuary. Otherwise it was deserted.

It was very cold and my coat wasn't warm enough. It's getting a bit tight as I seem to have got a lot taller and less skinny since Kate bought it for me, all that time ago. I felt sad and angry. Kate had been kind and thoughtful some-times, but she had been horrible too. I didn't know what to think.

I was quite far down the promenade now, it was feeling even colder and I wondered what I was doing. I should be with people. There was nobody here, except for that person on the bench. As I got a bit closer I saw it was a boy.

And then I realised. The boy was Jimmy. He was wearing a cagoule and jeans, and skateboarding plimsolls.

He hadn't seen me; he was still looking over at the sea, with his hands in his pockets. I wondered if I could just run back in the other direction without him knowing I was ever there, but I couldn't move. I just stared at his trainers.

And then he turned round.

I lifted a hand in a sort of wave. •

'Lydia?' he said, sitting more upright and taking his hands out of his pockets. He craned forward at me, frowning. 'What's the matter?'

'I . . .' I couldn't speak. For the first time probably in my entire life I couldn't get the words out.

Jimmy got up quickly. 'What's happened?' he said, coming towards me.

'My stepmother has just left for good,' I managed to get out, still gripping the note. 'I don't know what to do. There's no one at home.' I swallowed and started shivering almost uncontrollably.

And then Jimmy was in front of me and he put both his arms round me and pulled me into his cagoule, and he smelled nice, of washing powder. He didn't say anything for a bit, just held me until I stopped shivering.

'Your coat's too small for you,' he said into my hair.

'I know,' I said, and couldn't help laughing a bit.

Jimmy gently pulled away from me, but his hands were rubbing my arms. 'Where's your dad?' he said. 'Is he coming home from work?'

I shook my head. 'I'm not sure. He doesn't always come straight home.' I didn't tell him that Dad didn't go to work any more and could be anywhere.

'What about your brothers?' said Jimmy. 'And your sister?'

'Harry's out sailing, and Sam is . . . probably on *Philomena* with Ben,' I told him. 'And Elsa is far away in Cambridge.'

'Elsa's a nice name.' Jimmy paused. 'Not as nice as Lydia though.' I could have sworn he went slightly pink in his cheeks when he said that.

I stared at him. His hands were still gently rubbing my arms and it felt nice. 'It's not just Kate going,' I said. 'It's Jake and Sally and Erica. I quite liked them.'

'I'm sorry,' he said. 'Complicated families.'

I thought then of what Kay had said earlier about Jimmy's mum.

Jimmy did the top button of my coat up for me. Then he said, 'Shall we go back to *Lady Beatrice* and make a cup of tea. You're in shock.'

The thought of Jimmy somehow encountering my father was quite excruciating, but maybe it didn't matter right now. There were bigger things that mattered. I stuffed Kate's note into my coat pocket and let Jimmy put his arm around me.

Dad wasn't back on *Lady Beatrice*, but Harry came home from the boatyard, and he found Jimmy and me sitting on the sofa next to the stove, which Jimmy had stoked up.

'This is my friend Jimmy,' I said, as Harry hadn't met him yet. 'Jimmy, this is my brother Harry.'

Jimmy sort of smiled and nodded at my brother, who nodded back a bit suspiciously. Then Harry looked around the saloon. 'She's gone then?' he said.

'Did you know?' I said.

'Not exactly,' said Harry, taking off his donkey jacket and throwing it onto a chair by the table. 'But I've thought something was going on for months. Strange behaviour . . . that kind of thing.'

'And Dad's lost his job,' I said, before I could stop myself.

I looked at Harry in horror, who didn't seem surprised at all.

'Yes,' he said. 'And that.'

'I thought I was the only one who knew.'

'Oh, Lydia,' said Harry.

At this point Jimmy's eyes were wide open and he looked at Harry and then at me.

'My dad's got a drink problem,' I said to Jimmy.

'Lydia . . .' began Harry.

'There's no point in being in denial,' I said, realising what a daft idea that had been. 'But what if Dad doesn't come home?'

'He will.' Harry rubbed my knee. 'He always does.'

Jimmy was quiet and sipped his tea, but he very slightly knocked my leg with his, to show it was all right, and I thought he probably knew about Dad anyway.

'I don't blame Kate for leaving.' I reached over to my coat and got the crumpled note from Kate out of my pocket, holding it out to Harry.

'Oh God,' he said. 'I'm sorry. Maybe you should ask Kay if you can stay with her tonight.' Harry was obviously thinking of how Dad might be when he finally came home.

'I don't know . . .' I said, thinking of Kay's mum.

'You can stay at ours,' Jimmy told me. 'We've got a spare room.'

'Are you sure your mum won't mind?' I said, and glanced at Harry.

'She'll probably be asleep,' Jimmy said. 'She sleeps a lot.'

Harry nodded at us. 'Please look after her,' he said to Jimmy.

At that moment Sam came thundering down the stairs and through the saloon door. It was nearly 6.30 p.m. and he looked like he hadn't a care in the world. I bet he'd been hanging round on *Philomena* with Ben. He practically seems to live there now.

'She's gone, hasn't she?' he said. 'I knew it.'

'I'm sure you're very happy about it, Sam,' I told him flatly. 'It's what you've always wanted.'

Then Sam gave me a strange sort of guilty look. Maybe it was all a bit of an anti-climax for him. You know when you really want something to happen, but by the time it does you've found other things to be concerned about and you're not that bothered any more.

Harry looked at Jimmy. 'Go on, you two,' he said to us and I knew he wanted to talk to Sam about Dad and didn't want me there being unsettled. Sometimes it feels like Harry is the only grown-up one in our family. I suppose when you're the eldest you're often lumbered with all the responsibility.

It turns out that Jimmy lives on the other side of the prom, which we walked through after I'd packed a few books for school the next day and made Harry promise that he'll let the cats sleep in his cabin.

Jimmy carried my bag and held my hand the whole way. It felt quite innocent, and normal, nothing like I thought it would be to hold a boy's hand. I wondered if Jimmy and

I were now destined to be just friends, like me and Kay, united by our rubbish families. Except that I felt something else too, something sparky. Was it just me?

Jimmy lives in a flat on an estate. Somehow I had imagined a cosy little house, but it was a bit grim to be honest. Not his flat, which inside is quite nice with tasteful furniture, but the estate, which was full of dogs barking and kids in parkas cycling round and round.

'We used to live on the other side of town,' said Jimmy. 'But they sold our house when they got divorced, and this is all Mum can afford now.'

'It's nice,' I said. I wanted to hug him.

'It's not.' He laughed. 'But thanks for lying.' He went into a tiny kitchen and took two cans of Coke out of the fridge. 'Energy,' he said, handing me one.

'Is your mum in bed then?' The kitchen clock said it was 6.30 p.m.

'Yep,' he said. 'She's not feeling brilliant at the moment.'

Jimmy and I sat on quite a nice, shabby, velvet sofa in his living room. He drank some Coke and then just started talking. 'Mum's been a bit up and down since she and Dad split up. Sometimes she's OK, but every so often she has a bad patch. We told the school I had a virus and so I've had some extra time off so she's not alone.'

'So you look after her,' I said.

'We look after each other really,' he said, and I thought how lovely Jimmy is to put it like that.

'Sorry, Jimmy,' I said.

'It's OK,' he said.

'Well, it isn't,' I said, and he smiled at me.

'Got to do a bit of pretending,' he said. 'That things are OK, even when they're not.'

'Thank God I've got Kay,' I said. 'She's the only person outside of my family who knows what weird families are like.'

'Well . . . not the *only* person.' He finished his Coke.

'No,' I said, smiling a bit. 'Not the only person.'

'But after Christmas I might be going back to Cornwall,' he said. 'Mum's sister is coming to look after her, and my dad says he wants me to get to know the baby when it's born and bond with it or something. Everyone seems to think it's for the best.'

A boulder rolled on top of me, flattening me. I made myself say something supportive. 'Maybe it *is* for the best.'

Jimmy looked at me. 'I thought that, until a few weeks ago . . .'

But now I hardly heard him. I was too busy thinking that everything had returned to completely dismal.

'I've never talked to anyone about stuff before,' went on Jimmy. 'But I had a feeling I could talk to you. There was something about you . . . I even liked that your hair was a bit green.'

'Oh my God, Jimmy,' I said, blushing. 'That was only because I dyed my hair and it went wrong and the hairdressers tried to put it right!'

Jimmy laughed. 'I thought it was quite cool in a way.'

'Why?' I said, genuinely baffled.

'I don't know,' he said. 'I can't explain why. Do I have to?'

I laughed, and so did he, and then I nearly choked on my Coke.

We talked about lots of things, me and Jimmy. He made us pizza and oven chips and I wolfed them down, which he found funny. I must have looked like a proper glutton, but Jimmy kept fetching more and more things for me to eat, fussing over me a bit. And now I am in bed in his mum's box room, wearing a T-shirt Jimmy's lent me. It smells so clean and, like a house, it's nice. I'm very full, and confused, but safe. Are we friends now? Maybe a friend is good enough, and I should try really hard not to imagine anything else.

1981

I couldn't write for so long.

When I got home the day after Kate left, Harry and Sam looked exhausted and Dad was asleep having had an awful turn when he discovered what had happened. Since that day we've all had to keep watch to make sure he doesn't do anything silly. He doesn't talk to us, he just shouts about Kate and says that Elsa was right all along and that Kate was a 'shallow gold-digger'. I'm pretty sure Sam agrees with this, but Harry and I know that it wasn't quite like that.

Jake just disappeared from Oaks – and didn't come back after this half term either. I thought I might see him hanging about with Dean and Pete, and about asking them where he was but even though it's trivial considering, I'm still a bit mortified about the whole Dean thing and just can't bring myself to do it.

The worst thing is that Dad is definitely never going back to work. The truth all came out that Dad has hardly been to work for the past year, which is why he got sacked in the end. I'm frightened about where money is going to come from for food and electricity bills and nearly offered my Smuggler's Tavern money to help out, but the part of me that is angry with him doesn't see why Dad should have it. I know that's selfish, but Harry said not to worry anyway, and that with his boatyard wages we'll manage. But how can it possibly be enough?

'Maybe we should tell someone?' I said. 'Like a social worker.'

Harry and Sam exchanged a look. 'No,' they both said together. I wondered if that was because Social Services would put me in care or with a foster family if they knew, and Elsa's words all that time ago came back to haunt me.

Elsa came home at Christmas, which was probably the bleakest one ever and we didn't even have Christmas dinner: we had Spaghetti Bolognese and garlic bread from the supermarket. Actually, I didn't mind that bit, as I could easily live off garlic bread for the rest of my life, but it isn't really the Christmas spirit.

Aunt Lorna had called the pub about two weeks before, because Elsa wrote to her and she said that me, and Sam if he wanted, should come to stay with her and it was really tempting. Just the thought of her cosy little cottage and her little terrier, and pots of tea and Jamaican ginger cake was heavenly. But we couldn't leave Harry and Elsa with Dad – we just couldn't – even though all he does is prowl around trying to find bits of spare money to spend at the off-licence.

I have never felt so helpless. Elsa spent a lot of the time trying to get rid of Dad's bottles of vodka, only for Dad to go out and somehow buy more.

'How have you got the money to buy so much alcohol?' she asked him one night. 'How?'

But Dad just looks through us, never asking how *we* are? I soon realised that if I walked out of school tomorrow and refused to go back, my father would probably not do a thing about it. Sam of course was quick to remind me that if I did do that then this would certainly get Social Services involved, and we really didn't want them poking their noses in. He also said that now more than ever it was important for me to succeed. The pressure of it all makes my head ache.

Only Bob and Eugene seem completely unbothered by what's going on. They're being fed by Ben from *Philomena*, Sam says, which I am both grateful for and guilty about.

At school, Kay brings in leftovers for me, and she keeps offering to put my school uniform in with her mum's weekly wash as it looks the same as hers and her mum might not notice. But Kay is looking quite preoccupied herself these days, and I'm sure she's not telling me why because she thinks I have enough to worry about.

In the middle of all this I still wonder about Jimmy, who has been gone since after Christmas. The day after I stayed at Jimmy's I made a decision that made me feel quite grown-up but really sad at the same time. I decided that my heart wasn't able to worry about Dad and to be mooning over Jimmy at the same time, not just now, anyway.

But then Jimmy started sending me postcards, of Penzance where his dad lives, and pictures of a place called Sennen Cove and a little theatre built into the cliff called the Minack. He says his dad and stepmum are trying to be nice, but the baby has been born now, and he's all they think about. Jimmy asks me lots of things about my family, and how my dad is, but now that Jimmy is not here and not coming back, he feels too distant to tell the whole truth to.

The truth still makes my insides curl up cold and icy. Sometimes it feels like I'm falling from a great height and will smash into smithereens.

The head of English and Mr Turing both summoned me to an empty classroom today. I was sure that even though I have tried harder, it hasn't been good enough and that it is them who will ask me to leave in the end. But apparently I am doing better at maths and a lot of my other subjects, except perhaps the sciences which I find just too boggling.

I think I just sat there with my mouth open, until Mr Turing said right at the end, 'Now, is everything all right?' and I thought: Has somebody told him about Dad? Perhaps he was just being polite, or he took my stunned silence the wrong way. Either way he seemed quite satisfied when I said very enthusiastically that everything was fine.

This is just as well because apart from what's happening to Dad, Kay didn't come to school today and nobody has said anything. This is a bit odd, because Kay is never off school.

So when the final bell rang this afternoon, I went through the back gates and headed for Kay's house, hoping that her mum would be in a good mood. Kay told me her dad had recently painted the outside orange and had carvings of roses done above the front door. Apparently the neighbours and the council have been up in arms about it because it is not sympathetic to the other houses in the street. Kay said that this is like a red rag to a bull for her mum, and her parents are refusing to change it.

I wasn't prepared for quite how orange it would be though.

I thought Kay meant a kind of rustic orange, or terracotta – like a house in Spain or Italy, but it was actually a bright orange, like a tangerine.

They have a bay window which has the thickest, most detailed white lace curtains I've ever seen and a line of figurines on the window sill. On close inspection they are a mixture of Disney characters and shepherds and milkmaids with pails.

As soon as I got to the front door Gerta started barking, and I was having second thoughts when someone appeared behind the frosted glass and pressed their face against it.

'Who is it?' said the face.

Now I could see it was Kay's mum. She detached her face from the glass and opened the door. Kay's mum has eyes like Kay's, and today she was wearing a sort of housecoat and clogs. She looked eccentric rather than evil.

'Oh, it's you,' she said. 'Linda, isn't it?'

'Lydia,' I said, just as Gerta's barking approached the sound barrier.

'Never mind the dog, dear, she's in the back and she won't come out.' She looked me up and down. 'How can I help you?'

This seemed a bit of an odd question, as I obviously hadn't called round to sell dusters.

'Is Kay in?' I asked.

Kay's mum pressed her lips together.

'Only, because she hasn't been at school I thought I'd pop over and see if she's OK,' I said.

'Kay's not OK. She's not well,' she said. 'She's in bed.'

'What's wrong with her?'

Kay's mum was obviously having to think how to answer that, and while she was thinking a door behind her opened and Kay appeared in jeans and a jumper down to her knees and fluffy slippers. She did look a bit pale and puffy.

'It's all right, Mum,' she said.

'Kay,' said her mum sharply. 'Get back to bed.'

'You can't make me stay in my room,' said Kay angrily.

'You told me you had a temperature,' snapped her mum.

'I feel better now, to be honest,' said Kay.

'You little minx.' Kay's mum shook her head. 'What with your lies and staying out all hours. You're out of control.'

'No, Mother,' Kay said calmly. '*You* are.'

'Get to bed!'

Kay looked at me, aghast. 'I'm sorry,' she said. 'My mum has Munchausen's by proxy.'

'You cheeky madam!' Kay's mum looked exhausted. 'Go on then,' she said. 'I've had enough.' She pushed Kay outside and slammed the front door shut, leaving me and Kay on the doorstep, with Kay wearing just her slippers.

'Bloody lunatic,' Kay said, looking down at her feet.

'I've probably got some shoes you can borrow,' I said, feeling a bit stunned and wondering if Sam's feet were that much bigger than Kay's.

Kay shut her eyes. 'Sorry about that,' she said. 'She's making a mountain out of a molehill as usual.'

'What did she mean though? About you staying out all hours. Are you ill?'

Kay huffed. 'I caught a bit of a cold, and Mum acted like

I had the plague or something. It's the menopause,' she added. 'It's making her a bit doolally.'

It all seemed very odd to me. And I'm not exactly sure what the menopause involves, except that it must make women very bad-tempered.

'What do you mean?' I said.

'Not here.' Kay sighed. 'Let's walk down to the promenade.'

As usual the sky was grey, threatening rain, and Kay and I walked past the freshwater pool and then right down to the end of the promenade where there is a single bench. We sat down.

'Dad says that me and Mum are too similar,' Kay began. 'And now I'm growing up and Mum's finding it hard to accept.'

'Oh,' I said, wondering about my own mother and that she is never going to see me grow up. I stared at the little flag at the top of the mast on a wooden sailing boat and felt something awful in my heart.

'Is she jealous, do you think?' I asked Kay.

Kay sighed. 'Who knows? Dad worships her. For some reason he thinks she's the most beautiful woman ever to walk the earth. But it's never enough for Mum lately.'

'How do you mean?'

'Dad said I looked nice. About a month ago, Mum ordered a dress from Freeman's catalogue. When it came she took one look at it and said she didn't like it, and made me try it on. I think she was hoping it would look hideous, but it didn't. It suited me. That's because it was a dress meant for someone my age, not hers, and it did make my legs look nice. And Dad said I looked nice.'

'I don't get it?' I said, genuinely confused.

'Mum hit the roof when Dad said that,' Kay went on. 'She told me I looked like a prostitute. And then she said, but no, I was too ugly to be a prostitute.'

I was quite shocked. 'You are definitely not too ugly to be a prostitute,' I said without thinking.

Kay burst out laughing and at the same time she grabbed hold of my hand. 'You do make me crack up,' she said.

'But why didn't you tell me any of this?' I said. 'There was me mooching about and going on about my dad. I'm so selfish sometimes.'

'No you're not,' Kay said quickly. 'What's happening with your dad is really important.'

'I haven't been moaning or boring?' I asked.

'Jeez,' said Kay. 'You're a one-off, Lyds. No way are you boring. Never.'

'So,' I said, thinking of what she says in times of crisis. 'You need a plan.'

Kay smiled. 'I've got one,' she said. 'I'm getting out of this place the moment I finish at school. I'm going to America.'

'But we said we were going to go to London and get jobs?' I said, as me and Kay have often discussed this.

Kay shrugged. 'It's just my cousin told me I can definitely get a job in America . . . they love English nannies there, she says, as they're all obsessed with Mary Poppins.'

'They'll get a shock when you turn up then,' I said. 'I didn't know you liked babies and stuff.'

Kay shrugged. 'Why not? I don't *not* like them. And once I'm out there . . . maybe other things will come up?'

I was starting to feel a bit panicked at the thought of Kay going somewhere so far away and starting a new life.

'Still,' I said, 'it's years off, isn't it? You might change your mind.'

Kay sighed. 'I dunno. I'd think twice about leaving some people . . .' She hesitated. 'You . . . and Gerta, for example.'

'Oh, Kay,' I said. 'Everything just keeps changing all the time.'

'You can come with me, to America,' said Kay. 'We can both be nannies. Let's face it, neither of us is Einstein.'

'Me, especially. I think there's something wrong with me.'

'How do you mean?' Kay frowned.

'It's just . . . I can't do it. I can't do school without making a gigantic effort to remember facts. And even then they fall out of my head.'

Kay thought. 'Do you remember that kid in our form who got taken out last year and put in another school?'

'Marcus?' I did remember him. He had been very small and nervy and left quite soon after I started at Oaks.

'He got diagnosed with dyslexia,' said Kay. 'He doesn't see words and stuff in the right order – they're all a blur. That was why he couldn't do his work. It's like a kind of blindness.'

'But I can see words,' I said. 'I read all the time. Loads.'

'That's true,' said Kay. 'You've obviously just got a special brain which speaks a different language, and in the future they will dissect it for medical research. Sam's said as much.'

'When did Sam say that?'

Kay looked at me for a second. 'He's always saying things like that, isn't he?'

'Suppose,' I said, though I couldn't remember. This is another example of facts falling out of my head.

'You know what you are?' said Kay. 'You're an uncultivated prodigy.'

'That sounds like something to do with plants and gardening,' I said.

'It does a bit.' Kay smiled at me.

We lapsed into silence, until suddenly the rain came pelting down and we looked at each other.

'D'you reckon I could borrow some shoes then?' said Kay, whose slippers were now properly damp. 'I'm not giving Mother another reason to have a go.'

Saturday 14th March

Elsa came home again this weekend. She said Cambridge was 'getting on top of her' and I wondered if she's still having romantic troubles, but didn't ask. Elsa also said that she'd been pondering how important it is to check in on people you care about and take for granted.

'I keep thinking that this is all a bit much for you,' she told me when she arrived back. 'I know you've got your friend Kay, but I'm not sure I could stick living here constantly, with Dad like he is and with just Sam and Harry for company.'

'They're all right,' I said, as without my brothers I'm not sure what I'd do. 'I mean, Sam is weirder than ever. In fact, he's never at home lately.'

'God knows what goes on inside Sam's brain,' said Elsa. 'But he *is* seventeen. They're often a bit odd at that age.'

'Wow,' I said, cogitating. 'That means *you're* nearly twenty, Elsa. That's a proper grown-up woman.'

'Oh, don't,' Elsa groaned. 'Twenty is ancient.'

Today me and Elsa went into town because she needed women's stuff from the chemist and wanted to get some meat from the butcher's.

'Harry and I have clubbed together on money and I'm going to make a chicken and ham pie,' she said. 'Dad used to like that.' She looked a bit hopeless though. We both knew a chicken and ham pie wasn't going to cheer Dad up. In my heart, I know he can't help being like this, it's like he's on a slide of disaster that he just keeps going faster and faster down.

Elsa got some face bleach as she says she's got a moustache – which if you look really close up she has, but in an attractive way – and some tampons and moisturiser. Then we picked up some things from the market and a whole ham from the butchers, and finally we walked back down the hill towards *Lady Beatrice*.

'I don't fancy going home just yet and having to stare at Dad snoring in a chair all afternoon,' she said as we got down to The Smugglers' Tavern. 'Fancy a Coke or something? I've got a bit of change left.'

Of course, I seized on this as it's a rarity that I am allowed to be Elsa's companion, not to mention that I don't see much of her now.

'Rich will probably give us a discount,' I said proudly. 'Seeing as I am an employee.'

Elsa was amused. 'Get you,' she said. 'An employee!'

I went inside with Elsa, and Susan – who works behind the bar weekend lunch times – was there. Rich and Denise were at a hospital appointment, Susan said.

'On the house, sweetheart,' she said to Elsa, handing her a Shandy and me a lime and lemonade.

'Oh, that's so kind, thank you,' said Elsa. 'In that case can I have a bag of cheese and onion crisps too?'

'Elsa!' I whispered, while Susan was bent down rummaging through a cardboard box for the crisps. 'That's taking advantage a bit.'

'But we're living in near poverty,' she said. 'We have to take advantage.'

I wasn't sure this made sense but didn't dwell on it as

there was a man sitting on a barstool next to Elsa, giving her a look I didn't much like.

'Hcrc,' he said, and his beer sloshed around in the glass as he waved it at her. 'You're Charlie Thomson's girls?'

Elsa had been leaning on the bar and opening the crisps, but I watched her turn slowly, like a lizard, to look at him. 'Yes, that's right,' she said politely.

'In here the other night again, he was,' the man went on. 'Drunk as a skunk as usual. We had to carry him over the road and dump him on deck.' The man laughed a nasty laugh and then took a huge noisy slurp of his beer.

I held my breath and saw Elsa's furious face in profile. 'I'm glad you find it funny,' she said icily. 'Other people's misfortune.'

He laughed again, more this time maybe at Elsa's accent which was posher than usual and did make her sound a bit like the Queen.

There was a horrible atmosphere. Even Susan wandered down the other end of the bar and pretended to be cleaning all the optics.

'But it do make me laugh,' the man went on. 'A bunch of upper-class acting like they're superior and can't even hold their drink in public. A right state. Shameful.'

'Shall we go now?' I said shakily, the lime and lemonade suddenly tasting very bitter in my mouth.

But Elsa didn't move. 'How dare you!' she told the man, then very coldly and clearly. 'My father is worth a million of you any day. He's the nicest, cleverest man in the world.'

I stared at Elsa, and I could see her eyes were glittering a bit.

'Wasn't very clever the other night.' The man belched and raised his eyebrows at my sister. 'Shouting and swearing all over the place—'

But he never got further than that because at this point Elsa threw her drink all over him. Shandy dripped off his hair and his glasses and all down his shirt.

I made a dead face, even though inside me a huge cheer of pride for Elsa was happening. The man looked completely shocked. He looked over at Susan as though she was going to stick up for him and chuck us out or something. But Susan just looked at Elsa and then at me, and she folded her lips in a secret smile and went back to cleaning the optics as though nothing had happened.

'Sorry about that,' said Elsa calmly, putting her glass down on the bar. 'I obviously can't hold my drink either.' Her smile was icy. 'Lovely to meet you, but we'd better be going.' Then she picked up her bag of shopping and put her arm through mine. 'Come on, Lydia,' she said. 'We've got a pie to make.'

When we got back to *Lady Beatrice*, Elsa didn't behave any differently with Dad at all. She just returned to her usual slightly bossy self and told me not to get under her feet while she went about making the pie. It made me think of all that was going on inside Elsa that she didn't let on to anyone. Except for earlier, when I really saw it. How heartbroken she is.

Monday 30th March

Kay was much chirpier at school today. She said her dad's had a long talk with her mum, who's now making a big effort not to nag and cause scenes.

'She even said she's going to redecorate my bedroom,' said Kay. 'About time, as I've had the same *Magic Roundabout* wallpaper since I was six.'

'Phew,' I said, then I inspected the sandwich I'd made for myself this morning. It contained this green vegetable thing called an avocado pear, which I've not had before, but Elsa bought a load of avocado pears from the market when she was here and insisted they are a health food. I'm not sure about that, as after a few hours in clingfilm it looks a bit like rotting ectoplasm. Luckily I'd added in loads of Marmite to smother the taste. I took a bite and swallowed it really quickly.

'I don't know, maybe I was being a bit hard,' Kay went on. 'Dad says her hormonal changes have been making her a bit mental for years and she gets overheated all the time. Explains why she always has the flipping windows open even when it's snowing, and keeps taking her cardigan off. Anyway, they're going to see the doctors about it.' She chomped on her cheese sandwich. 'I wish they'd hurry up and do it though. I might end up in Juvenile Offenders for murder if not. Thank God for Gerta.'

I nearly spat out another mouthful of ectoplasm sandwich so as not to choke. Kay has a way of putting things that is so funny I'm surprised I haven't died laughing already.

'But still,' I said after a bit, 'at least you know for sure it wasn't about you. It was all about her hormones.'

'True,' said Kay. 'Same thing with your dad, Lyds. It's not your problem.'

I nodded. 'God, Kay, I'm not sure I want to be an adult if all that happens to you when you are one.'

'There must be some good times though,' she said. 'Otherwise who'd have the strength to carry on?'

We were sitting by the football field above the prom. It's quite hot for the time of year. Apparently we're in for a heatwave this spring.

'Anyway,' said Kay. 'Talking of your dad?'

'Well,' I said. 'He *says* he's not drinking.'

'That's good news, isn't it?' said Kay.

It is, I thought, as long as Dad isn't lying.

'We're still having to keep watch over him,' I said. 'Harry says he is very fragile.'

'Blimey, what a life.' Kay sighed. 'What about Jimmy the hero? Mum's gone quiet on that. Has he been in touch? Is he staying in Cornwall for ever?'

'Yes,' I said.

'I bet he won't,' she said. 'Or you should go and visit him over the Easter holidays.'

'I can't,' I said, 'Elsa's arriving then, with two of her friends from Cambridge, she says. A boy called Julius and a girl called Indy. Harry said we should take *Lady Beatrice* out on the river, maybe go a bit up the estuary. It might be fun, and being on the water usually cheers Dad up.'

'Well, that's nice,' said Kay. 'And it sounds like you're not missing Jimmy much at all. Like you hardly think about him.'

I knew she was giving me a sideways look, but I refused to meet it.

Sam is still in a funny, brooding mood and doesn't seem very pleased about Elsa and her friends coming today.

'That lot sitting round having conversations about Shakespeare and drinking Pimms on deck. You know we're going to have to give up our cabins for them to sleep in, don't you? What a load of fuss.'

I, on the other hand, was fed up of the gloom on *Lady Beatrice* and being the only girl. Elsa meant nice food and a bit of glamour.

'Well, I don't mind giving up my cabin,' I said happily. 'I'd be glad to.' Actually, I am glad to. I've never much enjoyed sleeping in my little corridor.

Sam gave me a look. 'What a treat for them,' he said. 'Who could resist a damp mattress and mouldy sheets.'

'Do you think I'll get arthritis from that one day?' I said. 'The damp and mould?'

'That will be the least of your worries.' Sam flicked my hair as though he was joking.

'We'll have to prepare,' I said. Since Kate left, the housework has gone to pot and the saloon mostly looks like someone has burgled it these days. 'We should do some cleaning.' I held out a raggedy old mop I had found in the bathroom cupboard. 'Clean the floors, things like that.'

Sam looked affronted.

'Sam,' I said, because he was bringing me down. 'How have you become so curmudgeonly about everything?'

'I'm not curmudgeonly,' he said, trying not to smile. 'OK.

I'll do the kitchen, you can do the bathroom – but I'm not laying out the red carpet just so that Elsa can pretend to her friends that we live on the Royal Yacht Britannia.'

'Thanks, Sam,' I said. 'I can't wait for this weekend. Kay is going to come to dinner on Sunday too. It's going to be so brilliant.'

Sam scratched his head and tried to smile at me.

'Oh, cheer up, Catweazle,' I said, waving the stinky mop head in his face.

At 1.00 p.m. Elsa burst though the saloon door wearing a big jumper and denim shorts and tights. She's had her hair cut really short and she's maybe even thinner than last time I saw her. She looks a bit like an elf. Elsa hugged me really tightly and suddenly I felt huge and awkward.

'Where is everyone?' she said.

Sam had vanished, of course.

'Around, I think,' I said, looking over her shoulder at a boy coming down the stairs. This was Julius. He was quite handsome and wearing a spotted cravat and a white shirt that billowed a bit and what looked very like silky pyjama bottoms and espadrilles. He made a sound like a squeal when he entered the saloon – which immediately made Sam, who was now hovering inside the galley, scarper as he is not good with theatrical types.

The last to appear was Indy, and as soon as I saw her I felt even more ordinary and pointless. Indy has long dark swingy hair, perfectly olive skin with huge brown eyes, and the longest legs I have ever seen.

'How fabulous,' said Indy who has quite a posh husky voice, looking around with her big eyes. She took a pack of Silk Cut cigarettes out of her shirt pocket and lit one up.

Indy even smoked beautifully. I found it difficult to stop staring at her.

She smiled at me. 'Is this your little sister?' she asked Elsa.

'Yes, this is dear Lydia,' said Elsa, completely unlike Elsa, and as though she had been taken over by an alien.

'Lovely to meet you, darling,' said Julius, very dramatically, shaking my hand.

'Is your father here?' Indy asked my sister, having already got bored of me.

'Somewhere . . .' Elsa said vaguely.

'He sounds fabulous too. A real character.' Indy puffed on her fag.

Elsa caught my eye. She knows Dad's not been fabulous for a long time.

At this point Harry came down below, followed by a girl with an earring in her lip and really short hair. Indy was looking very interested.

'Harry!' said Elsa. 'Indy, Julius . . . this is my brother Harry.'

Harry nodded at them. 'This is Jo,' he said as the girl with the lip piercing peered around him. 'My friend from the pub.'

Jo shot him a look then. She had nice eyes, almost bigger and browner than Indy's, but there was something odd about them at the same time; they were sort of darting everywhere.

I smiled at her but she looked right through me. I've seen a few of Harry's girls coming to and from *Lady Beatrice*. They never seem to last long.

'Are we having a drink then?' she said to Harry, but looking quite frostily towards Indy.

Harry patted his pockets and took out his tin of rolled cigarettes. 'There's probably some beer somewhere,' he said awkwardly, taking out a fag and lighting it.

Indy moved away from Elsa and towards Harry. 'Can I try one of those?'

Harry blinked before holding out the tin.

Jo was now looking very hostile indeed and crossed her arms over her chest. 'I'll get one myself then?' she said. 'The beer?'

'No, darling, we've got champagne,' said Indy. 'Much nicer.' She turned back to Elsa. 'It's in our bag – let's all have some. Can you fetch some glasses, Elsa?'

Elsa looked stumped for a second as we don't have much cause for champagne on *Lady Beatrice*.

'We have got a few real wine glasses,' I piped up.

'Fabulous,' said Indy, smiling at me radiantly. 'They'll do.'

Jo made sure she was sitting between Harry and Indy on the sofa and silently smoked one cigarette after another, staring into her glass of champagne suspiciously as though she thought it might be poisoned. I must admit that Indy did kind of take over, not because she talked a lot or was loud or anything, but because she is one of those girls who is just better than everyone else and makes everyone else go quiet.

I could see Harry giving Indy sidelong looks as I was sitting on a stool by the table, observing.

'I've never heard of the name Indy,' I said then, making conversation. 'Where does that come from?'

'India,' said Indy. 'I much prefer Indy. Don't know what my folks were thinking.'

'I like your name,' I said, catching Jo sneering at me, probably thinking I was trying to suck up.

'Thank you, darling,' said Indy. 'And yours is such a pretty name too.'

'A divine name,' said Julius emphatically. He loosened his silk cravat and shook his hair a bit like a little Shetland pony. I folded my lips, trying to stop myself from laughing.

Jo cleared her throat noisily and dug her elbow into Harry's ribs. Harry flinched and stubbed out his cigarette. The whole saloon stank of fags because everyone was smoking, even Elsa.

'And are you two together?' asked Indy, turning to Jo and Harry. 'As in a couple?'

Jo smiled for the first time but Harry looked perturbed. He hates personal questions like that.

'Jo's a friend,' he said finally. 'From the pub.'

Jo's smile disappeared.

'Oh look, Jo's got a piercing too, darling,' said Julius to Elsa. Harry raised an eyebrow at me.

Jo was getting more and more riled; I could tell by the way she was shifting around on the sofa and glaring at us all. I tried smiling at her again but that just seemed to make her scowl more.

'Where did you get yours done?' Elsa asked Jo politely.

'Market up town,' said Jo.

'I'm thinking of removing mine,' said Elsa. 'It's such a drag taking it out and cleaning it.'

Jo looked unaffected by this, and looked from Elsa to me as though we were from Mars.

Dad finally made an appearance at about 5.00 p.m. looking dishevelled and a bit alarmed to see Elsa and her little gang. Elsa quickly stuffed the champagne bottle out of sight and then introduced him proudly to Indy and Julius.

I felt very anxious that Dad would suddenly do something outrageous. I know that deep down he is still the same person who long ago read to me and put me to bed when I fell asleep on the stairs, but now he has such a dead look in his eyes, where once they twinkled.

'Do help yourselves to anything you need,' he told them tiredly, waving his hand at the table and the tattered old sofa. 'I'm afraid I'm not feeling too well so I'm just going to have a lie-down.'

While they commiserated, Elsa gave me the first real look she'd given me since she'd arrived. Dad was on his way to the door, but he stopped and turned back for a minute.

'Perhaps tomorrow we can take the *Lady Beatrice* out to sea?' he said. 'Now that we have a crew.'

'Fabulous,' said Indy. I was beginning to think that everything in Indy's life was *fabulous* and almost hoped that Dad would fall over so that she was forced to use another word.

By this time Jo and Harry had disappeared somewhere and Julius, who seems to have taken a shine to me, was helping me make tea in the galley. Julius is extremely dramatic. He seems to think that my job at The Smugglers' Tavern is fascinating, especially when I told him about the old orange cases filled with sorbet.

'Extraordinary!' he shrieked, which was quite satisfying and spurred me on to more stories from the kitchens of The Smugglers' Tavern.

Sam, who had just decided it was safe to return to the throng and had wandered into the galley to find food, rolled his eyes at this and sloped out again.

Later, Indy and Julius decided to go and walk up to the end of the promenade before dinner. Elsa was cooking tonight – thank God, as I miss her cooking. I've still not mastered it myself, not even out of necessity.

Elsa and I sat on deck as the sun was going down.

'Your friends are nice,' I said. 'Julius is funny.'

'Oh, Julius,' said Elsa, laughing. 'We only became friends a couple of months ago. He's been a great support to me lately.'

'Has he?' I said. 'In what way?'

Elsa smiled a bit sadly. '. . . Just being a good friend, that's all.'

I decided not to probe further. I didn't want to push my luck with Elsa.

'He's very kind and silly,' she went on. 'Such a sweetheart. I thought you two would get on.'

'I'm not very silly any more,' I said, which is definitely true.

'Lydia,' said Elsa, rubbing my knee. 'Life will be fun again, you'll see.'

I hoped so. Apart from Kay, I didn't feel like much was fun in my life at all.

'So have you got a boyfriend now?' I asked, more to change the subject than anything else.

Elsa blinked. 'There was someone . . . bit of a nightmare in a way.'

'Why?'

'He's quite hot and cold.' She laughed. 'I've been a bit of a wreck about it . . .' She stopped talking and lit a cigarette. I watched her; she looked sophisticated and sad. I wondered if it was the same man as Him who came and went from Carlos's party. Or was it a new one? Did Elsa have a thing for men like that?

'Can I have some of that?' I asked, nodding at her cigarette.

'No,' said Elsa immediately. 'It will kill you.'

We sat there in silence, staring at the tide that was rising and slapping against the quay.

'Dad still looks a bit ropey,' she said, breaking the silence. 'Is he drinking again?'

'He says not,' I said. 'Sometimes I don't care any more.'

Elsa frowned. 'Oh God, Lyds. Are you all right?'

'I'm OK,' I said. 'You know, just get on with it, I suppose.'

Elsa sighed, looking over to the prom where the figures of Indy and Julius were retreating slowly. Julius was waving his arms about, talking. Elsa smiled.

At this point Dad appeared at the hatch opening, rubbing at his chest. 'Bit of indigestion,' he said and belched slightly. 'Lovely to see you, Elsa.'

Elsa went slightly tense beside me. 'How are you?' she said.

'I'm managing to stay alive.' Dad laughed then, as though that was an exaggeration. His eyes gave him away.

'Dad, perhaps it's time for Alcoholics Anonymous,' said Elsa. 'They can help—'

'Absolutely not,' he cut her off. 'For Christ's sake.'

We were silent, all three of us then. Elsa got up and threw her cigarette into the mud. 'I've made a lasagne,' she said, looking at me. 'Followed by trifle.'

Dad looked quite uninterested – he doesn't eat much these days – but he rubbed at his forehead. 'Thank you, that sounds delicious,' he said vaguely. 'I'll just have my sleep before dinner.'

He disappeared back down the hatch and Elsa sighed, picking up her cigarettes and shoving them in her pocket.

'Somebody needs to do something soon,' she said. 'He's killing himself.'

Saturday 18th April

We only made it out as far as Osea Island today, as Harry and Sam agreed with me and Elsa that we definitely didn't want to be moored miles away from home with Dad so morose.

Osea Island is eerie and was famous a few years ago for its big rehabilitation institute where patients with depression and mental illnesses went to recover in peace and tranquillity. The house has been shut up for years now which is a pity as we might all have been tempted to drop Dad off and leave him there.

Last night, Elsa and I shared Sally and Erica's old cabin as it has two bunks one above the other, and Julius had my cabin. Of course, Indy slept in Jake's old cabin, which is one of the biggest and has been empty since Jake and everyone left, and Harry and Jo are in together, so Sam is having to sleep on the sofa.

Neither Elsa nor I slept very well – Elsa claimed I had snored and she had been kept awake for hours; but the truth is that neither of us slept as our cabin is right next to Dad's and he was mumbling all night.

As it was, Dad only appeared at breakfast and then went back to bed. Indy and Julius lounged around on deck drinking supplies of champagne that Elsa went up to Tesco to get this morning before we cast off. Apparently Indy's parents are loaded so she paid for it all.

Elsa seems to be in Indy's thrall a bit, and is some kind of slave. I'm starting to get annoyed actually as girls like

Indy are really just lazy and probably have servants at home to do their bidding, and I didn't like to see Elsa acting like a maid. Indy is obviously interested in Harry as she kept asking about tying knots and tides as though she was fascinated, which she can't possibly have been. This didn't please Jo, who appeared in the saloon about midday wearing Harry's shirt. I was watching the cats, who loathe being at sea and were unusually huddled together in their basket. Bob didn't even have the energy to sit on Eugene, who still stared at me as though I had betrayed him somehow.

'Are that lot still here then?' said Jo, who curled up on the sofa and immediately lit a cigarette.

'Up on deck, probably,' I said. 'I'm just making some tea.'

'Thanks.' Jo sniffed and fiddled with her lip ring.

'Is Harry still asleep?' I asked as I'd not seen him yet.

Jo shrugged. 'Talking to Lady Muck upstairs.'

I tried not to laugh. Obviously Indy wouldn't want herself described as Lady Muck, but she was a bit. A very pretty Lady Muck.

'Aren't you Harry's girlfriend then?'

Jo laughed a bit grimly. 'He thinks he can do better than me.' She lifted her eyes up to the ceiling to indicate Indy again.

I did think she'd got it wrong about my brother.

'Harry's nice really,' I said.

'A bit complicated,' Jo muttered.

'What do you mean?'

'Worries too much,' Jo said. 'About you most of all.'

'Me?' It felt very discombobulating to hear that Harry worried about me that much.

'I shouldn't have said that,' said Jo quickly, seeing my expression. 'Forget it.'

'That's OK, I won't tell Harry,' I said. Because I won't. But now I know I feel anxious too. Everyone seems to think I'm a problem teenager who requires a lot of worrying about.

At this point, thankfully, Elsa appeared at the bottom of the stairs. She glanced at me and then Jo and frowned.

'Everything OK?' she said to me.

I bit my lip. 'Fine.'

'Yeah,' said Jo. 'Fine.'

Elsa eyed Jo warily and went to the galley to get another bottle of champagne out of the box.

'Are we there yet?' I called to her. 'At Osea?'

Elsa came back through carrying two bottles. 'We're going really slowly as the engine's off and there's no wind. Probably be there in about three years.'

'What about Dad?'

'Asleep again.' She sighed. 'In a way I hope he doesn't wake up until we're back.'

Jo, who had been drinking her tea noisily, said, 'He's all right, your dad. He's a good bloke.'

Elsa stiffened and I knew exactly what she was thinking. Neither of us knew Jo existed before yesterday. It was a bit much having a stranger telling you things about your family that you actually know, thank you very much.

'He is,' said Elsa. 'Deep down.' She hesitated. 'But unfortunately he's having some sort of breakdown at the moment, so that's slightly beside the point.'

Elsa has this way of cutting a person to ribbons with her words. She's always had that over me as I often forget halfway through making a point what the actual point is.

Jo shrugged. 'Just think you lot treat him like he's not all there.'

'That's right,' said Elsa. 'Because he isn't.' She raised an eyebrow at me and then headed back up the stairs.

'I do mean it,' Jo said, when Elsa had gone. 'Your dad's got a good heart. He's always offering to buy us drinks down the pub. He listens. No offence, but maybe he doesn't feel like he's being watched like he is here.'

'Maybe,' I said, though inside it felt like another betrayal of Dad's. That he was only a silent wreck in front of us and managed to be normal and nice with other people.

The sun came out in the afternoon and we moored for an hour or two while everyone lay up on deck. Bob and Eugene appeared, having sensed that their lives were slightly less in danger, and Julius was very taken with Eugene and found his strangeness delightful. Julius seems to think I am the funniest person he's ever met and screamed with laughter when I reminisced about the troll collection I had back in Cottlesham.

'Darling, you mean those hideous gonks?' he said. 'What on earth attracted you to them?'

'I think I liked their smell,' I said. 'And because everyone thought they were ugly.' I couldn't imagine now what I loved so much about the trolls and blushed just thinking about it. 'But that was years ago.'

'Bonkers!' he said. 'I love it.'

Elsa, who had been reading the paper wearing her jet-black Ray-Ban sunglasses, glanced over at us. 'Lydia used to be so eccentric,' she told Julius. 'Drove me mad when she did her Disney impressions. They were quite good though, I have to admit.'

'Lydia, perhaps this is your vocation?' said Julius. 'An impressionist – or a troll ventriloquist!'

Elsa and Julius laughed and I joined in, though with the familiar feeling of not being taken seriously. And also that it was partly my fault from years of acting the giddy goat, as Dad used to call it.

Indy was wearing a skimpy bikini and seems to have absolutely no inhibitions about her body which goes brown straight away and is long and thin with medium- to large-sized boobs. She was watching Harry who was sitting by the wheel with Sam, the two of them having a technical boat chat, no doubt. Indy seemed gripped by the sight of them, particularly Harry, who kept flicking glances her way. I felt sorry for Jo, but maybe if she made an effort to be vivacious like Indy then Harry would be more keen on her.

'I can't imagine ever wandering around like that, practically naked,' I said to Elsa. 'I'm only ever going to wear a swimming costume in my life, one that goes really high up my neck and stops at my knees.'

Elsa laughed. 'You'll probably change your mind at some

358

point,' she said. 'But I must admit, Indy does make me feel huge at times.'

I looked at Elsa's tiny waist. 'Still, it's a bit insensitive, with Jo sitting downstairs feeling left out,' I said.

'Yes. But what is wrong with Jo?' Elsa had rolled onto her stomach and was covertly watching Indy. 'She's like a permanent black cloud.'

'It's because Harry's not taking much notice of her,' I said. 'She feels rejected, probably.'

Together Elsa and I looked at Indy, who was now smoking another one of her cigarettes and laughing in what I thought was quite a put-on way with Julius.

'We'd better not talk about it anyway,' I said solemnly. 'I think Jo told me that in confidence.'

Elsa looked amused. 'Hilarious, since you're about the most indiscreet person in the world.'

'Thank you so much,' I said sarcastically.

Elsa pretended not to notice. She picked up her paper and resumed reading, and I then felt quite restrained that I hadn't told her what else Jo had said, about Harry worrying about me. This, in fact, makes me quite a discreet person, so Elsa is wrong.

Sunday 19th April

This morning the sun shone through the Perspex skylight in Sally and Erica's old cabin, and I lay in the top bunk looking at a Pippa doll that Kate had accidentally left behind on top of their cupboard. For a minute I thought about Sally and Erica and how I hadn't seen them for nearly six months and I wondered where they are now. I've tried not to think much about what Kate did that day. I never imagined they'd mean anything to me, but I miss them, even silent little Erica and her blanket. Of course I miss Jake: his ironed T-shirts and the conversations we had.

But then maybe it's normal that people just come and go in your life. Jimmy has, I thought. It almost made me wish I'd never met any of them in the first place.

'Lydia,' came Elsa's sleepy voice from the bottom bunk. 'Fancy making me a cup of tea for a change?'

'Not particularly,' I said. I knew Elsa would complain about my tea as she likes hers weak as dishwater and I always do it wrong. All the same I sat up and then shuffled down the ladder with my duvet on my back as it was chilly down below, even though this April has been more like July.

I walked barefoot past Sam, who was lying face-up on the sofa with his eyes shut and his mouth slightly open and his hair sticking out as if he'd had an electric shock. He was only half covered by a blanket and had no pyjama top on and I couldn't help staring at his chest, which was slender and hard-looking, and the muscles on his arms and his long legs sticking out over the end of the sofa, and I realised that Sam was definitely not a pudgy little boy any more. I don't know why but this made me feel jealous. Sam has grown up without me realising.

I threw my duvet on top of him, but he didn't stir.

Then I stood in the galley and waited ages for the kettle on the cooker to boil because of the low-voltage generator and I thought about seeing Kay later and this did cheer me up immensely.

It was when I opened the fridge door for milk that something rolled off the top and smashed on the floor. I crouched down, careful not to move my feet because glass was everywhere, and then I saw what had broken. It was a big bottle of Smirnoff vodka, and from all the liquid on the floor it must have been nearly full up.

I stared at the mess and wondered where else Dad had hidden his bottles. I wanted to take a shard of glass and go and stick it in his head. Why is he ruining everything? I thought. We're all having to look on the bright side because of him but he never does anything in return.

'Morning,' said a voice behind me. Jo was standing on the step that goes up to the bathroom and Harry and Sam's cabin. 'What's happened?'

'Nothing,' I said, reaching out to take the bit of glass that had *Smirnoff* and *vodka* written on it and holding it behind my back. 'Just a bottle of water fell off the fridge.'

Jo sniffed the air. 'Smells like booze,' she said, peering at all the glass.

I felt the shame creeping over my cheeks.

Jo was putting on her plimsolls and lacing them up. 'Don't

move before I've picked all that up,' she said, and then she carefully removed every bit of glass and got the mop and bucket to clean the floor. When she'd finished she put all the cleaning stuff away and took the shrieking kettle off the hob. Then she made three cups of tea, even somehow ensuring that one of them was as weak as dishwater.

'He'll die, won't he, if he carries on?' I said suddenly. 'One day Dad will die from drinking all this.'

Jo hesitated, then she said, 'We're all going to die one day, girl. I reckon he'll come through this though. He knows what he's got to lose.'

'Thanks,' I said, as she handed me my tea. 'And for being honest.'

Jo smiled and she looked completely different. Pretty. She should definitely smile more, I thought.

She took a sip of her tea, then she said, 'Might make a curry, later. I do a good chicken and lentil, if I say so myself.'

'That's nice. I've only ever had curry in a restaurant.' I said, slightly worried that Elsa would be put out.

Jo grinned, reading my mind. 'Tell your sister it's a thank you for putting up with me,' she said. 'She needs a night off, the way Lady Muck's been bossing her about this weekend.'

'Poor Lady Muck,' I said. 'Elsa told me Indy ruined her expensive, Chinese silk dressing gown from Harrods by leaving it under the leak in her cabin. She'll never get the stain out, apparently.'

'What a shame,' said Jo, quite happily.

Me and Jo laughed, and I only felt slightly mean.

'Oh. Can you make extra curry please, as my friend Kay's coming?' I asked. 'Kay eats anything and everything.'

'Will do,' said Jo. 'Quite looking forward to making myself useful.'

I was mostly looking forward to seeing Kay. At least no one can take Kay away from me, I thought, comforted, as I took Elsa's tea to Sally and Erica's cabin.

While everyone is having breakfast I am lying in my bunk and making a note in my diary of Dad's smashed bottle and Jo being kind and us laughing over Lady Muck, as it's a good example of one of life's bitter-sweet moments.

Monday 20th April

I'm wide awake at 5.30 a.m. and it isn't light yet but I have so much to write down before I forget any of it, as yesterday still feels like an awful dream, even though it all really happened, every single bit of it.

Lady Beatrice arrived back to Maling at 5.00 p.m. yesterday and Indy was met by her personal driver almost straight away, who was taking her all the way to London to her family's mansion in Kensington. I'd earwigged on Indy and Elsa's discussion about this earlier and I wondered what it would be like to be as rich as Indy. I know money doesn't make you happy by itself, but all the hot baths would. And the carpets. And never having to get a train or a bus in your life if you didn't feel like it.

Julius was leaving too, but as he had a bit to go before his train, he and Elsa went to the Admiral to have a beer first.

When Julius said goodbye he enveloped me in his scarf and aftershave and made me promise not to forget all my stories.

Sam and Harry spent a long time tying the boat up safely while Dad watched them, looking quite morose. Of course, Bob and Eugene immediately leaped onto the quay and disappeared, desperate for dry land and creatures to chase.

While Harry went off to get Jo cigarettes from the pub and Dad had disappeared down below, I stayed up on deck waiting for Kay to arrive. At 6.00 p.m. a blue van with *Palmer's Plumbing* on the side came down the hill to the quayside, and I spotted Gerta sitting in the front seat, her head sticking out of the passenger window. When Kay's dad parked up, Gerta started howling up at the sky.

Kay got out and pushed Gerta's head back through the window, laughing. Then she said something to her dad and he drove off, giving me a little wave.

Sam had been tinkering around inside the electrics fuse box on the quay, but he stopped and looked over at Kay who was standing by the gangplank with a little rucksack over her shoulder.

'Is that thing a dog or a horse?' he called out to her.

'Lovely to see you, Kay,' I said. 'Don't mind Sam, he's an ignoramus on these matters.'

Kay laughed. 'Gerta's a trained assassin, if you must know,' she called back to Sam. 'I only have to say the word.'

'I bet you do,' said Sam, standing there with some kind of tool in his hand.

I could see that Kay was making that face where you're trying not to smile.

'Anyway.' I was anxious to go down below and tell Kay all about Julius and Lady Muck. 'I expect you've got work to do, Sam. We won't keep you.'

Sam eye-rolled me, while Kay clambered aboard.

Even though Sam had managed to turn the electricity on, Elsa said it might be cosier to eat by lamplight, so Jo went and put tilley lamps everywhere, and at 7.00 p.m. everyone ate with lamps and candles on the table. It was quite cosy, and because it was warm the boys had taken off the big skylight in the saloon and we could look up at the stars in the clear evening sky. Even Dad seemed less miserable and chatted to Harry about some work Harry's doing over at the boatyard.

Next to me, Kay was already helping herself to extra rice, while Sam sat opposite us, not really eating his food.

'Eat up, Sam,' said Elsa, who was sitting the other side of me. 'What's wrong with you?'

'Nothing,' he said rudely. 'Can't you shut up for once.'

'Honestly,' said Elsa. 'You're worse than ever. Shouldn't you be out with your girlfriend somewhere?'

Harry lifted an eyebrow, and Sam went the colour of tomato soup while Kay reached out and took a big drink of water from her glass.

'It's the curry,' she said, but I saw her flick a glance at Sam, and I felt bad as it must seem to Kay like all we do in our family is snipe at him, even if it does serve him right as he's been trying to embarrass me all my life.

Dad, who had been prodding at his food, looked up. 'Elsa,' he said wearily. 'Leave the boy alone.'

Elsa opened her mouth to say something caustic but then shut it again. She took a deep breath instead, and scooped up a forkful of curry.

I looked at my father. I thought of the smashed bottle of his Smirnoff vodka and standing in all the glass while Jo had cleared it up, and for a second I felt like screaming.

'This is delicious,' Elsa said to Jo then. 'Thank you.'

Jo looked embarrassed and pleased at the same time. 'No bother.'

For a bit there was the sound of cutlery scraping against plates, before Elsa piped up again. 'Whatever happened to that boy?' she asked me. 'Jimmy, wasn't it?'

Beside me I knew Kay was beaking in, hoping I would divulge information to Elsa that I hadn't to her, which of course I never would. Anyway, Jimmy seems a million miles away now.

'He went back to live with his dad in Cornwall,' I said, poking at a bit of chicken.

'Oh. Bummer,' said Elsa. 'He sounded nice.'

'Jimmy *is* nice,' Kay butted in. She elbowed my ribcage.

'Who's that?' said Sam.

'Jimmy,' said Kay. 'You remember?' And I saw her cock her head at me.

'Oh, him,' said Sam, and then I felt his foot pressing down on mine.

I finished my food. 'Me and Kay will do the washing-up, won't we, Kay?'

'Course,' said Kay, but Elsa shook her head.

'Kay's a guest, Lydia. We can do it together, you and I.'

'I don't mind—' Kay started, but Elsa was having none of it.

'Lydia is an expert now,' she said. 'So between us we should get it done in no time.'

At this point everyone except Sam had cleared their plates, and Jo and Harry were getting ready to go out to the Admiral. Dad and Sam just sat there and I noticed some dried paint up one of Sam's arms, which he hadn't bothered to clean off properly. He saw me looking and pushed his shirt sleeve down.

'What is it you've been doing on that boat anyway?' Elsa asked him. '*Philomena*, isn't it?'

'Painting, fixing things . . .' Sam said. 'We had to slow down over the winter, but we've finished now. It looks really good. Quite professional.'

'Excellent,' Dad said. 'Perhaps you can make a start on *Lady Beatrice* then?'

'Yes. What is your hourly rate, Sam?' Elsa was trying to keep a straight face.

Harry grinned while putting his jacket on. 'Only Sam would charge Dad for painting his own cabin.'

'I'd give a discount, obviously,' Sam said, quite seriously. 'I'm not that hard-hearted.'

Kay, who was having another drink of water, started laughing and then suddenly she was choking. She sprayed a mouthful of liquid straight over the table, where most of it landed on Sam's shirt.

'Kay!' I said, thumping her on the back. 'Please don't die and leave me with these people.'

Sam looked completely unbothered by his wet shirt; in fact, now he actually looked happy for once.

'Oh my Lord, Sam,' said Kay, getting her breath back. 'That was funny.'

Personally I didn't think it was *that* funny, but at least Sam had stopped looking so sour. I felt proud of Kay, who always dissolves a weird atmosphere and makes it better.

I saw Elsa's eyes flitting in amusement between Kay and my brother before she shoved a tea towel at me.

'Come on then,' she said. 'Washing-up.'

'Sorry,' I mouthed at Kay, who was still wiping tears from her eyes.

Jo had put a couple of the lamps on the counter in the galley but now it was dark outside so we couldn't see much. Elsa shut the door and turned the lights on and snuffed out the lamps, while I filled the sink with water that wasn't very hot and started washing up.

'Your friend Kay's got something about her,' Elsa said, as I handed her a plate to dry. 'A vast improvement on Donna.'

'I can't believe I stuck with Donna for so long,' I said. 'I was such a wimp, Elsa. I could never be myself with her. And she was quite mean.'

'Some good has come out of living here then.' Elsa started on the knives and forks. 'Even Sam seems to like Kay.'

'Yes,' I said. 'Actually, I think Sam might have a crush on Kay, and Kay feels bad so she's extra-nice to him, laughing at his jokes when they aren't funny, that sort of thing. Sam is not her type at all but she doesn't want to hurt his feelings, she's kind like that.'

'Hmmm,' said Elsa. She took the last plate from me and gave me an odd smile. Then she said, 'If only Dad would cheer up. All the self-pity, it's so depressing.'

I dried my hands on my dungarees, while Elsa bent and opened the cupboard under the counter to put away all the clean plates.

'Does anyone clean this cupboard, ever,' she said, crouching down. 'It's filthy—' She stopped abruptly and dumped the plates on the floor. Then she reached further inside the cupboard and took out two full bottles of Smirnoff vodka.

'Bloody hell,' she said quietly. 'I knew it.'

'I found one earlier,' I said. 'It fell off the top of the fridge.'

Elsa stood up with a determined look on her face and started to empty one of the bottles down the sink.

Then all the electric lights went out.

'How very symbolic,' Elsa said wearily in the darkness, pouring out the contents of Dad's second bottle.

I opened the galley door. 'Sam!' I called, walking through to the saloon, but it was deserted. The lamps and candles on the table were casting their shadows on the walls. I carried on through to the cabin me and Kay were sharing tonight, thinking she must be unpacking her little rucksack, but she wasn't there – only Mr Bear, leaning up on the pillow in the bottom bunk.

'Everyone's gone,' I told Elsa when I came back to the galley.

Elsa was trying to relight a lamp with some matches. 'Dad's probably persuaded them all to go to the pub. Typical of him to flout the law and coerce Kay into drinking underage.' She paused. 'Though she is rather well-developed, so no doubt he'll get away with it.'

'No one asked *us*.' I was annoyed that as soon as my back was turned Kay had been kidnapped by my father.

'Oh well, the Admiral is literally two minutes away,' Elsa said, exasperated. 'You can go over there now. Someone who knows what they're doing needs to come home and fiddle around in that fuse box.' She put the empty vodka bottles in the swing bin. 'And get me a Kit Kat while you're at it.'

'Yes, my lady,' I muttered, putting my plimsolls on.

Up on deck, Bob and Eugene sprang down from the hatch and trotted after me as I ran across the gangway and onto the quay. It was quite cold now that the sun had gone, and the sky was very dark with no stars out at all. I was shivering slightly in my T-shirt but I was only going to be gone a minute, so I just rubbed at my arms as I walked. I could see the Admiral right at the end of the quay with all its lights on and I felt another twinge of resentment for my father, who just did exactly what he wanted and everyone went along with it.

Across the road at The Smugglers' Tavern, there was a sudden loud cheer and I remembered that Sunday night is quiz night. I could just glimpse Denise through the window, serving behind the bar.

Along the quay all the barges were quiet, and there was *Philomena*, which did actually look quite smart. Even in the dark the name *Philomena* on the bow was glistening, with a bright yellow swirl underneath it.

Two people were sitting further along from *Philomena*, with their backs to me and their legs dangling over the quayside, holding hands, and I thought: What a strange place to have a romantic interlude, and then, before I could stop him Bob ran over to them, as he's always on the lookout for attention, even from strangers. One of them put out their free hand and turned to stroke Bob's back. And I stopped walking.

Kay. And it was Sam holding her hand.

I put my hand up to my mouth to stop anything from coming out of it.

A hundred yards away was the Admiral, and Harry and Jo – and Dad, who was oblivious to everything. He didn't know because he never really noticed me now. He didn't know that this moment was probably the worst one of my life apart from being told about Mum. Mum, who's gone for ever and can't look after me now.

Eugene, who had been obediently parked by my feet, let out a loud mewling sound and that was when Kay turned round and looked over and saw me, and my eyes filled with tears.

'Bob,' I said loudly. 'Come here, Bob.'

Of course, Bob is hugely disloyal, even when it is imperative that he isn't. He started cleaning his paws instead.

'Lydia,' said Kay anxiously, scrambling to her feet.

'You're a liar,' I told her. 'All that time you said you didn't like Sam, and you did. *Why did you lie?*'

I screamed the last bit, as rage suddenly got hold of me. Sam was looking terrified and stood up behind Kay.

'I don't care, you pigs!' I screamed even louder at them. 'I don't care if everyone hears me!'

Kay was walking carefully towards me, but I could see her eyes were still happy from holding Sam's hand. I thought that if she came any closer I would attack her.

'Don't,' I said calmly. 'I never want to see or speak to you again.'

'I'm still your friend,' Kay said. 'I'll always be your friend.'

'Well, I'm not *your* friend,' I told her. 'Ever again.'

Then I picked up poor confused Eugene and I turned and started running back to *Lady Beatrice*. I pushed open the hatch and it was pitch-black at the top and I stumbled, not caring if I fell down the stairs. My head felt full of stinking air. At the bottom of the stairs, by all the coats, my skull crashed against the lit lamp that had been hung there earlier, but the lamp swung away and I didn't feel anything. Eugene shot out of my grasp and back up the stairs in fright before I could stop him.

I came through the door to the saloon and there was Elsa, sitting at the table smoking a cigarette and reading the Sunday papers by candlelight.

'Did you find someone?' she said, looking up. She peered, almost sniffing me, and I thought, Elsa's like a bloodhound. 'What's happened?' She stubbed out her fag and got to her feet. 'Lydia? Is it Dad?'

'No,' I said, shaking.

'What is it then?' Elsa came to me, and tried to steady me with her hands.

Then I burst into tears.

Elsa put her arms around me. 'Tell me what's happened?' she said. But almost immediately she pulled away and I saw her eyes flickering at something over my shoulder.

'It doesn't matter,' I said.

'Something's on fire,' she said abruptly. 'Look!'

Through the saloon door, the shadows were alive and small flames were licking out towards Sally and Erica's old cabin, where Kay was going to have the bottom bunk and me the top.

Elsa walked cautiously towards the door, but even I could feel the heat now and she stepped quickly back. 'It has to be one of those bloody lamps,' she said shakily.

I remembered crashing down the stairs and my head hitting the lamp.

Elsa's eyes were darting around the saloon until she saw the fire extinguisher behind the stove.

'Has anyone ever used that thing?' she asked, going to get it and trying to get the safety catch off. 'Lydia, go and fill a bucket of water.'

'Shouldn't we get out first though?' I said a bit numbly, wiping at my wet cheeks with my hands. 'Call the fire brigade or something?'

Elsa, who was still struggling with the fire extinguisher, gave up and dumped it. 'But all your things,' she said. 'Maybe we can put it out between us?'

'I don't care about my things,' I said, as just then I didn't. Every few seconds a wave of hurt hit me, and in between the waves the flames outside the saloon door were dancing, getting bigger and making fun of me.

Elsa was in front of me now, her hands on my shoulders. 'Is that little hatch in Harry's cabin locked? Can we get out that way?'

'I don't know,' I said uselessly.

'Come on.' Elsa took hold of my hand then and said,

'Let's go together.' Holding on to me, she pulled me along, through the galley and up the step to Harry's cabin. A precarious ladder led up to the little hatch and Elsa climbed up and started shoving at it, trying to get a grip in the darkness. Then I heard the sound of it moving on its runners, and the night sky appeared above us.

Elsa looked down at me. 'Quickly,' she said. 'But be careful, this ladder's pretty much had it.'

On the quay, people were already gathering, and one of them was Ben from *Philomena*; he was the first person I saw when I got out of the hatch. Then there was Harry and Jo behind him, pushing past a couple of curious kids on bikes. And trailing behind, looking disorientated, was my father.

'I've phoned the fire brigade.' Ben looked anxiously at Elsa. 'Are you girls OK?'

'We're OK, thanks.' Elsa tried to smile at him. 'Let's get to a safe place,' she told me.

Nowhere is safe, I thought. Even dry land moves underneath you, and people who once felt solid can then crumble away.

When I looked at my home, dark-grey smoke was already pouring through the big open skylight in the saloon and beneath it the glare of orangey-red flames lit up the mast and the big brown sail.

I followed Elsa towards where Dad was standing, looking silent and helpless with Harry and Jo, who had spotted us. Harry broke away and I found myself sandwiched between my brother and sister, both of them holding onto me as though I would vanish if they didn't. Maybe Elsa and Harry are solid, I thought, even if the pig Sam isn't. And Kay. I couldn't think about her because it hurt so much.

I had so many feelings circulating inside me I couldn't really take in what was going on. My home was on fire and all I could do was be full of fury about something most people would probably think was trivial.

Jo appeared, pale-faced as she craned to see the fire. 'I put one of them lamps by the coats,' she said, frightened. 'It's all my fault.'

'No, Jo,' I said quickly. 'It's all *my* fault.'

'It's nobody's fault,' said Harry firmly.

'Sam!' said Elsa bit frantically. 'Where is he? Is he OK?'

'He's off somewhere,' Harry said. 'But he's safe.'

'Too bad he won't be burned alive,' I said nastily then.

Elsa looked at me in horror. 'That's a vile thing to say, Lydia,' she said. 'And not like you at all.'

'Well, maybe you don't know me very well,' I said angrily. 'You all think I'm some daft clown whose feelings don't matter. Sam does anyway. I hate him.'

'What—?' Elsa started, and looked at Harry as though he would provide an explanation for my inappropriate outburst. Harry shook his head at her, and I felt his hand squeeze mine. I felt bitter in my throat for being so horrible about my brother but I couldn't stop myself either.

All around us people were gathering, now that the fire was properly visible. Because it wasn't just *Lady Beatrice* that was in trouble – all the boats along the quayside were too, and a group had gathered and were trying to untie them and get them to safety. Even Rich and Denise had come out from The Smugglers' Tavern and they and a few strangers were gawping at the fire. I saw Denise look over at me and then she blew me a kiss. Denise is such a matter-of-fact person normally, and quite bossy. I realised that people do care, even if it seems that they don't think about you much.

As I was turning back to *Lady Beatrice*, I saw my father, looking confused and sad, and I thought about the Ridiculous car journeys and the carousel fiasco in the toy shop, and Dad always being so kind and good-natured and knowing what I meant by things even when nobody else seemed to, and I felt my heart expand painfully as though it would come out through my chest.

Dad's eyes met mine then and I took a breath and moved behind Harry and Jo and Elsa and went to stand next to him.

'This is really entirely my fault,' he said.

'But you weren't even on *Lady Beatrice*,' I said, not understanding.

Dad's eyes were glassy, and I could see a bit of sweat on his forehead. 'I mean, everything . . . Lydia,' he said, in a strange wobbly voice. 'All my fault.'

I swallowed, unable to comfort him.

'Are you warm enough?' he asked then, looking at my clothes – my dungarees, my thin T-shirt – and my filthy plimsolls.

I wasn't anywhere near warm enough. 'I'm OK,' I told him.

Three fire engines were driving onto the quay, deafening us all with their sirens and that was when we spotted Sam. He was alone, standing right on the quayside in front of *Lady Beatrice*, and I could see the silhouette of that little tuft of hair on his head that never lies flat.

I wondered if Kay had been collected already by her dad in his *Palmer's Plumbing* van. There was another wave of hurt and I turned back to Dad, but he had just vanished.

I looked round me but he wasn't anywhere. I'd lost sight of Harry and Jo and Elsa too; more and taller people were blocking my view, and above our heads plumes of smoke continued to cloud the night sky. I started to panic, standing on tiptoe. It was like when you're very young and you let go of your mother's hand and then she's gone. I was surrounded by strangers, all chattering as though it was November the 5th and Bonfire Night, and then in the middle of all the chatter I heard someone shouting and it was unmistakeably Elsa and I came to life. I pushed past two big men to get to her.

'Harry!' Elsa was practically screaming, standing about three feet away from the quayside. Her face was lit up by the fire and wet with tears. I couldn't help looking around for Sam, too, but he had vanished.

Harry appeared, coming towards Elsa, and it was then that I saw Dad, on board *Lady Beatrice*, standing right over by the hatch at the top of the stairs. Even though we could all see the black smoke below him, he hardly seemed to register it. He looked almost calmly over at us.

'It's Sam,' he called. 'The silly boy has gone back down

below. I must go and get him. Don't worry, children, I'll put out the fire while I'm down there.'

'Jesus,' gibbered Elsa beside me. 'He's drunk. What is he doing?'

'Dad, no! Don't be an idiot—' Harry started after him, just as three firemen moved him out of the way to run on board where Dad had disappeared down the stairs, and now Elsa had her head in her hands.

'Sir!' one of the fireman was shouting down from the top of the hatch. 'Sir, please don't go any further. We'll deal with this.' He glanced at the other two firemen and nodded, and then all three of them climbed down after Dad, and my brother, wherever he was.

Why did Sam go back onto *Lady Beatrice*? I thought, imagining him down there with the flames and the poisonous smoke. I felt unexpectedly, violently sick, while beside me Elsa was shivering and crying.

Everything in the world had gone to hell.

'There's a tank full of fuel down in the engine room,' said Harry. 'If the fire spreads that way . . . It's incredibly dangerous.'

Harry was doing his best to be calm and grown-up, but when I actually looked at his face I realised, he's young. He's only twenty-one. Despite what Elsa said, that isn't ancient at all.

'They will rescue them, won't they, Elsa?' I asked, feeling real fear for the first time. 'The firemen will get them out?'

Elsa clasped hold of my hand. 'Of course they will, darling,' she said.

It seemed like so much time went by before anyone

appeared back upon deck and then finally, they all came out. Two firemen were helping Dad, who was coughing quite badly, and another had hold of Sam, and they were led across the deck and off the boat. Then the fireman on board gave a thumbs-up to the rest of them on the quay, who ran to get some more equipment off one of the fire engines.

'Daddy,' I said, touching his arm as he went past, still coughing. He stopped and put out his arms and clutched both me and Elsa against his smoky shirt, and I thought I could still smell a tiny bit of cologne even though he never wears it any more. I knew he was still there, some-where.

An ambulance had arrived, and the ambulance people came to take Dad and check him over. I snuck a look over at Harry, who was hovering by Sam, and I saw him grab Sam and kiss the top of his head as if Sam was six years old again, and I fought off tears of relief because I still bloody hate Sam.

'I'm going to sit with Dad,' Harry called over to us. 'Jo's gone to see about accommodation for us.'

'You go too, Sam,' Elsa called back. 'You're in shock. And they'll want to check your lungs.'

Then Elsa and I watched as the firemen clambered care-fully over the boat with all their paraphernalia, and within half an hour they had extinguished the fire and the boat was still there – in one piece, just smoking a bit.

I didn't look at where my cabin was, but everything had gone, I was sure about that.

'Lydia,' Elsa said then. 'What has Sam done to make you say that awful thing?'

I shook my head. 'Nothing,' I said.

Elsa doesn't normally let things lie, but this time she somehow managed to. 'Where did Kay get to?' she said instead.

'I think her dad picked her up earlier. Harry said . . .' I lied.

'Oh,' Elsa smiled. 'Thank goodness she hasn't been dragged into all of this.'

I forced a hugely relieved expression, as it wasn't really the right time to tell Elsa that Kay is a sneaky, lying cow and I couldn't care less.

Lady Beatrice was resting, looking almost serene after all the excitement, like it would take more than this to unsettle her. I remembered about Dunkirk and the War.

'Pity the tide's down,' said Elsa. 'But the mud will help cool her down, I suppose.'

'I used to fantasise about *Lady Beatrice* exploding,' I said. 'But then we would have nothing – we wouldn't have a home at all.'

Elsa wiped at her eyes. 'I had that fantasy too.' She put her arm round my waist, just as Ben came towards us with a tray of mugs. 'I hope he's put some whisky in whatever that is,' she said.

It was hot tea. Ben told us we were welcome to sleep aboard his boat, and also that he'd picked up Bob and Eugene, who had been prowling across the quay, wondering what all the fuss was about.

I couldn't believe I hadn't given Bob or Eugene a thought!

Bob has always dashed like a cheetah from anything that threatens him, I thought cats are obviously a whole lot better than humans at running off and protecting themselves; that must be what people mean when they say about their 'nine lives'.

'I might have known those selfish little sods would be all right,' said Elsa, reading my mind. And then we laughed, as though this wasn't really happening to us, but was something we were watching on telly.

'I need to see Dad,' Elsa said after a bit. She had drunk her tea and was much calmer. 'You should head for *Philomena*, and try and go to sleep.'

I watched her disappear into the crowd. Then I turned back for another look at *Lady Beatrice*, but someone was in the way.

Sam was standing in front of me, looking slightly more dishevelled than usual, wearing an over-sized coat with enormous pockets that someone must have lent him. I saw a reddish patch of skin on his forehead.

He gave me a wary smile.

I didn't smile back; instead I then deliberately craned my head to see past him, as though anything else was more interesting and important than Sam.

'I've got something for you,' he said.

'I don't want it,' I said automatically and coldly, refusing to look at him.

But I did see Sam put his hand in one of his huge pockets and take something from it and hold it out to me a bit shakily.

It was my diary.

I opened my mouth and took it from him, but I couldn't speak.

'I put the photo of Mum in there too, the one with you in it,' he said. 'It's a bit of a miracle that it didn't get burned up actually. The odds were completely against it.'

Professor Yaffle.

'How did you know?' I said, meaning my diary.

Sam paused. 'Kay reminded me about it . . .' he said. 'I don't know, I just thought I could run down below and get it and it wouldn't take long.'

'Thanks,' I said.

'I'm sorry, Lydia—' he began.

'I've got to go, actually,' I cut him off. 'I need to check on Bob and Eugene . . . et cetera.'

'OK then.' Sam nodded. 'Good idea.'

Then, before I could weaken, I turned, and as I ran through the crowds to *Philomena* I couldn't help remembering what Sam had said that time to my father – about taking risks, and what a terrible idea that seemed to him.

Aside from everything, tonight Sam had actually risked his life for me.

Now it's 7.00 a.m. and last night me and Elsa shared Ben's master cabin with the cats, and I'm finishing writing everything down now that Elsa's awake and is in the bathroom. It's the most I have ever written.

Elsa said last night that she and Harry and Jo had taken Dad to The Smugglers' Tavern, where Denise had a couple of spare bedrooms waiting for him and Sam and Harry if they needed them. Dad had sat down in his room and wept, Elsa said, and told them that in the morning he's going to get some help. She told me that for the first time Dad talked properly about Mum and how much he missed her.

'He's going to try,' Elsa said as she got undressed. 'That's the main thing.'

She didn't say everything would be all right, because no one knows that, but I have to believe that Dad will get better. I can't lose him as well as my mother.

Saturday 2nd May

Me, Dad, and Harry have all been staying in a rented flat in town while *Lady Beatrice* is being fixed up after the fire damage. The day after, Sam announced he was going to Aunt Lorna's for a few weeks, as our schools have said neither of us have to go in for a while but can come back in after half term. They've given us work to do at home instead, so I'm having to manage on my own with maths and physics stuff, but my hatred for Sam has turned to awkwardness and I don't know how to be with him any more, so it's just as well.

The good news is that Dad has been to the doctor, who prescribed him tablets. To help him function, he said. Dr Marsh also gave him leaflets on how to overcome his addiction to alcohol, so Dad is now going to Alcoholics Anonymous meetings three times a week. Dad says that though it is hard to sit in the Church Community Centre with lots of strangers and talk about why he drinks so much, some of the people there have such dreadful lives it has made him quite thankful for things in his.

'What dreadful things have happened to them?' I asked, wondering if there could be anything worse than somebody dying, or losing your job and all your money and your home.

'I'm not going to tell you that, Lydia,' said Dad. 'Everything is talked about in complete confidence. I certainly wouldn't want any of them to be gossiping about me.' He drank from one of his many daily cups of tea. 'Needless to say, many of these poor people have sunk right to the bottom.'

Somehow I pictured the gloopy mud and the marshes on the estuary.

'What are you thankful for then?' It seemed to me that Dad honestly didn't have much.

'Well, you, Elsa and the boys, for a start,' said my father. 'That's an awful lot. Everything, in fact.'

Knowing you're someone to be thankful for is strange and wonderful. Also, it's funny how one person can really hurt you and another person will make up for it. I remembered what Alice our cleaning lady used to say: 'God closes a door and opens a window.' Or something like that.

The older I get, the more I can't believe God exists, but it's true that brilliant things can arrive in your life just when you really need them to.

Like Kay, for instance.

I still can't think about Kay without feeling mostly angry. At least I am not forced to see her or have to avoid her at school, but I want to tell her about my proper bed and the window with curtains in my room, and Bob and Eugene who prowl around sniffing everything. Eugene keeps trying to escape up the chimney in the living room. Kay would find that so funny.

I just don't know what to do about it all.

Ben from *Philomena* came over to the flat today and brought us post that has been gathering in the box on the quayside, and amongst a lot of official-looking letters for my father, there was also something for me. It was an envelope, addressed in handwriting I didn't recognise at first, but when I peered at the postmark I saw it was from Cornwall and my heart fluttered a bit because I only know one person who lives in Cornwall.

I went straight to my room and made myself carefully open it.

Dear Lydia

I've been wanting to write again for ages, but I didn't know if you wanted to hear from me any more.

Anyway, the baby is a bit older and not as boring as he was. I can hold him now without thinking I'm going to break his neck by accident. I'm getting on OK with my dad, and I know he's trying to be responsible and all that kind of thing. I talk on the phone with Mum a lot though. In a way that's why I'm writing. She told me about the fire on Lady Beatrice, and that you'd lost all your things and then I thought I'm going to write to you anyway whether you like it or not, because I'm really sorry and I want to know if you are OK and how your dad is.

Mum also mentioned that Kay's mum is worried about Kay, and that the two of you have fallen out. Kay won't tell her mum or dad or anyone why, but she's really down about it. It must be something quite bad, to break you two up?

You don't have to tell me what's happened either, Lydia, but if you do I won't tell anyone. The baby wouldn't understand what I'm talking about anyway as he has a limited grasp of English and can't speak.

Whatever it is that you and Kay have fallen out about, Kay thinks the world of you and I know you feel the same about her. That's all I'm going to say, other than, please write back – a letter or a postcard, anything you want. Tell me about your life. And your sister and your cats. Please.

Love, Jimmy.

I sat on my bed, while beside me Eugene tried to nibble at the envelope before realising it wasn't actually food. First I thought how perfectly straight and even Jimmy's writing is, not like mine which starts off normal-sized and seems to get smaller and smaller the more I write, and not like Sam's, which isn't even joined up and looks like a five-year-old's and is quite surprising as Sam is clever in other ways. Then I smelled the paper, as I do with new books before I read them. And I just wanted to sit and feel happy for a bit that Jimmy had written a letter to me and thinks about me. I re-read the bits about Kay, and tried to imagine never speaking to her again ever. And I knew that was more painful than anything. More than seeing Sam holding her hand.

I got up and went out into the living room where Dad

was going through all his letters at the table, tucking into a bar of Bourneville chocolate. I saw him break off a tiny bit and feed it to Bob, who began feverishly licking it.

'That's your lot,' Dad said, and tugged gently at one of Bob's ears.

I stood in the doorway with Jimmy's letter in my hands, watching them. And then Dad looked up and saw me and took off his glasses.

'All right?' he said.

'Dad,' I said. 'I think I'll go back to school soon.'

'I see,' he said. 'Are you sure?'

'I'm ready to face the music.'

'Are you?' He smiled. 'Me too. Shall we face the music together?'

'And dance.' I remembered a song he used to sing in the car.

'And dance.' He held out his packet of chocolate. 'Care for a square of Bourneville?'

Monday 18th May

As Dad was under-insured, for the past few weeks I have mostly been wearing clothes from the Sally Army charity shop, but Denise from the Smugglers' poured me a Coke just before I started my shift on Saturday and I told her about going back to school next week, and she said did I think my father would be put out if she bought me my school uniform.

'No offence, my love,' she said, looking me up and down. 'But you really can't turn up in that sort of clobber.' I hadn't thought about my uniform, and to be honest it's one of the things I'm quite glad got burned in the fire, but Denise did have a point.

'Dad probably won't mind at all,' I said, which he wouldn't. 'But I promise I'll pay you back out of my wages.'

'Don't be silly,' Denise said briskly. 'I won't hear of that.'

Of course, Juliet Huntley-Smith was straight in with all her questions during Registration this morning. I think everyone must have been ordered to be nice to me though, as no one whispered or laughed. In fact, even some of the normally very immature boys in my form said hello quite politely. In a way I would have preferred it if they'd just been immature, as usual, so I wouldn't feel so pitied.

Juliet handed me a big Tupperware box. 'Mother made brownies,' she said.

'Thanks,' I said. 'That's really kind of her.' Sam will eat all of these, I thought instantly, then remembered he wouldn't as he's gone away.

Before Juliet could pounce on me to sit with her in the canteen and eat lunch after maths – my last morning lesson – I ran out of the classroom really quickly to go and sit on the playing field and read Jimmy's letter again, which I've been carrying around with me since it arrived.

I lay on my front in the grass and felt the sun on my back, and went over Jimmy's letter for the fifteenth time. And then I saw someone coming through the school gates holding what looked like chips and walking past the prefab classrooms, and before I could look away she saw me.

Kay stopped, and even from a distance I saw a chip hanging out of her mouth and my stomach rumbled as I'd not brought any lunch with me and Mrs Huntley-Smith's brownies were in my locker.

I watched Kay eat a few more chips, obviously thinking how to approach the situation and whether to just turn round and pretend she hadn't seen me. Then she wrapped up her chips and started walking over, and my heart began beating very fast. I put Jimmy's letter down the waistband of my school skirt and sat up on my knees.

'All right, Lydia,' Kay said carefully, standing over me so I was enveloped by her shadow. 'I didn't know you were back. They said you might be off till at least after half term.'

'I just wanted to be normal,' I said awkwardly.

'How's your dad?' she asked.

'He's OK,' I said. 'He's going to Alcoholics Anonymous.'

'That's brilliant.' Kay stared at her wrapped chips and I could see her thinking of what to say next.

'It's OK. You don't have to make conversation with me,' I said.

'I don't *make conversation* with anyone,' said Kay. 'As you well know.'

I really wanted to smile, but I resisted.

'I want to say something important and that I really mean,' she went on. 'If I could take back what happened I would. If I could time travel back to before—'

'—Before you sneaked around with Sam and lied?' I interrupted her, unable to stop sounding angry again.

Kay hesitated. 'Yes, before that.' She dropped down to sit beside me. 'But I didn't mean to lie. And in a way I wasn't. I wasn't sure how I felt about Sam. I knew I liked him, but I didn't know for sure it was in *that* way. When you saw us that night . . . that was the first time I knew.'

I didn't say anything. I really wanted to see things from Kay's point of view, even though I didn't yet. I remembered about going round to hers that time and what her mum had said.

'When you were ill and off school,' I said. 'Your mum mentioned you were out all hours and you never really explained about it. Were you with Sam then? Was that why you didn't explain?'

Kay sighed. 'Sam sometimes came and chatted to me when I was at the kiosk and we went for little walks and stuff. And I did see him the evening before you came round . . . but nothing, you know, had happened or anything. I knew Sam liked me, I just didn't know what I felt, and what was the point of saying about it when it might all be nothing.

I knew you'd hate me, and I felt really bad. So I just bunked off school the day after, so that my mother could suffocate me with her attentions.' Kay sighed. 'I made a right hash of it all.'

In a way I felt sorry for Kay as she most definitely had made a hash of it all.

'I thought Sam wasn't your type of boy though,' I said quietly.

Kay shrugged. 'He's not. But, I don't know . . . he makes me laugh and he's clever.' She paused and then added awkwardly, 'And we both love you.'

I was silent for a bit.

'I'm really sorry about Mr Bear, Kay,' I said finally. 'In the fire . . .'

'Thanks,' said Kay. 'I did love Mr Bear. But you've lost everything, Lydia.' She smiled at me, a bit sadly. 'And you're not even moaning about it.'

'But I haven't lost everything,' I said, realising that the really important things to me are safe. My family, the cats, my photo of Mum. And my diary.

I looked at Kay's nice eyes. 'You reminded Sam about my diary.' I said then.

'I know how much all that writing stuff means to you,' she said.

My heart lurched. It was the kindest thing anyone had ever done for me.

'Anyway,' she said awkwardly, shifting the subject, 'I haven't seen Sam since the fire, and not talked to him either.'

'He's not here,' I said. 'He's staying with Aunt Lorna.'

'Jamaican ginger cake Aunt Lorna with the little terrier?' asked Kay.

I nodded and smiled.

'Sam said he's going to join the Merchant Navy anyway,' Kay said. 'So he'll be away for years, won't he?'

I'd forgotten about that. Somewhere inside me I knew I had to make it up with Sam again before he went or I would be sad for ever.

Kay unwrapped her chips. 'Want one?' she said.

'Yes, I'm starving,' I said, and took four big ones, cramming them in my mouth.

Kay laughed and then I did the same and we sat together like we do, just stuffing our faces.

'Still going to America?' I said at last.

'Think so,' said Kay. 'As soon as I've done my O-levels I'm out of here.'

'I don't think I'll come,' I told her. 'But I'll visit.'

'You'd better,' she said. 'When you've got a job as a librarian.'

'If I pass any exams.'

'Did you ask your dad about the dyslexia thing?' Kay said.

'Not yet. I don't want to send him spiralling into another depression of failure or something.'

'I don't think dyslexia is anyone's fault,' said Kay.

I wasn't sure I wanted to find out if I was dyslexic. What if I wasn't and I was just dumb?

'Oh,' said Kay. 'Mum saw Mrs Jones in the Co-op the other day.'

'Jimmy's mum?'

'Mum said she was looking really well, really chatty.'

'Did she say anything about Jimmy?' I said, thinking of the letter in my waistband.

'Well, that was the weird thing. She was buying loads of food, pizzas and fish fingers and stuff, and Mum said, "Are you feeding the military, Val?" And Val said, "It's amazing how much boys eat, Diane." But she rushed off with her trolley before Mum could ask any more.'

'What do you think that means?' I said.

'Dunno . . .' Kay hesitated. She ate the last of the chips and screwed up the wrapping and then gave me one of her knowing smiles.

'I'll be OK,' I told her then. 'I just need time to get used to things that I can't do anything about. I know you didn't do it to hurt me.'

'I would never do anything on purpose to hurt you,' she said. 'Never.'

Then we lay down on our fronts and closed our eyes and the sun felt like a piping hot bath does after you've spent ages out in the cold.

Saturday 23rd May

As one of my possessions that survived the fire is the bike that Jake gave me for my birthday last year, I've been out cycling a lot. I like going down the big hill that leads out of town and over the little bridge on the estuary to the sea wall, where it's quiet – except for the gulls that shriek incessantly, of course.

I was lying there today on my back, feeling really hot as the weather has been amazing for weeks, and I'd bundled my sweatshirt into a ball so that I could rest my head on it while I stared up at the cloudless sky and tried hard not to daydream about Jimmy coming home. And then I heard the sound of a bike bell ringing and I sat up, and someone was waving and grinning at me like mad.

'Jake?' I said, shocked. I honestly thought I would never see him again. I scrambled up self-consciously.

Jake got off his bike and said, 'I thought it was you cycling over the bridge.' He hesitated. 'I didn't want to scare you though, so I kept my distance.'

He stood there for a minute and then he stepped forward and gave me a hug, and though it felt a bit awkward I was just so glad that Jake didn't hate me because of my father.

'I heard about the fire,' he said. 'It was on the local news – we saw pictures of you all standing on the quayside. We were all really worried until then.'

'Were you?' I said.

'Did you think we could just leave and not worry about you all? Mum was in bits about you in particular. But you're not her kid. You belong with your dad, and Harry, Sam and Elsa.'

'Yes,' I said. 'We are sort of stuck with each other.'

'You look a bit different,' Jake said then.

I grimaced. 'Same old hair unfortunately.'

He laughed. 'No . . . You look nice. More grown-up somehow.'

'Where did you go, Jake?' I said. 'You just vanished. Sometimes I wondered if I imagined you.'

'Mum wanted a clean break. She said it would be too complicated otherwise.'

I thought about everything that had happened since Kate left and how maybe she had been right.

'Do you still live in Maling?' I asked.

'We moved to the outskirts,' he said. 'A few miles or so away, and I'm at Thurstall school.'

There was a tiny awkward silence then we both said at the same time:

'*Sorry.*'

Then we both laughed.

'Why are *you* sorry?' I asked.

'Just that I am sorry – about everything,' said Jake. 'I really wanted to write or talk to you on the phone, but it seemed like it might make matters worse.'

'I understand why your mum left,' I said.

He smiled. 'How is your dad? Is he OK?'

'He's trying to be. He's going to Alcoholics Anonymous now.'

'That's really good news,' Jake said, looking genuinely

pleased. 'They should never have got married,' he added. 'We should never have moved onto *Lady Beatrice*. Even though I miss it every day.'

'Are you joking?' I said.

He laughed. 'I loved it. It was an amazing place to live. I'll never forget it.'

'Well, we're in rented for now,' I said. 'I've got a proper bed and actual curtains, Jake.'

'Wow,' he said, and then we both laughed again and Jake got out a can of Coke and we sat down on the grass together and shared it, and talked about the cats and Bob's stubborn ways and his adorable evilness. I asked about Sally and Erica, and Jake said they were fine but Sally still asks if he ever sees me about.

'So how's your friend Kay?' Jake asked.

'She's OK,' I said. 'We fell out because it turns out that she and Sam *really* like each other.'

'Sam?' Jake was agog. 'Your brother Sam?'

I laughed. 'I know. I was furious about it, but I'm coming to terms with it now.'

'He chose well though, Sam,' said Jake. 'Wouldn't you say?'

'Yes,' I said. 'He did choose well.'

Then Jake said he really should get back. Kate had got a new table delivered apparently and he'd promised to help her put it together today.

'You know, you'll be OK, Lydia,' he said as he got to his feet. 'You're pretty strong, I reckon.'

I thought of how many times I've felt scared stiff over

the past couple of years. How can you be really scared and strong at the same time?

'*Adios* then, Addie.' Jake brushed at a bit of dirt off his saddle, then he climbed on his bike and grinned at me. 'See you on the other side.'

Sunday 24th May

Today after lunch, at 3.00 p.m., I went out to collect the glasses and rubbish and sweep up all the dropped basket food from under the tables outside the Smugglers'. Eugene would love those bits of scampi, I thought, brushing them into a dustpan. Poor Eugene's going a bit stir-crazy in the flat, especially as hostile relations have resumed with Bob.

I was just shoving the last of everything into a bin bag when out of the corner of my eye I saw someone cycle slowly past down the hill. I wouldn't have looked again but for the skateboarding trainers.

I know it's a cliché, but my heart skipped a beat. It was Jimmy. Getting off his bike and staring at me.

'Jimmy,' I said, completely caught off-guard.

'Lydia,' he said back.

'Are you back for a holiday?' My throat was very dry; I had nothing at all interesting in my head, just a blank fuzz.

'No, I'm here for good, with my mum,' he said, grinning. 'I've been cycling round town today trying to find you. Did you get my letter?'

'Sorry I never wrote back,' I told him. 'I was going to.'

'Doesn't matter.' Jimmy smiled.

'Kay and I have made it up though,' I said. 'It was all a bit daft, thinking about it.'

'Good.' Jimmy hesitated, then he said, 'I wish I'd never gone back to Cornwall.'

'What about Sennen Cove?' I said. 'And the Minack theatre?'

'They're all right,' said Jimmy. 'But not the same.'

'Not the same as what?' I said. 'The boring old prom and the marshes?'

'As . . .' I saw the colour coming to his cheeks. 'Well, I did think about you a lot, Lydia.' He looked straight into my eyes, daring me to look away. 'Most days, in fact.'

'Oh . . .' I said. My stomach felt strange, sort of hot, like someone had lit a fire inside it, and the heat was spreading nicely through my body. I wondered if perhaps I was asleep and dreaming this conversation.

'Anyway . . .' said Jimmy, as I'd not spoken for a while. 'I—'

But just at that moment, someone appeared behind him, stood on tiptoe and clamped their hands over his eyes.

'Boo!' said Kay as Jimmy nearly jumped out of his skin. 'Fancy seeing you here, Jimmy.'

'Jimmy's back for good,' I told her.

'Yes, Mother told me,' said Kay. 'That woman's a human satellite in regard to people's comings and goings.'

Jimmy laughed.

'Time to celebrate, I reckon,' said Kay. She opened her rucksack and shook a giant bag of Monster Munch in our faces. 'Afternoon tea, while we watch the tide come up.' She waved across at Sam, who's back from Aunt Lorna's and was cleaning his boots off with the quayside hosepipe. 'See you in a bit then,' she told us and ran over to my brother, and I didn't want to watch as I'm still slightly weird about all that.

Instead I went and dumped the rubbish in the Smugglers'

bin area and went inside to scrub my hands while Jimmy sat down on one of the benches to wait for me.

When I came outside with my little envelope of wages, me and Jimmy sat for a minute looking over at Harry, who was painting *Lady Beatrice*.

'Mum says you're welcome to come and stay with us if it ever gets too much,' Jimmy said then. 'She says that only a person who has been down to the bottom knows what it's like to be there.' He paused. 'She definitely has her bad days, but she's a nice mum.'

'Thanks,' I said. 'I'm sorry I've behaved a bit madly around you.'

'I kept wanting to tell you I liked you, but I couldn't be sure . . .' Jimmy hesitated, 'if you liked me in the same way.'

I thought about the latest postcard I'd got from Elsa: a black and white picture of Dorothy from *The Wizard of Oz*. On the back, Elsa told me her news and asked how Dad was getting on, but there was a P.S. at the end, in Latin: *Carpe Diem*, which Dad said meant 'Seize the Day' and was pretty good advice in general.

I looked at Jimmy, at the little mole by his mouth and his nice blue eyes.

'Well. Now you know,' I said bravely.

Carpe Diem and all that.

Jimmy reached out for my hand and his felt so warm and solid. 'Come on then.' He looked over at Sam and Kay down by *Philomena*. 'Shall we go and have tea and stare at the mud?'

The four of us sat in a row with our shoes off, snacking on Monster Munch and listening to Harry and the workmen shouting at each other on *Lady Beatrice*, and the seagulls shrieking across the marshes over on the other side of the estuary. As Jimmy and Sam made awkward boy conversation, me and Kay caught each other's eye and made faces at the wafts of sulphur coming up from the riverbed.

Then I gazed down at the stubborn, dark-brown slimy substance below us and inhaled it as though it was Elsa's Opium.

What *is* this strange ugly sludge that has always seemed a bit pointless? Mud is always there, never-changing, cushioning *Lady Beatrice* when the tide is down, making the cats furious when they are caught in it. It cools you down, it sticks to you like armour . . . and it might suck you under, if you let it.

But then that's up to you, I suppose.

Acknowledgements

Thank you so much to all those who have supported me in the writing of *Mud*. To my agent, Gillie Russell, for believing so much in this book and for being so consistently articulate about why. To my publishers, Andersen Press, particularly Charlie Sheppard and Chloe Sackur, for liking it as much as they do, and for all their editorial expertise and thoughtfulness and belief – and patience. To Louise Lamont for her early guidance. To all my kind friends who listened to my angst and cheered me on. To my unusual and brilliant family. To 'Kay'. And to my parents, wherever they are now.

Too Close To Home

AOIFE WALSH

Minny's life is a complicated whirlwind of unbearable PE lessons, annoying friends and impossible-to-live-with siblings. She's desperate for some space in a house spilling over with family and hangers-on. She has to contend with her autistic sister Aisling's school bullies whilst trying to keep her self-absorbed BFF Penny happy, and look normal in front of new boy Franklin. And on top of this, now Dad has announced that he's returning to London – with his new girlfriend.

Secrets, lies and home truths will out in this beautifully warm and witty novel about the pain of being from a large and very complicated family.

'A contemporary version of *Little Women*. Excellent' *Lovereading*

'Wonderfully authentic family drama, funny and complicated as real life relationships are' *Scottish Book Trust*

9781783443000

GIRL ON A PLANE

MIRIAM MOSS

Jordan, 1970. After a summer spent with her family, fifteen-year-old Anna is travelling back to her English boarding school alone. But her plane never makes it home. Anna's flight is hijacked by Palestinian guerrillas. They land the plane in the Jordanian desert, switch off the engines and issue their demands. If these are not met within three days, they will blow up the plane, killing all the hostages.

The heat on board becomes unbearable; food and water supplies dwindle. Anna begins to face the possibility she may never see her family again. Time is running out . . .

'Nerve-shredding'
Independent

'A unique and extraordinary story, exceptionally well told'
Books for Keeps

9781783443314

Out of Shadows
Jason Wallace

**WINNER OF THE COSTA CHILDREN'S BOOK AWARD,
THE BRANFORD BOASE AWARD AND THE UKLA BOOK AWARD**

Zimbabwe, 1980s
The war is over, independence has been won and Robert
Mugabe has come to power offering hope, land and
freedom to black Africans. It is the end of the Old Way
and the start of a promising new era.

For Robert Jacklin, it's all new: new continent, new country,
new school. And very quickly he learns that for some of his
classmates, the sound of guns is still loud, and their battles
rage on . . . white boys who want their old country back,
not this new black African government.

Boys like Ivan. Clever, cunning Ivan.
For him, there is still one last battle
to fight, and he's taking it right
to the very top.

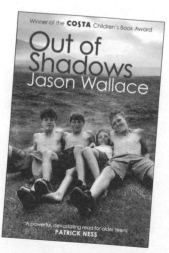

'Honest, brave and devastating,
Out of Shadows is more than just
memorable. It's impossible to
look away.'
*Markus Zusak, author of
The Book Thief*

9781849390484